BOOKS BY TINA FOLSOM

Samson's Lovely Mortal (Scanguards Vampires, Book 1)

Amaury's Hellion (Scanguards Vampires, Book 2)

Gabriel's Mate (Scanguards Vampires, Book 3)

Yvette's Haven (Scanguards Vampires, Book 4)

Zane's Redemption (Scanguards Vampires, Book 5)

Quinn's Undying Rose (Scanguards Vampires, Book 6)

Oliver's Hunger (Scanguards Vampires, Book 7)

Thomas's Choice (Scanguards Vampires, Book 8)

Silent Bite (Scanguards Vampires, Book 8 1/2)

Cain's Identity (Scanguards Vampires, Book 9)

Luther's Return (Scanguards Vampires, Book 10)

Blake's Pursuit (Scanguards Vampires, Book 11)

Fateful Reunion (Scanguards Vampires, Book 11 1/2)

John's Yearning (Scanguards Vampires, Book 12)

Ryder's Storm (Scanguards Vampires, Book 13)

Damian's Conquest (Scanguards Vampires, Book 14)

Grayson's Challenge (Scanguards Vampires, Book 15)

Lover Uncloaked (Stealth Guardians, Book 1)

Master Unchained (Stealth Guardians, Book 2)

Warrior Unraveled (Stealth Guardians, Book 3)

Guardian Undone (Stealth Guardians, Book 4)

Immortal Unveiled (Stealth Guardians, Book 5)

Protector Unmatched (Stealth Guardians, Book 6)

Demon Unleashed (Stealth Guardians, Book 7)

Ace on the Run (Code Name Stargate, Book 1)

Fox in plain Sight (Code Name Stargate, Book 2)

Yankee in the Wind (Code Name Stargate, Book 3)

Tiger on the Prowl (Code Name Stargate, Book 4)

A Touch of Greek (Out of Olympus, Book 1)

A Scent of Greek (Out of Olympus, Book 2)

A Taste of Greek (Out of Olympus, Book 3)

A Hush of Greek (Out of Olympus, Book 4)

Venice Vampyr (Novellas 1 – 4)

Teasing (The Hamptons Bachelor Club, Book 1)

Enticing (The Hamptons Bachelor Club, Book 2)

Beguiling (The Hamptons Bachelor Club, Book 3)

Scorching (The Hamptons Bachelor Club, Book 4)

Alluring (The Hamptons Bachelor Club, Book 5)

Sizzling (The Hamptons Bachelor Club, Book 6)

VENICE VAMPYR

NOVELLAS 1 - 4

TINA FOLSOM

Venice Vampyr

Novella One

NEW YORK TIMES BESTSELLING AUTHOR

TINA FOLSOM

CHAPTER

ONE

enice, Italy - early 1800s

Raphael di Santori never thought he'd lose his life by drowning. A stake through the heart, maybe, or burnt to ash by the sun—but never drowning. Not that it wasn't something many vampires feared: their cells, after all, were so dense and solid that their bodies were much heavier than water and therefore sank instantly.

That was exactly what had happened to him. One minute he'd been wandering along the canal. Now he was enfolded in its icy-cold depths. He could paddle and splash all he wanted, but his weight pulled him under the water without regard for his efforts. All his strength worked against him.

There was nothing to hold onto. The canal was lined with Venetian homes without ledges or docks, without the entry doors on the water level —mainly used for deliveries—that were customary at the larger merchants' homes. The homes that bordered this narrow, insignificant, yet deep canal in the labyrinth of Venice didn't have this luxury. Their inhabitants entered from the streets above, streets he'd walked earlier.

The noise of the carnival's revelers drifted to him, deadened by the water in his ears. Even if he screamed, they wouldn't hear him. They were too drunk to take any notice. It was one of the reasons he'd been prowling the streets despite the large number of people out. In a drunken crowd, there were more than a few morsels that would turn into prey, more than a few juicy necks he could feast on without being discovered.

All year he'd been careful, never feeding when the streets were busy, always making sure his victims wouldn't remember what had happened. Only during carnival, when masks were the ultimate accessory to any garment, did he gorge himself on the plentiful buffet of humans.

Had he been careless this time? Had somebody seen him? Why else had he felt a hand on his back, pushing him into the canal? Merely an accident by a drunken passerby or a deliberate act by someone who knew what he was? Had the Guardians of the Holy Waters finally caught up with him?

The Guardians—he and his brethren feared them. Nobody knew how the secret society of merchants and nobles had come into existence. However, for the last one hundred years of his life, he'd seen more and more of his fellow vampires fall prey to them. Many of his friends had vanished one night, never to be heard of again. They'd either died at the end of a stake through their hearts or drowned just as he was about to.

Had the hand that he'd briefly felt on his back belonged to one of the elusive Guardians? Elusive, because despite all investigations he and his kind had engaged in, all they'd ever been able to discover was their symbol: a cross intersected by three waves. His brethren had only ever captured one member of the Holy Waters, but he hadn't disclosed much more than their name and the symbol, which he wore on a black onyx ring, before he'd escaped them by killing himself and taken his secrets to the grave.

Were the Guardians behind his ordeal? Had one of them pushed him, knowing he'd drown? And what did it matter now? In a few minutes, he would be dead, his immortal life over. He would rot on the bottom of the canal, his body never rising to the surface, even as it decomposed, the denseness of his cells and bones making sure nothing of his being would ever come to light.

Raphael reflected on his long life, a life longer than any human could have wished for. He was leaving his brother Dante behind. But there was no woman who loved him or would cry a tear for him. His life was empty. With a last breath, he gave up his struggle and allowed the water to take him.

~

ISABELLA TENDERINI HEARD the sloshing of water in the otherwise quiet canal and asked her trusted gondolier to go faster. The Canale Grande was busy due to the festivities surrounding the carnival, and she'd instructed Adolfo to take her home via the quiet backwaters.

"Yes, Signora," he now answered and propelled the gondola forward effortlessly.

Her eyes peered into the darkness, the occasional light from the houses lining the canal throwing eerie shadows along the narrow passage. "Do you see anything?"

"There seems to be a disturbance in the water, just ahead of us," Adolfo answered.

"Quickly, pull alongside." Her heart beat faster at the thoughts that entered her mind. "Tell me what you see."

"Somebody appears to be in the water, Signora."

The tight fist of fear gripped her, and before she knew it, she divested herself of the cloak that kept the chill of the night air from her body and dropped it onto the seat next to her. "A child?"

"No, larger. A man."

A sense of *déjà vu* struck her, her heart reminding her of her own loss. Without hesitation, she undid the laces of her bodice, then felt Adolfo's hand on her shoulder.

"No, Signora, he'll be too heavy for you. You can't rescue a man. A child, yes, but not a grown man."

Isabella turned to him. She wouldn't be deterred by his concern. He had to understand that she had to do this so no other woman would feel the pain she had to endure. So no other woman would become a widow as she had. "I can't let anybody drown, you know that."

He nodded and, acknowledging his sad expression. But he wouldn't stop her. Her own husband, a wealthy merchant, had drowned in one of these canals less than a year ago. The money he'd left her did nothing to appease her loneliness.

As she stripped off her richly embroidered gown and dropped the petticoats to the bottom of the gondola, the cold February air blew through her chemise. But all she could think of was the man whose hands were the only things now visible above the water as if he was trying to hold onto some invisible rope. If she could save him, maybe she would finally be at peace and accept what had happened. Accept Giovanni's death.

"Hold on," Isabella begged, "just hold on a few more seconds." She prayed she wouldn't be too late.

"I will help you," Adolfo's voice came from behind.

She shook her head. Just because she needed to do this foolish thing didn't mean she would endanger her loyal servant. "No. You're not a strong enough swimmer."

As he pulled the boat alongside the drowning man, Adolfo released his oar and stepped behind her. A moment later, she felt his hands on her.

"What?" Was he trying to stop her after all?

"A rope. I'll tie it around you."

He expertly tied a rope around her waist while she scanned the dark waters for the man. His hands were gone. He'd slipped under the water. Only ripples remained on the surface. "Hurry."

"Ready."

Without a glance back, she jumped into the canal, feet first. The icy cold water hit her like a slap in the face. She held her breath and let herself be pulled into the depths of the canal's murky waters. She felt the pull on the rope and knew Adolfo would make sure she was safe.

Isabella didn't open her eyes—there was no use. All it would do was hurt her, but she wouldn't see anything. It was too dark. Even by daylight, there was little chance that her eyes would be of any assistance in her search for the drowning man.

She kicked her legs and reached her hands out, feeling for resistance. Nothing. Frantically she dove deeper, turned to her left, then her right, stretching her arms out further. Finally, her fingers encountered some material. She grasped for it, her hand latching onto a piece of fabric, a coat-tail or a sleeve. The soaked woolen cloth was heavy. She pulled on it, and to her relief, the weight behind it confirmed that she had found him.

The pressure in her lungs built. She fought against her body's instinct to come up for air, knowing if she dropped her hold on him and gave into her own need for air, he would be lost.

Isabella slipped one hand under the man's armpit. He was heavy despite the buoyancy of the water—heavier than she had expected. Gathering her remaining strength, she signaled Adolfo with a pull on the rope. She had just enough time to hook her second arm under the drowning victim's and kick her legs before she felt herself being pulled upwards. The man in her arms was big. His massive body pressed against her, her arms barely reaching around his chest.

The moment she breached the surface, she sucked in a much-needed breath of air, filling her lungs. The cold stung her chest, but she ignored it, just the way she ignored the dead weight of the man she was holding in her arms. Was he still alive?

"You were down for so long," she heard Adolfo proclaim, his voice more tense than usual.

"He's so heavy," Isabella pressed out and tried to paddle toward the boat. But all she could do was hold onto the man and let Adolfo do the hard work. She figured Adolfo deserved a few extra Lira as a bonus after this ordeal.

As her gondolier pulled on the rope, she felt the stranger slip from her grip. Without thinking, she spread her legs and wrapped them around his hips to hold him in a vice grip. It wasn't ladylike, nor was it anywhere near appropriate, but the man was unconscious and certainly wouldn't remember what she'd done.

When she heard voices drift to her from further down the canal, she prayed help was coming. Adolfo wouldn't be strong enough to pull both her and the man into the gondola. For once, her prayers were heard.

Her limbs were frozen when she finally landed in the gondola, helped by a couple of friendly delivery men who dragged the half-dead stranger into the boat right behind her.

Adolfo instantly covered her with her cloak, but she knew she wasn't the only one who needed warmth. Isabella scrambled closer to the man she'd just saved and wrapped the cloak around them both, holding him tightly to her soaked body to preserve any heat that was left.

She felt shivers go through his body and could only echo them. He was alive.

Isabella tore the wet clothes off the stranger's body as her maid Elisabetta stood by wide-eyed. "Don't just stand there, get a fire going," she ordered.

"Signora, shouldn't you let one of the footmen do this?"

Isabella shot her an annoyed look. "There's no time for modesty." Already she'd wasted precious minutes by ridding herself of her own wet clothes and drying off before stepping into a chemise and a dressing gown.

Adolfo had helped get the stranger up into her own rooms and placed him on the divan in front of the fireplace. She'd instructed him to keep quiet about the man. Having a stranger who was neither her husband nor a close relative staying with her would start all tongues in Venice wagging. Still, she knew it was only a matter of time before one of her staff gossiped and spread the scandalous news.

Despite the fact that she'd grieved for her husband for almost a year without taking a lover, without so much as allowing any man to even woo her in the most acceptable of manners, even she, a respectable widow, would not get away unscathed. If anyone found out a stranger was at her home—worse, in her own bedchamber—she would have to deal with the consequences. They would be harsh. Were they worth it? She hadn't craved a man's touch or attention, only her husband's. Until now.

As she gazed upon the tall stranger whose clothes she peeled away layer by layer, she was grateful for the fact that her maid was busy with stoking the fire, for she didn't want to be watched as she devoured the handsome man with her eyes.

Isabella allowed her hand to travel over his muscled chest and felt the raw power he represented. She wondered what kind of work this man did to have such strength in his body. But she knew he wasn't a common laborer who worked in the warehouses or on the docks. His clothes were too well made and too expensive for that. He had to be a gentleman, a very well-built gentleman.

The moment she opened the flap on his breeches, easing open button after button, her own body heated, despite the chill she'd gotten in the freezing water. No man had ever been able to ignite that kind of response in her body, not even her late husband. They'd had a loving marriage, a very comfortable one, but she'd never lusted after him like she lusted after this stranger.

The fabric clung to him. She told herself that she needed to rip it off him so he wouldn't die of a chill, but she knew better. The reason she tugged forcefully at his soggy clothes was so she could feast her eyes on what was beneath. She stripped him and dropped the wet garments onto the rug.

"Give me a bowl with warm water and a sponge."

Behind her, Elisabetta shuffled closer. A gasp told her that her maid was looking at the naked man. Isabella shifted her body to obstruct her maid's view. She didn't want to share him. What a strange thought, she reflected. He wasn't hers, yet she wanted to be the only one who saw him like this: vulnerable in his nudity.

"Signora! It is not decent!"

Isabella spun her head and snatched the bowl of water from Elisabetta's hands. "Leave us. And not a word of this to anybody if you value your position here. Do you hear me?"

She nodded nervously and fled the room. Isabella looked back at the beautiful naked man in front of her and took a deep breath. She should let one of her male servants do this, but she couldn't bring herself to relinquish the intimate task.

With the sponge she bathed him, starting with his face. His dark hair, sleek and shiny as that of a raven, clung to his skin. As she gently washed his face, she wondered what kind of eyes lay behind those dark lashes. Were his eyes as dark as his hair? And would those lips smile at her if he knew what she was doing? She sighed. It had been so long since she'd touched another person. And to touch him felt more exciting than she could have imagined.

Isabella cleaned every inch of his body with warm water, then dried him with a large bathing sheet. And all the while she marveled at the beauty of his nude form. Strong, powerful thighs, a muscled chest covered in just a light dusting of dark hair, arms that looked strong. But what truly captured her attention was what lay at the juncture of his thighs.

In a nest of black, coarse curls, a large shaft rested against his sac, which looked as if it held two small eggs. She knew all about the male form —her husband had been a virile man and had taught her about the pleasures of the flesh, how to arouse him and how to pleasure him.

When she looked at this stranger now, she wanted to do just that: arouse him, pleasure him. Her hand stroked over his manhood, exploring his soft skin. How she missed touching a man. How she longed for the invasion that stretched her channel to its capacity. And this man would stretch her. Even in its relaxed state, he was of a formidable size. Once aroused, she knew he would be magnificent.

Suddenly, he shifted under her touch, startling her. Isabella instantly reached for the thick blanket and pulled it over him, covering his gorgeous body.

Somebody had made a mistake. For all intents and purposes, he should be in hell. But from what Raphael could see, he'd made it into heaven. He'd never expected there to be a heaven for vampires. But he wasn't going to complain—no, he would not voice his concerns, even though he knew he didn't deserve this.

The woman was clearly an angel. Her raven hair was loose, not held up high on her head with hundreds of pins as was the current fashion. And her clothing was indecent at best. She wore a long red dressing gown of rich brocade embroidered with golden roses. It was pulled tight at her waist, but the top gaped open as she leaned over him. He noticed the soft white fabric beneath clinging to her generous breasts.

No, she could not be a mortal. No woman in Venice would dress this scandalously in the presence of a man who was not her husband. It was proof positive that he was in heaven. Why he lay on a divan in a very feminine boudoir, he couldn't yet explain, but he would get to the bottom of it. Nor could he explain why he felt cold. In fact, he positively shivered.

"I'll have Elisabetta put more coal on the fire in a moment," the angel said.

Coals in heaven? Raphael had thought they would have invented something a little more advanced. When she reached out and stroked his face, he realized that her skin was almost as cold as his. He certainly could do something about that.

"You're awake. Finally. We were worried." Her voice was like the most beautiful music he'd ever heard.

Worried that he wouldn't make it to heaven? "My angel, you won't have to worry any longer. I am here now." He reached for her hand and pulled it to his mouth, kissing her palm. The floral bouquet of her skin barely masked the heavy, rich scent of the blood in her veins. Despite the fact that he'd fed just before his death, he felt his fangs itch and his stomach clench with thirst for the angel's blood.

The beauty pulled her hand from his grip. "Signore, there is no need for such familiarity."

Raphael dropped his gaze to her neckline. "Familiarity? Maybe you mean formality?" He gave her a charming smile, the same kind of smile he used to lure his female victims to him. As he locked eyes with her and gazed into her green orbs, his hand went to her face. That was when he noticed the absence of clothes on his person. Why was he naked?

Surely, if he was without any clothes beneath the blanket and with the most gorgeous angel bending over him, there could only be one reason for it: he was here to make love to her. After all, this was heaven. "You're right, my angel, why kiss your hand when your lips are so red and full?"

Raphael pulled her to him and brushed his lips against hers. A gasp was her answer. "Shh, my angel, let me love you."

He captured the lovely creature's mouth and snaked his free arm around her, pressing her against him. She seemed to want to protest, but he didn't allow it. Instead, he greedily slipped his tongue between her parted lips and explored her.

Her tangy taste was enthralling, her lips soft and yielding. She tasted as enticing as her scent had hinted at. Yes, he would make love to her and take her intoxicating blood into him at the same time, gorge himself on her to celebrate his arrival in heaven.

His tongue coaxed her to respond to him, to dance with him in the intimate dance of two lovers. When he stroked against it for the first time, his cock pumped full with blood, readying itself for her. He pressed her body closer to make her aware of his urgent need.

When her hands pushed against his chest, he thought it was so she could free herself of her clothes, but she separated herself entirely from him instead and jumped up from the divan.

She took a few steps back, her body trembling, but he doubted that it was from fear. Her look was scolding as she glared at him. "Signore! Is that the thanks I get for taking care of you after you nearly drowned? Being attacked by you in my own home?"

CHAPTER

THREE

Isabella pressed her hand to her chest. Her heart beat frantically. He'd kissed her! The stranger had kissed her and made her feel things she'd never experienced. But she couldn't allow this, couldn't receive the pleasure he offered when she knew nothing about him. He was a complete stranger, a scoundrel for all she knew—very likely, considering his behavior. If she gave into his advances, she would turn into a common whore. She'd already gone too far by touching him. She should have never brought him here. He was a danger to her body and her heart.

"My life was saved?" His voice was full of disbelief. He sat up, dropping the blanket to his stomach, exposing his muscled chest.

Isabella averted her gaze. "Yes, you were one of the lucky ones."

"So this is not heaven?"

"Heaven?" Was that what he'd thought? "No, this is Venice. Do you remember anything about what happened?" Her pulse settled a little. Had this all been a misunderstanding? He'd called her *Angel*—several times in fact. Had he truly believed himself to be in heaven and thought she was an angel? Was that why he'd kissed her?

"Signora, my sincerest apologies," he said, and attempted to rise, then seemed to realize he was unclothed. "I would get up and bow in order to ask for your forgiveness, but it appears I find myself without the proper attire to do so."

Despite his sincere words, there was a smirk on his face, bringing out dimples in his cheeks. He looked young, younger than she thought he was. She followed his gaze to the heap of wet clothes that lay on the floor.

"It appears my garments are unusable at present." Then he looked at her, one side of his mouth tilting up in a smile. "Did you help me out of them?"

Isabella felt herself blush down to the roots of her hair. He knew! Had he been awake when she'd undressed him? Had he felt it when she'd caressed his naked body, washed him, dried him? She sucked in a much needed breath of air, afraid she would faint from the acute embarrassment that swept through her. She'd been a fool. Her reputation would be destroyed forever, and she would have to leave Venice because decent society would shun her.

A soft chuckle came from him. "Ah, I see. Well, Signora, then it appears I have nothing to hide." She heard the blanket being tossed to the floor and instantly turned her back to him.

He rose, and a second later, she could sense him a step behind her. "Signore, I will have my servants bring you some of my husband's clothes," she rushed to say.

"Husband?" he asked, sucking in a sharp breath.

"My late husband's, yes." She walked toward the door, trying to leave temptation behind her, but he followed her. When his hands grasped her shoulders, her breath caught.

Relief seemed to color his voice when he spoke again. "I'm very grateful for all you've done for me. Very grateful," he emphasized.

Then he spun her around to face him. "Raphael di Santori, at your service."

She turned her head to the side, making sure her gaze didn't drift lower, because she knew what she would see: his very tempting naked body. And if she allowed herself to feast her eyes on him once more, she would succumb to the temptation of touching him.

"Signore, this is hardly the time for an introduction." She tried to pull from his grip, but his hands cupped her shoulders firmly.

"When then, if not now? Or would you rather I ravished you before I found out your name?"

His arrogant suggestion made her snap her head back to him. "There will be no ravishing, Signore di Santori. I'm a respectable widow. Once you're dressed, you may come down to the parlor so we can talk."

Isabella pulled free of his grip and turned to the door. He didn't follow.

"Your name, Signora." When she hesitated, he added, "Please."

The softness in his voice made her relent. "Isabella Tenderini." Then she swept out of the room, holding her head high, trying to hold onto her dignity. When she closed the door behind her, his laughter followed her. *Insolent, arrogant rake!*

~

RAPHAEL COULDN'T STOP LAUGHING. Oh, this woman had fire in her belly. She made him feel alive. Hell, he was alive! And he had hundreds of questions. Had one of her servants pulled him out of the water? But, more importantly, who was this alluring woman who had clearly undressed him?

And not only that, now that her intoxicating scent wasn't flooding his nostrils any longer, he noticed that his own skin didn't smell of the murky waters of the canal as he would have expected. Somebody had bathed him. His eyes scanned the lavishly decorated room, his gaze instantly homing in on the four poster bed and the endless possibilities it suggested. Down, boy, he cautioned himself and continued his perusal of the chamber. Clearly, her chamber.

When his eyes fell onto a bowl with water and a sponge, he smiled to himself. Isabella had been the one who'd washed him, taken the sponge into her elegant hands and laved his body with it. Had she cradled his balls? Had she taken his cock into her hand as she'd performed this intimate task?

No wonder she'd blushed like a debutante. Now he understood. She'd touched his body intimately, more intimately than anyone had in a long time, and now she felt embarrassed about it. Had she liked what she'd seen? Had she maybe even stroked him, caressed him? Had her lips followed where her hands had explored first?

By God, he was hard just thinking of all the things she might have done to him while he was unconscious. He didn't feel violated in the slightest by the knowledge that she'd exploited his vulnerability. No—all it served was getting him aroused. All he could think of was whether she would do it again.

Clearly, as a widow she was familiar with the pleasures of the flesh. She was no shy virgin, but a grown woman who must recognize her own carnal needs. He'd felt them boil under her skin, those passions she kept locked away. Finding the key to unlocking those desires, and ensuring she unleashed them on him, would be his greatest challenge. Yes, that's what he would do: seduce her into his bed (or hers, as the case might be) and make her surrender to him.

He hadn't had a challenge like this one in a while. Most women fell into his arms and his bed without much ado, without much more than a smile and a wink on his part. Despite the kiss she had allowed him to steal, she wouldn't fall easily. Her stern reprimand had made that clear. She'd brought herself under control again. And he'd do anything to snap that control, like a mere twig a hunter crushed with his feet. All because he could. And because she was the choicest morsel he'd tasted in a long while.

FOUR

Raphael found the elegant parlor in which Isabella was waiting for him after he'd gotten dressed. The clothes of her late husband fit him perfectly, and the fellow had had taste, too. And just as perfectly as he'd slipped into the man's breeches, shirt and coat, Raphael wanted to slide into his widow. He was sure she'd fit him just as perfectly.

Isabella stood near the fireplace with her back to him as he entered. Her hair was now tied in a tight bun low at the back of her neck. And she was dressed in a gown that was fit for any noble in Venice. If she wanted to pretend that she was all prim and proper, he'd let her, and then he'd expose what lay beneath her respectable exterior: a passionate woman.

"Signora Tenderini," he greeted her.

A visible shudder went through her body. Had she not heard him come in? Perhaps he was so used to being silent when approaching humans that it had become a habit he barely noticed. He made a mental note to try not to startle her again.

Isabella turned and looked at him. Her features were tense as if she'd been thinking long and hard about something. A frown disturbed her pretty face. Her pursed lips were evidence that she contemplated her next words.

"I'm glad to see that your near drowning seems to have produced no lasting injuries." While she spoke, her spine remained stiff, as if she was forcing herself to remain formal.

Raphael nodded and gave a slight bow. "I'm grateful to your servants and would like to bestow the man who pulled me out of the canal with a little monetary gift if you allow me." Whoever had been so brave as to jump into the icy waters and had the strength to pull his heavy body out of it should be rewarded.

"My gondolier has already been rewarded by me. No further reward is necessary."

He would still give the fellow a handsome sum of money. His life was worth it. But to Isabella, he only nodded, not wanting to alienate her. "I thank you for your generosity. And if I may, I profusely apologize again for my inappropriate behavior toward you. Let me assure you that—"

"No assurances are necessary," she interrupted him. "The traumatic circumstances explain your behavior. I'm a respectable widow and have a standing in Venetian society I care not to jeopardize. I trust in your discretion."

Raphael bowed and grinned to himself, wiping the grin off his face as soon as he straightened. She'd asked for his discretion? It could only mean one thing: She wanted him to be her lover.

He hadn't expected her to make an offer like this. Maybe he had under-estimated her. Maybe she was a widow who took lovers frequently. The thought disturbed him—why, he didn't know. "My discretion precedes me, Signora."

"Good. Then I bid you farewell. My gondolier will take you home."

She'd dismissed him? But hadn't he just assured her that he would be discrete? That nothing of their affair would reach Venetian society's ears?

"Signora? I don't understand. As I've just assured you, my discretion is unparalleled. Nothing of our affair will seep—"

"Affair?" she shrieked and took a step back. "You thought I was proposing an affair?" Her bosom heaved, and her cheeks turned a beautiful shade of red again. And not only that. He could see the vein at her neck throb. It was a sight that made him want to sling her over his shoulder, throw her onto the nearest flat surface and toss up her skirts before he fucked her and sank his fangs—

"I advise you to leave my house immediately. I'm a respectable woman, not a trollop."

The indignation in her voice gave him pause. It appeared his challenge wouldn't be as easy to win as he had assumed.

He bowed again as he retreated. For now. He would figure out a way to win her—sooner rather than later.

The gondolier was awaiting him at the dock. "Signore, where to?"

Raphael stepped into the boat and took a seat before he gave the man an address close to his house. He was careful never to disclose his actual location to anybody. His life depended on it.

"Very well, Signore."

Raphael leaned back and let his thoughts drift back to Isabella. Why he'd suddenly thought she was making him an offer to start an intimate affair, he could only blame on what had happened in her bedchamber. Why take him there, undress him, most likely fondle him while he was unconscious, when she had no intention of going through with it?

And why had she dressed that provocatively when she'd taken care of him? Why not remain in her prim and proper dress? Because all her scandalous attire had done was provoke him into kissing her. Damn that kiss. He couldn't forget it, no matter how brief it had been. He could still taste her on his tongue.

"We're here, Signore." The gondolier pulled up alongside a dock.

Raphael looked up at the man. "If you'd wait here for a few minutes for me to retrieve some coin, I would like to reward you for saving my life."

The gondolier gave him a startled look. "But, Signore, I wasn't the one who jumped into the water to pull you out."

"Then who was?" He stared at the man, but the gondolier hesitated.

"I'm sorry, I've misspoken," the man claimed.

Raphael could see a lie when it hit him in the face. Suspicion crept up his spine. He raised his voice. "Who jumped into the canal to rescue me?"

The gondolier lowered his gaze. "The Signora."

Shock coursed through Raphael's body. Isabella had braved the cold waters of the canal to save him? "Signora Tenderini?"

"Yes, Signore. She was the one who saved your life."

~

ISABELLA SIGHED DEEPLY. She hadn't been able to go through with it. More than anything, she'd wanted to ask him to conduct an affair with her, a very discrete, very short affair, just so she was reminded of what it was like to sleep with a man's arms around her body. But the thought that they would be discovered at some point had made her hold back.

Her late husband's cousin Massimo was keeping close watch on her, always trying to find a way to take from her what her husband had left her: his merchant business. As a male relative, he'd expected to inherit after his death. Yet, her beloved Giovanni had had other designs. He'd always seen her for what she was: a strong and intelligent woman more than capable of running a business by herself. His will had said as much.

After being left out in the cold, Massimo had taken it upon himself to pry into her personal life and dig up any dirt there was to find. There was none. She'd been virtuous before her marriage and remained virtuous after Giovanni's death. If she slipped only once, Massimo would be there to take advantage. He'd spread the gossip amongst Venetian society and make certain not only she but also her business was shunned. She knew it was his plan. Once she was down and cast out of polite society, he would take the business off her hands for a pittance.

No, she could never let herself slip and give into the desires that had started boiling up in her. Only another marriage would do. However, she hadn't met any man since Giovanni's death who she even remotely wanted as a husband.

And the scoundrel who'd just left her house? He was not the kind of man who'd make an offer for a decent woman like her. She had seen it in his eyes: the lust, the passion, the heat. All he wanted was to satisfy his carnal urges, to tumble her. And even if she hadn't seen it in his eyes, his words had made it clear. He'd expected an affair.

Her own body had almost betrayed her when he'd stood there in front of her. She'd wanted to run into his arms, ask him, beg him to make love to her, to pin her under his beautiful naked body and drive her wild. To feel his hard shaft in her, filling her, satisfying her. It had taken all her strength not to give in. Her life as she knew it would be over if she did.

Already, by bringing Raphael—oh, what a wonderful name—into her home and tending to him personally, she'd risked too much. She could only hope that Elisabetta would heed her threat. Adolfo she trusted one hundred percent. He was her ally, the only one of her servants who was completely loyal to her. Elisabetta was new in her employ and, Isabella hoped, too intimidated by her to go against her strict orders. She'd researched her background thoroughly before employing her, making sure she had no connections to Massimo. Massimo kept enough spies in her household.

Now she could only hope that no word of what had transpired in her home tonight would reach the outside world.

FIVE

Isabella waited until Elisabetta had undone her corset and stepped out of it. She was left with her chemise and drawers. Her hair was already relieved of the pins that had held it up and now hung loosely around her shoulders.

"That'll be all for tonight." She met Elisabetta's gaze in the mirror. "And don't forget, one word of what happened here tonight and you will never find another position in Venice."

She curtsied. "Yes, Signora."

When the maid finally left her bedchamber, Isabella let out a quiet sigh. All she could do was dream. At least she'd saved a life tonight. She hoped it had been worth it.

"Finally, I thought the chit would never leave." The deep voice came from behind the curtains.

She swiveled on her chair and saw Raphael di Santori step out from his apparent hiding place. Gasping, she pressed a hand against her chest and frantically reached for her dressing gown. "Signore, this is an outrage! How did you get in here?"

He motioned to the window. "I climbed in. And don't worry, nobody saw me. I understand how you value discretion."

Isabella pressed her dressing gown to her front to cover up as much as she could. Her heart beat in her throat. Only a rake would enter a woman's bedchamber without invitation. "I would value it even more if you disappeared just as discretely." She paused for effect. "This instant."

Raphael took a step closer. "I can't do that."

"Of course you can," she insisted. "Surely, if you managed to climb in, you'll manage to climb back out."

He smiled his insanely crooked smile and flashed his brilliantly blue eyes at her. She'd never seen a man with such hypnotic eyes. "What I meant to say is I won't. Because you, Signora, lied to me."

She shot up from her seat. "Lied?" What was he accusing her of? And besides, what did it matter? He was trespassing on her property.

"You risked your own life to save mine. Why did you lead me to believe that your servant rescued me?"

"Oh, that."

"Yes, that."

Before she knew what he was about to do, he crossed the distance between them and clasped her shoulders with his hands. "Don't you understand what kind of danger you put yourself in? You could have drowned with me, woman! How could you be so careless with your own life? Do you know how heavy I am? Did you even think?"

With every word he appeared to get angrier. She couldn't understand why. After all, they were both safe. "But we're both alive."

"By whatever stroke of luck! You could have given your life for me, a stranger. You don't even know whether I was worth saving." His eyes grew darker by the second, his voice harsher with every word.

"I couldn't let you drown. Every life is worth saving."

WHY THIS RAVEN-HAIRED beauty could infuriate him like this, Raphael had no idea. Yet, she did. The moment he'd heard the gondolier say that she'd been the one who'd jumped into the frigid waters to save him, he'd felt as if an ice-cold hand had squeezed his heart. For the first time in his life, true fear had traveled through his body. Fear for another person. Fear of what could have happened to her.

And when the gondolier had told him how long Isabella had stayed under water and how hard it had been to pull them up, all he could think of was paddling her stubborn ass to teach her a lesson so she would never again put herself in the path of danger as she had.

"Damn it, woman, if I were your husband, I would make sure you never jumped into another icy canal and risked your life." Yes, if Raphael were her husband, there'd be a hell lot of things he'd do, starting with—

"And how would you try to achieve that, you arrogant, ungrateful man!" Isabella spat and pushed off his hands.

Arrogant? Maybe. But ungrateful—no, Raphael wasn't ungrateful for having been given a second chance. But he was incensed about her apparent lack of concern for her own safety. As for keeping her from jumping into canals to rescue drowning strangers? He had just the right remedy for that.

With one swoop, he pulled her into his embrace and ripped the dressing gown from her grip, dropping it to the floor. "When I'm done with you, you won't have any energy left to swim in dirty canals and save undeserving strangers."

His mouth captured her plump lips. She'd parted them, clearly to voice her protest, a fact he now used to his advantage. Greedily, Raphael swept his tongue between her lips and dove into her. The delicious cavern of her mouth greeted him with the intoxicating flavor of an aroused woman.

He'd noticed that he didn't leave her cold, and it pleased him tremendously. He wasn't taking a shrinking violet to bed. No, the hot-blooded woman in his arms knew full well what would happen now—or at least her body did. And her body didn't protest anymore. On the contrary, her arms came around his neck, a hand slipping into his hair as she held him closer.

Raphael felt her generous breasts crushed against his chest with only her thin chemise and his own clothes impeding a closer contact. She was soft in all the right places and warm, so deliciously warm. He felt her heat seep into his body. Hunger attacked him, hunger for Isabella's body—and her blood. He tamped it down, not wanting to scare her. If he wanted more than just one night, he'd have to hide his bloodlust from her. And he wanted more than just this one night.

The moment she stroked her tongue against his, a bolt akin to a lightning strike hit him. A deep rumble started in his chest, his body wanting to give voice to what she did to him. When she stroked against him a second time, he freed his mouth from hers and let out the moan that had threatened to choke him.

"Angel," he whispered against her lips, his voice hoarse and breathless, his pulse racing.

"Nobody can ever find out," she said with a shaking voice.

He nodded eagerly. "I promise you." He'd keep their affair a secret. Nothing would compromise her standing in society. He'd make sure of it. The longer he could keep their affair hidden from prying Venetian eyes, the longer he would have her, devour her, consume her.

Raphael lifted her into his arms and carried her to the four-poster bed, where he laid her onto the crisp linen. She looked up at him with wide eyes, eyes that were full with the knowledge of what was going to happen.

"You're beautiful. I'm going to worship you with every fiber of my body."

Then he shrugged off his coat and dropped it to the floor.

CHAPTER

SIX

He undressed in plain view. Isabella realized that he wanted her to watch as he peeled item after item from his body and exposed his naked skin to her.

Was she making a huge mistake by allowing him to seduce her? When he'd intruded into her chamber, she had at first been shocked. But her shock had soon turned to desire. And a possibility had started to emerge. If it was true that nobody had seen him, then maybe she could risk this just once. He would leave the same way he'd entered, and nobody in her household would be the wiser in the morning.

For one night she could indulge in passion and pleasure. It would sustain her for many years to come: a pleasant memory, a few hours of bliss. And knowing what lay underneath Raphael's clothes, she knew it would be bliss. His body was made for sin.

She held her breath when he snapped the first button of his breeches open. Her decision was made when each button was released, revealing more of his flesh. First, dark curly hair came into sight, then his cock sprang free from its confines. Hard and big, it curved slightly upwards.

God, he was so much bigger than when he'd been unconscious. Much bigger than her late husband. In fact, it appeared his impressive shaft seemed to have more than doubled in size, or was she hallucinating? She licked her lips in anticipation. This was more than she'd expected, and she'd be a fool to turn down such a gift.

All she could think of was feeling his powerful instrument in her, of impaling herself on it. The mere thought made her perspire.

"Patience, my angel," he whispered with a knowing smile on his face. "This is all for you, and only for you."

Isabella met his gaze and shuddered. There was so much raw desire and lust in his eyes, she should be scared by its intensity, yet all it did was stoke the flames in her body higher. Instinctively, her own hand trailed to the juncture of her thighs, to that hidden place that throbbed with uncontrollable need. The place where wetness had already spread.

When Raphael inhaled visibly, she knew he realized it too. His nostrils flared, and his eyes grew darker. His voice was a growl. "You slay me."

His words didn't mean anything, made no sense, but she drank them in and relished the knowledge that he'd soon unleash his desire upon her. Like a barely-tamed beast, he stood before her, fully naked now, his chest rising and falling with every breath. His eyes traveled over her, then rested on the place where her hand lay over her quivering mound.

"I want you," she whispered, not caring if she sounded forward.

He took another deep breath as if he was drinking in her perfume. In the next instant, he leapt onto the bed, planted each of his knees to the outside of her hips and hovered over her. "My angel, you'll have every single inch of me in whichever way you please."

Then he took a hold of her chemise and, without any effort, ripped it open from the neckline to its hem. Isabella could only gasp at his boldness. Gasp and shiver with delight.

THE MOMENT RAPHAEL tore the thin chemise in two and exposed her breasts to his hungry eyes, he felt his cock jerk. She truly was beauty personified. Never in his long life had he seen a woman with such perfect breasts made of creamy skin and topped with the hardest nipples possible. He blew a hot breath against one nipple, eliciting a strangled moan from Isabella.

She was so responsive. When he'd undressed in front of her—moving deliberately slowly to give her a chance to feast her eyes upon him—he'd enjoyed seeing her become aroused. Her nipples had tightened under her thin chemise, and the aroma that had drifted into his nostrils had almost made him spill, so strong was the scent.

So delicious that it made his fangs itch despite the fact that he'd fed plenty before his unexpected nocturnal swim. He'd have to restrain himself so as not to bite her and drink her blood. The last thing he wanted to do was frighten her. All he wanted for tonight was to sate his carnal urges and make this angel come apart in his arms until she collapsed, unable to move another limb. Maybe then she would understand that she couldn't risk her life anymore by jumping into canals.

The thought of what she'd done still made him shudder. If she were his woman, he'd never allow it. He'd never let her out of his sight for fear something bad could happen to her. He'd protect her day and night.

Raphael stopped his thoughts. Why was he being so possessive about her? She wasn't his—in fact, she would never be his. It would only be a short affair, during which he'd be lucky enough to call a woman like Isabella his own, a woman who looked at him now, her eyes full of desire. He wouldn't disappoint her. She would experience ultimate pleasure in his arms tonight, even if it cost him his last breath.

He dropped his head to her breasts and let his tongue lick over one nipple, then the other one. She arched toward him. With an appreciative grunt, he sank his lips onto one breast and sucked the hard little nubbin into the depths of his mouth. His hands weren't idle either. They palmed her gorgeous globes and gently squeezed the firm flesh. Despite her generous proportions, she fit his palms perfectly. Just as he'd thought.

The nipple in his mouth tasted more delicious with every lap of his tongue over it. God, he couldn't get enough of her warm flesh, nor of the woman beneath it. As he switched to the other breast to lavish the same attention on it, he quickly glanced at Isabella's face. Her flushed face was framed by her long dark hair, strands of which clung to her glistening skin.

Her eyes were half closed, her long dark lashes resting against her skin. She'd captured her lower lip between her teeth.

Raphael smiled. "My angel, there'll be no holding back tonight. Whatever you feel, I want to hear it."

Isabella's eyes flew open, pinning him with a surprised stare. "But it's not decent." Her voice was breathless.

"There's nothing decent about what we're going to do tonight. So, let go and show me who you are." He wanted to see the passionate woman beneath the proper exterior, the courageous woman who'd recklessly risked her own life to save his.

Again, he sucked her nipple into his mouth and tugged on it.

"Oh!" she yelped.

"That's it, angel," he praised and moved lower, nibbling his way further south. When he reached the top of her drawers, he pulled on the strings and loosened the garment. Without effort, he freed her from it, laying bare the treasure beneath.

And what a treasure it was. Her dark curls glistened with her honey. Without coaxing, she spread her thighs, and he accepted the invitation and settled between her legs. He planted small kisses on the dark thatch of hair, then placed his hands on her thighs and urged her to part them further. She twisted under his grip. His mouth moved lower and hovered over her moist cleft.

"You shouldn't do that," Isabella said.

He looked up and met her gaze. "Do you not like it?"

"I don't know."

Surprise hit him. "Your husband never—?" He let the question hang in the room.

She shook her head. "He taught me what to do to him. But he never ... it's not clean."

What kind of husband had he been? Taking his own pleasure, but not giving her the same in return? Raphael inhaled sharply, taking in her enticing scent. "It's more than clean. Your scent drives me crazy, and you'd be depriving us both if you won't let me taste you."

Her eyes widened. "You want this?"

"More than anything." Then he simply sank his mouth back over her warm pussy and snaked out his tongue to take his first taste. As her honey spread over his tongue and ran down his throat, his gut constricted at the lightning bolt that charged through him. He growled and licked again.

Isabella was a feast the likes of which he'd never partaken. He would even forego blood if she allowed him to gorge himself on her honey. He felt like a pirate, plundering her sweet cave of its treasures. The intimacy of his action wasn't lost on him. He was her first, the first man who tasted her this intimately, who drank from her. A rush of heat went through him at the thought.

With leisurely ease, he lapped against her moist folds, tracing his tongue along her slit. When he moved higher, he recognized the instant change in her breathing. The moment he reached the engorged nub that rested just above the entrance to her channel, she twisted under his hold. He could feel her frantic heartbeat, hear her panting breaths. Then he licked over her little button. His name exploded from her lips as her hips bucked against him.

"That's it, angel," he praised and sucked the bundle of flesh into his mouth and tugged.

Now her moans and pants became more pronounced. Lick after lick he dealt her, nibbling, sucking, kissing, and devouring her sweet pussy. And with every touch she became more sensitive, reacting more urgently to his caresses. Under his hands and his lips, he felt her come alive, like a flower that suddenly started blooming.

With his fingers, he spread her wider, alternately fucking his tongue into her channel, then sweeping it over her center of pleasure. When he felt her tense up, he doubled his efforts until he sensed her shudder. He held onto her as her body shook from her climax and drank in the cream she released, not wanting to leave the paradise her body represented.

"Raphael," she whispered, her voice colored with disbelief and wonder.

Reluctantly, he lifted his head from her core and slid up her body, aligning his hips with hers. His erect cock was poised at her moist channel, which still quivered from the aftershocks of her orgasm. He couldn't resist and plunged in without a word or a sign of what he would do.

Her eyes widened. "Oh, yes."

He nodded, the cords on his neck tightening from the effort it cost him to ward off his imminent release. She was too tight. Nobody had visited her warm and wet cave in a long time. He tried to hold back, but of their own volition, his hips drew back and plunged back in. The sound of flesh on flesh only fed his hunger for her.

"Angel, I need to fuck you hard."

On the next stroke, she slammed her pelvis against him, intensifying his actions. Then his body's rhythm took over, his cock thrusting into her as if there were no tomorrow. All he could think of was possessing her, marking her, branding her.

Raphael looked at her face, wondering if he was hurting her with his frantic rhythm, and the sight that greeted him filled his heart with pride. Her lips were parted, her eyes dark with lust and desire. "Oh, yes, Isabella, yes!"

"Fuck me!" she whispered. Her words did him in. Never had he heard a lady utter such words, but when they came over her lips, he couldn't help but rejoice. His balls burned and tightened at the knowledge that she gained as much pleasure from their coupling as he did.

Dropping his hand to her pussy, he pressed his thumb onto her pearl. The widening of her eyes told him he was reigniting her sensitive flesh. "Yes, once more. Let me feel you milk my cock."

Her interior muscles clenched a second later, and his control shattered. With hot and eager spurts, he filled her tight pussy with his seed, pumping into her again and again, before he allowed himself to collapse on top of her, bracing himself on his elbows.

CHAPTER
SEVEN

Isabella rested her head in the crook of his neck and breathed in his spicy scent. Her entire body felt boneless. If somebody asked her to get up right now, she was sure she'd be incapable of moving even one limb.

Raphael turned his face to her and pressed a soft kiss on her forehead. It surprised her. She hadn't expected him to have a tender side.

"And now I'd like to know what in hell you were thinking when you jumped into the canal to save me," he said in a calm voice.

She jolted and tried to pull away from him, but his strong arms kept her imprisoned.

Isabella sighed. She didn't want to be reminded of what could have happened, how he'd almost slipped through her arms and drowned. She would have never experienced the kind of pleasure he'd given her in the last hour.

"Please," he added softly.

She pulled herself up and looked at him. "I couldn't let you drown."

"But you didn't even know me," he protested.

"It didn't matter."

"Why, Isabella? You must have had a reason."

She swallowed back a tear that threatened to push to the surface. "My husband drowned in the canal."

Shock registered in his eyes. Then he pulled her close to him and cupped the back of her head, pressing her against the crook of his neck. "Oh, my angel, I'm so sorry. I didn't mean to stir up bad memories."

"It happened almost a year ago. And I'm fortunate in many ways. But ..." Her voice became thick with the threatening tears.

"You miss him," Raphael whispered into her hair.

She nodded.

"Tell me what happened."

"Giovanni was good to me, generous and kind. He taught me how to run his business. I think he did it merely because it amused him, not because he knew how much it meant to me. He spent lots of time with me, despite the fact that he and Massimo often went out without taking me along or telling me where they were going."

"Massimo?" Raphael asked.

"Giovanni's cousin. They were close. But then, about a month before my husband's death, something changed. He started avoiding Massimo, made excuses when he came by. I had to lie for Giovanni when he didn't want to see him. He avoided me too. Suddenly, he didn't want to share my bed anymore. He stayed away all night. I think he might have had a mistress."

The thought still hurt, even after all this time. "He lost interest in me. He stopped loving me."

Isabella felt Raphael's hand on her chin as he tilted her face up to make her look at him. "I can't imagine how any man could ever stop loving you. I've never met a more lovable creature than you, my angel." He planted a tender kiss on her lips.

"You flatter me, but I can't ignore the truth. He was gone almost every night, until that one cold December night. Nobody knows what really happened, but by the time two footmen managed to pull him out of the canal, his lungs had already filled with water, and his heart had stopped beating. They said they were lucky to even find his body. Had his coat not gotten tangled up in some fishing hooks that hung over a moored boat, he would have drifted away."

"So you thought if you saved me, you'd save your husband. Why?"

"I was so angry with him. I wanted another chance. If I'd done something wrong that made him pull away from me, I wanted a chance at undoing it. Don't you see? When he drowned, I never got to ask him why he didn't love me anymore." She'd cried so many nights, trying to understand all that had happened.

"I'm sure there was some other explanation for him being away at night. A man married to you would not need a mistress. Believe me when I tell you that if I had you in my bed every night, there'd be no reason to ever seek pleasures elsewhere." Raphael traced her lips with his thumb, then slipped it between them. She instantly sucked on him and saw him close his eyes. "See? That's what I mean. With your lips on any part of my body, I would never have the strength to leave your bed."

When Raphael opened his eyes, his gaze collided with hers. His eyes had gone dark with passion. He pulled his thumb out of her mouth and lowered it to her breast, where he rubbed his digit over her nipple.

Her breath hitched.

"I want you to ride me. You've got me under your thrall, and I'd like to offer my body to you. Take your pleasure. I'm here to serve you."

His strong hands supported his words as he pulled her on top of him. Her legs automatically fell to each side of his hips, and her core aligned with his hard length. Isabella sat up and looked down to where their bodies were joined. His manhood was swollen, almost purple in color, evidence of the blood pumping it full. She reached for it with her hand and stroked against it.

He jerked at her touch and moaned. "Tell me, Isabella, did you touch me when I was unconscious?"

She felt her cheeks color with embarrassment.

"Please, I want to know. There's no need to be ashamed."

She avoided looking at his face when she answered him. "I washed you and dried you."

"Did you stroke your hand over me as you just did?" His voice was hoarse. She snapped her gaze to him and could see excitement shine in his eyes.

Isabella nodded. "Just once." She felt herself get wet at the memory.

"Did you touch my balls? Did you cradle them in your palms?"

She ran her hand along his shaft again, up and down. "I only let my fingertips slide over them."

"Did you like it?"

"Yes."

"And now, do you like it that I'm awake?"

Isabella wrapped her hand around his cock and squeezed, eliciting a groan from him. "I like it more now, because now you're hard and big." She pressed his shaft to her center, sliding against him so he touched that place where her pleasure concentrated, the place that throbbed uncontrollably now.

"I like it more now too," he offered, "because now I can feel what you're doing. Yet, the thought of what you did when I was unconscious excites me. It makes me want to do the same to you: to touch you when you're asleep. To slip into your tight sheath when you're not even aware of it."

The thought shouldn't excite her, but it did. To be taken by him when she had no defenses, no way of fighting it. To allow him such liberties with her body that not even her late husband had taken. "What would you do?" she heard herself ask.

She noticed his eyes flicker with lust. "I would slide my cock into you from behind, drive myself into you to the hilt. You would still be slick from earlier in the night. Then I'd hold onto your hips and pump into you, slowly and steadily, without any haste until you found yourself waking up."

Isabella pressed his cock closer to her and slid up and down, the liquid heat that flooded her with every word he spoke dripping from her onto his balls.

"My angel, I can feel you weep for me." He pumped his cock in her hand. "Ride me."

When his hands came to her hips, she lifted herself and aligned his cock at her moist entrance. With one long slide she pushed down, sheathing his hard length within her body. She welcomed the fullness.

"Yes," he groaned and pressed his head back into the pillow. "This is heaven."

Isabella smiled at his comparison and lifted up before lodging him deep inside her again. She fell into an easy rhythm, and judging by the sounds of pleasure he released and the hungry look he raked over her, he was more than pleased with what she was doing.

When his hand came and found her center of pleasure, he rubbed against it. With every downslide, his thumb grazed the little bundle of flesh, igniting the flames in her body. She felt moisture build on her face and neck and run like little rivulets between her breasts. They ached to be touched.

"Touch me." She was shocked to hear herself speak in such a lusty manner. But instead of being disgusted by her wanton ways, Raphael smiled back at her.

"I can only touch one of your breasts as you can see." He pointedly looked at where his thumb stroked her pearl. Then his other hand captured her nipple and pinched it. "Touch your other nipple."

Her eyes widened in shock. She couldn't do such a shocking thing.

"Do it," he ordered, "and don't stop riding me." He thrust his cock upward, plunging deep into her. "I want to see you touch yourself," he continued, his voice hoarser now. He pinched her nipple again, and it turned hard. "Just mimic what I'm doing. Like this." And again he rolled her nipple between his thumb and forefinger, sending a bolt of heat through her body and straight to her pearl.

She threw her head back and did as he asked. With her eyes closed, she touched her other breast and hesitantly rubbed over her nipple. It beaded.

"More," he urged her.

Without thinking, lust guiding her actions, she pinched her own nipple and cried out at the intense sensation. "Oh, God!"

Of its own volition, her rhythm sped up, and she rode him as if her life depended on it. The slide of flesh on flesh was like a symphony in her ears, and his hands pinching and rubbing her drove every sane thought out of her mind. She was like a rutting animal, barely recognizing herself. She suddenly was a wanton creature only intent on her own pleasure, on finding that delicious release he'd given her earlier.

Harder and harder, Isabella impaled herself on him. With every thrust, he drove deeper into her, filling her more. And she gripped him, not wanting this to end, not wanting him to escape. And then, with a breathless moan, she greeted the onslaught of her climax. The waves that swept over her nearly knocked her unconscious.

She felt the heat inside her channel and realized that Raphael had joined her in release, his hot seed pumping into her, before she collapsed onto his chest.

His arms instantly imprisoned her. His chest heaved from the effort it seemed to cost him to breathe. She felt a warm puff of air against her temple when he spoke. "You've slain me."

CHAPTER

EIGHT

Raphael had never had such an elaborate dream as this one: of angels and heaven, of ripe woman and sexual bliss. Even his sense of smell was still drugged with the scent of her, the beautiful Isabella who'd rescued him. He couldn't even remember how he'd gotten home after their intoxicating encounter. Had he taken her again after she'd ridden him into oblivion? And to think that it had been his hands and his mouth that had coaxed all that passion out of her.

He shifted in bed and encountered lush curves and warmth so familiar, he instinctively pulled her into the arc of his body, delighted to realize that his dream wasn't over yet. Yes, he could indulge once more, take the sleeping woman in his arms and make sweet love to her again while she slept. He could drive his aching cock into her and impale her with it until his orgasm claimed him. And then he would do what he couldn't do to her in reality: drink from the plump vein on her graceful neck, gorge himself on her rich blood.

Yes, even in his dream he could feel the draw her body had. And even now, with the ghost of her form pressed into him, he was getting hard. Hard for her body and thirsty for her blood.

Raphael took a deep breath. Her scent was still around him, and it felt so real it nearly undid him. Not wanting to wake up from this, he kept his eyes closed. His hand traveled to the soft globes of the imaginary woman in his arms and squeezed. Her nipple rubbed against the palm of his hand and tightened.

His cock pressed against her warm buttocks, and he pulled back to readjust himself. Yes, he could slide into her, his dream woman. Because in his dream, she'd be all wet and ready for him, open to any kind of debauchery he had in mind. He could ravish her even without her knowledge, because she was merely a figment of his imagination. A very beautiful figment.

With his hard length poised at the entrance to her cave, he noticed the warmth and wetness of her honey and pushed forward. Like a tight glove, she engulfed him in her dark depths.

"Oh, yeah," he grunted to himself. "Let me fuck you."

The woman in his arms stirred. Her ass moved back to take him deeper.

"Yes, take my big cock into your cunt." To his dream woman he could talk dirty, and it excited him. He didn't have to pretend he was refined. "And after that, your ass is next."

A startled cry came from her as she pulled away. He gripped her hips harder and pushed her back onto his cock.

"Raphael!" Isabella's voice was so real, it made him stop in his tracks.

Then he felt her hand on his—too real to be a dream. His eyes flew open. Despite the dim light, he could clearly make out where he was: in Isabella's bedchamber. He'd never left.

Raphael cursed and pulled himself out of her, for once not listening to his throbbing dick. A quick glance at the windows confirmed the worst: it was daytime, and while the shutters and the drapes kept out the rays of the sun, he could see light seep through the sides.

He'd slept in her arms—and slept better than he'd ever had—and missed sunrise. He was in a quagmire.

"You promised you'd leave before sunrise," Isabella said. He couldn't even fault her for the accusatory tone in her voice.

When he looked at her, he saw fear in her eyes. He knew what she was thinking: if anybody saw him leave her house now, her reputation would be ruined. And if he stayed, sooner or later her servants would discover him.

But what she didn't know was that he didn't have a choice in what to do. His only choice was to stay. The rays of the sun would burn him, and within minutes he'd turn into a pile of ash. He knew, because there had been moments when he'd taken short dashes from one hiding place to another—mere seconds—but nevertheless, his skin had burned painfully. He wasn't keen on repeating any of it.

He couldn't leave, no matter what. And somehow, he had to make this clear to her without exposing what he was.

"I'm so sorry, my angel. I fell asleep in your arms. I don't know how it happened."

"You can't stay here. My servants. They'll find out. You have to leave. Please. But nobody can see you." Her voice shook, and her eyes darted around the room as if to try and find a way out for him. Then she gasped.

He followed where her eyes had traveled. The clock over the mantle showed it to be past ten o'clock.

"Oh, no!"

"Please, Isabella, calm down. We'll find a solution to this. But I can't leave the house. Not now. The streets will be teeming with people. There's no way I can leave unseen." *And remain alive.* As much as he hated his next suggestion, it was the only possible solution. "You'll have to hide me here. Maybe in a dark storage room nobody uses?"

ISABELLA'S MIND CLICKED FRANTICALLY. How could this have happened? Hadn't they agreed this would be only one night, and nobody would ever find out? And now she was facing a disaster. How could she hide him from her servants? The only one she trusted was Adolfo; all others were liable to gossip.

"Maybe Adolfo can hide you in the small workshop he keeps for the gondola. But how will I get you down there without you being seen?" She pushed back tears of desperation.

A moment later, she felt his hand cup her cheek. "We'll figure it out. Now, let me help you get dressed."

Raphael jumped out of bed. Her eyes followed his nude form as if drawn by a magnet. His firm buttocks flexed as he walked to her dressing table. He pulled a fresh chemise and silky drawers from one of the compartments.

When he turned, he grinned unashamedly. How he could find humor in the situation, she couldn't fathom. "How can you—?"

"Because this allows me to spend another few hours with you that I wouldn't have had otherwise." He stepped toward the bed and turned back the covers, exposing her to his hungry eyes. Yes, she could clearly see the hunger in them and was instantly reminded of how she had awakened: with his hard length inside her, thrusting deep, and the most indecent words whispered in her ear. Words that had excited her nevertheless. More than she wanted to admit to him. If she did, she'd be no better than a common whore.

Raphael's hands were gentle as he helped her into her undergarments. Her corset followed. As he laced her up in the back, she felt his loins press into her buttocks. His cock was as hard as before.

"You're gorgeous," he whispered into her ear, then started nibbling on it. For a moment, she lost all senses.

A commotion on the stairs brought her back to reality. She jolted, and so did Raphael. He'd heard the voices outside in the corridor too.

"Quickly." He snatched her dressing gown and helped her into it.

"No, Signore, you can't see her now!" Elisabetta's indignant voice penetrated.

But a moment later, the door swung open without a knock, and Massimo burst into the room, his valet on his heels.

Elisabetta tried to push into the room too, but was prevented by the two men. "I'm so sorry, Signora, I tried to stop them."

But Isabella didn't listen to her maid, because Massimo's booming voice took all her attention.

"Look at you, you whore. How you drag my cousin's name through the mud!"

"Massimo," she echoed in shock.

Raphael grabbed her and pushed her behind his naked body as if to shield her from Massimo. But he couldn't shield her from the accusations that rolled off his tongue.

"Caught with her lover, still aroused and ready." Massimo sneered and pointed his finger at her while Raphael held her behind his broad back, seemingly unconcerned about his nude state. "By tonight, all of Venice will know what a whore you are! I can't wait to attend the ball."

Then he turned on his heels and left, slamming the door shut behind him. She was ruined. Not only was it her word against his, he'd brought a witness. Everybody would believe him. Her whole life was lost because of one night. Nobody could help her now. Not even Raphael.

"Leave," she choked out and turned away from him.

CHAPTER

NINE

Raphael stood frozen, still staring at the door. Massimo, she'd called him. Her dead husband's cousin. But none of that mattered, not after Raphael had seen the ring the man wore. He'd recognized the symbol on it. The black onyx was graced with a cross intersected by three waves—the sign of the Guardians of the Holy Waters. Holy Waters, because they had made it their mission to eradicate vampires and drown every single one of them.

He and his brethren had not been able to find out who the members of their secret society were, at least not so far. They were far too careful. This was the first time he'd actually seen someone wear the elusive sign. He could only imagine that it had been an oversight by Massimo to wear the ring in public and give himself away. Unless, of course, he didn't consider Isabella's house to be a public place, but rather a place where his secret was safe. Or had he simply been absentminded?

Had fate just handed him the key to dealing with the threat the Guardians represented? Was this why he'd been given a second chance and been thrust into this house and this woman's arms? So he could discover who they were?

A sob behind him made him turn. Isabella sat at her dressing table, trying to comb her hair, a look of anguish on her face. The woman who'd given him such pleasure only hours ago was a bundle of nerves.

When he met her eyes in the mirror, she looked away. "You should leave. There's nothing more to do for you. By tonight, all of Venice will know what a whore I am."

Her lips trembled as she spoke, and Raphael couldn't help himself. He walked to her and lifted her into his arms.

"No," she protested, "it's no use. You'd better go."

He tipped her chin up with his hand and made her look at him. Unshed tears rimmed her eyes. He wouldn't let her cry them. "There is something I can do."

A flicker of hope appeared in her irises.

"Do you have a servant you trust implicitly?"

She gave him a curious look, then nodded. "Adolfo, my gondolier. He's loyal to me."

"Good. Send him for a priest."

"A priest?" She tried to pull away from him, but he didn't allow it. Her eyes widened, and he knew then that she understood. Her breath rushed out of her lungs. "No. You can't do that. I won't allow it."

He hadn't pegged her to be this stubborn, but no matter, she would not win this fight. "You have no choice. Only if we can prove that we're married can a scandal be averted. You know it as well as I do."

She shook her head. "But you can't just offer for me and sacrifice yourself. All you wanted was a tumble. It's not fair to you."

"Fair? Isabella, I put you in this position. I ruined you. I would be a cad if I didn't take you as my wife now that our affair has been exposed. Surely you don't want a scandal?"

She was backed into a corner, and he could kill two birds with one stone. By marrying her, he could insinuate himself into her family. He would be able to get close to her despicable cousin, and, with some luck, find out who the other members of the Guardians were. Nobody would suspect him. However, he would have to be careful.

"Of course, I don't want a scandal, but I'm not going to ruin your life in addition to mine."

"Ruin my life?" He pulled her closer to his chest, crushing her bosom against him and sliding his hand onto her ass. "My sweet angel, if I get to spend every night with you in the way we spent the last one, I can see how my life would indeed be ruined." Yes, his second reason for marrying her was right there: he didn't yet want to let go of the passionate woman in his arms.

Raphael smirked and ground his cock against her. It was still semi-hard, and the way her barely-covered ass felt under his palm made sure all available blood was flowing to it now to bring him to another raging hard-on. "So, here's your choice: marry me so we can spend every night of our future giving each other pleasure, or ..." He paused and stroked her intimately, knowing he had no second suggestion.

"Do you mean it?"

"Yes. Now get dressed before I drag you back to bed. The next time I'll ravish you, it'll be as your husband." His chest swelled as he said the words, words which should have scared him and made him run the other way. But to know she would be his wife in a few short hours filled him with unknown pride.

Isabella spent most of the day in a trance. Raphael had done the honorable thing and married her. She hadn't expected it. There was no reason why he should. He had nothing to lose—only she did. But she wasn't brave enough to reject his kind offer, despite the fact that she feared his kindness would wear off soon when he was stuck with the reality of marriage. For a brief moment, she wondered whether he would have married her if she weren't a wealthy woman, but she pushed away that thought. Everything about his appearance and manners told her that he didn't need her money.

She allowed Elisabetta to fuss over her hair as she piled it high on her head. She'd chosen a dress made of red silk for the ball. It had been made for her only weeks before Giovanni's death, and she'd never before worn it.

But when Raphael had discovered it in her closet, he had assured her it would be the right gown for the occasion. She needed to make a statement: she wouldn't cower in the face of vicious rumors.

"Ready, Signora?" her maid asked and met her eyes in the mirror.

She nodded and stood.

Raphael waited for her at the foot of the stairs. She watched him as she slowly glided down, step-by-step, holding her gown slightly off the floor so she wouldn't trip.

Isabella looked at her new husband, who seemed frozen where he stood, his lips slightly parted, his eyes glued to her person. His attire was of the latest fashion. These weren't the clothes she'd lent him the night before. It appeared he'd sent a servant to retrieve some of his own garments.

She let an appreciative glance travel from his head to his feet and felt her sex clench. She'd never seen a more virile man, who could ooze sex like a poppy oozed opium, and who was just as dangerous and forbidden. His eyes were darker now, and they pinned her with a stare so intense she wondered whether she'd done something wrong. Was he angry with her?

As she reached the foot of the stairs, he took her hand and pressed it to his lips for a kiss. Then he took a step closer. His voice was low when he addressed her. "Angel, you take my breath away. I wish we didn't have to go to this ball to save your reputation—I'd much rather continue ruining you."

Raphael dipped his head to kiss her cheek, then whispered into her ear, "You make me so hard, I can't guarantee that the next time I ravish you will be in a bed."

Her breath hitched at his words. She didn't care where he took her next, as long as he took her. Her cheeks flushed at her scandalous thoughts. Where had all her manners gone? Had she thrown them to the wind?

When he straightened and looked at her, a knowing grin flashed over his features. He offered her his arm, and she took it, not only because it was expected of her, but also because her stomach was a nest of butterflies and her knees made of pudding.

"Now try not to think of what I'm planning to do to you later or your rather flushed face will attract every scoundrel at the ball like a pot of honey." He dropped his voice to a deep gravel. "And this honey is mine."

Isabella shot him a shocked glare. He responded by laughing. A full, uninhibited, happy laugh.

The Doge's Palace was illuminated as if a fire were blazing within. All of Venice was assembled: nobles, wealthy merchants, and foreign dignitaries. It was *the* event of the year. Raphael had never attended before. He lived a life that didn't allow for exposure. Living at the edge of society—albeit in pure luxury—made it easier to conceal what he was. Tonight, he would brave society's scrutiny for one reason and one reason only: to save his lovely wife's reputation.

Wife. What a strange concept. He'd never thought he'd get married, let alone in such a hurried way with not even his brother Dante in attendance. When he'd sent a servant to their house for garments with a quick note that he was all right, it was still daylight and therefore impossible for Dante to join him. He'd therefore refrained from telling him that he was getting married, because most certainly, his dear brother would have tried to get him to stop this foolish undertaking.

Isabella fidgeted next to him as they neared the entrance to the hall and edged forward in the line, so their arrival would be announced to all assembled. He dropped his head to hers and noticed for the first time that he was a good head taller than her. He liked that—it made him feel even more like her protector.

"Don't be nervous. I promise you, all will be settled." He clasped his hand over her fingers, which she'd hooked under his arm. They were ice cold. "And when this is over, I'll get you so hot, you'll never have cold fingers again." He loved rattling her, and the jolt in her body told him he'd succeeded again. By the end of the evening she would be panting for release, and he'd be only too happy to oblige his darling wife.

"Names," the tall announcer prompted him as they reached the top of the line.

Raphael bent toward him and gave him their particulars. A moment later, the booming voice of the man announced them to the room: "Signore Raphael di Santori and his wife, Signora Isabella di Santori, formerly Signora Tenderini, the widow of the late Giovanni Tenderini."

Dozens of heads snapped in their direction, and the collective gasps traveled through the crowd, like a ripple on the water's surface when disturbed by a pebble. Just as he'd expected, Massimo had already spread the news about Isabella's ruin. Just as well. This way, Raphael could undermine his credibility.

Keeping Isabella close by his side, he made his way down the stairs and waded into the mass of people whose curious and doubting stares followed them. His goal was single-minded: they needed to see the Doge. His authority alone would silence their wagging tongues. Merely announcing one's marriage wasn't sufficient in this case. They had to prove it.

As they approached the place where the Doge sat on his throne to hold audience, they were stopped by one of his attendants. Raphael looked past him and caught the Doge's eye. The man waved toward him, curiosity flashing in his eyes.

"Let them pass."

Raphael bowed in front of the older man and noticed how Isabella fell into a deep curtsy. From where the Doge sat, he could surely see deep into Isabella's neckline and get more than a glimpse of her ample bosom. Raphael took her hand and pulled her up.

"Your Excellency," he greeted the powerful man, who would help them restore Isabella's reputation. "May I introduce my wife and—"

"No introduction is necessary. I caught your name well enough as you entered." Then his eyes settled on Isabella. "Nasty things have been said about you, Signora."

"All untrue," Raphael offered.

The Doge gave him an impatient glare. "I addressed your *wife*, if she is indeed your wife."

Raphael held his tongue and squeezed Isabella's arm in reassurance.

"Your Excellency, all rumors are untrue, and I'm certain no harm was intended. However, it merely appears that the person who spread those rumors was misinformed about my status," Isabella said.

"And would you care to correct this misunderstanding now?"

"Indeed. My wedding to Signore di Santori took place yesterday, and it appears the notices I was planning to have delivered to Venetian society have been delayed. I will make sure my personal attendant makes haste." Her voice was steady now, and only Raphael could feel the light tremble in her body. He tried to soothe it by gently stroking her arm.

"And you have proof that such a wedding took place? I hope you don't mind my being a little cynical, but as you can imagine, once a claim has been made, it is up to me to verify it."

Isabella nodded. "I wouldn't expect anything less."

Raphael reached into his pocket and handed her a folded piece of paper. She smiled at him when she took it. Then she looked back at the Doge, who motioned her to approach.

When the man took the paper from Isabella's hands, Raphael could fairly hear her heart pounding. She wouldn't have to worry about anything. The ceremony as well as the priest had been genuine. The only thing he'd manipulated with his powers of persuasion was the date on the wedding certificate.

When the priest had signed and dated it, Raphael had sent his suggestions into the man's mind and made him write a different date: one day earlier. That way, Massimo couldn't claim they'd only gotten married after he'd discovered them in Isabella's bedchamber. They could claim that Massimo had intruded the morning after their wedding night. The scandal would be all his.

After many long seconds, the Doge looked up and rose from his chair. He nodded to one of his attendants, who pounded a long staff onto the floor to ask for silence in the hall. The chatter of the crowd subsided.

"My dear friends, I would like you to join me in congratulating Signore and Signora di Santori on their recent nuptials."

Gasps went through the crowd yet again, but before any kind of cheer could break out, a man pushed through. Raphael recognized him immediately: Massimo.

"That's not possible!" he cried as he rushed toward them.

"Are you calling me a liar?" the Doge asked, his voice tight and threatening.

Instantly, Massimo bowed. "Of course not, your Excellency." Then he straightened. "I am merely saying it appears rather sudden. And as a close relative, I was not informed." He glared at Isabella, and Raphael tightened his grip around her arm to pull her closer.

"You are informed now," was the Doge's reply before he turned. "Dismissed." The man had clearly lost interest.

When Massimo turned back to him and Isabella, his eyes were full of hatred. "You scheming, no-good—"

Raphael snatched the man's throat so quickly he had no time to react. He ignored the stares of the people around him. "Say the word, and I will call you for a duel. Just to warn you, I'm an expert in any weapon you might choose. So I would tread carefully now when you speak about my wife."

He sensed a tightening of his jaw, evidence that his fangs itched to descend, ready to attack. Quickly, he dropped his grip and turned away from Massimo. He couldn't risk public exposure.

"Isabella, would you like to dance?" Not waiting for her answer, Raphael pulled her into his arms and twirled them onto the dance floor. Her body pressing against him soothed his anger. He'd been close to killing her cousin right there in full view of everybody. It wouldn't do. The man would die, soon, and without any witnesses.

CHAPTER

ELEVEN

Isabella waited for Raphael to retrieve their cloaks and accepted another couple's well-wishes. After a few dances with her new husband, during which he'd plied her ears with scandalous words not suitable to be repeated anywhere, he'd finally declared that they'd spent sufficient time at the ball and could return home.

She was relieved. Despite the fact that the Doge had declared their marriage legitimate, she didn't like the stares people gave her. Was it her gown, or was it her husband they looked at? Or maybe it was the fact that she felt flushed, not by the warmth in the large hall, but by the words Raphael had whispered to her on a continuous basis. And by his hard length, which she'd felt while dancing with him.

She shivered when she felt Raphael's hands on her shoulders, spreading her cloak over her, then tying it at her throat.

"You were the most beautiful woman at the ball." His breath caressed her neck, and she tilted it slightly, offering it to him. He pressed a soft kiss against her skin, and she felt her blood warm. A moment later, he turned her to face him.

"Here, put this on."

She looked down at his hands and took a mask from him. "Why do you want me to wear a mask?"

"I'll explain later."

He put his own half-mask on and helped her tie hers. It hid most of her face, but her mouth remained free and unimpeded. When she turned and looked into the full-length mirror in the hallway, all she saw was a stranger in a long red dress covered by a black cloak. The black mask made her face unrecognizable.

"Come," Raphael urged her and led her into the night.

The streets were teeming with revelers, many wearing masks, some elaborate, others as simple as her own. Everybody was the same. Class was forgotten. It was how it was meant to be. During carnival, a pauper could be a prince. A noble could be a pirate. A whore could be a lady.

Isabella looked with wonder at the different people and masks as Raphael led her through the busy alleys around Piazza San Marco. The further they walked, the quieter the streets became. She barely noticed how far they'd gone because she was so fascinated with the activities in the streets.

She was surprised when Raphael suddenly stopped under an arched walkway and pressed her back to a wall behind her, his body flush against hers. "And now, my sweet wife, it's time to consummate our marriage. I think I've waited long enough." The predatory glint in his eyes was unmistakable.

Isabella gasped in shock. "Here?"

His lips ghosted over her skin, his breath caressing her as he answered. "Yes, my beautiful angel, right here. That's why we're wearing masks. I'll ravish you here, where any passerby might see us. Yet, they won't know who we are. All they'll think is that a man is fucking a whore, and they won't care. Maybe they'll simply watch."

She tried to push him away, and with him her own scandalous desire to do just what he was suggesting. Her body already responded to his salacious words, her sex clenching in anticipation of his body claiming her. And the thought that somebody could see them sent a hot flame through her core. No, she couldn't allow this to happen.

Raphael encircled her wrists and held them to the wall, then dipped his head to where her bosom heaved. He licked his tongue over her twin swells in a low and sensual stroke and inhaled. "I can smell your arousal, my love."

Panic gripped her. If she allowed him to do this, he would realize that she was no lady, that she was no better than a whore, because only a whore would allow herself to be ravished in such a public place. And then? Would he toss her away when he saw what she really was? A deeply disturbed woman with lusty feelings, more debauched than any whore in the city?

"Please, Raphael, let us go home," she pleaded, but knew her voice was hoarse with the lust she could barely contain. She didn't understand why he conjured these feelings up in her. Her first husband never had. She'd been the dutiful wife, and while she had enjoyed when Giovanni had bedded her, she'd never lost control or felt the desire to do scandalous things like those Raphael proposed.

Isabella felt her bodice loosening and realized that Raphael was undoing some of the hooks that held her dress up. She tried to protest, but couldn't because his lips on her skin made her brain unable to form any words. When his hands pulled down her bodice by only a few centimeters, it was sufficient for her breasts to pop out of their cage. Cold air blasted against them, tightening her nipples instantly.

Greedily, Raphael clamped his mouth over one nipple and sucked, while his hand cupped her other breast and kneaded it. Isabella couldn't stop the moan from leaving her lips, just as she couldn't stop the liquid that pooled between her legs. "Oh, God," she whispered breathlessly.

Her nipple popped out of his mouth, and he used his fingers to pull on it. Then he looked at her, his eyes clouded with the same passion she'd seen in him the night before. "Open my breeches and take my cock out."

Without thinking, she followed his order while he sank his lips onto her other nipple. With shaking fingers, she reached for his flap and started unbuttoning it. Her hand grazed his hard length. His moan was so deep and loud, she heard it echo in the archway. But by now she didn't care who would see or hear them. She wanted him, wanted his hard shaft to drive into her and claim her.

When his trousers were finally open, she wrapped her palm around him and squeezed the velvety skin covering his marble-hard manhood. She loved the feel of it, soft on hard. Two opposites, yet one incomplete without the other. So perfect and beautiful.

She felt Raphael's hands on her shoulders, pushing her down. "Suck me," he ordered.

Isabella dropped to her knees in front of him and found his shaft pointing right at her mouth.

"Yes, suck me like a whore. Because tonight, my dear wife, you're my whore, and you'll do whatever I want."

The words should have shocked her, but all she thought of was to put her lips onto his flesh and make him beg for release. She didn't feel degraded because he'd called her a whore. Instead, she felt powerful, because by being on her knees she would bring him to his. She licked her lips and took her first taste of his flesh.

Raphael's control nearly shattered when Isabella's lips closed around his cock and slid down on him. White hot heat surrounded him, nearly paralyzing him. He braced himself against the wall behind her, trying to steady his shaking legs. She would be his undoing.

Never had a woman's mouth given him such instant, overwhelming pleasure. "Fuck," he let out, his brain unable to form any other word since it had turned to the consistency of molasses. He tried to steel himself against the onslaught of sensations she unleashed on him, but to no avail.

Like a barrage of cannonballs, they plowed into him: burning him, searing him, branding him. Yes, she was branding him with her mouth, with the laps of her tongue against his hard flesh, with her breath that whispered against his length, the hands that stroked him in concert with her mouth. She was spoiling him for any other woman, making certain he would never want to be touched by anybody else, never feel another woman's mouth on him but hers.

Like a witch, she spun her spells around him, her cheeks hollowing as she sucked on him harder, her fingernails scraping against his tight sac where his balls burned like hellfire, the pressure mounting like in a volcano. God, she would suck the life out of him if she could. And at this point he wasn't so sure it was beyond her capabilities.

Another lick against his mushroomed head and he pulled himself out of her mouth, hissing sharply. He couldn't take any more.

"I wasn't done," Isabella complained.

Without a word, Raphael grabbed her and lowered her onto the stone bench he'd seen in the corner, high enough so he could remain standing when he fucked her. Then he tossed up her skirts and reached for her drawers. With one swoop, he ripped them into shreds, ignoring her surprised look. He had no more patience than a sailor who'd spent the last months at sea.

Her arousal engulfed him. "Now I'll fuck you, my beautiful whore! I'll fuck you until you scream." And with one single thrust he seated himself in her drenched pussy. She convulsed around him, making him still instantly. "Oh, yes, you love being ravished out here, don't you?" When she didn't say anything, he ordered, "Answer me!"

Isabella's breathless "Yes" was more of a moan than a word. It suited him just fine. And strangely enough, it helped him gain his control back. No, this delectable, passionate woman would not gain the upper hand.

Slowly, Raphael pulled his cock from her silken heat, only to let it slide over her little pearl. She twisted underneath him, but he held her hips in a vice grip so she couldn't escape his torture. He would make her confront her desires. Now. Here. He would break down her defenses and free the passionate woman inside her.

Not giving her any indication of what he was about to do, he plunged his hard length back into her, making her release a startled cry. "Oh, yes, never think you're safe from my cock. Because I'll take your wet cunt with it whenever and wherever I want." He deliberately used crude words to shock her, all the while sliding back and forth in her tight sheath, her honey so slick, he felt like drowning all over again. Only this time, it was a pleasurable kind of drowning.

When he heard a sound behind him, he twisted his head. "It appears we have company." He briefly glanced at the well-dressed gentleman, who'd entered the covered archway and was looking at them.

Raphael felt Isabella's instant reaction and recognized it as her flight instinct. But he wouldn't allow her to follow it. Instead, he continued to pump into her sweet depths and reached for her ample breasts, which bobbed with each of his thrusts.

"When you're done with her, I'll take her," the man behind him offered.

Raphael growled. "I won't be done with her for a long time." A very long time. "She's mine for the night. I bought this whore, and I'm going to make certain I'll get my money's worth." He grinned at Isabella when he noticed her shocked face. "So, no, you can't fuck her, unless, of course, she consents."

Isabella's protest was instantaneous. "No!"

Raphael chuckled. "As you can see, she only wants my cock. But if you care to watch, step closer for a better view." He didn't care whether the man watched or not, but he would never allow him to lay one single finger on her. Isabella would not be shared with anybody. But while her mask provided her anonymity, and him as well, he would drive her lust higher by the knowledge that they were being watched.

The man's footsteps confirmed that he'd accepted his offer. Raphael could see how he stood only a short distance from them to the side, so he could see both Isabella's naked breasts as well as her cunt and how Raphael's cock plunged in and out of her.

"She has a beautiful cunt, this whore, don't you think?" he asked the stranger as he sliced back into her heat, kneading her breasts in his palms.

But the man didn't answer. From the corner of his eye, Raphael could see why: the man's hand had freed his own cock. Hard and thick, it strutted from his breeches as he now pumped it in his right hand.

"I see you agree," he commented and brought his attention back to Isabella, who'd followed his glance. Her mouth dropped open.

"Yes, he's stroking himself, wishing it was your hot cunt he's pumping into. Does that excite you?" He delivered a hard thrust, and she snapped her gaze back to him, dropping her lids as if in shame. With another thrust, he jolted her. "Oh, no, you won't look away. I want you to watch him watch you as I fuck you." Her eyes went wide behind her mask. He knew she wanted to watch, but was too ashamed to admit it.

He pinched her nipples hard until she cried out, her lips quivering, her breath at a fever pitch. "Now watch him. But remember, it is my cock that's inside you. My cock that fills you."

He wanted to possess her, every cell of her. And he wanted the whole world to know she was his, his to drive to ecstasy, his to pleasure. His body set his rhythm now, plunging deep and hard into her with long strokes.

He noticed her pull her lips between her teeth as she watched the other man stroke his own cock. Raphael heard the grunts the man let out, but he only saw her, his beautiful angel, ecstasy written all over her body. He released one of her tits and dropped his hand to her pearl. She snapped her head back to him as he rubbed his thumb over it. A moment later, she cried out, and her muscles clamped around his cock, igniting his own climax.

His seed shot from his balls through the length of his cock and exploded from its tip, pumping into her channel, flooding her with it. But he barely noticed any of it as his entire body was gripped by his orgasm, shaking him to the core. Nothing had ever felt as raw and earth-shattering as the consummation of his marriage.

TWELVE

Raphael kicked the door to his home shut with his foot even as he cradled the sleeping Isabella in his arms. He'd removed their masks and tossed them shortly before they'd reached his house. He carried her into the parlor and laid her onto the large sofa.

"You brought dinner. I guess that's the least you could do after making me worry about you," his brother droned from the corner, where he sat in his favorite wingback chair.

"Dante, I was hoping you'd be home. We need to talk."

His brother rose from his chair, his long legs eating up the distance between them without effort. "Yes, that we do. But after dinner." He glanced down at Isabella. "Have you tasted her yet? She looks positively delicious." Dante licked his lips.

Raphael blocked his brother from approaching her. He would have liked to give Dante the news in a less abrupt way, but the cad didn't leave him any choice. "She's my wife. And you'll do well keeping your hands and fangs to yourself. As well as your dick."

"Your wife?" Dante's voice filled the entire room. His doubtful look would have been amusing if Raphael didn't have other things on his mind —like her family connections.

"You got married?"

He couldn't miss the accusatory tone in Dante's voice. "That's my own business."

"Not when it affects us both. She's human." His brother squared his shoulders, but Raphael wasn't intimidated. When he ran his hands through his thick, black hair, Raphael knew that Dante wasn't planning on a fight. "Why in hell would you do such a thing?"

"She saved me."

"What?"

"She saved me from drowning. Pulled me out of the canal when I'd already slipped under. She risked her own life." There was a certain pride with which he said it. His wife was a brave woman.

Dante took a step back in shock. "You nearly drowned? What happened?"

He shrugged. "I'm not sure. I felt a hand on my back and fell into the canal. But there were lots of drunken revelers around, a rowdy crowd. It could have been an accident."

His brother raised an eyebrow. "What if it wasn't?"

"Then you and our friends will help me find out who's behind it."

"I could venture a guess." Dante gave him a pointed look, and Raphael knew immediately that he was thinking about the Guardians of the Holy Waters. A moment later, Dante glanced at Isabella still lying motionless on the sofa. "By the way, what's wrong with her? What did you do, drug her?"

Raphael grinned. "Multiple orgasms."

The laugh that followed echoed in the entire mansion. "You scoundrel!"

"Not likely—what I did was entirely proper. After all, she is my very respectable wife." Respectable—yet with a lusty streak he didn't mind a bit. "Now, let's let her sleep. She's exhausted." He pulled his brother away toward the sitting area in front of the fireplace.

"Yes, and sore, I'd imagine. She looks petite."

"She's stronger than you think. And don't worry about my wife. I know how to take care of her." Yes, she would be a little sore from the ferocity with which he'd ravished her, but he'd make it up to her by eating her sweet pussy and soothing her flesh with his tongue soon.

Raphael let himself fall into his armchair as Dante settled back into his own. He had to forget about his new wife for a moment. "I discovered one of the Guardians."

His brother sat forward with a start. "Of the Holy Waters?"

"Yes, the very same." He motioned his head toward the place where Isabella slept. "Her late husband's cousin is one of them. I saw the ring. He wore their symbol."

Dante's face flashed with surprise. "In public?"

"Not exactly. He burst into Isabella's bedchamber just as we were ..." Raphael cleared his throat. "His name is Massimo Tenderini. I want you to follow him, find out everything you can, what he does, who he meets, where he goes. Everything. He will lead us to the Guardians. We just have to be patient. Can you do that?"

Dante nodded. "Yes, nothing simpler than that. I'll put a man on him. However—" He paused and gave him a long look. "—has it crossed your mind that your meeting Isabella and then her cousin was not by accident?"

"In what way?"

"What if she was put in your path so you would then in turn lead the Guardians to our kind? Don't you think it was a little too convenient that you were pushed into the canal, and she just happens to come along and rescue you? What if it was a setup? Her connection to the Guardians can't be ignored. What if she is their spy? Their very delectable spy, if I may add."

A stab like a giant pin prick attacked his heart. "You can't possibly believe that. She's an innocent."

"Famous last words of a fool in love," Dante chastised. "You can't trust her."

ISABELLA FELT warmth penetrate her as her consciousness returned. The voice that had jolted her out of her sleep was unfamiliar.

"She's my wife," she heard Raphael proclaim.

"Which is still something you'll have to explain to me," another man said. "What are you going to do when she finds out?"

"She won't find out."

Isabella's heart stopped. What did Raphael not want her to find out? What did he have to hide?

"You can't keep it a secret from her forever."

"I'll be careful," Raphael assured him. "She'll never need to know. And besides, she'll help me get close to Massimo."

Massimo? Why did her new husband want to get close to her cousin? What did he want from him? She'd married a man she knew nothing about. Had she made a huge mistake? Would it have been better to be ruined rather than find herself married to a man who was using her for some wicked scheme?

"Unless of course she was planning all this. Didn't you say that her cousin burst into her bedchamber when you were fucking her? Who would do such a thing? It's further evidence of her involvement."

Raphael had told the man such a private thing? How could he?

"Are you suggesting that she engineered this situation so I would have to marry her?" Raphael asked, his voice full of disbelief.

"And why wouldn't she? If Massimo is a Guardian, he might have power over her and direct her to do what he needs done. She had to have known. No offense, little brother, but despite your considerable charms, a respectable woman doesn't just fall into bed with you without considering the consequences."

What were they trying to accuse her of? Massimo wasn't her guardian. She was an independent woman, or at least she had been until earlier today when she'd married Raphael. Perspiration built on her face. What had she done?

"I concede that the situation was unusual, but you can't ignore the fact that with her falling into my lap, our battle might soon be over."

Isabella pushed back the tears that threatened to burst to the surface, tears of disappointment. She'd thought Raphael desired her, maybe would even fall in love with her, but all he wanted was to use her for something she didn't even understand. She couldn't open her eyes, didn't want to face reality. She was married to a man who cared nothing about her.

"Fine, I will contact our friends and see what we can find out. In the meantime, you'd better take good care of your wife. And I suggest you don't let her out of your sight. If she's scheming against us, you know what you'll have to do."

Isabella held her breath, but there was no answer from Raphael. Instead, she heard him get up, heard his heels on the wooden floor come closer. When the sofa depressed beside her hip, she knew he'd sat down. When his hand stroked over her arm, she flinched.

"Wake up, my angel." He pulled her up to a sitting position and held her in his embrace, stroking his hands over her back.

She couldn't pretend any longer to be asleep, but was unable to form a word. "Hmm."

"Open your eyes, Isabella. I'd like to introduce you to somebody."

Her eyes flew open, and she met Raphael's gaze. He smiled at her and kissed her softly on her cheek. She tried to push away from him, but he held her too tightly. Suddenly, she was afraid of him. He was a strong man. If he wanted to hurt her, or if the man who'd called him brother ordered him to hurt her, he could do it, and there was no way she could avert it.

Raphael released her partially, allowing her to turn to the side. "Isabella, this is my brother Dante."

Isabella looked up at the tall man who stood near the sofa. His hair was black like a raven, his figure broad. She could instantly see the resemblance between him and Raphael, only that this man was a little taller and his facial features more rugged, less elegant than Raphael's.

"It's a pleasure to welcome you into the family," Dante drawled.

She knew it was a lie. Only minutes earlier, he'd told his brother not to trust her. But she knew she couldn't let either one of them know what she'd overheard. If she did, she was doomed. Even though she'd barely understood half of what they'd discussed, she'd understood enough to know that Dante was dangerous and would probably kill her if she got in the way of whatever they were planning.

"Thank you, Signore," she responded and lowered her eyelids.

"Now, now, Isabella, you'll have to call me Dante. We're not very formal here. And you're my sister now."

"Of course," she added hastily, not wanting to upset him.

"Enough of the pleasantries for tonight," Raphael interjected. "Why don't I show you upstairs and have a bath sent up for you? I'll join you shortly."

Her pulse raced. "We're staying here?" She'd assumed this was Dante's house. And she didn't want to stay under his roof. She'd rather be at her own home where at least she could summon help if she needed it.

"Yes, we're spending the night at my house," Raphael answered.

"Your house?"

He nodded. "Yes. Or did you think you married a pauper? This is Dante's and my house. We've lived here all our lives. Come, I'll show you to my chamber." He cleared his throat. "Our chamber."

Isabella swallowed hard and placed her shaking hand in his outstretched palm.

THIRTEEN

Not even the warm bath a servant had prepared for her could calm Isabella's nerves. She tried to piece together the things she'd overheard, but nothing made sense. What did Raphael want from her, and what did he want from Massimo? Did he really believe she was under Massimo's command? She'd always hated the man, even when Giovanni had still been alive. She hated the way he snuck around and considered her house his own, how he ordered her servants around and pretended to be the master of the house whenever he visited.

For anybody to think that she would do his bidding was ludicrous.

She won't find out. Raphael's words still echoed in her mind. What was he hiding? Was he a gambler? Did he already have a wife somewhere else? What was it that he didn't want her to know?

Clearly, he hadn't married her for her money. As she perused his bedchamber, she couldn't help but admire the rich furnishings, the expensive rugs, the beautiful paintings. Everything in his possession fairly screamed of wealth. Her own home looked like a pauper's in comparison. No, it wasn't her money he wanted.

Which brought her back to Massimo. What did Massimo have that Raphael and his brother wanted? She had never really figured out what

Massimo did. But she'd always hated the fact that when he came to call on them, he would take Giovanni with him, and they'd be out all night. Giovanni would come home disheveled and exhausted. But not once had he answered her questions about where he'd been.

Isabella slipped under the covers of the large bed and forced her eyes shut. Somehow, she would get through this. Tomorrow, she'd go back to her own house and try to figure out how to extricate herself from this situation. Maybe she could appeal to the Doge and ask for protection. Protection from her own husband? What would Venetian society say? No, she couldn't make this public. What if Raphael made it known how he'd taken her in that public archway in full view of a stranger? Her reputation would be in shreds, despite the fact that she was married.

No, she couldn't enlist anybody's help. She was alone in this. Alone and frightened of her own husband. A stranger, a man she knew nothing about.

When Isabella heard the door open and footsteps on the floor, she knew Raphael had come to join her. Since he'd led her into his own bedchamber and not given her a separate one, she'd known he'd be joining her eventually. She would feign sleep so he would refrain from ravishing her again. Surely, he must have had enough for tonight after what he'd done in that archway.

A rustle of clothes confirmed that Raphael was getting undressed. Moments later, he slipped under the covers and instantly pulled her into his arms. He was naked.

"Mmm, you smell amazing." He nuzzled at her neck, planting small kisses along her pulse. She let out a breath. "So you're still awake. I was hoping you would be."

"I'm very tired," Isabella answered, hoping he would leave her alone. She didn't want him to touch her when she knew something was wrong.

"I know, my angel. Are you sore?" His hand slipped to the place between her legs that instantly started throbbing.

"Yes, yes, I'm sore," she lied and wished he'd remove his hand so her body wouldn't turn wet and needy.

But instead of leaving her alone, Raphael pulled up her chemise. She didn't have a night rail, so she'd decided to wear her chemise instead to have some sort of protection. It appeared that her new husband didn't care for it.

"Let me make it better then. Now, let's get you out of this." He tugged on the chemise and lifted her toward him, then pulled the garment over her head.

"But," she protested. Hadn't he heard that she told him she was sore? Would he not give her reprieve?

He put his finger on her lips. "Shh, Isabella. I won't penetrate you. I'll merely soothe your flesh. I would be a poor husband if I didn't take care of my wife's needs." Then he stroked his hand over her hair. "You've pleased me tonight, more than you can know. To see you in such ecstasy, to watch your passion, to feel it surge through my body. You amaze me with your generosity."

She heard his words, and they were colored with admiration. How could he be the same man she'd overheard talking to Dante, the same man who'd admitted to his brother that he was using her? Her chest tightened, and a feeling of despair swept through her. She tried to hide the tiny sob that stole from her lips, but he heard it nevertheless. And misinterpreted it.

"My love, you don't have to be ashamed of what we did. Nobody will ever find out. You're my wife, and I'll protect you from all others." He let his hand trail to her full breasts, palming them gently. "You were so beautiful tonight. Your bosom pushed out of your bodice, your skirts lifted, your pink pussy glistening. I've never seen a more beautiful sight. And to know that all this is mine and mine alone, it makes me proud."

He was making love to her with his words. She didn't understand it, but her body responded against her will. It heated under his caress as his hand moved lower and stroked over her belly. She gasped when his fingers tangled in her triangle of curls.

"Yes, you were so responsive," he continued in his soft voice. "Your honey was so plentiful; it engulfed my cock, and I've never known a more welcoming home for it. Even now, just thinking about it, I'm so hard, I'm ready to burst."

God, how she wanted this man even though she feared his motives, feared what he was planning. But she had to fight him, fight her own body. She tensed.

"Don't be scared, Isabella. I promised you, I won't penetrate you tonight. I don't want to damage your sensitive flesh any further. But when your flesh is soothed again, I'll take you and plunge my cock into you so deep I'll be touching your womb."

She let out a moan, unable to keep it inside her any longer.

"Yes, you like that. You like my cock. I could tell by the way you sucked me today."

How was she supposed to resist him when he brought her body to boil, when he sent those delicious sensations through her with just a few words, while his hand rested almost innocently on her sex? He was barely touching her, yet her pleasure spiked and drove her body higher.

"Please," she whispered.

"Please what?"

She couldn't stand it any longer. "Take the ache away."

"Yes, my angel." Raphael made his way down her body and spread her thighs to settle in between them. Then he dipped his head and licked his hot tongue against her moist petals. And with every lick and every kiss, the pleasure in her body built. Forgotten was the conversation she'd overheard and the implied threat within it. All she felt was Raphael's eagerness to give her pleasure and make love to her.

Within seconds, she felt the heat in her body spiral out of control. His tongue was relentlessly lapping against her pearl, turning it hard. With every lick and every pull, little explosions ignited in her belly.

Isabella buried her hands in the bed linen, grabbing the fabric in her fists as she fought against her own body's reaction to him. But there was no fighting what he did to her. He gave her pleasure and catapulted her into a world of bliss without asking for anything in return. It made his intimate ministrations even sweeter. When his lips closed around her center of pleasure and tugged, she let go and allowed herself to surrender to him. The waves that followed lulled her into sleep.

The last thing she felt was Raphael pulling her into the curve of his body, pressing her back against his chest, whispering into her ear, "I'll never hurt you."

CHAPTER

FOURTEEN

Raphael woke in the early afternoon with Isabella still tucked into his chest. She hadn't moved all night, and it pleased him. He'd felt her apprehension the night before and feared that she regretted what they'd done. That's why he had made love to her with words alone. He didn't want her to feel regret. He wanted her to know how much he appreciated what she'd given him.

Despite the things Dante had said, he wasn't going to let anything get between him and his wife. Not even his hunger, a hunger he'd felt immediately upon waking. He hadn't fed since the night he'd nearly drowned, and could now feel his body craving the blood it needed to sustain itself.

He would have to feed tonight. Not from the lovely neck of his beautiful wife, who still slumbered in his arms, but from a stranger. Because about one thing Dante was right: he couldn't ever let her find out that he was a vampire. She would run from him. And he didn't want to lose her.

By the time Isabella woke, Raphael was dressed and had arranged a meal for her. He knew she would be hungry. When he joined her in the dining room, which was kept in relative darkness by keeping the shutters closed but every candle in the room blazing, she had almost finished her plate.

He took a seat opposite her. She appeared nervous when she looked at him, her eyelids slightly lowered as if trying to avoid him. Was she still embarrassed by what had happened the night before?

"Shall I prepare a plate for you?" she asked and made a motion to get up toward the small buffet one of his servants had prepared.

"Thank you, my love, but I ate while you were still asleep."

How long he'd be able to hide from her that he wasn't eating, he had no idea. His vampire body only tolerated blood and liquids but never solid food. He would have to come up with all kinds of excuses so Isabella didn't become suspicious.

"Oh. I've never slept that long." She blushed a delightful pink.

"I exhausted you last night." He paused and noticed how she lowered her gaze even further as her cheeks turned darker. "And I'm planning to do it again tonight." He ignored her shocked gasp. "Now, eat. So you'll have your strength."

He loved rattling her, making her lose her composure. Yes, most of all he loved peeling away those layers of proper lady she piled so high onto herself, because underneath was a woman who harbored raw passion and unbridled lust. Just the way he liked it.

"When will we return home?"

"Do you not like it here?"

"Your house is very luxurious, very grand. But I have a business to run, and all my things are at my home."

It was a fair reason. He couldn't argue with it. Besides, in order to find out more about Massimo, who surely would want to intrude on her again soon, it would be better to remain at her house. "Very well, my angel, we'll return to your home tonight."

"Why not now?"

He raised an eyebrow. "Why the rush? Do you hate it here so much?"

Isabella hastily shook her head. "No. Of course not." But her expression said otherwise.

"It's Dante, isn't it? You don't like him." Not that his brother was the most charming man. He could be downright annoying when he set his mind to it. And clearly, he had his reservations about Isabella, and maybe she'd picked up on those vibes.

"No, no, he's nice."

Raphael rose and walked around to her, then took her hand and kissed it. "I want you to be happy. We'll go home at sunset. I promise."

"I'm having the servants prepare Giovanni's old room for you."

Raphael turned at the sound of Isabella's voice coming from the door to the study. After returning to her house, she'd excused herself to attend to some warehouse business and left him to his own devices.

"That won't be necessary."

She graced him with a surprised look.

"I'm perfectly happy staying in your chamber."

Her chest heaved, and he couldn't tear himself away from the enticing site of the creamy skin of her breasts. The dress she wore wasn't quite as low cut as the red gown she'd worn the night before, but it wouldn't take much to lower that bodice and make those nipples pop out. His trousers tightened at the image.

"But it's not proper. Married couples have separate chambers."

He stood and walked toward her, his gaze zeroing in on her plump lips. "*We* won't. I didn't marry you to spend my nights alone." He stroked the back of his hand over the swells her neckline exposed. Tiny goose bumps formed on her skin. Then he lowered his head and placed a kiss at the line where her breasts pushed together to form a more than ample cleavage. He soaked in her scent and felt his hunger push to the forefront again. He still hadn't fed, and until everyone in the household had retired for the night, he wouldn't be able to sneak out and hunt for a meal. Maybe a quick ravishing would take off the edge.

Raphael pulled her fully into the study and closed the door. Her eyes went wide as if she knew what he intended to do. And maybe she did. By now, she should be able to read his face and know when sex was on his mind.

"Raphael, I have more work to do. So, if you'll excuse me." Isabella attempted to turn, but he merely pulled her back. His eyes darted around the room before he pulled her to the desk and bent her over it face down. "Are you still sore?"

"Y-yes," she stammered.

"Don't lie to me."

She hesitated, and he let his hand run over her ass. A hitched breath escaped her.

"I ask again. Are you still sore?"

A couple of seconds passed before she answered, "No."

"Did you like how I licked you last night? How I ate your pussy?"

He sensed her heartbeat speed up and knew his talk excited her. His hand squeezed one cheek before he started gathering her skirts to pull them up. "Did you not hear my question?"

A choked breath escaped her. "I liked it."

Raphael tossed up her skirts to her waist, then started untying her drawers.

"You can't do this here. The servants!" Her voice sounded panicked now, but he wouldn't be deterred. He pulled her drawers down to expose her perfectly round ass. When he stroked over it with his palm, she sucked in a breath.

Then he dipped his finger into her crevice and slid down to the apex of her thighs, where warm moisture greeted him. "So little encouragement, and you're already wet. I'm surprised your late husband ever got any work done, considering he had to keep you satisfied." He drove his finger into her inviting channel, making her gasp.

"You're right, the servants can intrude on us at any moment," he continued. "Do you know what they would see?"

"Raphael, please," she protested, but there was no heat behind it, rather, it sounded like a plea for more. A plea he was more than willing to answer.

"They would see how the mistress of the house was being fucked from behind as if she were a common whore. And they'd hear her pant like a bitch in heat." He pulled out his finger and unbuttoned the flap of his trousers. "And they'd hear her ask for more, they'd see her begging to be fucked harder, to be filled by her new husband's hard cock."

Raphael pulled out his shaft and guided the hard length to the entrance of her channel. "Tell me, Isabella, is that what the servants would see if they came in here?"

Her response was a mere whisper, but he heard it nevertheless. "Yes."

With one smooth thrust he glided into her, balls-deep. Underneath him, she panted heavily.

"Fuck me," she suddenly whispered, her voice barely audible.

"What was that, my angel?" he asked even though his superior hearing had picked up the words.

"Fuck me," she said, this time louder.

Her words were music to his ears. She was losing control and shedding the mantle of propriety, allowing herself to give into her wanton feelings, letting him satisfy her debauched needs. Yes, he was controlling her now, nobody else. Even if she was doing Massimo's bidding, he'd make sure she would defect to his side, because he'd give her exactly what she needed.

With every thrust into her sweet depths, her pulse became more uncontrolled. Her skin perspired, and her channel convulsed around him, trying to grip him and keep him there. As the sound of flesh slapping against flesh reverberated in the room, and her moans mingled with his, all he could hear was his own heart. Not simply beating in the frantic rhythm of their fucking, but telling him that whatever the outcome of all this was, he would have her, even if it meant making her one of them. One day—because he could not allow her to grow old and die.

Raphael rode her through her orgasm without giving her reprieve. As he continued pumping into her, he slipped a moist finger back to the crevice of her ass and found her puckered hole, which marked the entrance to her dark channel. He rimmed it, and it quivered.

Her mouth voiced a protest, but he ignored it, because her body was telling him otherwise. As he pressed against the rim, Isabella eased back against him, seeking, wanting this invasion. His finger slipped in one knuckle deep, and her muscles clenched, tightening around him. When she stilled, he moved his cock with renewed vigor, distracting her from what he was doing to her ass.

Isabella pushed back again, and this time, she took his finger deep into her. Slowly, he pumped his finger in the same rhythm as his cock, and her body mimicked his movements, moving back as he moved forward.

He'd never felt anything as tight as her ass. The knowledge that he'd soon take her there, that he would soon plunge his impatient cock into that forbidden hole, undid him. His release crashed over him in a torrent of sensations, and in the middle of it, he felt both her channels tighten around him in spasm after spasm.

CHAPTER

FIFTEEN

Isabella placed her earrings in the jewelry box on her dresser. Before she could close the lid, Raphael gripped her wrist from behind.

"Whose is this?"

She followed his look and saw him pointing at the black onyx ring that nestled in one corner. "Mine, of course."

Raphael pulled in a sharp breath. "Yours?" He sounded accusatory. And like a stranger, the same stranger who'd told his brother he was merely using her.

The cold blast suddenly blowing against her neck did nothing to assuage her sudden fear of him. Trying to stamp out the uncomfortable silence between them, she added hastily, "It was my late husband's. I inherited it."

He appeared to relax at her words. "May I look at it?"

She nodded and watched him take the ring out of the box and examine it. "It's unusual. Is this the family seal?"

"No. I don't think it was his favorite ring either. He rarely wore it. And then he stopped wearing it completely." She'd always wondered what Giovanni had liked about the odd piece of jewelry. She'd certainly never liked the ugly thing. But what intrigued her more was why Raphael seemed so interested in it. Did it have anything to do with his interest in Massimo and her husband's family? "Why are you asking?"

"Just curious since it seems to be such a gaudy piece. So you said he stopped wearing it. When was that?"

"The month before his death. He was different then." Isabella remembered how her husband had suddenly seemed changed. He'd been distant and unapproachable. And he'd started avoiding her. She'd wondered at the time whether he'd taken a mistress. He'd stayed away most nights.

"... Isabella?"

Raphael's voice pulled her out of the depressing thoughts. "I'm sorry, what were you asking?" She met his gaze in the mirror and noticed how intense it was. It reminded her again of how he wanted to use her. His questions about her late husband only cemented the suspicion that not everything was as it seemed with her new husband.

How she could have allowed him to take her so fiercely in the study only a short hour earlier and to explore her in the most debauched way, was unfathomable to her. But her body had reacted to him in the only way it seemed to know: with unquenchable lust. She felt her face flush with embarrassment as she relived the memory of his possession. Her nipples beaded, and she felt her skin turn into gooseflesh.

When Raphael's fingers suddenly grazed her nape, she flinched. He pulled away and met her with a surprised look in the mirror. Then he cleared his throat. "I was wondering if you could tell me more about him, about your late husband."

"Why?" Her spine tingled with the unpleasant feeling of being interrogated.

He smiled at her now. "Because I don't want to make the same mistakes in our marriage as he did."

Isabella turned her head to him. She hadn't expected his answer. "Mistakes? What makes you think he made mistakes? We had a perfectly agreeable marriage."

"Agreeable," he snorted. "I don't want an agreeable marriage. I want a happy one."

"Isn't that the same thing?"

"No, my angel. Now tell me, what was he like?" He took the hairbrush out of her hand and started brushing her hair with it. She was startled by the intimate action.

"Well, if you must." Then she sighed. "He never brushed my hair."

Raphael's smile was warm, and it extended to his eyes. The almost predatory, tense way with which he'd questioned her about Giovanni's ring was gone. Maybe she had just imagined it.

"He was a good man. He provided for me, taught me how to help him run the business. I learned much from him. He was kind." She paused, not knowing what else to say about him.

"Yet he never licked your pussy," Raphael whispered close to her ear.

She dropped her lids. "He wasn't that type of man."

"What type, Isabella?" His breath ghosted over her shoulder.

"That ... that," she stammered, unable to concentrate when he was deliberately trying to make her body react to him.

"Passionate?" he helped.

"He was a measured man. Everything had its time and place. That's why it was so strange ..." So strange when he changed.

"What was strange?" Raphael continued brushing her hair with long and gentle strokes.

"Before his death. He was not the same man anymore."

"In what way?"

"I'm not sure, but he was different. He avoided being alone with me. He had terrible mood swings, outbursts of temper. And he would stay away all night, then shut himself away all day. It wasn't normal. He even shunned Massimo, and they'd always been as close as brothers. One day he tossed the onyx ring in the corner as if it was worth nothing. It was his temper."

The smooth strokes with which Raphael brushed her hair soothed her memories. But something else still bothered her. "I think he took a mistress. He didn't bed me anymore. Maybe that's what happens to men when they are married for a few years. They lose interest in their wives."

Raphael set the brush on the table and turned her body to him. "Is that what you're afraid of? That I'll lose interest in you?"

She didn't want to answer him. What would it serve? Only to expose her heart. He would break it one day—one day soon when she discovered his true motives for marrying her. She didn't want to meet his eye, but he shelved her chin on his hand and tilted her face up.

"I'll never lose interest in you. How could I? You're the most engaging and passionate woman I've ever met."

His kiss was tender, but within seconds it turned heated and consuming. Despite her reservations about him, her uncertainty of what he wanted from her, and from this marriage, she melted into him.

Raphael lifted her into his arms and carried her to their bed, where he covered her with his own body. "Now, my sweet wife, let me show you how much you interest me."

CHAPTER

SIXTEEN

This was the third night that Isabella had awakened and found herself alone. Raphael was nowhere to be found. Just as the two nights before: he'd come to bed and made love to her, only to disappear sometime while she slept. At first, she'd thought she would find him downstairs in the study or the parlor having a glass of grappa or reading a book, but the house was empty, except for the servants.

Yet, every morning he was by her side again, sleeping, his body pressed closely to hers as if he'd never been away. Despite his assurances that he wouldn't lose interest in her as Giovanni had, she couldn't help but speculate where he went in the middle of the night.

But she wouldn't make the same mistake she'd made with Giovanni. She wouldn't allow him to treat her like this. If he disappeared again, she would follow him and find out what he was hiding from her.

RAPHAEL ENTERED the parlor in his own home and noticed that he had a visitor. Lorenzo, one of his closest friends, was sprawled in one corner of the sofa.

81

"Lorenzo, it's good to see you."

Lorenzo gave him a crooked grin, mischief twinkling in his blue eyes. His loose, shoulder-length hair and open shirt attested to the fact that he'd been waiting for a while, and the drops of blood on his chest indicated he'd fed recently. Very recently.

"Likewise. I hear congratulations are in order."

Raphael's nostril's flared as he scented the fresh blood. In fact, it was very intense. He glanced around the room and found Dante in his favorite chair in front of the fireplace, a young woman in his lap. Her gown was open in the front, exposing her small but firm breasts, which Dante fondled while he suckled from her neck.

Drops of blood ran down Dante's cheek, evidence of how greedily he drank from the woman. Her soft moans drifted to his ears. She was under Dante's thrall. Raphael knew that she wouldn't remember anything his brother did to her. The persuasion skill his brother used was what had helped him and his fellow vampires avoid detection over centuries. Every vampire used it when feeding.

He felt his trousers tightening at the thought of feeding from a woman. Not just any woman. Isabella. With a grunt, he pulled himself away from the sight and embraced Lorenzo who'd risen from the sofa.

"Thank you, my friend."

Lorenzo made a sideways glance at Dante. "Would you like some? I brought her for Dante, but as we both know, he doesn't mind sharing. Do you, Dante?"

As much as he would have liked to accept the offer, he'd decided to only feed from men now that he was married to Isabella. He didn't feel that it was right to touch another woman.

"No, thank you."

"My brother is smitten with his wife, you must understand, Lorenzo," Dante drawled, having dislodged his fangs from the woman's neck. "It appears he doesn't want to give into temptation by touching another woman."

"And Dante seems to stick his nose into things that don't concern him. Who I feed from is entirely my business," Raphael shot back. "Now, if you're quite done with feeding, can we get down to business? What did you find out about Giovanni Tenderini?"

Dante licked the puncture wounds on the woman's neck, got up and carried her to the sofa where he laid her down. Then he wiped his mouth and looked back at Raphael, his face serious now. "He was a Guardian all right. But I'll let Lorenzo tell you the story. It's quite interesting, by the way."

"Yes," Lorenzo confirmed. "A Guardian turned vampire."

Surprise registered with Raphael. "What?"

"You heard right. He was chasing a group of us together with a couple of other Guardians, but we managed to separate him from his brethren. We cornered him in a dead end. There was no way out for him. Nico had the brilliant idea of handing out the ultimate punishment."

Raphael held his breath, guessing what was coming.

"And what fitting punishment it was for a Guardian to become the very creature he hunts, don't you think? Nico turned him. He struggled, he fought—a very brave man, if I may add. But to no avail. In the end, the deed was done. He'd made him one of us. We heard of his death a month later. I wonder whether he took his own life. He must have known he would drown."

"It all makes sense now." Raphael ran his hand through his hair.

"What makes sense?" Dante asked.

"Isabella noticed a change in him in the month before his death. And he never wore his Guardian ring again. But I don't believe that he committed suicide. More like somebody close to him hastened his demise."

"His wife?" Lorenzo asked.

Raphael gave his friend a scolding look. Isabella wouldn't harm a fly. "No. Isabella would never hurt a soul."

"You seem so sure, my brother. Didn't I tell you not to trust your wife? Watch out or you might end up like her first husband."

Raphael glared at his brother. "Isabella has nothing to do with this. I rather suspect that his cousin Massimo was involved in his demise. Have you had somebody follow him?"

Dante nodded. "He's careful. No suspicious meetings with anybody so far. And we haven't spotted the ring on anybody else. I suspect the Guardians only wear it in private or when they meet with each other."

Which could mean that Massimo considered Isabella's house his private domain. "We'll just have to be patient." Raphael glanced at the clock over the mantle. "I have to get back before she wakes."

Dante *tsk*ed. "I think you should leave her. We don't need her to get to Massimo. Now that we know his name and whereabouts, you shackling yourself to her isn't necessary. She'll only become a liability and put you in danger."

Raphael snarled. "She's mine. And she'll remain mine."

CHAPTER

SEVENTEEN

Knowing he had to feed again, Raphael peeled himself out of the arms of his sleeping wife and slid out of bed. Maybe he should have accepted her offer to take Giovanni's bedchamber, but he couldn't bring himself to sleep without her and only visit her to make love. He liked having her in his arms at night when she slept. It soothed him.

Trying to be as quiet as possible, he snatched his clothes from the chair and left the chamber, closing the door behind him without a sound. He felt like a thief as he got dressed in the corridor, but he knew if he didn't leave now, he was liable to attack his wife.

Lorenzo's offer to feed from his female victim the night before had had a certain appeal, but the thought of putting his hands on another woman had actually disgusted him. It was better to sink his fangs into a man. It felt less like a betrayal. The fact that he was thinking in these terms scared him. He'd never been a one-woman man, but it was important to him to be faithful to Isabella. She deserved it. He wanted this marriage to work.

Raphael was quiet when he left the house and pulled the side door shut behind him. He looked up at the full moon, which flooded the narrow alleys with light. Too much light for his liking. He preferred it darker so it was easier for him to hide. But he didn't have much choice. His hunger dictated his actions.

He'd fed the night after Isabella and he had stayed at his own house. Over the last three days, his hunger had been building. More than usual. The fact that he was making love to his passionate wife several times a day or night was one of the reasons for it. She was draining his energy, but he didn't mind. He couldn't stop himself from cornering her whenever the urge overcame him. Throwing her skirts up in the study had been just the beginning.

During the day, he fucked her fast and frantic, but at night, when they were cocooned in her chamber, he took his time and made sweet love to her, with words, caressing hands, and soft kisses. He couldn't tell what Isabella liked more, the way he ravished her in every conceivable place in her house, or when he worshipped her body at night.

Sometimes she glanced at him with the look of a frightened doe, but the moment he laid his hands on her, that look always vanished and was replaced by a sparkle in her eyes that he'd come to love. Once he'd fed, he'd return home instantly and wake Isabella by making love to her.

Raphael sighed and trained his eyes on a movement ahead of him. It was a man, who staggered along the alley. The scent emanating from him confirmed that he was drunk. That would make it even easier. He wouldn't even have to enthrall him to approach and feed from him. The drunk would never remember. And the alcohol swimming in the man's blood wouldn't make him drunk.

Raphael approached the man. "Good evening, my fellow."

The man turned his head, his eyes barely focusing, his mouth tilted up in a stupid grin. "Huh?"

The time for conversation being at an end, Raphael put his arm around the drunk's shoulder, then turned him into his chest before his fangs descended and drove into his neck. There was barely a shudder by the man. His fangs were coated with a substance that dulled all pain, thus making it possible to feed from a human without causing screams of pain.

As the rich, alcohol-infused blood coated his tongue and ran down his throat, Raphael let his senses relax. He closed his eyes and only listened to the demands of his body. He drew on the vein, long and hard, taking the life-sustaining liquid into him. His only thought was how much he wanted this neck to be Isabella's. To drink from her, nourish himself with her fragrant blood, gorge himself on her essence, while he drove his insatiable cock into—

A scream pierced the silence in the alley.

Isabella only realized she'd screamed when she saw Raphael's head snap in her direction, releasing the neck of the man he'd had his teeth locked into. When his piercing eyes pinned her, she saw the blood drip from his lips and run down his chin. His mouth was open, and she could clearly see the white of his fangs. Paralyzed, she stared at him.

She'd heard stories about creatures like him but never believed any. She'd always thought they were mere fairy tales to frighten children. But what she saw in front of her now was not a fairy tale, not something she could dismiss.

She was married to a vampire. A creature that drank blood and sucked the life out of humans.

The moment Raphael let the man sag against the wall and came toward her, she found her strength again and ran.

"Isabella," he called behind her, "Stop!" The voice came closer, and she knew he was chasing her. She was glad she wore breeches, making it easier to run. She'd hidden them under the bed, knowing it would take her less time to get dressed in the dark than if she had to step into a dress. The moment Raphael had left her chamber, she'd jumped out of bed and gotten ready to follow him.

But now, she almost wished she'd caught him with a mistress instead. It would be easier to deal with—and safer.

Her thighs burned as she continued to flee even though she knew she could never outrun him. The sound of his boots on the cobblestone street closed in on her. Her lungs stinging, she pushed herself harder and ran faster than she ever had.

"Isabella, please!" Then his hand gripped the collar of her coat and pulled her back.

"No!" She slipped on the wet stone and would have fallen had Raphael not pulled her against his chest and imprisoned her within his arms. Like chains, they closed around her, cutting off any movement of her upper body. But she still had her legs. She kicked them back, trying to make him loosen his grip on her, but to no avail.

"Stop struggling, Isabella. I would never hurt you. Please trust me."

"No, let me go, you monster!"

His mouth was at her ear, his breath caressing her neck, when he answered her. His voice was low and soothing. "I'm sorry you had to find out like this, but I'm not a monster. I'm still the man who loves you."

Tears threatened to burst to the surface, but she forced them back. "No. Let me go. Please let me go."

She felt him shake his head behind her. "Never, my angel."

Then Raphael started moving, carrying her in front of him. Renewed panic gripped her. He'd take her to a dark place and then drain her of her blood. She kicked her legs back again, hitting his shins. "No! Where are you taking me?"

"Stop struggling, it's no use. We're going home."

But the direction he took wasn't where her house lay. "You're lying. Home is the other way."

"My home," he corrected and slid his lips against her cheek. A shiver ran down her body, and she didn't know whether it was caused by fear or was merely her body's usual reaction to his touch.

Isabella gave up her struggle against him, knowing it was useless. He was bigger and infinitely stronger than she. It was better to preserve her strength so she could attempt an escape later.

Now some things made sense. Dante had been concerned that she would find out that Raphael was a vampire. And his nightly absences? Clearly, he'd been out to attack people and feed on their blood. And she would be next, now that she'd uncovered his secret, and he wouldn't have to hide it from her anymore. Would it hurt? How long would it take until he'd drained her? Would he toss her lifeless body into one of the canals?

Isabella shuddered at the ugly thoughts. She'd married a stranger to save her reputation, and now she would lose her life because of it. Was this the punishment she would receive for the days and nights of unbridled pleasures she'd indulged in with Raphael? Would she have to pay for her sins in this world, and not the next?

Just remembering the things she'd allowed him to do to her made her shiver. All the forbidden pleasures he'd unleashed, the way he'd ravished her—and she'd loved every debauched second of it, had even asked for more, dared him to go further. She'd allowed him to use her body as only a whore would, yet it had given her more pleasure than she'd ever known existed.

"We're here." Raphael pushed a door open and carried her inside. The light was dim, only a few wall sconces illuminated the hallway, but she recognized it nevertheless. They were back at his home, his den, his lair. Whatever a vampire called it. She was at his mercy now.

EIGHTEEN

Raphael released Isabella and closed the door to his bedchamber behind them. She instantly moved away from him, and he couldn't really blame her. She was frightened after what she'd witnessed. He shrugged off his coat and tossed it on a chair.

"Sit down, my love, make yourself comfortable."

She straightened her spine and glared at him. "I'd rather stand."

"I think it's only fair to tell you that any attempt at trying to run away from me will be a waste of your time. I'm faster, I'm stronger, and I'm motivated."

He opened a drawer and pulled out a clean handkerchief, wiping the remaining blood off his face. "I'm sorry you had to see this. But you shouldn't have followed me."

When he took a step toward her, she took several back. "Don't come any closer," she warned, her voice shaky. He could hear her frantic heartbeat.

"It's very hard to make love from a distance like this."

Her eyes widened. "I won't let you touch me."

"You will, and you will do it willingly."

"Never. I won't let a monster like you touch me."

"Isabella, please think for a moment. I know you're in shock, but try to remember the last few days. Was there ever a time when I hurt you?"

He felt her hesitation and knew she couldn't answer his question in the affirmative. But her lips remained sealed. Instead, she lifted her chin in defiance.

"Are you afraid of me?"

There was an almost unperceivable nod of her head.

Raphael swallowed. The last thing he wanted was a wife who was afraid of him. He had to convince her that she had nothing to fear from him. The only way to achieve this was to make himself vulnerable to her. It was a risk he had to take. If he didn't, he would lose her for good.

"Fine, Isabella, you win." He opened the buttons of his shirt.

"What are you doing?" There was panic in her voice again.

"I'm undressing." He tossed his shirt to the floor, then stepped out of his boots.

"I told you I won't let you touch me."

His trousers dropped to the ground, and he stood naked in front of her. "I won't touch you, but you'll touch me."

She shook her head, pulling back further.

Raphael walked to the bed and opened the drawer of his nightstand. He lifted his gun out and placed it on top of it. When he pulled out the leather restraints and turned back to her, she shrieked.

"Oh God!"

"Isabella. Those are not for you. They are for me. Inside the leather, there's a thin lining of silver, a metal no vampire can break. I want you to tie me to the bed. I will be at your mercy, and you can assure yourself that I'm no danger to you." He glanced back at the nightstand, and he noticed her follow his look. "The gun is loaded with silver bullets. They'll kill a vampire. If you think I'm a danger to you, use it."

Isabella shook her head. "It's a trick. As soon as I come close to you, you'll attack me."

"No." He went to the bed and laid down. "I will tie my ankles to the bed first, then you'll do my hands. I trust you. Now I want you to trust me."

Raphael knew he was crazy proposing this, but he had to make her trust him. If she killed him, it really didn't matter, because a life without Isabella made no sense anymore. If she couldn't accept him like this, then it was better if she ended his life now and didn't let him suffer the loss of her love.

Continuously watching her, he tied first one ankle, then the second one to the foot of the bed, keeping enough length so he could still bend his legs. Then he held out his hand with the remaining two ties. "Take them. Bind them tightly."

There was hesitation in her steps as she approached. He saw her glance at the nightstand with the gun, then back at him.

"Tie me up, Isabella." He placed the leather straps onto the bed next to him and held his arms up against the headboard with loops which had been fashioned as restraints.

Another few steps and she stood next to the bed. He nodded as she reached for a strap. He could see her perspire, a thin lining of moisture building on her brow. He inhaled her scent and felt himself harden. Instinctively he dropped his eyes to his cock. Hard and thick, it rose.

When he looked back at Isabella, he caught her staring at his erect shaft. Then she reached for his wrist and tied the first leather strap around it. She secured it tightly against the restraining hook despite her shaking hands. Not letting him out of her sight, she stepped around the bed and did the same with his other wrist.

"Thank you," he whispered. He tested the restraints. They held. He'd never been so vulnerable in his life. But Isabella had saved his life once, and he hoped she'd find it in her heart to not take away the life she'd given him.

RAPHAEL HAD ALLOWED himself to be tied up, but would he truly not be able to break the restraints? What if he was lying to her? Isabella stepped around the bed, keeping close watch on him. When she reached the night-stand, she looked at the gun. From the corner of her eye she could see him watch her, but he didn't move, made no attempt to free himself from the leather straps. But it wasn't proof enough that he was truly tied up.

Isabella gripped the gun and turned to him, pointing it at his chest.

There was a flicker of surprise in his eyes, only to be replaced by disappointment. He lowered his lids. His voice was flat when he spoke. "I gambled, and I lost. I had hoped your love would be strong enough, but I was wrong." He looked at her. "I love you, Isabella. The last five days were the happiest of my entire life. I'm sorry that you don't feel the same for me. Aim for my heart and make it quick."

Then he closed his eyes and inhaled.

"Why did you allow yourself to be tied up by me?"

"It doesn't matter anymore."

"It does to me."

His eyes remained closed. "You've made your decision, my angel."

But she needed an answer. "Open your eyes. Look at me. Tell me why!" Isabella swallowed back a sob.

When his eyes flew open, he pinned her with a surprised look. "You want to know why? I let you tie me because I need you to understand that I'm prepared to do anything for your love. I need you to trust that I would never harm you. And the only way I can do that is to show you that you hold all the power. And now that I've satisfied your curiosity, please end my misery, because a life without your love is worse than a merciful death."

She recognized it then: Raphael loved her, more than anybody had ever loved her. She could feel it deep in her heart. How could she kill a man like that? How could she allow this love to slip through her fingers? Did it matter that it was the love of a vampire? Yet—

"Do you kill the humans you feed from?" She voiced the fear she carried in her heart. Was he a bloodthirsty murderer?

"No, my love. I don't kill unless my own life is threatened. I only feed from them."

Isabella exhaled the breath she'd been holding. He wasn't a killer. She allowed her eyes to wander over his naked body, sprawled out in front of her: vulnerable, yet aroused. His tied hands didn't look like those of a monster. They were the hands that had caressed her, given her pleasure beyond belief.

Dropping her gaze lower, she feasted her eyes on his cock. Hard and heavy it curved upwards and lay against his flat belly. With it, he'd driven her to ecstasy every single day since she'd met him. Could she really kill somebody that perfect, simply because of what he was?

Isabella dropped her arm and tossed the gun to the foot of the bed where it landed in the soft sheets. When she crawled onto the bed, his eyes widened. "Isabella?" There was hope in his voice.

She closed in on him, then straddled him without another thought, before meeting his lips with hers. His startled moan was drowned out by her own.

"My angel."

"Kiss me, my husband," she whispered against his parted lips. She felt no fangs when he took her mouth in a fierce kiss, only soft lips and a hungry tongue that devoured her. She licked against him with firm strokes just the way she knew he liked it.

Raphael broke the kiss and stared at her with those dark passion-filled eyes. "Take off your coat and shirt, and let me see your beautiful tits."

She divested herself of the pesky garments within seconds, only keeping her breeches, reveling in the hungry look in his eyes. When she was bare, he licked his lips. "Now feed them to me." He looked up to meet her eyes. "I won't bite. Not unless you want me to." There was a hesitation in his voice, as if he was unsure if he'd said the right thing.

"Would I want you to?" she asked, curiosity overwhelming her.

"Maybe one day. But believe me when I tell you that even if you never let me taste your sweet blood, I'll always be your faithful husband. Never doubt that."

She didn't. The sincerity didn't only shine through his words, but also radiated from his eyes. It was the moment when she realized that he would never be able to lie to her again, because she would always know by looking into his eyes whether he was sincere. The thought warmed her heart.

"Now let me suck those tits before I burn up with desire for you." He gave her a crooked smile, and Isabella lowered her breasts to dangle above his face. He strained to lift himself closer to her, but the leather straps on his wrists didn't allow for much movement.

"You want my tits?" she teased him. "How much do you want them?"

He pushed his hips upwards, pressing his hard length against her sex. Liquid heat traveled to her pussy as it clenched in response. "That much."

"Oh," she answered him, trying her most coquettish voice. "That's indeed quite impressive, Signore." She lowered herself another inch. Instantly his tongue snaked out and lapped at one nipple. "Signore, do you think that's proper?"

"Very proper, Signora," he joined in her game. "Now if Signora would just lower herself a little bit more, I could show her how proper this is."

"Signora can do better than that." She cupped one breast and led the nipple to his mouth.

Raphael sighed contentedly and sucked it into his mouth, his eyes never leaving her face, showing her how much he appreciated her gesture. Greedily, he sucked, turning the little nub into a hard peak, transforming her insides into mush. She pulled up, not being able to take any more.

"The other one," he begged. Unable to resist him, she led her other breast to his mouth. This time, he sucked on it harder as if he was intent on never letting it out of his mouth again.

She panted heavily. "Signore, this cannot possibly be proper."

Raphael let her nipple pop out of his mouth and ran his tongue between her breasts, licking her as if he were devouring a sumptuous dessert. "Proper would be if Signora lets me fuck her tits."

Not knowing what he meant, interest rose in her nevertheless. "And how would such a feat be accomplished?"

He gave a rakish smile. "Slide down on me until your tits meet with my cock. Then take me between them and press them together with your hands."

A delicious shiver danced along her skin at his description. "Why, Signore, this sounds positively debauched."

"Yes," he rasped. "So, do it, my beautiful Signora. Capture my cock between your wonderful flesh and make me come."

Isabella's entire body vibrated as she slid down his muscled torso, dragging her sensitive nipples against his skin. Every word Raphael said made her hotter and hotter. All her fear was gone. Left was the passion and love she felt for him. And the knowledge that he would fulfill all her fantasies.

The crevice between her breasts was wet from when he'd licked her. Now she knew he'd done it deliberately so his cock would slide smoothly into place. When she pressed her hands against the outsides of her breasts, he let out an uncontrolled moan.

"Oh, fuck!"

Isabella shifted, making his cock slide toward her throat, then back down again. It felt good to feel his hard, hot length pulsate between her ample flesh. "Yes, Signore, is that proper enough for you?"

"More than proper." His hips flexed, and he started pumping up and down. "Yes, my angel, this is all very proper." His voice became more and more slurred and unrecognizable with every thrust of his cock.

When she felt him stiffen and his cock jerk, she knew he was right at the edge. Isabella released him from the prison of her breasts and took him into her mouth with one smooth slide. It was clear he hadn't expected it.

"Oh, God, Isabella! Fuck!" Raphael cried out and shot his hot seed into her mouth as his body spasmed and rocked against her. She swallowed some of the salty liquid, but his spurts came so hard and fast, she couldn't keep up. She lifted her head and released him.

Her hand steadied his cock, pumping him, the escaping juices lubricating her actions as his climax ebbed. She looked at his face. His eyes had rolled back, his lips were parted, beads of sweat ran down his forehead and neck. She'd never seen a more erotic sight than that of her very satisfied husband.

Her hand released his cock and trailed to his balls, making him jerk. "Isabella, are you trying to kill me?" he whispered breathlessly. Then he opened his eyes and smiled.

"I love touching you."

"And you can touch me all you want," he assured her.

"You don't mind that I'm not a proper wife? That I act like a whore with you?"

"You're my wife. You can act any which way you want with me. Nothing is taboo between us."

"Nothing? Do you mean whatever I want you to do to me—even if it is debauched—you will do it?"

He groaned. "Yes, my angel. And anything you want to do to me, I want you to do it."

Isabella licked her lips and fondled his balls with her moist hand. "Do you remember what you did to me in the study?"

Something flashed in his eyes. "You mean when I took you from behind?"

"Yes." She let her fingers trail lower behind his balls.

"Did you like it when I finger-fucked your sweet ass?" He breathed faster now.

"Yes." She slid a finger further back toward the crevice of his buttocks. A moment later, Raphael pulled his knees up as much as his leather constraints allowed, setting his feet flat onto the bed.

"You want to do the same to me?" he guessed.

Isabella nodded, not being able to voice her wish.

"Slide your finger back."

"You don't mind?" she asked, surprised that he gave into her request without protest.

His eyes were dark with lust when he looked at her. "Finger-fuck me, my angel, and make me surrender to you."

She slid her finger, still slick with his cum, further back and found the puckered hole. She rimmed it, timidly at first, but then with more determination. When she placed her fingertip at the entrance, she felt him push against her.

"Yes," he encouraged her. "Let me feel you inside me."

She eased her finger in, slipping past the tight ring. The seed on her finger eased her entry and made her glide inside without difficulty. "Is this ... good?" she asked, unsure of herself.

"It's so much better."

"Better?" Isabella asked and pulled her finger back slightly. He squeezed his muscles together, trying to hold her in.

"Don't stop."

She slid back in, but she hadn't forgotten what he'd said. "Has somebody else done this to you before?" She'd hoped that she'd be the only one to touch him like this.

His gaze collided with hers. "No. I've never allowed anybody this intimacy before. You're the first. The only one. But I've used toys before."

"Toys?" What did children's toys have to do with this?

"Metal implements, rounded and curved, to stimulate myself with. But I find that I much prefer your fingers inside me than any toy I could dream up."

"Fingers?"

"Yes, my love, slide a second finger into me." He paused and smiled. "Take the ache away," he repeated her words from a few days earlier.

Raphael moaned when she complied. And she couldn't help but find what she did to him exciting. He was at her mercy, a vampire wild with desire, yet chained by straps he couldn't break. She'd never felt the kind of power she felt now: the power a woman had over a man. The power he gave her.

"I love you," Isabella whispered and slid her fingers back and forth inside him, thrusting in and out of his dark passage as he gripped her tightly. His moans filled the room, drowning out everything else in her mind. She was driving him to ecstasy and giving him what he needed.

When he chanted her name, his body bathed in sweat, she added a third finger and pressed harder. His muscles clamped onto her and contracted as his entire body convulsed.

She felt his orgasm to the last cell of her body, and it was the purest feeling she'd ever experienced from another person.

As he stilled, she pulled herself up to him and kissed his lips. He breathed heavily, his eyes closed. "Isabella," was all he said, but she knew what he wanted to say. He loved her.

She planted another kiss on his mouth.

"You whore! That's how you drag my cousin's name through the mud! If I hadn't seen it with my own eyes, I would have never believed it!"

Isabella's heart stopped at the menacing voice she recognized instantly.

CHAPTER

NINETEEN

His body exhausted from multiple orgasms, shock coursed through Raphael as his head snapped to the intruder: Massimo. This was the worst possible scenario he could have ever imagined. He'd been too lust-drugged for his senses to register his enemy until it was too late.

Now Massimo stood near the door, a gun pointed at him. And considering he was a Guardian and knew how to kill a vampire, Raphael was sure it was loaded with silver bullets.

From the corner of his eye, he saw how Isabella had snatched the bed sheet and pressed it against her naked breasts. His own modesty was the least of his concerns now. He calmed his mind and tried to think the situation through. If he could stall Massimo long enough, either his brother or one of his friends would show up. If they'd continued tailing him as they'd done the nights before, they would be here soon. Very soon.

"Massimo! What are you—?" Isabella's question was a mere gasp.

"My love, I think you should know something about your late husband's dear cousin," Raphael drawled and glanced at the man. "Would you like to explain it to her or should I?"

"Please do," Massimo replied with an evil grin. "It'll be the last time you speak to your whore, so enjoy."

"I'd appreciate it if you didn't call her a whore. She's my wife."

Massimo only snorted.

"Isabella," Raphael addressed her, "Massimo is here to kill me. I suspect he already tried a few days ago by pushing me into the canal."

"Alas, I can't take credit for that. One of the other Guardians deserves that praise."

"What Guardians?" Isabella interrupted, her voice high pitched.

Raphael kept his voice calm as he answered her, knowing her nerves were at a breaking point. "Massimo is part of a group of men who hunt vampires and kill them. Just as your late husband was."

Isabella gave him a shocked stare. "Giovanni? No! That can't be. Giovanni was a good man. He wouldn't kill anybody."

"Yes, he was a good man, that's why he was one of us. A protector of the human race, a Guardian. Until *they* made him one of them. Until *they* turned him against his will." Massimo's voice was full of hatred. His jaw clenched tightly when he continued, "He came to me and told me what you monsters did to him, how one of you bit him and fed him vampire blood. He told me he'd continue fighting against your kind, but it wasn't possible, of course."

"Oh God!" Isabella gasped. "Not Giovanni. Please, say it's not true."

Raphael saw the tears building in her eyes as she looked at him. Would she hate him now for what his kind had done to the man she'd once loved? He searched her eyes for a sign that would tell him whether she would remain his. But her tears made it impossible to see beyond her immediate grief.

"Yes," Massimo droned. "*He* did that to you. *He* made you a widow." He pointed at Raphael. "*He* took the man we loved."

"I did no such thing," Raphael protested. "Yes, a vampire turned him, but it wasn't I, and it was certainly none of our kind who killed him." He took the gamble. If he was right in his assessment of Massimo, the man wouldn't be able to resist the bait.

"Killed?" Isabella echoed. "But he drowned."

Raphael nodded. "Yes, he drowned because he was a vampire, and vampires don't have any natural buoyancy. They can't keep themselves above water. Just as I couldn't."

"Yes, and Giovanni knew that," Massimo interrupted. "He knew when I pushed him into the canal that he wouldn't survive. He looked at me. He couldn't believe that I'd done it, but he should have. He of all people should have known that I couldn't let him live. He'd become a creature so vile, there was only one thing to do. He should have understood. I loved him like a brother. I did it for him."

A sob tore from Isabella's chest. Raphael looked at her, but she turned away from him and let herself fall face down into the sheets, facing away from him. Had he lost her? Was this what this meant, that she would hate him now for what one of his brethren had done?

"Isabella. I'm sorry."

She didn't respond.

"Well, it appears all has been said." Just as Massimo cocked his gun, Raphael's sensitive hearing picked up the sound of the front door opening.

"Wait." He had to stall him just a few more seconds until help arrived. "At least tell me how you figured me out. I deserve that much, don't you think?"

Massimo chuckled, but it wasn't a friendly sound. "Nothing easier than that. A servant told me that you nearly drowned in the canal. So I made inquires and found out that one of my fellow Guardians had pushed a vampire into the water that same night. It was easy to figure out from there that it was you. You might have escaped death once, but now, vampire, you'll die."

A shot rang out the moment the door burst open. Raphael closed his eyes and steeled himself against the pain the silver bullet would inflict on him seconds before his life force would drain from his body.

"I love you, Isabella," he whispered his goodbyes as the shouts of his brother and Lorenzo filled the room.

"What in hell?" Dante cried out.

"Raphael!" Lorenzo called to him. "Are you all right?"

Raphael opened his eyes. He felt no pain. "I don't know." Then his eyes searched for Isabella. She sat up, the sheet that had covered her breasts pooling in her lap, his gun in her hand, still pointing toward where Massimo had stood.

"He's dead," Dante said. "Massimo's dead."

"Isabella?" Raphael tried to get her attention. Finally, she turned to him and ran a long look over his body.

"I thought I was too late." Then she threw herself into his arms—or rather, against his chest, since he couldn't embrace her with his wrists still tied.

"You saved me."

A clearing of throats made him snap his head toward his brother and Lorenzo. He gave them a scolding look. "And what took you guys so long? I thought you were following him."

"We were, but the crafty fellow tricked us with a decoy dressed just like him. We lost him. When we noticed, we had a hunch he'd go for either you or Isabella. And since we didn't find either of you at Isabella's house, we instantly came here," Lorenzo replied.

"And now that that's cleared up, would you care to explain why you're tied up in your own bed?" Dante grinned.

"That's between me and my wife."

Isabella raised her head, then pulled on the bed sheet to cover her naked torso.

"Would you like me to untie you?" Dante offered.

Raphael looked at Isabella and smiled. "That's for Isabella to decide."

The sparkle was back in her eyes, the tears forgotten. Without turning to Dante, she answered, "I'm not done with him."

His heart skipped a beat at the underlying promise in her voice. "You heard my wife, Dante. So, if you would be so kind as to leave our bedchamber and take the body with you. My lovely wife and I have things to ... discuss."

Dante shook his head. "As I said before: a fool in love. A very lucky fool."

When the door closed behind Dante and Lorenzo, it was quiet again. All he could hear was Isabella's breathing. "My angel, this is the second time you've saved me. I hope you realize that now my life belongs to you."

"And your body?" she negotiated.

"My body was already yours long before that." He kissed her gently. "Now untie me so I can hold you in my arms and thank you properly."

"Not yet. I want to ask you something first."

"Then ask."

"Does it hurt?"

"Does what hurt?"

"Your bite."

A hot flame shot through his body. Was she contemplating what he thought she was? "When I feed from a human? No, it doesn't hurt. My fangs are coated with a substance that dulls the pain to a point where there's none."

"The nights you left our bed, did you go out to feed from humans?"

"Not every night. I only need to feed every three days. Why do you want to know all this?"

"Do you want to feed from me?"

His heartbeat doubled in an instant. "Oh, God, Isabella! I can't think of anything I want more, except to make love to you. But you know you don't have to do this."

"I want to."

Could he be so lucky? And if she allowed him this, would she one day allow him to turn her into a vampire so she wouldn't age or die? So they could spend eternity together? His heart filled with hope for a happy future. Pulling on his restraints, he whispered, "Then get me out of these chains."

Isabella sat up, and suddenly her breasts dangled right in front of him. His mouth closed over one nipple and sucked on it. Isabella's moan echoed in the room. He let the nipple pop from his mouth.

"Quickly, my love."

As soon as she'd untied him, Raphael ripped her breeches from her body and brought her underneath him. She was slick with her arousal, a scent that teased his nostrils. "Thank you." He slid into her with one smooth glide, seating himself balls deep in her tight sheath.

Isabella tilted her head to the side in invitation. "Feed from me, my love."

His gaze drifted lower, away from the vein on her neck, down to her gorgeous tits. He hesitated. Then he sensed her watch him.

"You want to feed from my breasts?" she asked with surprise in her voice.

"Only if you allow it." He looked up and locked eyes with her. "Your tits are so perfect, so full and ripe, I can't think of anything better than having my face buried in them when I take your blood inside of me." He licked over her nipple. It stiffened in response.

"Then do it. Nothing is taboo between us," she repeated his own words from earlier.

Slowly, his fangs descended, and he grazed her skin with them. He felt a shiver go through her body. At the same time as he pulled back his hips and pumped into her pussy, he sank his fangs into her plump flesh and sucked. The rich liquid coated his tongue, the taste and scent of it nearly making him delirious.

As he fucked in and out of her warm and moist channel, he took her essence into his body. There would never be any other taste he wanted for the rest of his life than Isabella's sweet blood.

~

Venice Vampyr

FINAL AFFAIR

NEW YORK TIMES BESTSELLING AUTHOR

TINA FOLSOM

CHAPTER

ONE

enice, Italy - early 1800s

At first, she thought her physician had made a mistake.

Three months—the doctor had given her only three more months to live. During the last two, she'd likely be confined to her bed with blinding pain.

It wasn't possible.

Just days earlier, her governess had warned her that, despite her pretty face and graceful figure, her outspoken manner and outlandish ideas were scaring away potential husbands. Viola hadn't cared. She'd figured that if a suitor couldn't stand up to her, then she'd rather not be married at all. Plus, she was barely one and twenty, and while she was still on the shelf when it came to marriage prospects—which was due to her impetuous nature—she had her whole life ahead of her. So she'd thought.

Three months wasn't a life.

Yet, despite her brain tumor, she'd make the most of it.

At first, she'd thought to prove her physician wrong. She'd already traveled to Switzerland—leaving in the dead of night and without a chaperone—and consulted another expert. But the answer remained the same: she was dying.

That's why she'd come to Venice. No longer to prove him wrong, but to live.

She hadn't told her family where she was going; they would have stopped her. They would have called her foolish and scandalous. But she would not be stopped. Viola had accepted that she would die, but there was one thing she wanted to experience before she left this world.

She refused to die a virgin.

But she was also practical: a scandal wouldn't serve her family. Already, her sudden disappearance would have to be covered up, something her over-eager mother was more than capable of handling. She would simply let everybody know that Viola was staying in the countryside to tend to an elderly relative. There were plenty from which to choose.

Viola had decided to go where nobody knew her or any of her relatives, where her scandalous behavior would not have any repercussions for her parents. She had sent them a letter from Switzerland, telling them that her condition had worsened and that she was confined to a hospital bed. She had also told them in no uncertain terms that she wanted to be left alone and be remembered for who she was before her illness had started.

She had threatened to create a scandal in Florence should her wishes not be respected. Her threat would ensure that her mother complied with her wishes and impressed upon Viola's father not to make any attempts to fetch her. Besides, her mother was probably happy to be rid of her. After all, Viola had never been able to live up to her high expectations. By rejecting the first—and only—suitor who'd ever dared to court her, Viola had extinguished any goodwill her mother had ever felt toward her.

Viola had arranged for her parents to receive a letter in three months, indicating that their daughter had passed away peacefully. Of course, it would be a lie, because she would take her life much earlier. Once she had accomplished what she'd come to Venice for.

Once she was no longer a virgin, she would take the pistol she carried in her bag and end her life before the pain would debilitate her. She had no intention of suffering a long and painful death.

Viola smoothed a hand over her skirts and righted her cloak. Filling her lungs with a deep breath, she pushed the heavy oak door open.

The place she entered was a club of sorts. According to her information, gentlemen who were looking for female companionship frequented the surprisingly clean establishment. While it was not a brothel, many of the women who joined the men at the club to seek carnal pleasures did so for money. However, the man who'd guided her to this club had assured her that on occasion, women of the higher classes were seen there, seeking diversions in which their respectable husbands were unwilling to indulge their wives.

She hoped the man had been correct, and the story she had rehearsed would be believable. The last thing she wanted to do was to draw attention to herself. It was hard enough to overcome her embarrassment at having to approach a stranger and ask him to bed her. Being sent on her way without achieving her goal would be worse. Because there was one rule the men at the club insisted on despite their debauchery: nobody was to bed a virgin.

The place smelled of cigars, alcohol, and perfume. Viola took a shallow breath and let the door snap in behind her. A burgundy curtain of heavy velvet separated the foyer from the main rooms behind. Music and laughter drifted to her. She took a step forward when a hand on her arm held her back.

Her breath caught in her throat as she snapped her head to the side.

"There's a fee, Signora," the heavy-set woman in the richly embroidered dress said. Her breasts spilled over her low-cut gown, and the large baubles around her neck sparkled in the candlelight.

"Of course," Viola answered and reached into her purse, retrieving a coin. The man who'd told her about the club had prepared her for this. It would not do if she behaved like an innocent who'd never done this before. It would only create suspicion.

The hostess took the coin and made it disappear in the folds of her dress. "Very well then."

A moment later, she parted the curtain and allowed Viola to step through.

The room was larger than she'd expected. In fact, it was as large as her parents' ballroom. On the sides, booths had been built to provide a semblance of privacy for anybody who wished it, but in the middle the chaises and sofas as well as their occupants were in plain view. Large chandeliers with blazing candles provided light, and a small string quartet supplied the ambiance.

Servants circulated to supply the guests with beverages and, by the state some of the guests were in, it was clear that alcohol flowed freely. Men lounged on sofas, some fully dressed and perfectly respectable, others with their cravats loosened and their chests partially exposed. Women could be found draped over men's bodies in more than indecent poses.

Hadn't her informant said this wasn't a brothel? Viola felt her heartbeat rise. She was nothing like the women she saw in this place. They seemed unconcerned with modesty or privacy. This was not what she'd expected. Maybe the man had misunderstood her. She'd sought a place to find a man who would bed her in the privacy of a bedchamber and let her experience what it was like to feel a man's body joined with hers.

This was a mistake. Viola took a step back and bumped into something solid behind her. She swiveled.

"Ciao, bella," the handsome stranger greeted her as he swept an appreciative glance over her.

Viola swallowed, unable to answer, the pulse at her neck beating so frantically she was sure her vein would burst and drench the man in her blood.

Her silence didn't seem to bother him. "I see you're new here." His hand came up and traced along the seam of her décolleté. Viola gasped at his boldness and pulled back.

"I'm Salvatore. And I'm happy to spend the evening with you."

She took a steadying breath and gave him an assessing look. He was slightly taller than the average man. Well groomed in his dark suit and fashionable necktie, not even her mother would have any objections to him were he to come courting. But he wasn't here to court her. Nor did she want him to.

All she wanted was a tumble. Was he the right man for it? Would those elegant hands caress her and make her feel like a real woman, or would his touch leave her indifferent? Was her fluttering heartbeat indication of her interest in him or merely telling her she was scared of actually going through with her plan?

She couldn't be sure. But if she simply stood here without making a decision, she'd never attain the goal she'd set herself.

Viola summoned her courage and forced a smile onto her lips, pushing back her rising doubts. "That would be charming."

TWO

Dante was furious.

He looked at the bruises on Benedetta's face. "How often have I told you not to go to that club?" Sure, she was only a girl who sold her father's carvings on the street, and he was only very loosely acquainted with her, but somehow he felt protective toward her. She was poor and so young. Every time he passed by her stand, he felt compelled to purchase one of her father's ghastly carved figures.

"I'm sorry," the girl whimpered, her split lip making her speech slurred. "But business was so bad this month. We needed the money."

"Who did this?"

Benedetta looked away, but Dante took her chin and made her meet his glare. She winced. "I asked who did this."

"Salvatore."

"Fuck!" Dante ran his hand through his dark hair. "Have you no sense of self-preservation? Of all people, you had to let Salvatore touch you?" He wasn't acquainted with the man personally, but he knew he wasn't fit company for Benedetta.

She closed her swollen eyes. "He was the only one willing to pay."

"Damn it, girl. If you were my daughter, I'd lock you up at home for your stupidity. No woman in her right mind would let Salvatore touch her. Why do you think he was willing to pay for it? Everybody knows of his reputation. He loves to beat women."

Tears ran down Benedetta's face. Dante pulled out a handkerchief and patted her face with it.

"Thank you."

"Now, go home. I'll buy all the carvings you have left for tonight." Dante glanced at her cart. Tonight, the wooden figures she was selling were particularly ugly. They'd serve as firewood in his home just as all the others before them.

Her face lit up. "Oh, thank you so much, Signore di Santori. You're so kind."

Kind? It wasn't an adjective he was often graced with. No vampire was kind, least of all he, but if Dante hated one thing, it was men who beat women. He loved women in every shape and form they came. Especially when they came—in his bed.

He liked them even more when he fed from them.

A woman's blood was richer than a man's. And it was even more intoxicating when he fed from a woman while he was fucking her into oblivion. In fact, it was his preferred way to have dinner. There was nothing kind or civilized about it. When it came down to it, he wasn't that much better than Salvatore—a mere human—but he drew the line at hurting women.

In fact, he lived to give them pleasure.

His bite was painless, and his powers of suggestion made it possible for him to conceal what he did. After a night in his arms, the women he bedded didn't remember the passionate man who'd driven them to ecstasy or the bloodthirsty and insatiable vampire who'd gorged himself on their necks.

Dante's anger had failed to simmer down by the time he reached the club where Salvatore usually spent his evenings. He arrived spoiling for a fight. A real fight, not one where he would use his superior vampire powers to crush the human. He longed for a brawl in which he'd use his fists to pummel the man.

He pushed inside the club, ignoring the demands of the hostess to pay the fee. He would only stay long enough to find Salvatore and beat the living daylights out of him, and make him look much worse than he'd made Benedetta look.

Dante's entrance and the hostess's angry complaints behind him caused several heads to turn in his direction. He ignored them and instead scanned the room. It didn't take long for him to spot Salvatore in one of the booths that lined the room. And Salvatore wasn't alone. He was already working on his next unsuspecting victim.

Dante took no notice of the other guests' stares and marched straight toward Salvatore, stopping only a foot away. The man had his hand on the woman's skirts and his head close to her ear, undoubtedly whispering sweet-sounding lies to her. Dante cleared his throat loudly.

Without looking up, Salvatore tried to dismiss him. "I'm busy."

Dante clenched his jaw. "You won't be for much longer."

The woman snapped her head to him, her eyes widening in fear. She'd clearly heard the threat in his voice. Dante ignored her and snatched Salvatore's wrist, ripping it away from the woman's skirts and yanking him up. Startled, Salvatore glared at him.

"What the hell?" Salvatore's eyes narrowed. "Get your own woman. This one's mine."

"I'm not interested in your tart. I'm interested in you."

Salvatore tried to wrestle from the grip Dante had on his wrist but couldn't. "Leave me alone, you fag, or I'll beat the shit out of you."

"You mean the same way you beat the shit out of Benedetta?"

At Benedetta's name, a flash of fear crossed his face. He knew he was caught, but the bravado hadn't left him yet. "None of your damn business."

"She's a friend. So it's my business." Dante released the man's wrist and swung. His fist landed in Salvatore's face, snapping his head back in the process.

Collective gasps went through the assembled guests. In the background, Dante could hear the hostess's shrill voice. "Gentlemen, take your disagreement outside."

But it was too late for that. Salvatore had recovered from the first blow, and now swung his fist at Dante, grazing his chin. Dante laughed. "That's all you've got?" The human was weak. This would barely be any fun at all. No wonder the asshole liked to beat up on women since men were no match for him.

Dante launched his fist into Salvatore's stomach, making him double over. "Next time you decide to beat a woman, you'd better think twice." With an uppercut to Salvatore's chin, Dante turned. Before he could walk away, the man jumped him, slamming him to the ground.

Inside, Dante rejoiced. Finally, the jerk was fighting back, making this a little more interesting. Jerking his elbow back, Dante jabbed him in the ribs, then rolled, throwing Salvatore off his back. Within seconds, they dealt each other blow after blow. Dante barely felt any pain, but the human winced with each punch he received.

"Stop it! Stop beating him!" a woman's voice came from behind him.

Holding his victim down with one arm across his neck, Dante turned to look at the woman Salvatore had been with. She stood over him, her fists at her hips, a scowl on her face. "Signorina, you'd do well to keep out of this."

"I will not let you beat up my companion."

"Well, would you rather he beat *you* as he did the last woman he fucked?"

A red blush colored her skin at his crude words. He gave her another look. Now that he perused her closely, he noticed something strange about her. She didn't belong here. She wasn't the kind of woman who frequented clubs like these. Her manners seemed refined, her dress understated yet expensive. Her face was fresh and innocent, her hair held up in a tight bun at her nape with not a single loose strand framing her elegant features.

He inhaled her aroma. Yes, she smelled of innocence and goodness. But there was something else—something foreign that seemed to cloud her rich scent. And it made him want to protect her. And keep her close.

Dante tried to shake off the strange sensation while his gaze lingered on her face for a few seconds longer. The most striking things about her were her eyes. Their green color combined with her porcelain skin and those red lips made her look like an enticing tableau. What was a woman like that doing in a hell like this?

"You should leave," he advised her and turned back to Salvatore.

With one last blow, he knocked him unconscious. As he rose, the hostess blocked his way. "Signore, I do not tolerate this kind of behavior in my—"

Dante held up a hand. "I'm leaving."

With long strides, he left the club and stepped into the cool night air.

CHAPTER

THREE

Viola stared at the hostess. "But you can't throw me out. I had nothing to do with this."

The hostess pressed the coin back into her hand and pointed to the door. "Out."

Suppressing her tears of desperation, she walked outside, pulling her cloak tightly around her. If that terrible man hadn't beaten up her companion and knocked him unconscious, she would have lost her virginity tonight. And now? She was back where she'd started. And worse: she was banned from the club. It was the only place she knew where she could find what she wanted. Where would she go now?

Viola let out a frustrated huff and raised her head. Her gaze fell on the man who'd started the fight. He was standing a few yards away, arranging his cravat. Before she could lose her courage, she approached him.

"That was a terrible thing you did."

He gave her a bemused look. "You should be grateful to me, not badgering me."

"Grateful? You got me thrown out of the club."

"As I said, you should be grateful for that. You don't belong there. You're an innocent."

Anger churned up in Viola. "I'm not an innocent," she lied. "I'm a widow, and I'm here to find some ... pleasures." It was the same lie she'd given Salvatore, even though *he* hadn't questioned her motives.

The man arched an eyebrow and raised one side of his mouth, mocking her.

"Now you've destroyed my chances of being with a man tonight."

The man took a step closer, his body almost touching hers. His voice was low when he replied, "And you listen to me now, woman. The man you wanted to be with tonight beats the women he beds. It's part of what get's him off. He's violent, and he enjoys seeing women suffer. Was that what you were looking for?"

Instinctively, Viola took a step back.

Was the stranger telling the truth? Had he truly saved her from being beaten? She shook off the thought. No, the two men probably had had some prior quarrel. "No matter. Now I have to go somewhere else to find what I need."

"Are you crazy? Didn't you hear what I just said?"

"I heard you loud and clear. Now, would you please direct me to where I might find another place like this? You owe me that much." She thrust her chin up and waited.

The stranger shook his head. "I will do no such thing. Go home and be glad you didn't get hurt tonight."

She narrowed her eyes. "Fine ... Maybe somebody else can advise me." Viola turned on her heel but before she could even take one step, a hand clasped over her forearm and pulled her back. She snapped her head back to him, surprised by his boldness, and clenched her jaw.

"Signore, I suggest you remove your hand now."

He didn't yield to her threat. "You have no idea of the dangers out there. A woman like you shouldn't be prowling the night alone."

"It's none of your business. So, unless you want to bed me yourself, let go of me." The moment she issued her threat to him, she realized that it was exactly what she wanted. When she'd watched him beat up her companion, she'd seen the raw power in his body. But she'd also seen that he'd held back. He was much stronger than he'd let anybody see.

And the eyes that stared at her now in disbelief were the most sensual ones she'd ever seen on a man. They were a brilliant blue, which stood out in stark contrast to his black hair. His face had sharp angles, more rugged than elegant, and his shoulders seemed to bulge from his coat. He was tall, and the thought of his touch on more intimate places excited her. Where Salvatore had been handsome, this man was beautiful.

However, the frown on his face suggested that he had no intention of accepting her impromptu offer. Well, maybe her looks didn't appeal to him. She tried hard not to take his reaction personally. But to realize that she couldn't get this man to tumble her did put a chink in her carefully built armor.

"So let me go then," she repeated, not wanting to hear his rejection. His face had said enough. Viola jerked her arm, trying to get him to loosen his grip on her, but he didn't relent.

"You want me to bed you?" he asked.

She swallowed away her surprise at his question. Was he considering it? Her heartbeat sped up. "I've been a widow for a while and miss the touch of a man."

"Is that so?" His voice sounded as if he didn't believe her. Was her story not good enough? She'd rehearsed it many times, and Salvatore had believed it.

"Well, clearly, you're not interested. So, don't concern yourself. I'm sure I'll find somebody." Where and how she would accomplish this feat, she wasn't certain.

"Who says I'm not interested?"

Viola looked up at his face and noticed how he let a long gaze travel down her body. She shivered and wet her lips. Yes, this man was stirring something in her. For some strange reason, he was breaking through the uncertainty she'd felt when she'd been in Salvatore's company. Despite the sweet things Salvatore had whispered in her ear, she hadn't warmed to him. Whereas this man—

"There's a place down this alley we can go to," he suggested. "What's your name?"

"Signora Costa." Her throat felt dry as sandpaper.

"Your given name."

Her brain stopped working under the intense stare he gave her. "Why would you want my given name?"

"Because I'd like to call out your given name when I thrust into you."

CHAPTER

FOUR

Dante let the door to the inn's simple bedchamber shut behind him and watched as the lovely Viola took off her cloak. He hadn't planned on ravishing anyone this evening, but he never looked a gift horse in the mouth. And Viola was more than just an unexpected treat: she intrigued him.

What had driven her to that disreputable club? She seemed too refined, too well bred for an establishment like that. Frankly, he was extremely glad to have arrived there when he did, because the more he looked at her, the more he wanted to be the one to satisfy her secret desires. The thought that she'd gone out to invite trouble sent a severe chill racing down his spine.

Even as a young widow who knew about the pleasures of the flesh, she had no idea what dangers lurked outside. In his eyes, she was still an innocent. And he had a thing for innocent women. Just as he'd always tried to protect Benedetta, a girl of merely fifteen, he now wanted to protect this woman.

To a certain extent, anyway. He wouldn't hurt her, but while he was fucking her, he would also taste her. Despite the fact that he'd fed earlier in the night, he never turned down dessert. And if her blood tasted anywhere near as intoxicating as the scent of her skin promised, it would be a very sumptuous dessert indeed.

"Well," she said, her voice trembling in concert with her fingers. He sensed her nervousness and assumed her late husband had been the only man who'd ever touched her. Clearly, this was difficult for her.

Dante walked to her, tossing his coat onto a chair in midstride. "Let me help you with your dress."

Viola flinched when he put his hands on her shoulders. "I... can do that myself," she stammered.

"But I would like to do it, if you'll allow me." He tipped her chin up with his hand and dipped his head. Her breath mingled with his, and he inhaled the scent. "I'd also like to kiss you."

He didn't wait for her answer. Instead, he pressed his lips to hers and nudged them open. Without much ado, he swept his tongue inside her mouth and issued his demand. Her answer was timid. Dante went after her tongue and growled his disapproval. If she wanted to be bedded, she sure wasn't showing it in her reaction to him. Was he not to her liking? The thought that she might prefer Salvatore's more elegant features to his rougher ones inflamed him.

He ripped his mouth from hers. "Kiss me back, damn it."

Her eyes glittered with uncertainty.

"Or have you changed your mind?" He would let her off the hook if she had. He wasn't the kind of man to force a woman.

The shake of her head was quick but determined. "No!" Just as quickly, she laced her hands around his neck and pulled him back to her.

"That's better," he praised and snaked his arms around her back. "Now, let's try that again, shall we?"

Viola closed her eyes as if steeling herself for his onslaught. It surprised him. Did she see him as some kind of rough beast? Dante paused for a moment. She knew nothing about him but what she'd seen him do: violently beat up another man with his fists. Had that scared her?

"I won't hurt you."

Her eyes flew open. "I know."

This time when he kissed her, he gently pressed his lips against her soft mouth and tugged on her upper lip, then ran his tongue over it. Slowly, her lips parted. Dante continued nibbling on her lips until he heard a tiny moan coming from her. Now he understood: she wanted gentle and slow. That's what she responded to. He could do that.

He stilled his lips. "You should have told me you wanted it gentle. Because a woman walking around dingy clubs trying to find a man for sex generally wants some frantic fucking."

Viola gasped and seemed to want to protest, but he pressed a soft kiss onto her lips before he continued. "It doesn't matter to me. You want it soft and gentle, I'll do it that way. But when you want me to fuck you fast and hard, you'll let me know, won't you?"

Her nod was barely noticeable.

Dante explored the warm and moist hollow of her mouth, swept his tongue against hers and savored her taste. She was a delicious morsel, and her gentle and measured response to his searching tongue only fed his excitement. Coaxing a response from her was a challenge, and he liked a challenge more than any other man.

The more he kissed her without letting his demanding self take over, the more Viola awakened in his arms. Her hands on his neck were hot to the touch now, and her entire body seemed to radiate heat. He welcomed it and slid his hand up to the exposed skin of her shoulders. She trembled when he stroked his knuckles against her pulse, and he heard her heartbeat quicken. Her blood charged through the vein underneath his fingertips, a feeling that made his cock harden in an instant.

Yes, bedding this shy young woman would be an unexpected delight. And taking her sweet blood would make it all the more enjoyable.

Dante lowered his hand and cupped one breast, eliciting a gasp from her. He eased his lips from hers. Her green eyes seemed to be even darker than before. And her lips were swollen from his kisses. He rather liked the sight. "May I help undress you?"

~

His words pulled her out of her passion-drugged state. No man had ever kissed her like that. In fact, no man had ever kissed her other than on her hand or her cheek. This was more than she'd ever expected. And she didn't want to stop. "I want to kiss some more," she mumbled and averted her gaze.

"We'll kiss plenty more, I promise you. But first, take off your dress so I can touch you while I kiss you." His eyes seemed to devour her. And the huskiness in his voice carried the promise he'd spoken.

"Will you undress too?"

He chuckled. "Would you like to help me with it?"

The thought of undressing him excited her. She licked her lips in anticipation. From what she'd felt under her hands when she'd held him close to her, Dante was a big man with strong muscles. They'd felt hard, yet comforting.

"I'd say that's a yes." His smile was warm, and she smiled back.

He started unlacing her bodice. Since she'd come to Venice without a maid or a companion, she'd chosen a dress that she was able to put on and take off without anybody's help. However, when she felt his fingers stroke over her torso while he loosened her dress, she didn't mind his help in the least. She enjoyed the tingles that spread over her skin with every press of his hands. And he was merely touching her through the many layers of her garments. What would it be like once he touched her naked skin?

As Dante peeled away her bodice and let her skirts fall to the floor in a rustle, she stood before him in her chemise and drawers. She'd not worn a corset since she'd known she'd be unable to lace herself into it without help. Now she felt exposed, knowing he could see through the thin white fabric of her chemise. Instinctively, she crossed her arms over her chest.

"No," he whispered, "let me see you." He took her arms and uncrossed them. "You're beautiful. You have no reason to hide."

His palm cupped one of her breasts, then the other. The touch felt as if a lightning storm went through her. "I love the way they feel in my hands." He squeezed, and her heart rate spiked.

"Oh, God."

"It's Dante," he corrected. Of course, she knew that. He'd told her his name on the way to the inn. But for some reason her brain wasn't working when his hands were on her.

"Dante," she whispered. "I want to undress you too."

Viola put her hands on his chest, making him let go of her breasts. Slowly, she eased button after button open, revealing a muscled chest with a light sprinkling of dark hair. In the middle of his chest it concentrated and then narrowed toward the top of his breeches. Her eyes followed the dark path.

"Yes," he encouraged her. "Open my trousers, and take my cock out."

Nobody had ever spoken that word in front of her, yet she knew what it meant. Her eyes drifted lower to the bulge hidden beneath the fabric. The very large bulge. Did he wear padding? She hoped so, because what the hard outline under his breeches suggested would be physically impossible, she was certain.

Viola hesitated, but Dante simply took her hand and laid her palm over the bulge. Startled, she tried to pull away, but he held her wrist and forced her to cup his erection. The flesh under her palm was warm, and it pulsated. She'd never felt anything that vibrant. Now she had her answer: he wore no padding.

"Open the buttons."

She followed his command without thinking. Moments later, his breeches were open. He pulled them down and stripped completely. Viola averted her eyes, even though she wanted to look at him. But embarrassment swept through her. She'd never seen a man naked.

"Look at me." Dante's voice was calm and soothing.

She lifted her eyes to meet his gaze. But he shook his head. "Look at my cock."

She swallowed at his bold statement. How could she simply look at him in such an obvious manner?

"Please, look at my cock and take me into your hand."

She collected her courage and lowered her gaze to his stomach, then lower. In the midst of a dark nest of curls, his shaft stood erect, curved slightly upwards, its purple veins pulsing, its mushroomed head glistening. She'd always expected men to be ugly there, but nothing could be further from the truth. His veined shaft was like a sculpted piece of art. Beautiful, proud, and perfect.

Her hand reached out of its own volition, her fingers grazing the underside of his cock. The skin was as soft as a baby's, yet when she wrapped her hand around him, she could feel how hard he was. Like a phallus chiseled from marble.

Dante hissed. "Fuck."

At his curse, she released him with a surprised gasp.

"No. Don't stop. I like the way you touch me."

Tentatively, she took him into her hand again. Then she felt his hands on her, opening the top buttons of her chemise so it easily slid over one shoulder, exposing one breast to his view. He bent his head down and licked his tongue over her nipple.

Her hand released him as she tried to deal with the new sensations crashing over her. His tongue felt warm and wet, the texture of it creating a delicious friction on her breast. Her nipple had turned hard and was aching for more. Viola threw her head back. When cool air blew against her skin, she realized that he'd pushed her chemise over her shoulders and let it drop to the floor. Then she felt his hands on her drawers, ridding her of those as well. She should have felt embarrassment, yet she only felt the rioting sensations he urged through her body.

His mouth was suckling on her nipple, drawing it deep into his warmth. It created an equally strong ache between her legs, where she felt a warmth and wetness, something she'd never experienced before.

Viola dug her hands into his shoulders to keep from swaying, her balance impeded by his ministrations and her own body's order to simply let go. Dante growled and lifted his head from her breast.

"No," she protested, wanting more of what he was offering.

"Shh, my sweet." He lifted her into his arms and carried her to the bed. When he lowered them onto it, she felt the finality of her actions. A hint of panic struck her, and she stiffened.

"What's wrong?" he asked.

Viola opened her eyes and looked at him. This was the man who was about to take her virginity and make her a woman before she died. She was scared, but she knew she needed this, needed to know what it meant to be a woman. Despite her fear, she forced herself to smile. "Nothing."

Dante settled on top of her, spreading her thighs with his body. His hard shaft was poised at the apex of her thighs, where the throbbing ache she couldn't describe was getting stronger.

"You get me so hot and so hard," he pressed out, his jaw clenched as if he were exerting a strong force on something or someone. "I can't wait any longer."

Then she felt his thick cock at her entrance just before he plunged into her.

Dante felt himself breach her barrier and froze when he heard Viola cry out.

"You're a virgin?" He braced himself on his elbows, taking his weight off her. "You lied to me." Fury coursed through him. The woman underneath him was no shy widow but a blushing virgin. No wonder she'd been so tentative when he'd first kissed her.

Viola averted his angry gaze. "Would you have done it if I'd told you I was a virgin?"

"Of course not." He rolled off her with a huff. "I'm not in the business of deflowering innocents."

"And neither are those men at the club, so I figured—"

"You figured you'd lie to me. I get it. If this is some trick of yours to get me to marry you then—"

Her eyes widened in shock, and she sat up while nervously pulling on the bed sheet to cover herself. "How dare you insinuate I wanted to trap you? I have no interest in you. All I wanted was one night of passion." She jumped out of bed and snatched her chemise from the floor.

He noticed how her hands shook as she pulled it over her body. "Viola, stop. What are you doing?"

She pulled on her drawers and reached for her dress. "I'm leaving."

"And where are you going?"

"What does it matter? I got what I came for. You've done what I wanted you to do." She sniffed, and he rather suspected she was on the verge of tears. Damn, how he hated crying women.

"I haven't done anything yet. You think that was all there's to it? You truly are an innocent." And for some odd reason, he liked her innocence. So did his still-hard cock.

Viola pulled her dress up, and he was surprised at how fast she tied the laces on the front of her bodice. "I'm not an innocent anymore."

Dante jumped out of bed, unconcerned with his nudity. "All I did was penetrate you. This wasn't fucking."

"Well, I don't care to know about the rest." She grabbed her cloak and the small satchel she'd brought with her and dashed for the door.

Dante stood frozen. What had just happened? He'd deflowered a virgin who'd hightailed it out of his bed before he had even properly fucked her. All she would know was the pain associated with his invasion of her entirely too-tight channel. Damn, how she'd gripped him for so brief a time. Had he known, he would have prepared her better. What was he saying? Had he known, he would have never touched her.

Damn it to hell, this was not how he wanted to be remembered: as the man who'd hurt her.

Dante cursed and grabbed his clothes.

THE MOMENT the cold night air hit her heated body, Viola sensed a dull ache in her head. Like a clenched fist, the pressure in her head built: as if the growth inside her were trying to push through her skull and crack it as a chick inside its egg.

It had all been too much for her after all: the anticipation and nervousness when she'd first entered the club, the fear and devastation when the fight between Dante and Salvatore had broken out, and now the loss of her virginity. It had been painful, even though the sharp pain had lasted only a moment. The moment he'd penetrated her with his manhood, which was clearly too large for a woman like her, all the delicious sensations his kisses and caresses had caused had fled her body. If this was what sex was, then she was no longer interested.

Well, at least she wouldn't die a virgin. Now that she knew she had experienced everything she had set herself to do, she felt empty. But instead of a pleasant emptiness in her head, she felt a throbbing ache. For hours, she would be in the throws of excruciating pain if she allowed this to continue.

But she didn't have to allow it. All the items on her list were ticked off. There was no reason to stay. It was better to end it now.

Viola walked to the next corner, where a gas lamp provided more light, and stopped. She loosened the bow to her small bag and opened it. Apart from a handkerchief, a few coins and her pills, the only other item in it was the pistol she'd taken from her father's study. She'd watched him often enough when he'd cleaned and loaded it. She'd even shot it once before in Switzerland to make sure it was working. Then she'd reloaded it.

Her fingers suddenly felt icy when she pulled the weapon from her bag. She recognized her slow movements as a symptom of her cowardice. She was a coward for taking her own life, but she was also a coward for hesitating to put the pistol to her temple.

She forced herself to steady her trembling hand. It had to be done. She would not sit idly by, waiting for her death when there was nothing more that she wanted from life, when all that was going to happen from now on would be painful. No more joy would come her way.

Viola gave a rueful smile, remembering the few moments of sheer and utter bliss she'd felt when Dante had kissed her. Those were the minutes she wanted to remember in her hour of death, not the pain that had followed or the ugly words he'd hurled at her.

A tiny sob tore from her chest as she raised the weapon to her head and closed her eyes. She cocked the pistol, and the sound echoed in the alley, ricocheting off the stone walls to tell all the world that she was leaving. Her finger on the trigger trembled, but she took a steadying breath, then another one.

Tears pushed passed her closed lids and rolled down her cheeks. She squeezed her index finger and felt something impacting her body the moment the shot rang out.

The shot echoed in the alley just as Dante slammed his body into Viola and simultaneously jerked the pistol from her hand. They crashed onto the cobblestone street, Dante landing on top of her. He instantly rolled off her, but she didn't move.

His sensitive nostrils picked up the scent of her blood immediately. "No!" he screamed. He'd come too late. When he'd seen her standing there under the gas lamp, he'd hesitated to approach her. He hadn't figured out what to say to her. Too late had he seen the pistol in her hand. Only when she'd lifted it to her temple had he reacted and started to run.

Dante looked at the wound on Viola's head, pushing away the hunger for her blood at the same time. He should be ashamed of himself. Even now, with blood oozing from her head, he wanted nothing more than to taste her. He shook the thought off as a dog shook his pelt free of water.

Hesitantly, he smoothed his hand over the wound, wiping away the blood, afraid of what he'd find. But his fingers didn't encounter a gaping wound. On the contrary, all he felt was an abrasion. It was bleeding mildly. He bent his head closer, training his eyes on the wound. The gas lamp provided some light; his superior night vision compensated for the rest.

There was no hole. The bullet had only grazed her, and most likely the violent way with which he'd knocked her to the ground had made her faint. Dante pressed his hand to her chest and felt for her heartbeat, even though he could hear it. But he needed to reassure himself. Instinctively, his hand moved, cupping one breast. He jerked it away from her.

Gods, he was so depraved, he'd even fondle an unconscious, injured woman. His stomach growled, the scent of her sweet blood assaulting his senses. There was no use, as long as she bled, even slightly, from her head wound, he wouldn't be able to concentrate on anything else. He brought his lips to her wound and licked over it with one single swipe of his tongue, forcing himself to pull back from her immediately.

His saliva closed the wound and healed the skin, but he took no notice of it. He was too distracted by the taste of her on his tongue. Her blood was sweet and rich just as he'd expected, but there was another taste in it, and he couldn't determine what it was. It seemed foreign, just the way her scent had struck him as foreign when he'd first inhaled it at the club. He tasted something threatening. Dante shook his head. His mind was probably addled, still confused from the shock he'd been dealt.

Viola had tried to kill herself because of what he'd done to her.

Had he been such a cad? Maybe he wasn't any better than Salvatore. At least the wounds Salvatore left on women were visible and would heal over time, but the wounds he'd left on this innocent woman were internal. He hadn't seen just how much he'd hurt her. But he had hurt her—so badly that she'd wanted to take solace in death.

The knowledge hit him in the gut. She'd tried to take her life minutes after she'd left his bed, minutes after he'd accused her of lying and trying to trap him. Minutes after he'd been inside her, had physically hurt her. She'd wanted to leave this world with the misconception that sex was a terrible thing, that it hurt women. And that he was a terrible lover.

That particular knowledge hit his ego.

No woman he'd been with had ever done this—at least he hoped not. He'd always tried to make sure the women he fucked enjoyed themselves. Frankly, it was more fun for him if they did. But Viola—he'd disappointed her so badly that she couldn't even bear to go on living. What did that make him? More than just a bad lover—it made him an accomplice in her death. And that was one thing he didn't want to be.

Yes, he'd killed—but those had been men who'd threatened his life or that of his fellow vampires. He'd never killed an innocent, and he wasn't about to start now. He needed to convince the woman who still lay unconscious on the cobblestones that life was worth living. And that sex was worth having. Again and again and again.

Knowing what he had to do, he put the pistol in his coat pocket and gathered Viola in his arms. He barely felt her weight as he carried her the fifteen minutes it took to reach his home.

Lights were ablaze when he entered, and voices and laughter drifted to him through the open door of the parlor.

"Dante?" his brother Raphael called out to him.

"Not now." Dante headed for the stairs, but his brother was already at the door and stepped into the foyer.

"Rumor has it you had a fight at the—" His brother interrupted him. "Did you have to bring dinner home? I thought we'd discussed—"

Dante swiveled and faced his brother. "She's not dinner." He was surprised at the defensive tone in his own voice.

"I smell blood."

"She's injured."

Behind him, Isabella emerged. "What's going on?" His sister-in-law looked as ravishing as ever. Dante noticed how Raphael instantly took her hand in his. Honeymooners, Dante grumbled internally.

"Nothing. I'm merely helping an injured woman."

At that, even Isabella raised an eyebrow. It appeared that his new sister-in-law had already figured out he wasn't the good Samaritan kind.

"Since when are you so charitable, Dante?" his brother mocked.

Dante took a deep breath. "May I remind you that this is my house too, and that it's my business what I do?"

"Granted. However, I'd like to assure myself of the girl's safety while she's in our house."

Dante's patience snapped. "Well, look at my suddenly proper brother.

No offense, Isabella, but it appears your husband has forgotten what he was like before he married you. I distinctly remember that—"

"Be that as it may, things have changed." Raphael led Isabella's hand to his lips and kissed her knuckles. "We agreed that we wouldn't subject Isabella to the more gruesome aspects of our kind. And that includes bringing unsuspecting humans into our home and—"

Dante took a step closer. "And what?" Then he looked down at Viola's face, which was cradled against his chest. "I mean her no harm. If you must know, she tried to take her own life tonight."

Isabella gasped in shock. "Oh, no. Poor girl!"

"What happened?" Raphael asked, his voice full of compassion now.

Dante closed his eyes, warring with himself about how much to tell his brother. "She was a virgin. But she lied to me and told me that she was a widow looking for some... carnal diversions." He looked at Isabella's face, wondering how much more he should say. His brother's wife merely listened with bated breath. "It wasn't... well, it wasn't pleasant for her. She tried to kill herself ten minutes later. I was lucky to stop her. The bullet only grazed her temple."

For a moment, nobody spoke. The silence in the foyer was deafening.

He waited for a snide remark from his brother, but it didn't come. "What, no comeback?" Dante asked.

"You'd better take her upstairs. I'll inform the servants to watch what they say. I'm assuming she doesn't know what you are?" Raphael's voice was calm and collected.

Dante shook his head. "No. It's bad enough she thinks sex is a terrible thing. How do you think she'll react if she realized one of our kind took her virginity?"

He gazed at Viola's face and drew her tighter to his body. She seemed so fragile, and he felt as though he were a beast that had attacked her.

And he wanted to do it again.

CHAPTER
SEVEN

Viola felt a warm cocoon surround her and snuggled deeper into the softness. She hadn't expected the afterlife to feel so soft and warm. In fact, she'd rather thought that as a consequence of her desperate act of committing suicide, she would wake up in hell. But this didn't feel like hell. There was, to be sure, the smell of a little smoke from a fire burning nearby, but no smell of sulfur, no screams. Instead, she could smell a lingering scent of cologne—a man's cologne. It was odd.

She opened her eyes to take in her new surroundings. Shock made her sit up.

She was in a large four poster bed in the middle of a richly decorated bedchamber—a very masculine bedchamber.

"Ah, you're finally awake."

Viola snapped her head toward the male voice and froze. Dante. He sat in an armchair near the fireplace and now rose to walk toward the bed. She grabbed the sheets and pressed them against her body, realizing instantly that she wore only her chemise.

"I had to make you more comfortable." His tone was apologetic, and even his eyes looked sincere.

"Where am I?" she pressed out, panic gripping her. Had he kidnapped her? What had happened? She distinctly remembered pressing the gun against her temple and pulling the trigger.

Dante reached the bed and sat down at the edge. Viola eyed him suspiciously. "You're in my home. I didn't know where you lived, so I brought you here."

Instinctively her hand went to her temple. She felt a tiny abrasion, but nothing else.

His eyes followed her hand. "The bullet only grazed you. I jerked it from your hand."

Her heart pounded at the knowledge that he knew what she'd done and that he'd prevented her from succeeding. "How dare you?"

"Excuse me?" His forehead crinkled with confusion.

"You heard me. How dare you stop me? It was my choice." She hit him with a furious glare.

"Choice?" He stood up with a start. "You didn't know what you were doing. You can't just kill yourself over something so trivial."

"Trivial?"

"Yes, trivial. No woman's first sexual experience is all that enjoyable. Don't you know that?"

He thought she'd wanted to kill herself because it had hurt when he'd penetrated her? She'd had to deal with more severe pain in her life than the little ache that had lasted only a few seconds. How self-absorbed was he? "You pompous, arrogant rake! This has nothing to do with you."

Dante glared at her. "It has everything to do with me. There's no need to lie to me. In fact, it would be better for all involved if you told me the truth. You're obviously not a widow. I guess we've already established that."

Viola didn't like his commanding tone and decided not to make this easy for him. Maybe he thought he could command other women around, but not her. "I could very well have been married and still be a virgin if—"

He suddenly was at the bed and took her chin with his thumb and forefinger. "Lying doesn't become you. So stop, or I'll have to do this to shut you up." He pressed a kiss on her lips, a kiss so brief she could barely enjoy the sensation.

"I didn't give you leave to kiss me!" she protested and pushed him away, dropping the bed sheet in the process.

"You gave me leave to do a lot more than that." He grinned and lowered his gaze to her breasts.

With a jerky movement, she covered herself with the sheet. "Go, sit on that chair over there." She wanted him as far away as possible. When he was so close with his male scent wrapping around her, she couldn't think clearly. Why else would she want to pull him into bed with her and ask him to kiss her again the way he'd done before he'd used his enormous manhood on her?

The look he gave her could only be described as brooding. "If you wish." Dante let himself fall into the armchair and stared at her.

"Now, if you tell me where my garments and my bag and pistol are, I'll be getting ready to leave."

"You will do no such thing."

Viola narrowed her eyes. "Are you keeping me captive?"

"It's for your own safety. As for your pistol: you must be crazy to think I'd simply hand a deadly weapon back to you after you tried to kill yourself with it. No, you, young lady, are staying here until I can make sure you won't try it again."

She inhaled sharply. "This is not up to you. My life is mine, and I'll do with it as I please."

"Not if I can help it," Dante snapped and rose. He looked like a caged tiger as he approached the bed again. Instinctively, she scrambled toward the other side of the bed.

"You can't do that."

"I can do a lot more than that. For starters, I'm going to show you that sex can be just as pleasurable for a woman as it is for a man. And once you realize that, you won't have any reason left to take your own life."

Viola simply stared at him. He couldn't be serious. The man had an entirely overblown sense of self-centeredness which wouldn't allow his addled brain to understand that he wasn't the reason for her desire to leave this world. And of course, she wouldn't tell him the truth. It was none of his darn business. Besides, she wanted nobody's pity. As for him proving to her that sex was pleasurable for women... "How will you do that?"

Sometimes she wished her brain was faster than her tongue, because clearly she'd spoken too soon again. Judging by his smug grin, he was enjoying the situation.

"Very slowly and very thoroughly." The look he raked over her made her shiver. God help her if he meant it.

"You can't—"

"—do that?" he finished her sentence and jumped onto the bed on all fours. "I wouldn't be so sure if I were you."

A second later, Dante was straddling her hips and pressing her back into the pillows, his face only inches from her. Viola's body heated, and her pulse raced. Knowing how she had reacted to his kisses and his touch before made it impossible for her to push him away. She felt paralyzed.

His knuckles stroked softly over her cheek. "As we both know, I'm stronger than you. So, save your breath for when you find yourself panting for release. But now, I'll have the servants prepare a bath for you. And once you're done, I'll expect you downstairs for a meal."

Her fighting instinct hadn't left her yet. If he thought she was easily intimidated, he didn't yet know how stubborn she was. "I will do no such thing."

"Fine, then I'll bathe you myself."

Shock coursed through her. "You wouldn't—"

His grin stopped her. He would.

"Fine."

"Now, that's a good girl," he praised, or was he mocking her?

When he jumped off the bed, she should have been relieved, but her body instantly missed his warmth.

He walked to the door. "And if you take too long with your bath because you're trying to avoid me, I will pull you out of the tub myself and dry you off."

When he let the door snap in behind him, Viola threw a pillow at it.

"You are not as irresistible as you think!" she mumbled under her breath and could have sworn she heard him chuckle as he walked down the stairs. Yet, there was no way he could have heard her through the closed door.

CHAPTER

EIGHT

"**A**re you crazy?" Raphael ground out.

Dante shrugged and kicked his foot against the grill of the fireplace, making the fire hiss in response. "What would you have me do? Let her loose, and have her try it again? I won't do that."

"You're surprisingly protective of the girl. It's not like you. Are you sure you're quite all right?" Raphael's insolent grin did nothing to calm Dante's constitution.

"You're one to talk. You've gone soft since you got married."

"You do know I can hear you, Dante, don't you?" Isabella asked from the sofa.

"I was merely trying to get your husband off my back, dearest."

"So he wouldn't question your actions?" she asked.

"I'm my own master. What I do shouldn't be any of your or your husband's concern."

"What of the girl?" Raphael interjected and took a seat next to his wife.

"I promise that no harm will come to her. I'm not a complete bastard."

"That remains to be seen," Viola said from the door.

Dante jerked from his seat and spun around. She walked into the room, wearing the gown she'd worn earlier, the same he'd stripped her of many hours ago. The memory of it was still fresh and made his pulse race. He tamped down his heated reaction to her presence.

"I would have left, but it appears somebody bolted the door accidentally, and I can't find a way to open it." She turned toward Raphael, who'd risen from the sofa. "Maybe you would assist me so I can take my leave? My parents will be worried that I've been gone so long."

Her smile was sugary sweet, but Dante knew Viola was anything but. And he wouldn't fall for it.

"Raphael di Santori," his brother introduced himself. "Dante is my brother." Then Raphael turned to his wife who'd moved to his side. "My wife Isabella."

"Pleasure. Viola Costa. I'm sorry to have inconvenienced you. If you please, I'd like to return to my accommodations." She gave another sweet smile and shifted her body toward the door.

Her last words echoed through Dante's head. She wanted to return to her accommodations, not her home. Odd. He took a gamble. "If you allow me, Viola, I'll be happy to accompany you to your hotel to make sure you're safe. Where are you staying?"

"The Aristo—" She snapped her mouth shut quickly, but Dante had heard enough.

"Just as I thought. You're not going home to your parents. I'd venture a guess that your parents have no idea where you are." By the way her cheeks colored, Dante knew he was right. "Well, well. In that case, I'm sorry, my young lady, but I feel it is my duty to keep you here under my supervision where no harm can come to you. I'll be happy to contact your parents in the meantime so they may come to collect you."

Viola narrowed her eyes. "That won't be necessary. I will find my own way home."

"No, no. I insist. Once your parents have arrived, I'll be more than happy to release you into their care." He turned to his brother. "I think that's the least we can do as hospitable Venetians, don't you think so, Raphael?"

For once, his brother agreed, albeit with a frown. "I'm afraid it would be unwise to allow a young lady without a chaperone or a companion to leave our house. If you give me your parents' name and address, I will personally send a messenger and make them aware of your whereabouts, Signorina Costa."

Viola huffed and took a few steps toward Dante. He'd hit the nail on the head. She was a runaway and had no intention of being found. Just as well because he wanted her here with him. Until, well... until he was done with her.

"You, you..." Her skin glistened, and her lovely bosom heaved with every breath she took. With her index finger, she jabbed him in the chest. "You, you..."

"Running out of words, my dear?" Dante snatched her finger and led it to his lips, giving it a soft peck. "Now, how about some food? All that lying must have made you hungry."

Viola huffed once more and turned away. Dante couldn't help but laugh. She was too much fun to spar with. Damn, he liked that in a woman.

Isabella put a hand on Viola's arm. "Come, Signorina Costa. Cook prepared a nice spread for us. Let's leave the men to their talk."

Viola had no choice. She could not allow Dante or his brother to contact her parents. If they did, her parents would shepherd her home, despite her earlier threat that she would cause a scandal. By the time they were all back in Florence, too much time would have passed, and her health would have deteriorated to the point where she would have no strength left to execute her threat. And her parents knew that. No, she could not risk a message being sent to them. Let them believe she was in Switzerland.

If only she'd thought before she'd spoken, but Dante had immediately caught her tacit admission that she was staying at a hotel. He'd beaten her at her own game.

She would have to devise a strategy to gain back some ground, but first, she needed to eat. She felt famished. Her stomach growled as if commanded.

"You must be starving," Isabella said and pointed to a chair opposite hers at a large dining table.

Viola took the seat and folded the napkin over her lap. "I'm not sure why though. I already had supper."

"Not tonight. You slept for almost twenty hours after Dante brought—"

Startled, Viola stared at her. "I've been here since yesterday?"

"You were unconscious when Dante put you to bed. I dare say, he was quite worried about you. It's not like him." There was a puzzled look on Isabella's face. She was a stunningly beautiful woman with silken skin, mesmerizing green eyes, and long dark hair which was piled loosely onto her head.

"He has no reason to worry about me. I'm quite capable of taking care of myself."

"Since you raise that subject, why did you attempt to kill yourself?"

Viola clenched her jaw. She hadn't expected the outwardly pleasant woman to be so blunt. "Nobody in this household seems to have any tact."

Isabella made a dismissive hand movement. "Oh, that. Blame my husband and his brother. Their behavior tends to rub off on others. We are a very unconventional household to say the least."

"Does that mean Dante kidnaps unsuspecting women quite often?" She crinkled her nose and lifted her chin in a blasé kind of way. If the lady of the house couldn't keep up proper decorum, why should she? She was merely a prisoner, not even a guest.

"Whatever you want to know about Dante, I'm sure he'll be happy to tell you. But it's not my place to do so." Then she changed the subject. "Do you enjoy the pheasant?"

Viola chewed the divine meat thoroughly and swallowed. "Passable."

"I'll have cook prepare something different tomorrow if you're not partial to fowl."

"I'll be gone by tomorrow, so don't trouble yourself." They couldn't watch her every second of the day and night. She'd sneak out soon when their defenses were down. But in the meantime, she took another fork full of meat. There was no reason to go hungry.

"Making plans without me, Viola?" Dante drawled from the door.

How had he managed to sneak up on them like that? She didn't give him the satisfaction of showing him how startled she was by his appearance and took another bite instead.

"Well, eat up then, my sweet, we're going out. I'll see you in the foyer in five minutes."

She snapped her head in his direction, but he'd already left. What in hell was he planning?

CHAPTER
NINE

Dante waited for Viola, his long black cloak slung around his shoulders, the girl's cloak in his hands. He needed to get out of the house. If he stayed under the watchful eye of his brother and his sister-in-law any longer, he'd never get to kissing the girl and starting her education in the carnal arts.

It was time to remind her of what they'd done the night before—not when he'd penetrated her without much preparation, but when they'd kissed. If he wasn't mistaken, she'd liked the kissing part well enough.

He picked up her scent even before she exited the dining room. Just as her blood had tasted different when he'd licked it off her temple, her scent had something foreign to it. Something that made him want to protect her. He didn't understand his strange sentiment. After all, he was a self-proclaimed rake whose only interests lay in fornication and imbibing in rich blood until he felt the same kind of high drugs would produce in humans.

When he laid eyes on Viola as she resolutely swept into the foyer, his protective instinct toward her increased even more. The aura he sensed around her seemed fragile and in stark contrast to the sharp tongue she wielded against him so easily. Not that he minded. He'd spar with that tongue any day—or night.

Dante cleared his throat and pushed his thoughts back into the dark recesses of his debauched mind. "There you are."

"Where are we going?" Her voice was assessing.

He took a step toward her and secured the cloak around her shoulders, tying the ribbon under her throat. Then he dipped his head to whisper in her ear. "Exploring."

Before she could protest, he swept her outside into the night. Minutes earlier, he'd secured a gondola and a gondolier who'd promised him a smooth ride through the canals and a discrete look in the other direction when necessary.

Dante helped Viola into the gondola and squeezed onto the comfortable high-back bench next to her. She was a dainty thing, yet his massive proportions assured there wasn't an inch of space between them.

As the gondolier pushed off and navigated them down the canal, Dante made himself comfortable and slid his arm around Viola's shoulders to press her closer to him.

"Signore!" she protested.

He dipped his head to hers. "Please call me Dante. I'd hate for you to scream 'Signore' when you come apart in my arms. Now, enjoy the ride."

She didn't respond, and he didn't expect her to. For now, all he wanted was for her to enjoy the tour. Since she'd admitted that she was staying in a hotel, he knew she was not native to Venice. It had given him the idea of taking her on a little sightseeing tour along the picturesque canals. Even at night, she would be able to see many of the magnificent mansions and palaces the city was famous for.

As he pointed out different buildings and retold little anecdotes about the inhabitants, he felt her relax next to him. From the corner of his eye, he noticed how she looked at many of the impressive homes with awe, her mouth open in obvious admiration. Illuminated on the inside by massive chandeliers, Dante and Viola caught glimpses of the grandeur inside.

"Beautiful," she whispered.

Dante was pleased with himself. Viola seemed to enjoy the gondola ride. It was part of his plan to show her that life was worth living, that there was beauty and excitement all around her.

When she suddenly shivered next to him, he pulled her closer. "Cold?"

She nodded, and he reached for her folded hands. They were like ice. He cursed himself. Just because he didn't feel the cold as severely as a human would didn't mean he could forget about her well-being. "I'm sorry, Viola."

He opened his own cloak.

"No, you'll be cold then," she protested.

"No, I won't. Come." Before she could protest, he lifted her into his arms and settled her on his lap. He scooted back onto the bench before he closed his cloak over both of them.

"But—"

He killed her protest by pressing her closer to his chest, keeping his own arms inside his cloak, away from prying eyes. "This way we'll both be warm."

"Is that why?" She tilted her chin up in challenge.

"There's a second reason."

"Which would be?"

"Did you like it when I kissed you last night?"

She dropped her lids at his question but said nothing.

"Do you want me to kiss you again?"

An almost unperceivable nod was the answer. Excitement coursed through him. He hadn't misread her the night before. He had another chance. "Then lift your head and offer me your lips."

She did just that. But instead of stealing a passionate and demanding kiss, he pushed back his hunger for her and only lightly brushed his lips against hers. They were almost as frozen as her hands. He nibbled on them, stroking over them with his hot tongue in an attempt to warm her.

VIOLA CLOSED her eyes and savored the gentle touch. Dante was different than the night before, less urgent, less demanding. Gentler, softer. Yet in no way less intoxicating. She breathed in his rich scent, a mixture of musky cologne —the same she'd smelled in his bed—and a deep earthy and leathery scent.

His lips were tentative against her, merely touching lightly, barely pressing against her. A frustrated moan escaped her. She wanted him to kiss her the way he'd kissed her the night before.

"Something wrong?" he whispered against her lips.

"No." She couldn't very well tell him what she wanted. Instead, her hands went to his shirt and pulled, forcing him to put more heat behind the kiss. Hadn't she just told him she was cold? Did he think his little timid kiss would get her warm?

When she pressed her lips against his mouth, a startled moan came from his throat. Suddenly, he angled his head and nudged at her lips, requesting entry with his tongue. On a relieved sigh, she parted her lips and welcomed him.

Her hand dug into his shirt to hold him close to her so he wouldn't stop too soon. In seconds, his kiss had turned from innocent to demanding. Instantly, she felt heat build in her belly and ripple through her body, reaching all her cells. She relaxed into him, melted against his mouth and tongue, opened up for him so he could explore her more thoroughly. All the while, her hands stroked him through his shirt. She marveled at the hardness of his muscled chest and the warmth radiating from his body. She wanted to soak up all of it and cocoon herself in his warmth and closeness.

When his hand moved up the side of her torso and reached the under-side of her breast, she gasped into his mouth. But he didn't stop. On the contrary, he increased the demand in his kiss, making her forget where she was.

His hand cupped her breast and gave it a soft squeeze. She yelped and pulled away from his mouth. "No, not here. People can see."

"Nobody can see what I'm doing under the cloak," he assured her, and took her mouth again, stifling her next protest. As if to underscore his statement, he tugged on the bodice and managed to free her breasts, letting the material bunch just under them. It now provided a shelf on which her breasts rested for him to do with as he pleased.

"Dante!" She tried to tell him that it wasn't decent but he kissed her again. With every kiss, she was less able to resist him. Her body seemed to melt more and more every second he exerted this sweet torture on her.

When his hand brushed over her breast and grazed her nipple, a bolt of lightning shot through her core. It liquidized everything in its path and left an unknown ache behind. Viola writhed under his touch, trying to soothe the want his touch left behind.

"Easy, my sweet," he cooed and nibbled kisses along her neck while his fingers teased her naked flesh, turning her nipple into a hard peak. "I'll give you what you want."

How could he know what she wanted when she didn't know it herself? All she knew was that she didn't want him to stop touching her. So when his hand left her breasts and lowered to her waist, she protested. "No. Please. I want—"

His hand squeezed her thigh, the warmth flooding through her making her forget her thoughts. "I know what you want."

Did he? She hoped so, because she was burning up. Her insides were aching, the place between her legs throbbing with desperate need. Her heart beat frantically, and her lungs burned as she panted.

A moment later, she held her breath. Dante's hand traveled down her leg and scooted under her skirts. Panic gripped her. "What are you doing?"

"Making you feel good." He nibbled on her ear, biting on it lightly. The sting distracted her from the movement of his hand, but only for a moment.

When his fingers suddenly reached the apex of her thighs and tunneled underneath her drawers, she gasped at his boldness. "Dante," she whispered, less in protest than encouragement, for his fingers had reached the dewy moisture that was oozing from her. She tensed when she felt him probe at her cleft, afraid of the penetration that had hurt the night before. She froze, steeling herself against the pain, but nothing happened. He'd stilled his fingers.

"Shh," Dante breathed into her ear. "I won't enter you. I just want to feel your wetness and caress you."

Slowly, Viola relaxed against his hand. Warring emotions filled her mind. She should push him away, not allow him such intimacy. Yet, the night before she'd allowed him much more than that. She had no strength to resist him, because just as she had the night before when he'd kissed her, she wanted more of what he was doing now.

And wasn't this what she'd come to Venice for? To experience the pleasures of the flesh? The loss of her virginity the night before had been unpleasant, but what Dante was doing with his fingers now felt more than pleasant. The caress of his fingers against her intimate flesh made her body heat further and her heart increase its frantic beat.

"You like that?" Dante's husky voice unleashed another heat wave in her body.

Before she could stop herself, she admitted, "Yes."

"I like it too. You're so slick, so soft. And then..." He drew his dew-covered finger further up, away from her folds to a spot just below her curls. "Then there's this." He rubbed against the sensitive flesh, making her gasp. "Yes, I think I've found just what you need."

As he swirled his finger around the bundle of flesh that was more sensitive than any other part of her body, it throbbed even harder than it had earlier. She felt more moisture oozing from her core. Her head fell back against his shoulder, and she let out a ragged breath.

"So responsive," he praised and continued his sweet torture. She felt boneless in his arms. Her thighs spread wider to allow him better access to this special place. His growl told her that he approved of her action.

As if to thank her for it, his caress became more urgent, the pressure harder. Something was happening. Her body tensed, both in fear and in anticipation. She didn't know what to expect. Viola only knew one thing. "Don't stop!" she cried out.

Seconds later, her body erupted. The tension splintered into waves of unknown pleasure and delight, flowing through her in ripple after ripple. Behind her eyes, she saw an explosion of white light so intense she thought she would die. This was her end.

CHAPTER

TEN

For the second night in a row, Dante carried Viola into his house. While she'd been unconscious the night before, this time she was merely asleep. After he'd brought her to climax in the gondola, she'd collapsed against his chest and drifted off to sleep. And all he could do was smile as he looked at her peaceful face. This was the first time he'd seen her completely at ease and relaxed. And he liked the sight. A lot.

His ears perked up when he heard his brother's voice. But this time, he knew he wouldn't be disturbed, because Raphael's voice came from his bedchamber. And his wife was with him. Dante blessed the fact that the two lovebirds couldn't keep their hands off each other. For the next few hours, they wouldn't interfere with his plans.

He quietly carried Viola upstairs to his room where he laid her on his bed. Somehow, the picture looked right: her dark blue gown contrasted against the white linen, and her long, dark hair fanned out around her head like a halo. Dante shook his head. He was getting soft. Her wanting to kill herself right after she'd left his bed, had crushed his ego. He wouldn't let her leave his presence until his ego was built up again and as strong as before: so it could act as a stone wall around his heart.

As he undressed her, his hands took advantage of her lush curves, caressing, cupping, squeezing everything she had to offer. After what she'd allowed him in the gondola, he could see no wrong in it. When she finally lay on his bed in the nude, he stripped himself of his clothes and joined her.

The fire in the fireplace was burning brightly and provided a comfortable warmth. He'd instructed a servant to ensure his room was well heated. He wanted her to be comfortable without the benefit of thick bed covers. Because what he had in mind was best done lying on top of them.

"Viola," he whispered to her and planted small kisses along her mouth.

Finally, she stirred, her eyelids opening but a sliver. "Hmm?"

"Your lesson in the pleasures of the flesh isn't over yet." It was only fair to give her a warning. Then he slid down her body and put his hands on her thighs, pushing them apart. He settled in the space he'd created for himself.

Viola reared up. "What?" Suddenly fully awake, her eyes wide, she stared at him in shock. "Where are my clothes?" She tried to cover herself with her hands, but he pushed them away.

"If you remember, I've seen everything before. So, there's no need to cover up. Now lie back and enjoy."

Her mouth opened, then snapped shut again, her eyes searching his face for a long moment. He couldn't tell what she was thinking, but something was going on in that pretty head of hers. When she finally lay down again, he sank his mouth onto her sex.

He inhaled deeply, wanting to drink in the enticing flavors of her body. Her curls tickled his mouth, so he shifted lower until his lips aligned with her moist cleft. Whether she was still wet from when he'd made her come in the gondola, or whether she'd creamed again because he'd stripped her naked, he couldn't tell. But she was wet, her honey dripping from her slit.

Dante sensed her muscles tense as if she was afraid he'd hurt her. But he had no intention of doing so. All he wanted was her pleasure, merely to stroke his ego—so he told himself.

He stuck out his tongue and lapped against the moist female folds, parting them in the process. Her plentiful juices ran over his tongue, igniting his taste buds and setting his body on fire. She tasted like a spring morning, fresh and innocent.

"Oh!" Her panted exclamation pleased him, and the fact that she relaxed her muscles at the same time was confirmation that she wanted him to continue. Not that he would have stopped at this point. The restoration of his ego was too important. And besides, licking her delightful cunt made him as hard as a board and stiffer than a morning breeze.

The delicious morsel he feasted on had no idea about the effect she had on him, and he wasn't about to tell her. No, he'd never wanted to give a woman that kind of power over him. Most likely, his reaction to her was only temporary anyway. The only reason she aroused him like this was because she'd bruised his ego and made him needy for her approval. Once this issue was dealt with, she'd represent no temptation for him.

He'd had more experienced women in his bed—women who knew the most amazing things about how to pleasure a man. And he'd never said no. Viola wasn't that kind of woman, and even if he taught her, there was no way she'd do the things he expected from a woman, especially one who wanted him to stick around for a while.

Viola's soft moan drifted to his ears, and he increased the pressure of his tongue on her soft flesh. Lapping up her cream, he swiped his tongue upwards toward the little bundle of flesh he'd teased with his fingers earlier. He'd been surprised at how responsive she'd been to his touch and how easy it had been to find the right rhythm for her to climax so violently. He could still feel the tremors that had wracked her frame. And even now, he felt a shudder go through his own body at the memory of it.

Her pearl was swollen, more so than it had been earlier. When he captured it in his mouth and stroked his tongue over it lightly, she twisted under his hold, her breaths coming in shallow pants. From the corner of his eyes he could see her hands fisting in the sheets, her knuckles nearly white from the intensity with which she seemed to fight against her body's reactions.

It only made him work harder. With one hand, he spread her wider, opening her up to him more fully. With one finger of the other hand, he teased along her slit without entering her.

Her hips rocked against him as if she wanted to force him inside her. But he didn't give in. Instead, his tongue sparred with her pearl, the little button now fully erect. Dante shifted between her legs, adjusting his own cock that rubbed against the sheets. He was coiled like a tight spring, ready to go off at a second's notice.

This had never happened to him, but he could come just by licking her sweet cunt. He pushed back his desire and concentrated on her body. Again, he pulled the plump bundle of flesh into his mouth and sucked. Viola let out a loud moan and bucked against him.

A second later, her body convulsed. He slipped his finger into her channel in the same instant and felt her muscles contract around him as her orgasm claimed her. Only when her body stilled—something that seemed to take an eternity—did he release her and slide up her body, cradling her in his arms.

"Oh."

He pulled back and rolled to his side, looking at her flushed face. He found that he liked the sight more than he should. But he hadn't forgotten his own needs. In fact, his cock throbbed painfully now. When he wrapped his hand around it and started pumping, she dropped her gaze to it.

"Yes, watch me, my sweet." Her eyes on him excited him. "See what you do to me? You make me so hard, I can't hold back."

The pressure in his balls built, and his hand—moist from Viola's honey—moved rapidly up and down his cock, squeezing as tightly as he knew her virgin cunt would squeeze him. His heart started beating frantically, and his breathing became ragged. But his breaths weren't the only ones filling the room.

Viola's breathing matched his own. Her skin glistened from the moisture that built on her forehead and neck, the tiny rivulets starting to run down her breasts. He looked at those breasts as he continued pumping his fist. When a moan escaped her, he lifted his gaze and looked at her face.

The sight undid him. She was licking her lips, her pink tongue snaking out as if she wanted to taste him.

"Oh, God, Viola." His cock jerked and, a second later, his seed shot from his cock, bursting against her belly and his own skin. Again and again, more semen released until his climax ebbed and he collapsed onto his back.

CHAPTER

ELEVEN

Viola was still mesmerized after Dante had wiped his seed off both of them and pulled her against his chest. She'd never seen a man touch himself like that. And by God, she'd liked the sight. It had made her mouth water for a taste. Just as he'd tasted her. She'd never thought something like that was possible, that a man would put his mouth onto a woman the way he had.

But when he'd done it, her brain had shut down, and all her body had done was react to him. The thought of what utter bliss her body was capable of made her both rejoice and despair. Now that she knew true pleasure, how could she not despair at the fact that she was going to die soon? She gave a small sigh.

Dante's chest moved under her hands. "Didn't you like it?" He tucked his hand under her chin and urged her head up. There was a concerned look on his face when his gaze collided with hers. "It disgusted you when I touched myself?"

"No," she protested instantly. Nothing could be further from the truth. But how could she tell him that it had excited her when she felt embarrassed by her own debauched feelings? "I—"

"You don't have to spare my feelings. Next time I'll take care of it when I'm alone."

And deprive her of the sensual sight of his body in ecstasy? "Why would you do that?"

He gave her a surprised glare. "Men need release, just like—"

She put her finger to his lips to stop him when she realized he'd misunderstood her question. "No, why would you want to hide this from me? Don't you like me watching you?"

His eyes changed instantly. His blue irises shimmered golden, but it was probably the glow from the fire that made his eyes shine in such a beautiful hue. "You liked watching me?"

Viola gave a small nod.

"Did it excite you?"

More than anything. "Yes."

Dante lifted his head and brushed his lips against hers for a soft kiss. "I love it when you look at me. To know you watched me while I pleasured myself made me so damn horny." He paused and inhaled sharply. "I haven't come so hard in a long time."

Just thinking of what he'd looked like made her feel hot all over again. Without thinking, she lowered her hand and moved it down his chest. She felt his muscles tense under her as she continued her path south. She stopped when she reached the nest of curly hair.

"Please," Dante mumbled against her lips. "Touch me."

Viola allowed her hand to slide down further and encountered the hard flesh she'd watched him touch earlier. And it was hard, just as hard as when he'd touched himself. Just after he'd come, his manhood had decreased in size somewhat, but now, only minutes later, it stood erect again and was as hard as marble.

Dante let out a ragged breath. "Viola."

She wrapped her tiny hand around him, not quite reaching all the way around. "Why is it so hard?"

He chuckled. "Because of you."

"What do you mean?" She propped herself up on one elbow while continuing to stroke his erection. She liked the feel of it. Despite its hardness, the surface was almost like velvet, so soft and smooth.

He flicked his finger lightly against her nose. "You're in my bed, as naked as the day you were born, and you smell so darn enticing that no man with any kind of heartbeat could refrain from getting hard at the sight of you. Do you have any idea how difficult it is for me not to sling you under me right now and fuck you so hard you'd faint?"

Shock coursed through her, and she couldn't help a slight flinch. She remembered the pain when he'd done that before, and she didn't want a repeat of it.

DANTE STARED into her widened eyes and realized instantly that he'd gotten carried away. He should have never said what he'd felt. She was still scared of being penetrated again, and he'd done the absolute worst thing he could by admitting he wanted to fuck her and drive his hard cock into her to the hilt.

"Oh, damn," he cursed. "Viola, I'm sorry. Please forget I said that."

Only now did he notice that she'd dropped her hold on his cock. But that didn't even matter now. He just didn't want her to be afraid of him.

She dropped her gaze and looked away from him. "I understand. And why shouldn't you get what you really want? You've been a good teacher. You've shown me what I wanted to know. It's only right that I pay for it." Her voice cracked.

"Stop."

"No, I owe you. And I'm not one to not pay my debts." She pulled herself out of his embrace and laid flat on her back. "Go ahead. Do what you want to do."

Dante jumped out of bed and rushed to the fireplace, far enough away from her to resist the temptation. "No. I won't do it."

"But I know you want to. You said so yourself. I don't mind."

She didn't mind? He ran his hand through his messy hair. "That's just it. I won't fuck you just because you don't mind it. I want to fuck you because you want me inside you. Because you desire me. Not because you don't mind." He spat the words, trying to rid himself of the bitter taste they left in his mouth.

What the hell was wrong with him? He'd never turned down an offer like that before. And his dick was as hard as ever. Not even her lukewarm offer had been able to make him deflate. Yet, here he stood naked as a babe and randy as a sailor, refusal spurting from his lips. Somebody should stake him for his stupidity.

And since he was already on the subject of his own stupidity, why on earth hadn't he bitten her yet? He'd had plenty of opportunities to take her blood without even using any of his powers of persuasion. Yet, he'd done no such thing.

Like a docile pet, he'd cuddled her and taken care of her needs instead of taking care of his own. Was that what happened to men when women trampled their egos?

Dante balled his hands into fists, wanting to kick somebody. He felt his jaw tighten and realized to his horror that his vampire side wanted to emerge. The itch that always accompanied the lengthening of his fangs was already spreading.

Feeling panicked, he searched for his clothes. When he stalked toward his garments and snatched them off the floor, he heard Viola's hesitant voice from the bed. "Have I done something wrong?"

He didn't look in her direction for fear he'd feast his eyes on her body and succumb to the temptation of taking her in the most savage way he could. And then he'd be no further than before. She'd never stroke his ego and build it back up if he hurt her now.

"Sleep. I'll be back later."

There were still several hours left in the night. After giving his servants instructions not to let Viola leave the house, he stalked into the night to hunt. He needed blood, and the more the better. Only when his thirst for blood was stilled would he allow himself to return home. Then he would be better able to control his carnal urges. Because unleashing those on Viola and hurting her would not appease his need to be forgiven.

Forgiven? Only when the word scrambled through his mind did he realize that guilt was driving him—guilt because he'd driven *her* to set the pistol to her head and pull the trigger.

That's when he knew his actions and his feelings had nothing to do with his ego. It had to do with the fact that he'd saved her life—even if he'd been the one who drove her to take it.

Preserving it was his mission now.

Viola awoke with a splitting headache. Had she been alone, she would have moaned in pain, but she found herself cradled in Dante's arms. He was fully dressed and asleep. The fire had burned down, but the embers were still glowing, providing sufficient warmth for the room.

Not wanting to alert Dante to her condition, she did what she always did to try to make the ache go away: she breathed in and out and wished herself in a peaceful meadow. She slowed her breathing and tried to concentrate only on the picture in her mind, but this time, the picture wouldn't come. All she could see in her mind was Dante: the way he'd touched her in the gondola, the way he'd put his mouth to her sex and licked her until she'd screamed out her pleasure. Dante, Dante, Dante. Like a chant, his name echoed in her head.

Instead of her breathing slowing down, it sped up. Instead of her body falling back into a peaceful slumber where no pain existed, she felt her skin heat and her stomach clench with need. The need to be touched. By Dante.

Her aching head was forgotten. All that existed now was his body close to hers. Viola clasped his hand and pulled it to her naked breast. The contact of skin on skin soothed her, but it wasn't enough. She needed him to stroke her, to tease her nipples the way he'd done it before. To squeeze her breasts and make the ache go away.

When she clasped her hand over his and squeezed, thus tightening his hand over her breast, he stirred. An incoherent mumble broke from his lips, but he didn't wake. She sighed in frustration. This wouldn't do.

She looked at his relaxed form, his face almost soft and peaceful in his sleep. And his manhood—the hardness that she'd felt under her fingers the night before didn't seem to be there. The bulge under the fabric was smaller. Viola cupped him with her palm and felt the heat beneath. When she squeezed gently, Dante suddenly stirred.

She raised her eyes to his face just as his eyes flew open, a startled look crossing his face. "Good morning," she whispered.

"If you don't remove your hand from its current position, I can't guarantee what might rise this morning other than the sun." He gave her a meaningful look. But instead of removing her hand, she squeezed him again. Something in his eyes told her that he hadn't meant his words as a threat.

"What if I don't?" she teased, suddenly much more sure of herself, because under her hand she could already feel him swell. It appeared that he hadn't lied the night before: her presence in his bed did excite him.

"What do you want?" His voice was lower now, and she recognized the rumble in it as arousal. The same arousal that now made her cup the hard length of his manhood.

"More."

"You want more of what we did last night?"

"Yes. But this time—" She hesitated, unsure of how to form her request.

"This time?" Dante prompted.

"I want to touch you too."

"Viola, you're going to kill me."

She wasn't going to be violent, he had to know that. "I won't hurt you. I saw how you did it yourself. I can do—"

He exhaled. "That's not what I meant. I know you won't hurt me. But you're going to make me lose all control if I let you touch me. Don't you see? How can I show you the pleasures of the flesh when I can't keep myself under control?"

She didn't understand how that was any different than what he'd done to her. "But I lose control when you touch me. It's not fair if I don't get to do the same."

Dante shook his head and sighed. "I guess I can't argue with that, can I?"

"Is that a yes?"

Excitement coursed through her when he nodded. She would get to touch his beautiful body, pump his hard shaft in her palm, and make him surrender to her the same way she'd surrendered in his arms when he'd showered her with his caresses. She licked her lips in anticipation.

DANTE LOOKED at Viola's parted lips and nearly felt his heart stop. She wanted to touch him, not because he'd coaxed her into it or kissed her senseless, but because... Well, why did she? Why would she want to caress the very instrument that had caused her pain two nights ago?

But the eager hands that now opened his breeches and took his fully erect cock out of its confines were testament enough that she wanted to give him the pleasure of her touch. And he was too far gone to stop her. The moment her soft palm wrapped around him, he closed his eyes and let out a deep moan. Nothing could possibly feel better than her hands on him.

"Is it all right like this?" she asked, her voice hesitant.

"All right?" he rasped, his throat suddenly as dry as sandpaper. "It's perfect." After that, he lost the ability to speak and could only grunt out his approval at her tender ministrations.

Viola had a magic touch. At least, that's how Dante perceived it. Her hand was firm yet gentle. Strong yet soft. She pumped his shaft master-fully, exerting the right pressure and speed, varying between long and short strokes, alternately squeezing hard, then merely running her fingers up and down his shaft. He loved everything she did.

Each caress drove him further toward insanity, because that's what this was. It was insane allowing her to pleasure him like that when he knew it would ultimately lead to one thing: him plunging his cock into her soft folds. Which wasn't what she wanted from him. She wanted soft and gentle, stroking and sucking, kissing and licking. And he would give her that, but when she stroked his cock like this, all he could think of was how it would feel if her cunt squeezed around him like that.

"Oh, God, Viola, I'm gonna come!" he cried out the moment the pressure in his balls built. Then his body bucked against her. His seed shot in the air and spread over her hand as well as his shirt and breeches. But she didn't let go. She continued pumping him until the last of his spasms subsided.

With the last ounce of his strength, he pulled her against his chest and pressed a kiss in her hair. "Thank you." He pressed her hard against him, not wanting to let go of the wonderful woman in his arms. She molded to him so naturally that he barely registered where he ended and she began.

"I liked that." Viola's voice warmed his heart.

"Not as much as I did." He chuckled and felt a broad smile build on his face. Who'd ever said that virgins were useless in bed? It turned out that this almost-virgin was a much better student than he was a tutor.

THIRTEEN

"We can't do that," Viola protested and blushed.

"Of course we can. They won't even know." For the last three days and nights, Dante had barely left the house to feed, so drawn was he to spending time with the increasingly insatiable Viola. Now that he'd introduced her to the sensations her body was capable of, she seemingly couldn't get enough of it. It was as if she was trying to soak it all up and store it away for lean times.

The only two things he hadn't done was truly fuck her or allow her to suck him. With the former he feared scaring her away, and if she did the latter to him, he'd never be able to control his body's reaction. Besides, there was no reason for him to think that she even wanted to suck him. However, she seemed to want to know more about sex, so he'd decided to show her what others did. Since it excited her to watch him stroke himself, maybe she would enjoy watching another couple.

"Come, I think you might enjoy this. It can be very arousing to watch someone make love."

He noticed her cheeks darkening even further. When she tried to lower her lashes to escape his gaze, he shelved her chin on his palm and made her look at him. "I will touch you while you watch."

Her lips parted, and her pink tongue appeared, licking herself. He recognized how her pulse was racing now. Then she nodded slowly. "But I want to touch you too."

Dante smiled and kissed her cute nose. "I should hope so." He'd never been in such a good mood as long as he could remember. Somehow Viola brought out his lighter side.

A short while later, after he'd instructed her what to wear—or not to wear for that matter—he took her by the hand. On bare feet, they snuck into one of the small storage rooms to the side of his brother's bedchamber. Years ago, Dante had discovered that the mirror over Raphael's fireplace was translucent on the other side, allowing anyone who knew about it to spy on him. Dante had only discovered it because he'd been searching for an old book in the room. And he knew nobody else had access to it because he kept the only key.

Not that he would normally spy on his own brother. It held no interest for him, however, it would provide some titillation for Viola, and it would be in a safe environment.

When they entered the room, Dante locked the door behind them so they wouldn't be disturbed. He noticed Viola's look zero in on the pillows that lay on the raised wooden platform which had initially been built for storage.

Dante had made sure the area was clean and had spread sufficient pillows on it for both of them to be comfortable while watching Raphael and his wife.

When Viola opened her mouth to say something, Dante put his finger on her lips. "Shh. We have to be quiet. My brother has exceptionally good hearing." All vampires did.

He led her up the four steps to the platform and pulled back a black curtain on the wall it was facing. The mirror behind it was a window into Raphael's bedroom where his brother was undressing Isabella.

"Oh!" Viola gasped and turned away in embarrassment.

"They can't see us," Dante assured her.

Hesitantly, she turned back and looked through the glass. Dante didn't watch the goings on in Raphael's room. Instead, he looked at Viola. He'd told her only to wear a corset, stockings and garters, and a dressing gown over it. And the dressing gown had only been so nobody would see her half-naked as they'd walked through the corridor.

He wore only a robe with not a stitch underneath. Already now, his cock was at full attention, and he hadn't even freed her of her robe and admired her scantily clad body. He would take care of that right now.

Viola sat down, folding her legs underneath her, her eyes glued to the action in the other room. Dante cast a quick glance in the same direction and saw how Raphael laid the naked Isabella onto the bed while he stood at the edge of it, naked and hard.

Dante put his hands on Viola's shoulders and tugged on the robe. Without coaxing, she undid the belt. He was sure she didn't know what she was doing, so mesmerized was she by the sight in front of her.

Dante stripped her of the robe. The corset he'd given her to wear was only a half-corset: it reached from the top of her pubic hair to just below the swell of her breasts, presenting them as if on a platter. For him. The matching black garter belt had lace strips running down her delightful ass cheeks. The strips held her stockings in place.

He put his hands to Viola's hips and lifted her onto her knees so he could truly admire her enticing heart-shaped ass. His hands slid down to caress her, and a soft moan came from her lips.

He swept her long hair to one side, exposing her pale neck. Without haste, he stroked his fingers over the plump vein that pulsated underneath her silken skin. His lips longed for a taste and descended onto her flesh. He greeted Viola's trembling with pure male satisfaction. To know that his touch excited her made him even harder than he already was.

"Whisper to me what you see."

"I can't."

He kissed her neck, briefly pulling the soft skin into his mouth. Then he slid his hand down to her tempting ass and caressed her perfect cheeks. A hitched breath was her answer.

"Please, tell me what you see."

He felt her heart beat frantically. "He's spreading her legs. Wide." Her voice was low, huskier than he'd ever heard her.

"I want you to spread your legs too," he ordered.

She moved her knees apart. Instantly, the aroma of her arousal became stronger, teasing his nostrils in the most enticing fashion. His hand dropped between her thighs and reached forward.

"He's in between her legs, and he's... he's slamming into her. Oh God!"

Dante slid his finger along her drenched folds, coating himself in her rich cream. Then he reached forward and circled her pearl. She whimpered, her body starting to tremble again.

"He's going back and forth, and she, she... likes it." There was confusion in her voice as if Viola hadn't expected Isabella's reaction to her husband's touch.

Dante pulled his hand away from her pearl and teased her wet slit with his fingers, sliding along the warm flesh in long and slow strokes, bathing himself in her honey.

"Yes, she likes her husband's hard cock inside her, filling her, stretching her tight channel. Does she want more? Is she encouraging him?"

He felt Viola nod. "Yes, she's holding onto his hips. She's pulling him toward her. She wants more. Deeper. Harder." Every word came in a pant. Viola's body moved rhythmically against his hand. "Deeper, harder," she chanted.

At her words, Dante lost his control. Without thinking, he slid his finger deep into her. She bucked against him as if she wanted more. A whispered "deeper" startled him, but he complied. Pulling back his finger, he plunged inside again. Her channel was even tighter than he'd expected and infinitely more tempting than anything else he'd ever been offered.

Dante drove into her again and again while his other hand captured one breast and pinched her hard nipple.

Viola cried out and threw her head back. "More. Yes, she loves his cock." Her words sounded as if she was delirious. "She wants to be filled. Stretched."

Then he understood. She was pretending to be somebody else so she could demand what she wanted. "Does she want his cock inside her?" he asked and held his breath. Would she want his cock?

Viola panted heavily. Her pulse raced. "She wants his big cock to fill her."

"Is she sure that's what she wants? His cock inside her?" Dante continued to fuck his finger in and out of her, increasing his tempo, not wanting her to come out of her trance-like state. Stretching her to prepare her for the invasion of his cock.

"Yes."

At her answer, Dante nudged her forward and pressed her into the pillows. Then he dislodged his finger from her cunt and spread her legs. The sight of her beautiful round tilted-up ass gave him a perfect view of her glistening petals, and nearly robbed him of his control. He ripped his robe off his body and settled between her thighs, his cock taut and ready.

"Now," she whispered. "She needs his cock now."

She was spread out before him for his pleasure. He couldn't wait any longer. Dante nudged his cock forward, pushing her moist folds apart. "More."

"Everything," he mumbled. "I'll give you everything." And then slowly, without haste, he drove into her. Her channel stretched, accommodating him, yet squeezing him like a tight glove at the same time. This was what heaven was like.

When he was balls deep inside her, she gasped. He stilled his movement and watched for her reaction.

Viola turned her head and looked back at him. "Dante," was all she said, but the way she said it with her breath rushing from her lungs, her lips glistening, her cheeks flushed, he knew everything would be all right. Her eyes confirmed it. The desire in them was undeniable.

"Viola, my sweet."

He sliced into her, and for a few agonizing seconds he thought he'd spill instantly. But he couldn't allow that, because he needed more from her than just a quick romp. He needed to look into her eyes and kiss her, know that she saw him, that she knew it was he, who made love to her.

Dante pulled himself out of her, ignoring her disappointed sigh, and rolled her onto her back before he thrust back into her. "I need to see you."

Not giving her a second's reprieve, he kissed her red lips and angled his head to capture more of her. She responded to him by stroking her tongue against his, inviting him into the delicious cavern of her mouth.

FOURTEEN

Dante's kiss brought her back to reality, and for once, reality was more beautiful than her fantasy. This was not like the coupling she'd experienced with him that first night in the dingy inn he'd taken her to. Neither was this like the things they'd done over the last three days, the touching, kissing, caressing. This was everything, and more.

This time, Viola felt no pain. Her body accepted him, the moisture that had already oozed from her channel allowing him easy entry despite his impressive girth. And he'd taken his time, slowly inching forward as if he'd been ready to pull out the moment she voiced a concern. But it had been perfect.

The fullness that she experienced and that made all her nerve endings tingle was different from the way her body felt when he touched her with his mouth and fingers. His cock inside her made her feel complete. She couldn't describe it any other way. And she wanted more of it.

When Dante severed the kiss, she gave him a startled look. "Something wrong?"

He smiled the most wicked smile she'd ever seen him unleash. "No. Just keep your eyes open. I want you to see who you're making love to."

The insistence in his voice surprised her and made her look at him with different eyes. Had something changed between them? Suddenly, he seemed more than just the tutor he'd become. Now he was simply a man whose eyes told her that he intended to take his own pleasure without holding back—and without leaving her behind.

A shiver went through her body at the underlying promise in his regard. She couldn't tear herself away from the sight. When she buried her hands in his hair and pulled him to her for another kiss, he started thrusting into her in a slow and steady rhythm. His tongue explored her in the same rhythm, thrusting, then withdrawing, mimicking the action of his shaft.

With every movement, her body's temperature turned higher. Sweat built on her forehead and neck. Her heart beat frantically, faster and more erratic than it ever had before, as if it was racing toward a finish line.

Her womb clenched, and she was certain his cock reached that deep with every thrust. She undulated her hips, wanting to increase the pressure, slamming against his body as he plunged into her. A rumbling moan came from his lips as he ripped them from her mouth. "Oh God, Viola, you're going to rob me of my control."

But he didn't slow or ease his movements. Rather, they accelerated. Their hips gyrated against each other, harder each time, making her body hum and her pearl tingle with excitement. She knew the signs of her body now. Dante had taught her well. She knew that the tension that now built in her sex, the heat that shot through her body as he filled her and stretched her, was the same sensation she had whenever he licked or touched her center of pleasure.

"Oh, yes, Dante, yes, please, more."

And he gave her more. He rode her harder, took her with more force, stretching her further than she thought her body was capable of. With his lips, he did the same: he captured her mouth as if he were a conqueror intent on claiming a new continent for himself. His hands stroked wherever they could reach: her face, her breasts, her neck. As if he couldn't get enough of her, just as she couldn't let go of him.

Dante's hair was wet from sweat, rivulets of moisture running down his neck and chest, bathing her in it, her breasts sliding against him, her sensitive hard nipples burning from the touch. Nothing had ever felt this good.

"Yeah, oh, yeah," he cried out, then trailed open-mouthed kisses along her neck. "You're too sweet. Too much."

She sensed his teeth graze her skin, the foreign sensation making her tremble with lust. She tilted her head, hoping he'd repeat the action, and again, his teeth grazed her skin.

DANTE NIPPED at the sensitive skin on Viola's neck and felt the plump vein throb underneath. His entire body was coiled like a tight spring, screaming at him to take her blood. And the way she tilted her head to the side to give him better access made resisting even harder. But resist he must.

If he drank from her, he'd have to use his powers of persuasion to clear her memory so she wouldn't remember—and that was the last thing he wanted. He wanted Viola to remember every single second of their love-making. He wanted nothing left out. For days, they'd only given each other pleasure through kissing and caressing. Now, finally, that he was deep inside her divine body, he couldn't throw these sensations away to still his thirst for her blood. He needed to experience his first climax inside her, and he needed her to be right there with him, sensing when his seed spilled inside her.

Dante pushed his desire for her blood back and kissed her neck, inhaling her intoxicating scent. His cock moved in and out of her body with long and eager strokes, driving deeper every time. Her channel was so deliciously tight, he couldn't remember why he'd ever been against fucking virgins. She was slick and hot, and her responses were so honest and real, he knew no other woman he'd had in his bed had ever truly reacted like this. No woman had ever opened herself up to him as Viola had. As she was doing now.

He lifted his lips from her neck and looked at her. Her eyes were dilated with passion, her skin flushed. She was the most beautiful sight he'd ever beheld. "Fly with me," he whispered against her lips and ground his hips against her, driving his cock deeper.

Then he took her lips and poured everything he had into that kiss. Every ounce of passion, lust, and affection he'd come to feel for her. His hand slid in between their bodies and reached down to her triangle of curls, where his fingers pressed against her pearl. A moan from her lips told him he'd found the right spot.

"Yes, come with me. Now."

He rubbed against her engorged button and drove his shaft deep into her. Her muscles gripped him as never before, clenching, then releasing. He physically felt the ripples that went through her body and let himself go. A second later, he joined her in her orgasm, shooting hot streams of seed deep into her welcoming cunt until she'd milked him of every last drop.

Without leaving her warm body, he rolled to the side, keeping her in his arms, pressed tightly to his chest. "I've never felt anything that perfect." He surprised himself with his words. He'd never been one to tell a woman of his feelings.

Her breath caressed his neck, and he realized he liked the sensation very much, when usually after sex he preferred some distance. "I liked it very much." Her words warmed his heart. And her next ones made his heart pound even faster. "Can we do this again?"

"Give me ten minutes, and we can do anything you want to." And everything Dante wanted too. Viola underneath him, Viola on top of him, Viola in front of him. Viola, Viola. Until he was drunk on her scent and her taste.

FIFTEEN

Despite the wonderful night she'd had with Dante, Viola awoke with a splitting headache. Not wanting to alert him to her pain, she snuck out of bed and took one of the pills from her bag. The doctor had given them to her but said they wouldn't help for long. Once the pain became too much, the pills would have no more effect.

Knowing it would take a while before the medicine dulled the pain, she went downstairs into the parlor wearing only her dressing gown. The house was quiet. Not even the servants seemed to be awake. It was a strange household, she had to admit. For starters, nobody rose before mid-afternoon, except maybe Isabella on occasion, but neither Raphael nor Dante ever left bed any earlier.

It was also strange that the two men never joined them for any meals. They always seemed to have other plans. It didn't appear to disturb Isabella, and she'd never noticed her complaining to her husband that he didn't have supper with her. However, Isabella was always happy to have Viola join her in the dining room. And considering the physical activity she and Dante indulged in most of the night, Viola was always famished.

What either Dante or Raphael did to make a living was unclear. But they both seemed ridiculously wealthy. Which made the fact that they shared a house very curious.

A new wave of pain interrupted her thought process and made her grip the sofa. She managed to sit before the pain brought her to her knees. She closed her eyes, thankful that even during the day the servants kept the shades drawn, allowing only minimal light into the house. While she'd found it odd at the beginning, she was grateful for it now, because light seemed to make her headaches worse.

Viola leaned back against the pillows and inhaled and exhaled slowly. Whether it was her breathing or the effect of the pill she'd swallowed, the pain waned and simmered down to a dull ache, which—while not pleasant—was bearable. It allowed her to let her mind drift back to Dante.

She'd been fortunate to meet him. Despite the initial pain he'd caused her—which she realized any man would have probably caused—she couldn't have found a better lover to introduce her to the wonderful pleasures men and women could give each other. Initially, she'd been embarrassed by her body's reaction to him, and by what she'd allowed him to do. But considering her unique situation, she had pushed those thoughts aside.

She had nothing to lose. Nothing that was important to her anyway. Her reputation meant nothing. It wasn't as if she had a long life ahead of her during which to regret the loss of her virginity or the debauched life she found herself living: sharing the home and bed of a stranger who, even if she lived, was never going to offer for her. Not when she'd been a virgin, and certainly not now after all the things she'd done. No man would want a soiled woman like her—not for a wife anyway.

Viola shook her head, trying to push the stupid thoughts away. She shouldn't think of marriage and all the things that came with it when she knew it was outside her reach. She should be grateful: at least she'd known true bliss in the arms of a man, a man so passionate, it made her knees weak and her heart flutter every time he raked that lusting look over her that told her that he wanted to eat her alive.

For a few more days, she would enjoy what he was giving her so freely. She would soak it up and cocoon herself in the sensations Dante conjured up in her. But she knew it couldn't last. Already now, she felt the pain in her head increasing. Maybe the end was coming sooner than her physician had expected. Her plan to end her own life before she was unable to take control of her own body was still in place. She would execute it when she knew the inevitable was imminent.

DANTE TURNED IN THE SHEETS, his hands reaching around him to pull Viola into his arms. But the bed was empty. He opened his eyes, a flash of true disappointment hitting him out of nowhere. After having experienced the most amazing sex in his life in Viola's arms, he wanted those arms around him again. Now. Instantly. His hunger for her was even stronger than his thirst for blood. And considering he hadn't fed in two nights and was close to being famished, that was quite a revelation for him.

He rolled onto his back and simply stared at the ceiling. What was happening to him? He'd never been the kind of man who spent night after night with the same woman. He liked variety. He loved all kinds of different women.

After last night, he knew his ego was firmly back in place, and the guilt that had plagued him for hurting her the first time had been wiped away by Viola's enthusiastic declaration that she wanted to do it again. And they'd done it again. And again. And again until he'd lost count. And every time, she'd looked at him with those sparkling eyes and smiled like a kitten that had just discovered an endless bowl of warm milk.

His chest swelled at the thought that he'd been the one who'd put that smile on her beautiful face. Dante grinned. He wanted to do it again, because he couldn't get enough of seeing her smile. Strangely enough, the thought didn't send him running for cover as if the sun was about to rise. Maybe spending more than one night with the same woman wasn't quite as bad as he'd always thought. For one thing, he knew her body so well by now that he could make her come apart whenever he set his mind to it—which was often.

Maybe his brother Raphael had had the right idea by settling down and marrying a good woman. He seemed happy, and by what Dante had briefly seen through the mirror the night before, their sex life certainly wasn't lacking, despite the familiarity they must be experiencing by now. He'd never thought about it before. Well, ideas like these were premature anyway. Maybe his infatuation with Viola would quickly fizzle out now that he'd finally fucked her so thoroughly.

Yes, thoroughly. And maybe that was exactly the reason why he wanted her again now: his body had gotten in the mood for sex and wanted more. He was almost sure that was the reason. Almost.

Dante rose and washed quickly before he dressed and stalked downstairs, his nostrils flaring when he picked up her scent. He found Viola in the parlor, stretched out on the sofa, her eyes closed. The gentle rise and fall of her chest indicated that she was sleeping.

He lowered himself onto the sofa and gathered her in his arms, lifting her onto his lap. She stirred, but he merely settled her against his chest and stroked his hand over her back. She mumbled something in her sleep, but he didn't have the heart to wake her. She looked so peaceful and content. He closed his eyes and relaxed. With Viola in his arms, everything seemed so much better.

CHAPTER
SIXTEEN

"You sure you two don't want to join us?" Isabella asked as Raphael put her black cloak across her shoulders and handed her a pair of long gloves.

His brother had finally realized that Dante had only Viola's best interest in mind. And if he interpreted Raphael's occasional smirks correctly, he was pleased with the developments between them. Raphael had said as much the day before.

"If I didn't know you any better, I'd say you're totally smitten with her."

Dante had merely snorted and declined to answer his brother's implied question.

"We're sure." Dante sat in his favorite armchair in front of the fireplace now, and what made the situation even more comfortable was the fact that Viola was snuggling against him, sitting on his lap. Why would he want to go out when he had everything he wanted right here? "Enjoy yourselves. I'll take Viola dancing some other night."

When the front door finally shut behind them, he looked at Viola's rosy cheeks and red lips, dying for a taste. "You didn't want to go, did you?"

She shook her long hair, which cascaded over her naked shoulders. She wore a low-cut dress he'd ordered for her in a hurry. She hadn't brought many clothes, and the blue dress she'd worn when he'd met her had started to become wrinkled and dirty. Besides, he liked seeing her in garments that revealed more skin than her own dress had.

They'd fallen into a comfortable routine over the last week and, to Dante's surprise, he was still not bored with her. On the contrary, the more time he spent with her, the more he craved her company.

"I'd rather be here with you." She paused. "Alone."

At her suggestive tone, his cock twitched eagerly. He knew that husky tone and what it implied. And he was more than ready for whatever she had in mind. "I'm your slave."

She chuckled. "You don't mean that."

Dante touched his finger to her nose. "I do mean it. You're the mistress of my body and my h—" Heart, he'd nearly blurted. Even if in jest, he couldn't allow himself to say something like that.

Sweet as Viola was, she didn't call him on it, didn't demand he declare himself. Instead, she placed a soft kiss on his lips and slid off his lap.

"Don't go," he begged.

Her smile was back on her face, mischief twinkling in her eyes. "I'm not going anywhere." She dropped down to the floor between his legs, shoving his knees farther apart so she could scoot closer.

When her gaze dropped to his crotch, he almost choked. She'd never sucked him. He'd never demanded it, never asked despite all the things they'd done in and out of bed. Somehow, he'd always felt she wasn't ready for it. Yet, she seemed ready now.

"You want to do this?"

She nodded.

"Here?"

Another nod.

"Now?"

His cock surged and pressed against his breeches, desperate to be let out of its confines. He ripped the first button open. Then her hand stopped him.

"Let me do it."

Dante let his head fall against the backrest of his armchair and exhaled. "Why now?" He felt as if he'd died and gone to heaven.

"I want to give you something you never asked for."

He stroked his palm over her face and slid his thumb across her lips. "You know you don't have to do that." But he wanted it. By God, how he wanted to feel her lips around his cock.

Viola eased the remaining buttons open and freed his hard shaft. "You're beautiful."

Her breath whispered against his naked skin, caressing him, teasing him. He watched her wrap her small hand around him and shifted in his seat to shove his breeches further down, allowing her better access not just to his cock but also his balls. She helped him pull the fabric down to his ankles so he could spread his thighs wide, opening himself up to her.

When she shifted closer and leaned over his groin, he let out a moan.

She giggled. "I haven't even started."

"I know, my sweet, but you have no idea what the power of suggestion can do to a man. If you don't take me into your beautiful mouth soon, I'm going to come without you even touching me."

"We can't have that."

An instant after her murmured response, Dante entered heaven. Instead of a first tentative lick against his cock, which he had expected, Viola closed her lips around him and slid down his entire length, capturing him within her warmth and wetness. Her moan bounced against his sensitive flesh, echoing his own. Her hand circled him around the base while she braced herself on his thigh with the other.

Dante cupped her head with his palms and steadied her gently without guiding her. He wanted her to suck him the way she wanted to: slow or fast, it didn't matter to him. Already now, he knew that he wouldn't last. His body was burning as if he'd stepped into the rays of the sun—but this was a pleasurable kind of fire. A fire he'd never felt before. Warming, coaxing, comforting. Not the fire that destroyed, but the fire that nurtured.

He recognized that it was Viola who stoked that fire in him and kindled that flame: with her tongue licking up and down his shaft, her lips sucking hard, her fingers moving up and down in concert with her mouth. She gave him softness and warmth. As for the desire he felt for her? He knew now that it would only grow with time rather than diminish. He could never let her go.

"Viola," he cried out. "I need you." It didn't matter how young she was and how inexperienced. All that mattered was that in her arms he felt whole.

Dante looked at her face. Her eyes were closed as if she truly loved what she was doing to him. He couldn't tear himself away from the sight of his cock disappearing between her red lips, then reappearing when she withdrew. "I've never felt this good."

For every other woman his words would have been spoken as an encouragement to suck him harder, but all he wanted to tell Viola was that she was bringing him to his knees. When she moved her hand and cupped his balls as gently as could be, he took one deep breath, knowing it would be his last before his climax ripped through him.

"I'm coming," he rasped, trying to pull out of her mouth. To his surprise, she kept her mouth firmly lodged around him. He exploded inside her and felt her swallow his seed. Not a single drop spilled from her lips.

As soon as he had his breath back, he pulled her up and into his lap, covering her swollen lips with his and plunging his tongue into her to show her how much this meant to him. He was breathless when he released her.

Dante rested his forehead against hers, trying to slow his racing heart, but he couldn't. Too much excitement was pumping through his veins, too many realizations hitting him all at once. "Viola?"

"Dante." His name rolled off her lips like a caress.

Whatever he'd wanted to say disappeared. Only one thought prevailed. "Marry me."

SEVENTEEN

Viola scrambled off his lap, her eyes wide in shock as if he'd said something truly frightening. Her mouth gaped open as she took a few steps back, her arm stretched out as if trying to push him away. Was she?

"Viola," he ground out while jerking up his trousers and rising from his chair.

"No, please. I don't believe—you can't—"

"Dante, there you are." At the voice, Dante swiveled on his heel and saw his friend Lorenzo enter the room. When Lorenzo's gaze fell on him and then on Viola, he bowed briefly. "I hope I'm not interrupting anything."

Dante could see him inhale and knew that by now he would have picked up the scent of sex in the air. It still hung heavy in the room. When Lorenzo's eyes flickered in interest, Dante shot him a warning glare. The lascivious suggestion that had clearly been on his friend's lips, died instantly.

At least one disaster was averted, because having his friend suggest they share Viola for an hour of unadulterated fun was not going to happen. Yes, he and Lorenzo had shared plenty of women—and in every way possible—yet there was no way in hell he'd allow another man to put his paws on Viola. Not even his best friend.

Dante cleared his throat. Lorenzo's interruption couldn't have come at a worse time. Hell, he'd proposed to Viola, something he thought he'd never do until the words had actually spilled from his lips. And by the looks of it, she didn't believe he was serious. But he was.

"Lorenzo, I see you can still smooth talk your way around my servants to allow you in even when I'm occupied with more important things."

Lorenzo approached with a smile. "If I didn't, I would rarely see you. Where have you been the entire week? Nobody's seen you."

Dante glanced back at Viola, who stood at the fireplace, her expression blank. He raked a long look over her. "I was occupied with more important things." He paused and locked eyes with her. "Much more important things."

The air prickled with tension between them. Severing the contact with her, he turned his head back to his friend, whose face was colored with surprise.

"May I introduce Signorina Costa to you? Viola, this is my friend Lorenzo."

"Charmed," Lorenzo answered and bowed in Viola's direction.

"Signore," she acknowledged him politely.

"Now that you've assured yourself that I'm well, I'd like to—"

Lorenzo held up his hand. "As much as I respect your privacy, you'll have to hear me out first. Something is brewing in the city."

Dante raised an eyebrow. "Brewing?" For once he wasn't interested in getting involved in anything that might be going on outside of his own four walls.

"Nico came to me an hour ago. Apparently, you pissed off some man who's now screaming bloody murder. Something about you stealing his woman." Lorenzo looked past him toward Viola. "Not that I can really blame him."

Dante didn't have to be a mind reader to know who might be having it in for him. "I'm assuming you're referring to a man named Salvatore."

He heard Viola's indrawn breath behind him.

"The very same."

"He's no threat to me."

"And to her?"

Dante sucked in a breath. "Viola is under my protection. She will not leave this house without me."

He heard her gasp behind him and turned. Her eyes were wide, but it wasn't shock anymore. It was disbelief. "I'm still your prisoner? I thought…"

"You're holding her captive?" Lorenzo asked before Dante could soothe Viola's concerns.

"Stay out of this, Lorenzo. And besides, it's not true."

"How could you?" Her voice was low, breathless. Unshed tears rimmed her eyes as she stormed past him toward the door.

He didn't try to stop her, but he would not drop the subject. "You've not given me an answer yet, Viola, and I will have that answer. We'll talk when Lorenzo has left."

She didn't acknowledge his words and swept out of the room. He listened as she stomped up the stairs before he turned back to his friend.

"An answer to what?"

"Since when have you turned into a nosy washerwoman?"

"Since you began acting strangely," Lorenzo retorted.

"I don't act strangely."

"Sure you do. And I suspect the chit has something to do with it. Since when do you give a damn about what some whore thinks?"

Faster than the blink of an eye, Dante snatched Lorenzo by his collar and bared his fangs. "She's not a whore! She's the woman I'm going to marry!"

The stunned expression on Lorenzo's face almost compensated Dante for the rude interruption—almost, but not quite. He dropped his hold.

"You? First your brother, now you. What the fuck is in the blood you guys are drinking? Because I'm sure going to avoid that source like the plague. Are you all going insane?"

"I assure you, I'm feeling quite well. Now if you would excuse me so I can talk to Viola and get her answer."

"You mean, she hasn't accepted you?"

"Yet," Dante corrected tightly. Yet. Because there couldn't possibly be any reason why she wouldn't want him. They'd spent an incredible week together, giving each other unspeakable pleasure. Why would she not continue that under the protection of being married to him? Why would she not want the security that marriage would grant her?

To be sure, the fact that he was a vampire would count against him, but she didn't even know about that. Obviously, it couldn't be the reason for her objection.

"Well, good luck to you. However, I'd like to bring your attention back to that Salvatore fellow. My suggestion is to nip the situation in the bud and take care of any threat before it escalates."

Dante ran his fingers through his hair and sighed. "What are you suggesting?"

VIOLA STUFFED her dress into the satchel and pulled the drawstring tight. She didn't know what Dante had done with her pistol, but it didn't matter. She would procure a new one shortly. All that mattered now was getting out of his house and away from him.

He wanted to marry her. How could he do that to her? How could he dangle this dream in front of her when she could never fulfill it, when she knew that she would be dead in a few short weeks? Viola sighed. She shouldn't blame him. After all, she'd kept her headaches a secret, making sure he never had any reason to believe she wasn't well.

Marry me. The words echoed in her mind, caressing her heart. They lifted her onto a cloud of temporary happiness only to make her crash land seconds later. He hadn't said that he loved her, but it had been in his eyes. Despite the fact that his climax had gripped him only moments earlier, she'd recognized that his offer of marriage had been genuine. It hadn't been merely the aftereffect of his lust-drugged state. His eyes had opened, and she'd looked into his soul.

A sob tore from her chest.

No, she couldn't allow herself to wallow in those dreams of what could be if only she were healthy, if only she weren't dying. It would only lead to more pain—both for him and for her. If she left him now, at least she wouldn't break his heart. He'd be angry and disappointed, but his love for her couldn't yet be deep enough to damage his heart. But if she allowed him to marry her, he would see her waste away over the next few weeks.

She didn't want to hurt him like that. He'd done too much for her. She wouldn't repay him by inflicting pain on him.

His explanation to his friend Lorenzo that she wouldn't be allowed to leave the house on her own had only given her the excuse she needed to push him away. It would make it easier to leave. He wouldn't pursue her if she insulted him by insisting he was imprisoning her. His pride would be hurt, his ego bruised, because he believed—rightly so—that by now she was staying of her own free will.

She may have been Dante's prisoner the first night, and maybe even the second, but after that, the choice to stay had been hers. They had never spoken of it, but she'd never heard him utter another word to the servants or his brother or sister-in-law that she wasn't allowed to leave.

Viola regretted that everything had to end so soon. She threw a last look at the bed they'd shared for a week, and her body instantly remembered the pleasure he'd given her, the tenderness he'd showered her with. Even now, her womb clenched with desperate need for his touch. For a last kiss. But she couldn't risk it. If she allowed him even one last kiss, one last embrace, she'd never leave him.

The tears in her eyes stung, but she cried them silently. No sound came from her lips when she walked down the stairs, her slippers in her hands so as not to make any noise. When she reached the landing, she stopped and listened. Dante and Lorenzo were still in the parlor. The door was ajar, and she could only hear their muffled voices.

As quiet as a church mouse, she reached the heavy oak entrance door and put her hand onto the handle. Viola held her breath while she pressed it down.

CHAPTER

EIGHTEEN

ante heard the thump of the front door closing and shot up from his armchair. Without sparing Lorenzo a look, he sprinted into the hallway and yanked the door open. His eyes instantly adjusted to the dark as he searched the badly lit alley.

Viola made it as far as the corner of the fifth house before he caught up with her and captured her in his arms.

"No, let me go."

Her struggles would be useless. He wouldn't let her go. He knew she had feelings for him. How deep they were, he wasn't sure, but he could sense that she wasn't indifferent to him. So why didn't she want to marry him?

"I can't let you go, Viola."

She wrenched against his grip, and he eased off the pressure so he wouldn't hurt her, but he didn't let go.

"Please," she begged, her eyes filling with tears.

"I love you." He took a leap of faith with his next words. "And I know you love me too. So, why are you leaving me?"

She lifted her chin, her gaze colliding with his. Her lips trembled, but she parted them nevertheless. Her sweet breath drifted to him, and he inhaled more of her. "It will never work. Please let me go."

He shook his head and clenched his jaw. She was keeping something from him, he could sense it. He couldn't suppress a jealous impulse. "Is there somebody else?"

"No!" Her protest was instant and vehement. "Please, Dante, if you really love me then you have to let me go."

"Why? Tell me why." His voice bounced off the walls of the neighboring buildings.

Viola dropped her head and her shoulders at the same time. She was defeated, but he felt no joy, because with her spirit gone, she wasn't the same.

Her voice was quiet and calm when she finally answered. "Because I'm dying, Dante. I have a brain tumor. In a few weeks, I'll be dead. That's why I can't marry you."

He loosened his hold on her, the shock of her revelation weakening him. She stepped out of his hold, severing her body from his. It was as if a cold blast of air hit him. For an instant, he felt dazed and confused. But then his blood flowed to his brain, and it started churning wildly.

Now he understood. The foreign scent and taste of her blood—it indicated her illness. It had been her body's way of telling him she was sick. And he hadn't recognized it. But he had felt that he needed to protect her, that she was vulnerable. How vulnerable, he only realized now. But he wouldn't allow her to push him away because of it.

"That's the only reason you don't want to marry me?" The step he was prepared to take demanded that he was sure of her feelings. If she didn't love him—

"Isn't that enough?" she whispered.

Dante drilled into her with his eyes. "Tell me the truth. Do you love me?"

A sob broke from her, but in the middle of it he heard her. "Yes, more than I want to."

His heart rejoiced. "Are you prepared to spend the rest of your life with me?"

"Dante, don't torture me."

"Answer me, Viola."

"Yes, I want to spend my last few weeks with you."

He shook his head. "That's not what I asked. I asked for eternity."

"I don't have eternity, Dante. Don't you understand? I've come to terms with it. Really, I have. But if I had eternity, there's nobody in this world I'd rather spend it with than you."

Dante nodded. "That's all I needed to know." She would be his. Now that he knew she loved him, everything would work out. He'd reveal to her what he was: a vampire, a creature of the night—an immortal creature. And he could make her immortal too—by turning her into one of their kind. Any illness she had would vanish as he drained her of her blood and fed her his. She would be as near indestructible as he was. And she would live. And be his wife. Forever.

"Come, let us go home, and I'll tell you about our life together. You'll—"

"Watch out, Dante!" Lorenzo screamed from behind him.

THINGS HAPPENED TOO FAST for Viola's tear-stained eyes to capture everything. Lorenzo had followed Dante from the house, but there was another shadow too, one that jumped out of an entryway. She recognized him instantly. Salvatore—the man who would have bedded her had Dante not interfered.

The moonlight was sufficient for her to see that he was armed with a pistol, a pistol he aimed at Dante now. She wouldn't allow it. She'd accepted her own death, but she couldn't allow the man she loved to perish. Without giving it another thought, she jumped in front of Dante as a shot rang out.

She barely felt the pain when the bullet entered her back. It was a mere pinprick, a sting. Maybe that was what death was like—all pain vanished. More shouts in the alley drifted to her ears, wrestling with each other as more people came running. But all she felt was Dante. His strong body holding her. His voice in her ear, "Oh, God, no!"

Other voices, Lorenzo's. "Take her into the house."

Footsteps, people running, voices echoing in the alley—her mind couldn't process all that was happening.

"I've got him—he's dead." Raphael seemed to appear from nowhere. When had he come back from the ball?

"—took the bullet." Fragments drifted to her.

"Hold on, my love." Dante's comforting voice again.

"—so much blood. She won't make it," she heard Isabella cry out.

Then Raphael's soothing voice, low and steady. "Dante will see to it."

She felt the movement of Dante's steps as he carried her, but her eyes were too clouded to make out his face. "So cold," she mumbled.

"I know, my love. Just hold on. Everything will be all right. I promise you." But she heard the fear in his voice, the desperation. The pain—the very pain she'd wanted to spare him.

"Forgive me, Dante," she pressed out, the few words leaving her breathless.

"No! You stay with me. You hear me?" he yelled.

"Here, on the sofa. You have to do it now," came Raphael's urging voice.

"She doesn't know."

"You love her?"

"Yes," Dante said, his voice firm and strong.

Then she felt his lips on her, kissing her softly. "I love you. Please trust me, I'm doing this because I love you." Then his lips drifted to her neck.

Her skin prickled. She felt his teeth graze her, reminding her of the night he'd truly made love to her for the first time. She moaned softly. "Yes."

When his teeth pierced her skin, she jolted, but Dante's strong body held her down. She struggled only for a second before giving into the sensation. It reminded her of sex—during sex, the initial penetration had hurt too, but only for a moment. Later, it had been pleasurable. Just like this.

Viola had never thought that she would experience her death so vividly, but instead of simply drifting off to sleep, she relived every moment of her time with Dante. Like a moving picture, it played before her mind's eye until all went black and quiet. Dark.

NINETEEN

Viola's blood was still on Dante's tongue when he pierced his own wrist with his fangs. He'd drained so much of her blood that her heartbeat was down to a mere twenty beats every minute. She was unconscious now, but still alive.

Despite the fact that his brother and Isabella stood in the parlor, it was eerily quiet in the house. Neither had spoken a word since Dante had started the process. All his concentration was on Viola. If he missed the moment her body would accept his blood, she would die.

His body tensed as he waited for her heartbeat to slow even further, and the whole scene in the alley played out in front of him again and again. He'd seen Salvatore a split second before Lorenzo had alerted him. He'd been unconcerned with his own safety—all he'd thought of was getting Viola out of danger. He'd never expected her to act so swiftly and shield him from Salvatore's assault. She'd sacrificed her life for his, with no reason. Salvatore's gun wouldn't have hurt him. Only silver bullets could have.

Viola's heart beat even slower now.

It was time. He raised his wrist and set it against her closed lips.

"No!" Lorenzo yelled as he burst into the room. "Stop, you're killing her!"

Dante reared his head and growled.

"The bullet is made of silver." Lorenzo stretched his open palm toward him. It held a ring.

Shock coursed through Dante. He pulled his wrist from Viola's mouth. He recognized the symbol on the black onyx ring: a cross intersected by three waves. The symbol of the Guardians of the Holy Waters, the group of wealthy Venetians whose mission it was to eradicate the vampires in their midst. A secret society that he and his fellow vampires had been fighting for years.

"I found it on Salvatore before I disposed of his body."

"He was a Guardian?" Raphael gasped.

Lorenzo nodded quickly. Knowing that Salvatore had been a member of the elusive society could bring them a step closer in their search for the remaining Guardians. Later, when Viola was out of danger.

"You have to take the bullet out before you turn her," Raphael said.

"Or she'll die," Dante whispered to himself.

If he left the silver bullet in her, the moment he turned her into a vampire, the deadly metal would burn her flesh from the inside and kill her. Had she been shot with anything else but silver, her new vampire body would merely expel the foreign object and heal itself.

Dante stroked his hand over Viola's face. By shielding him from Salvatore's bullet, she had truly saved his life. Now he had to save hers, or all would be in vain.

He gave his brother a desperate look. "Help me."

Without hesitation, Raphael was by his side, his fingers lengthening into sharp claws. Dante shook his head. "No, you hold her. I'll take the bullet out myself."

He shifted Viola and transferred her into Raphael's arms so her back and the gaping wound was exposed to him. Once she was a vampire, her body would heal itself within minutes. "Quickly," Raphael instructed.

Dante's fingers had already turned into claws. He sliced through the top layers of her skin and muscle, following the path the bullet had taken.

When he touched the bullet lodged next to a bone, the silver sent a bolt of pain through him.

Hissing, he clenched his teeth and curled his claw, dislodging the silver from the bone. With a groan, he drew the bullet from her body, then dropped it to the floor. His flesh was sizzling where it had come in contact with the metal. But he ignored the pain.

There was no time left. He could not lose her.

Taking Viola from Raphael, he placed his bleeding wrist at her mouth and forced her lips open. The blood dripped, filling her mouth.

"Swallow, Viola," he urged her. "Swallow, damn it."

Her mouth didn't move. His heart contracted. No, he needed her to live so he could live. She was all he wanted. "Please," he whispered. He bent over her face, and a solitary tear dislodged from his eye. It dropped onto her lips and ran to the corner of her mouth before it followed the path his blood had taken earlier. "Don't leave me."

A gurgle from her throat startled him. She swallowed. She took a breath.

"Viola!"

The relieved breaths of his companions filled the room. But all Dante saw was Viola. How her chest rose as she took another breath. How her cheeks turned rosy. How her throat worked to swallow the rest of his blood.

"Viola, my love." Her eyes flew open, and all he could do was smile at her.

"Dante, oh Dante, are you hurt? You're bleeding." Viola stared at his wrist.

He shook his head and laughed, full of relief. It figured that her first thoughts would be for him. "No, my love, I've never been better." Then he hugged her to his chest and squeezed her to him. "I love you, Viola, I love you so much."

"Salvatore," she stammered. "Did he shoot you?"

Dante pulled away just far enough so he could look at her face. "You took the bullet. You saved my life."

There was a puzzled look on her face. "But... I don't understand. I feel fine. Actually..." She paused. "I feel better than fine. He must have missed, even though... I felt the bullet hit me."

He gave her a soft kiss on her lips. "You did get shot. You almost died. I took the bullet out of you. But, that's not all." Dante looked at his brother. How should he tell her what had happened? How could he explain to her what he was? What she was now too?

"Just tell her," Raphael said.

Dante swallowed hard.

"Tell me what?"

Viola stared at Dante, who seemed insecure for the first time since she'd met him. Something was odd. While she could have sworn she'd felt the impact of the bullet and the pain that followed, she felt better than she had in a long time. She wasn't tired, and there wasn't even a hint of her usual headache. No throbbing, no dull ache, nothing. She felt the way she had before she'd gotten ill. No, better. She felt so full of energy she wanted to run a race, just for the fun of it.

All her senses seemed sharper too. Her eyesight was better—not that it had been bad before, but now she could see the smallest detail on Isabella's embroidered gown and even the intricate filigree on the buttons that graced Raphael's waistcoat. Not to speak of her sense of smell. Her nostrils flared as she tilted her head more in Isabella's direction. She smelled distinctly different than the three men in the room. She'd never noticed the difference before.

"My love." Dante's endearment jolted her out of her observations. "This might seem strange at first, but there's something important I have to tell you."

Viola raised her hand and cupped his cheek. The knowledge that he was alive and well was all she needed. Nothing else could be as important.

Dante turned his head and kissed her palm. "I made you into one of us."

Dante's words made no sense. "One of you?"

"Yes, you're like me, Raphael and Lorenzo now. Immortal."

She let out a soft laugh. "You're funny."

"No. I gave you my blood so you could live. Viola, I'm a vampire."

At his assertion, she jolted, her hand slipping from his face. She couldn't have heard right. "Sorry, can you say that again? I think I misheard."

Dante gave a slow shake of his head. "You heard right. I'm a vampire. And I turned you into one, otherwise you would have died. Even if you hadn't gotten shot by Salvatore. I'm sorry, but there was no time to explain. I had to act. Swiftly."

Viola listened to his words. Slowly, they sank in.

"You were slipping away. I couldn't let you die. I had to change you instantly."

She tried to understand the implications of his words. "You're a vampire? Immortal?"

He nodded.

"And I'm one too? But my brain tumor... I'll still die."

A warm smile curled around his lips and spread over his entire face.

Hope bloomed inside her. "Won't I?"

"No. Any illness you had was eradicated by the turning. You're healthy. Your tumor is gone. You're immortal."

Your tumor is gone. Those were the only words she truly understood. She would live. Her life wasn't over. She had another chance. Her heart filled with joy, making it so full it would burst if she didn't give her emotions free reign.

Tears pushed forward and escaped. "Oh, my God."

Dante's face twisted as if in pain. "I'm so sorry, Viola." He dropped his head and avoided looking at her. "Forgive me."

"Forgive you?" He'd given her a new life, the greatest gift she could have ever wished for. She'd never been happier. She took his chin and made him look at her. Regret was evident in his eyes. He'd misunderstood her tears. "I would like to give you an answer to your question now."

"My question?"

She smiled and drew closer to him. "I want to be your wife. For etern

—." Before she'd even finished the last word, his lips were on hers, kissing her breathless. He only lifted them long enough for a murmured "yes" against her mouth before he claimed her with his tongue, forging deep inside.

The clearing of throats in the room reminded her that they were not alone. Dante severed the kiss and turned his head briefly to the others in the room. "Go away."

Viola chuckled. "That's rude, Dante."

"I don't care. I want to make love to you now."

Raphael laughed out loud. "Last time I checked, you did have a bedchamber, my dear brother. I suggest you use it." He hesitated for a brief second before he continued. "And, Dante, the storage room next to my chamber is off limits from now on. Get your kicks somewhere else."

CHAPTER

TWENTY

The door closed with a loud thud that echoed through the entire house. Dante didn't care what anybody thought. He wasn't even surprised Raphael knew that they'd watched him and Isabella make love. After all, Viola had been quite vocal that night, and Raphael would have picked up the sounds with his superior vampire hearing.

But none of that mattered.

Viola was alive, and she'd accepted him for what he was.

Dante captured his soon-to-be wife between his body and the door at her back, pressing her against it.

"Is your brother angry with us?"

"Raphael? Hardly. I'm sure he got a kick out of it himself, knowing we watched him and Isabella."

"But we can't do it again?" A wicked smile curved around her pretty mouth.

Dante pressed his hardening cock against her soft stomach. "No. But I'm sure I can arrange other things for us to watch if you'd like."

His heart skipped a beat when he saw Viola raise an eyebrow in interest. Her breathless voice only underscored her excitement. "Yes?"

"Anything you want, my love. Because keeping you satisfied is my mission." He willed his fingers to turn into claws. Slowly, making sure she saw what he was about to do, he placed his claws at the spot where her décolleté revealed her lush breasts.

She inhaled, the action pressing the flesh closer to his sharp claws, but she didn't pull away. "What are you going to do?"

Not a question—not the way she said it. It was a challenge. One he was more than happy to meet. Faster than a human's eye could process, he sliced through the front of her bodice, ripping it in half.

"You mean what *did* I just do?" he corrected.

Viola looked down at her torn dress then raised her head and looked at him, her eyes shimmering golden. He sensed the power in her, the power of a vampire, and the knowledge that she was his—that she would be his for eternity—overwhelmed him.

"God, you're beautiful."

She raised her hand. Before his eyes, her elegant fingers turned into claws. She touched his neck with it, stroked down to where the top button of his shirt was undone. With a wicked smile, she sliced it down the middle. And her claws didn't stop there, only paused for a moment of anticipation.

Dante growled out his approval. She was his match—fearless, daring, and insatiable.

Viola sliced through the fabric of his breeches, carefully avoiding his hard length. He sucked in a breath when cool air hit his arousal and her suddenly-soft fingers curled around him.

"You're beautiful," she whispered in that husky voice he'd come to love, because it gave him a window into her soul, laying bare what she felt for him.

Unable to hold back, he tore her dress off her and exposed her nakedness to his hungry eyes. "Mine, all mine!" Pressing her harder against the door, he captured her thighs with his hands, and spread and raised them. The scent of her arousal was drugging now, overwhelming, impossible to resist.

With a deep groan, he positioned his cock at her core and thrust into her heat, pounding her against the door.

"Yes!" she cried out, her arms slung around his neck, her legs wrapped around his hips.

Lust and desire coursed through him, as did the knowledge that he didn't have to hold back anymore. It fired his loins to pound harder. Viola was a vampire now, as strong as he was, and as indestructible. He couldn't hurt her. Now he could finally show her everything he felt: the ferocity with which he loved her, desired her, and needed her.

She was his everything.

"Tomorrow," he ground out, "you'll be my wife."

Her eyes blinked in agreement.

"But tonight, I'll make you my mate." He raised his hand to her face and rubbed his finger over her lips, nudging them open wider.

"I want you," she said breathlessly. As if she knew what he wanted, she opened her mouth and bared her teeth.

"Yes," he encouraged her as his cock plunged harder into her.

Her fangs lengthened as instinct guided her. Her irises were a pure golden hue now, just like his.

He tilted his head to the side, offering her his neck. "Later, I'll take you out hunting," he rasped, "but right now, I want you to drink from me."

Dante would always remember the exact moment when Viola's fangs drove into his flesh for the first time. It was a moment of pure and utter bliss, and ecstasy. A celebration of love and passion, lust and desire. When she sucked his essence into her, his orgasm broke, washing over him like a tidal wave drowning Venice forever. And with it came another wave, as powerful as his: Viola's climax, her muscles clenching around his length, milking him, asking for the last drop of what he had to give.

And he would give her everything he possessed. His wealth, his body, and foremost, his heart.

For eternity.

"Forever," Viola whispered and kissed him with her bloodstained lips.

~

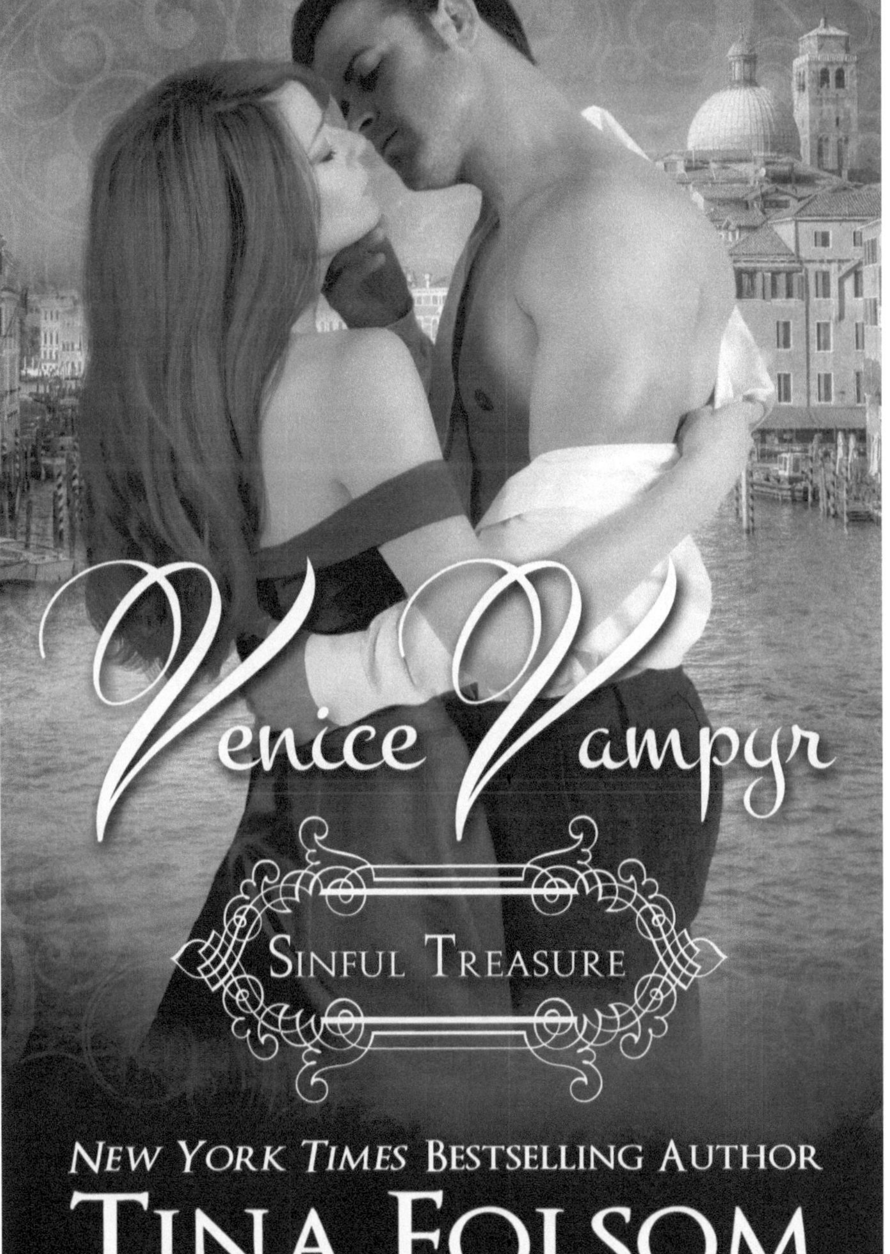

Venice Vampyr
SINFUL TREASURE
NEW YORK TIMES BESTSELLING AUTHOR
TINA FOLSOM

CHAPTER

ONE

enice, Italy - early 1800s

Lorenzo was late, yet he was sure his friends would forgive him, considering the good news he had.

Only a few weeks earlier, an attack by a Guardian had almost killed one of their own. With the Guardians of the Holy Waters, the secret society of vampire hunters in Venice, becoming more and more daring in their attempts to eradicate each and every vampire within the island city, he and his fellow vampires had decided on drastic measures to protect themselves against their threat.

Dante, his best friend, had suggested buying up all dwellings within the city block on which he and his brother Raphael lived, and turn the entire square block into a fortress of sorts: ten homes on this street, ten on the street behind them, and four each on the side alleys that completed the rectangle. By purchasing the houses that bordered each other, they would be able to create secret walkways between the buildings, thus being able to meet without having to exit to the streets or the canals. It would also provide them with easy means of escape and a way of coming to each other's aid during daylight hours without being exposed to the burning rays of the sun.

Tonight was their second meeting to discuss strategy on how to achieve their goal.

Lorenzo smiled to himself as a servant opened the heavy entrance door to Dante and Raphael's home. He was way ahead of the game. His friends would be very pleased with him.

There was a chill in the night air, and despite his vampire body not being as susceptible to the cold as humans were, he didn't like the damp, cold air that reached his lungs as he inhaled. He much preferred the subtle scent of the wood fire in the parlor that drifted into his nostrils as he stepped inside. He handed his gloves to the manservant and allowed him to take the heavy black cloak from his shoulders. The human servants were chosen carefully and often came from the same family that served their masters faithfully, taking their secrets to the grave. For that, they were paid extraordinarily well. Loyalty wasn't cheap.

His sensitive hearing had already picked up the voices of his friends. His enhanced sense of smell was able to distinguish them further: there were a dozen of them assembled.

Lorenzo entered the parlor and swept his gaze across the room. Besides the brothers Dante and Raphael and their wives Viola and Isabella, several of his fellow vampires were in attendance: Nico, Silvano, Enrico, Francesco, Paolo, Andrea, Carlo, and Marcello. While there were more vampires in Venice, the ones assembled represented the leaders of their various clans. They would instruct their followers on what to do.

As usual, his nostrils flared when he took in Isabella's scent. Raphael's wife was the only human among them, and her delightful scent always made his gums itch and his fangs tingle. His friend was one lucky son of a bitch. Not that Lorenzo would have liked the trappings of marriage, but to drink from a human without having to use his powers to make the woman forget what he was doing to her was a treat in which he'd never partaken. The thought of having a human woman underneath him and fucking her while she willingly offered her neck to him, fully aware of his intentions, made him hard.

"Evening, gentlemen," he said louder than was necessary, trying to distract himself from his debauched thoughts. Not that it would do any good. He'd have to venture out later and slake his lust with whatever trollop he could find at such a late hour. But while he would have no problems finding a willing woman who'd let him fuck her, taking her blood would have to be done under the veil of his persuasive powers, which would erase her memories of his act. A shame really, because a vampire's bite only heightened the arousal—both in the host as well as the vampire.

"Somebody tie you to a bed?" Dante chuckled and looked at him.

Nico laughed. "More like he needed seconds."

Lorenzo's appetite for women was well known among his friends, and instead of getting annoyed about their little jabs here and there, he wore them as medals of honor. "She simply couldn't get enough of me," he lied, making his friends roar with laughter. There was even a twinkle in Isabella's eyes. He winked good-naturedly. "But I had to take care of her friend too."

The second lie earned him an even louder reply.

"That's my boy!" Paolo proclaimed and slapped his own thigh.

And at most times, what Lorenzo was dishing out to his friends would have been the plain truth, but he'd had more important things to do these last hours. The negotiations he'd entered into had taken longer than expected, and hadn't allowed him to indulge in his favorite pastime: women.

"Find yourself a seat," Raphael instructed. "We started without you. You'll just have to catch up."

Lorenzo beamed. "Not necessary."

Several sets of eyes landed on him, curiosity flashing in them. Lorenzo didn't wait for their questions, too excited to impart his news. "I've purchased a house."

He could tell that Dante wanted to jump up from his seat, but Viola, his lovely wife, put her hand on his thigh. "Congratulations, Lorenzo!" she said and smiled.

"Thank you, Viola. That's very kind of you to say."

"Well, don't keep us on tenterhooks," Nico complained. "Where is it located?"

Lorenzo smirked and motioned toward the East. "Two doors down."

Suddenly Dante's apprehensive face turned to admiration. "How did you manage that? If I'm not mistaken, the owner only died three days ago. I was going to approach his heirs in the next few days."

"Beat you to it, my old friend. It turns out that I'd purchased one of the man's markers."

"He was a gambler?" Raphael interjected.

Lorenzo nodded. "A bad one at that. As soon as he died, I approached his solicitor and made it clear that it would be most beneficial to the heir if I received the house in exchange for my marker, considering the marker was for more than the house was worth. I threw in a small sum to pacify the solicitor and a slightly larger one for the heir."

"And the heir agreed?" Dante asked, raising an eyebrow in inquiry.

Lorenzo folded his arms across his chest, fully satisfied with his achievement. "She has no choice. There is nothing for her to inherit other than her father's debts, which I've now taken care of. The solicitor will explain it to her when she arrives in Venice. I'm sure it'll pose no problem. In any case, the solicitor had authorization to execute the contract."

"Excellent!" Dante stood and slapped him on the shoulder. "I applaud you on your initiative." Then he turned to the other men in the room. "That's exactly what I expect from the rest of you. Don't wait until a house is being offered for sale. Make an offer. We have the funds to make it happen. There are twenty-eight houses on this block and the one behind us. We need to own each and every one of them if we want to make sure we're protected from the Guardians."

All heads nodded enthusiastically.

"When are you moving in?" Nico asked.

"This Friday night."

Nico and Dante exchanged a conspiratorial look.

"I'm sure we'll find a suitable housewarming gift for you, won't we, Nico?" Dante grinned from one ear to the other and received the same wicked grin in response from Nico.

Lorenzo merely shook his head. He could be sure that whatever his friends had in mind would be either sinful or entertaining, and if he was lucky, both.

CHAPTER

TWO

Bianca Greco looked over her shoulder once more before she turned the key in the rusted lock and prayed for the first time in many years. The clicking sound announced that her prayer had been answered: the old key still worked. Nobody had changed the locks.

Before her luck could change, she slipped into her old home and shut the door behind her. Finally, she was able to breathe again.

As soon as she'd received the news of her father's sudden death, Bianca had packed her bags and traveled to Venice. But despite her hasty departure, the trip had taken several days, the muddy road conditions being to blame. She'd arrived too late.

The solicitor, Signore Mancini, had informed her with a beaming smile that he'd managed to sell her father's home and even extracted a little money from the buyer, who'd graciously paid off all of her father's debts. According to the solicitor, she should be happy to have received anything, particularly since the debts had far exceeded the value of the house.

But Bianca was fuming. And Signore Mancini had merely assumed that she was upset because this had once been her home and she had happy memories there. Bah! The few happy memories she'd had in her home were from her early childhood. But as soon as she'd developed into a young woman with a slim waist, wide child-bearing hips, and a generous bosom, her father had ferried in the suitors by the boatload.

It had turned into a cattle auction. She being the cattle to be auctioned off to the highest bidder. She could still taste the disappointment on her lips when she'd begged her father to choose a kind husband for her. He'd only looked at her with his cold eyes and ordered her to be quiet. Nothing of the gentle father on whose lap she'd sat for hours as a child was left. He'd become consumed with rising in Venetian society, and he was going to do it on Bianca's back by marrying her off to the most influential suitor.

She'd done the only thing she could: she'd fled.

After stealing sufficient coin from her father's purse to see her safely to the mainland, Bianca had made it as far as Florence before her money had run out. With no skills or talents to support herself, she'd done the very thing her father had tried to do for her: sold her body.

Thanks to her refined manners and her beauty, she'd attracted the attention of a wealthy benefactor who'd made her his courtesan. Once he'd tired of her, he'd handed her off to one of his friends. While the men Bianca had been with had treated her well and provided her with a good lifestyle, she had no delusions about what she was: a whore.

The fact that she didn't ply her trade in the dark streets and in dingy rooms that rented by the hour didn't diminish her feeling of being dirty. And despite the fact that she found relations with men enjoyable and had learned a great deal about how to please a man, and how a man could please a woman, she'd never loved any of them. Nobody had ever seen who was beneath the surface of the beautiful courtesan or had touched her heart. Because all they saw was the shell, the body that blinded them, the façade she'd erected in order to protect herself and the girl within. The girl whose father had betrayed her.

No, Bianca didn't want the house. But she wanted what it contained: the treasure her father had spoken of so many years ago. She remembered his words well.

"It's a great treasure," he'd claimed as she'd sat on his lap as a little girl. "And if I sold it to the right person, it would bring us more money than we could ever get for this house."

"More than for our house?" she'd gawked. "But it's a huge house!"

He'd smiled at her. "Yes, but the treasure is worth more."

"It must be big then, the treasure."

Her father had shaken his head. "No, it's small. That's why it's so easy to hide."

"Where is it?" she'd blurted.

"It's a secret. Nobody can know it even exists. If they do, they will hurt us."

"Shh," she'd hummed. "You can whisper it to me."

But her father had never divulged the hiding place, nor what the treasure even consisted of. And maybe it had just been a story to keep a ten-year old girl entertained. But she couldn't dismiss it. If the treasure really existed, then it still had to be in the house. And she needed to find it. It was her only way out of her current life. She wasn't going to remain a courtesan forever and give her body to men she didn't love.

Bianca set her bag on the floor beside her and ventured into the house. Everything was still the same: the furniture, the paintings, the rugs. Even the crystal glasses in the parlor where her father had liked to drink his Grappa were still in the same place as always. Signore Mancini had told her that the man who'd purchased the house had insisted on keeping the furniture and everything else. When she'd asked him when the new owner was going to move into the property, he'd shrugged and declared that the man had seemed in no particular hurry.

Well, considering that the purchase had only been recorded in the city's ledgers this afternoon, Bianca figured the new owner would most likely wait until Monday to hire workers to clean the place and bring his own personal items into the home. No Italian liked to work on weekends, not even the poorer classes. This meant she'd have the weekend to search the house from top to bottom and take everything apart to find what her father had referred to as the "treasure."

Bianca walked up the creaking staircase, her long dress picking up the dust on the way. Clearly, her father's servants had neglected the house even before his death, because there was no way this much dust could accumulate in a mere week. Now the house was quiet, devoid of any life.

The servants were gone, most likely glad that their back wages had been paid by the solicitor. It wouldn't surprise her if they'd taken some of the silver with them.

In a way she was glad this was how it had happened. Had her father's servants still occupied the house, she would have had to sneak around trying to hide what she was doing. With the house empty, she could conduct her search openly.

Bianca shivered as she reached the upstairs corridor. It had been an overcast day, and now that the sun was about to set, the dampness crept into the house and took hold. If she wanted to stay in the house for the weekend, she would have to get at least one or two fires going. She passed by the door to her father's chamber, but decided not to enter it. She had no wish to be reminded of him so intensely.

Instead, she opened the next door and stepped into her mother's old room. It was as though she'd died only yesterday, yet it had been over ten years. Her father had always made sure the servants cleaned and aired her room at least once a week, as if he were expecting her to come back. She glanced around. Fresh linen adorned the large four-poster bed, and wood was stacked next to the fireplace, ready for a maid to start a fire.

The remaining light entering through the window was sufficient for Bianca to see herself in the mirror. She looked a fright. Traveling all day, first on a dirty coach, then on a rocking boat, had shaken her. She hadn't had time to clean up since. The neat bun her long dark hair had been tamed into was no longer the elegant coiffure it had once been. Little strands of black curls tumbled down her neck and shoulders. Her dark blue dress was dusty, and its hem was caked with mud. Lifting her dress slightly, she noticed that her boots weren't faring any better.

As much as she wanted to start the search right now, Bianca couldn't help but yearn for a hot bath to take the grime of the trip off her body. Besides, she needed to get a fire going to warm up the room so she wouldn't freeze to death at night.

With a heavy sigh, she approached the fireplace and knelt down. Despite her sheltered upbringing, she knew how to kindle a fire. Early in her time in Florence, she'd learned everything she needed to survive. It didn't take long for her to get a fire going. She placed two large logs onto the flames and stepped back. In an hour, the room would be pleasantly warm.

In the meantime, she went back downstairs and made her way to the kitchen. The stove was a cast iron one. She had to get a fire started there as well if she wanted hot water for a quick bath. Pumping the water from the hand pump, she filled several large cooking pots and placed them onto the surface of the stove, then went about lighting a fire in it.

Sweat already accumulated on her brow from heaving the heavy pots onto the stove. It would be even harder to lift them off once the water was boiling. There was no way she would carry them all the way upstairs into the small bathing chamber next to her mother's room. Instead, she would use the tub that was located in the room next to the kitchen where the servants used to do the laundry. It would do for the night.

THREE

Lorenzo had planned on arriving at his new home just after sunset, however his friends had thwarted his efforts to take possession of his new residence by calling another meeting to discuss more details about the acquisition of the remaining twenty-six homes on the square block. He'd only listened half-heartedly, eager to inspect his new place. After all, he'd bought it sight unseen. He'd never set foot inside. For all he knew, the place was in shambles.

However, the solicitor had assured him the property was habitable and only needed some cleaning. It didn't matter much to Lorenzo. He was going to change the interior anyway. For starters, hidden exits would have to be incorporated into the layout of the home, and once the house between his and that of the brothers Dante and Raphael was in vampire hands, connecting tunnels would be built between the homes. Of course, these were not to be true tunnels, but covered walkways, above ground. Any attempt to dig beneath the level of the canals would result in immediate flooding. But such walkways would serve their purpose, allowing them to move around during the day.

It was well past midnight by the time Lorenzo reached the front door of his new home and turned the key. The smell that greeted him wasn't what he'd expected from a vacant house. It was welcoming, instantly feeling like a home. And he immediately realized why: somewhere in the house, a fire was burning in a fireplace. He was not alone.

Dropping his traveling bag in the foyer, he inhaled deeply, taking in the various scents of the house: smoke, soap, dust, and mold. And another very faint smell of something entirely unexpected.

A smile curled around his lips. Dante and Nico were the best. They knew him too well, and there was no doubt in his mind about what they'd gotten him as a housewarming gift. Emphasis on the "warming."

Lorenzo followed the alluring scent upstairs and trailed it along the corridor. In front of one door, he stopped and inhaled again. Yes, his gift was right behind this door, waiting for him. His ears captured every sound, but it was quiet behind the door except for the crackling of the fire.

Quietly, he turned the door knob and eased the door open, sliding inside the nearly dark room. Only the low fire in the fireplace provided some light, but Lorenzo's superior night vision didn't need bright light to make out the outlines of his present.

There, in the entirely feminine chamber, which at one time must have belonged to the lady of the house, a young woman slumbered under the sheets. Her dark hair fanned out like a halo around her porcelain face, her lips slightly parted, her breath beckoning him to approach.

He wondered what color her eyes were. Maybe as dark as her thick lashes, which seemed so long they caressed her cheeks.

Why had Nico and Dante kept him so long when they knew this enthralling beauty was waiting for him? It was inexcusable to let a woman like her wait and not give her the attention she deserved. He had every intention of making it up to her.

Without making a sound, Lorenzo took off his cloak and dropped it on a nearby chair before divesting himself of his shirt. When he opened the top button of his breeches, he realized that he was already hard. He stripped himself of his trousers and shoes, placing them next to the rest of his clothing. Then he looked back at the sleeping woman in his bed and touched his cock, trying to ease some of the tension.

His arousal was heavy and unstoppable. As much as he enjoyed looking at her, what he wanted even more was to touch her. And then wake her. Fuck her. Bite her. Not necessarily in that order.

Lorenzo released his erection and lifted the coverlet, revealing more of the woman's body. She wore a nightrail which revealed more than it concealed. The thin lilac fabric was virtually transparent, putting her dark nipples on display. With every breath, her full breasts rose and pressed the little buds against the fabric, the chafing action seemingly turning them hard.

He licked his lips at the sight and slid onto the bed. His eyes continued scanning her body, moving over her slender waist and further down. A dark thatch of hair shone through the fabric where her thighs met. Slightly parted, her sex was open to be explored if he chose to do so.

Her nightgown had ridden up, revealing a creamy thigh, the skin pink and unblemished, toned, yet not muscular. Surely, those thighs would grip him tightly when he thrust into her. Those were not the thighs of a virgin.

Lorenzo forced his gaze upwards again, past her tempting cunt and her luscious breasts to that little hollow at the base of her neck. Graceful, elegant. She was all that and more. The long column of her neck fairly screamed to be bitten, and her ears were petite and beautifully shaped, ready to be nibbled on.

He had to hand it to Nico and Dante: they knew what he liked in a woman. And this time, they'd outdone themselves. He would have to thank them for this thoughtful gift—later. After he'd devoured her and had his fill of her. And he wasn't going to wait a second longer, whether she woke up while he touched her or not. In fact, he liked the idea of her waking up only once he was thrusting inside her.

He would arouse her while she was asleep, then take her and continue when she awoke in his arms, surprised and delighted at his mastery over her body.

Lorenzo allowed his fingers to lightly glide over her breasts, making the fabric rub more tightly against her nipples. Even through the fabric, he sensed the heat in her body and the sensitivity of her skin to his touch. Without haste, he explored her. His eyes mapped her body for a later conquest while his hands forged ahead to touch her lush curves. Her breasts were firm and sitting high on her chest, evidence of a young and well-tended body. As he squeezed one of the round globes lightly, a soft breath rushed past her lips and bounced against him. The taste of mint and vanilla engulfed him, making him pause for a moment.

Mint and vanilla—the scents he associated with innocence when he knew that the woman in his bed was far from innocent. His friends had bought her for the night to please him with her body. And while she didn't look as if she'd been cheap, she was no innocent, but a seductress as sophisticated as they came. Her nightgown spoke to that effect. But as much as he liked the gown, it had to go.

Lorenzo wanted to feast his eyes on her skin, her curves, her sex. He wanted nothing impeding his mouth and hands, no barriers, not even as thin as the fabric of her gown. Three purple ribbons held the nightgown together in the front now that he looked at it more closely. In fact, it appeared the gown wasn't really as much of a gown as it was a robe meant to be worn over something else.

Had she waited for him only dressed in this flimsy robe, wanting him to simply untie those three ribbons before he'd throw her on the bed and drive his shaft into her? Had that been her intention? A present for which he would have simply had to untie three purple ribbons? How fitting.

As he released the top ribbon, the valley between her breasts was laid bare. He couldn't help himself: he had to taste her. His head dipped between her breasts, and his lips brushed against her soft skin as he placed a gentle kiss on the spot. When he inhaled, he smelled the soap she'd used only recently. It was the same scent he'd smelled upon entering the home. It appeared she'd bathed here. He appreciated the gesture. He liked a clean woman, and if she'd bathed, it could only mean that she would be more than happy for him to taste her beautiful cunt, something he was more than eager to do.

But he shouldn't get ahead of himself. First, he needed to unwrap his present completely and not act like a little boy who couldn't wait to get to what was underneath, tearing the wrapping in the process. No, he wanted to peel her out of it, reveal inch by glorious inch of her body to his hungry gaze. He wanted to revel in the anticipation, because he knew he'd climax so much harder if only he'd allow himself to wait until the last possible moment.

And she was a beauty to behold. When Lorenzo untied the last ribbon, he peeled each side of the gauzy robe to its side and laid her bare. Her breasts were as beautiful as he'd imagined, but when his gaze traveled over her flat stomach and down to where her womanly scent emanated, his heart nearly stopped.

Her sex was guarded by a neatly trimmed triangle of dark hair, but it was shorter and slimmer than what he was used to from other women. She'd shaped it into a long stripe, a little wider at the top, but slimming toward the bottom, almost as if it was an arrow pointing the way.

Not that he needed any directions.

His hand followed the arrow of hair and slid between her parted legs. Her sex was damp, either from her recent bath or maybe, already, from her arousal. Lorenzo glanced back at her face, but her eyes were closed and her breathing was even.

He smiled, liking the fact that she was still asleep, giving him the opportunity to explore at his leisure. Again, he dipped his head to her breasts and licked his tongue over one hard nipple. He loved the hard nipple grazing his tongue and took another lick before he closed his lips around it and sucked.

But his hand wasn't idle either. He rubbed one finger against her female folds, feeling the moisture spread under his ministrations. She shifted under him, and he realized it was to open her legs wider and give him better access. He thanked her by sucking her nipple harder before he released it and moved to the other breast where he unleashed the same treatment.

Whether it was him sucking her breasts, or his finger stroking her softly, her cunt released more moisture. He swept it up with the pad of his finger and stroked upwards, finding the little bundle of flesh that was now peeking from its hood. He slid his moist finger over it and simultaneously heard her moan out a breath.

She was responding to him in her sleep. Uninhibited, just like he loved it. Her aroma drifted into his nostrils, making his cock throb in anticipation. Soon, he promised himself. As soon as he'd tasted her.

Lorenzo slid down and settled between her thighs. As he spread them further, he opened up her cunt to his view. The beautiful pink flesh glistened in the light from the fireplace as if flames danced on its surface. He lowered his lips to her sex and lapped against it. When her juices hit the back of his tongue, he inhaled sharply and closed his eyes. By God, she tasted like paradise.

CHAPTER

FOUR

Bianca had always tended toward having erotic dreams, but this one was better than any of her previous ones. Maybe it was the exhaustion of the days of travel she had behind her, or the excitement of returning to Venice to start a new life with what she would find in her home, but her entire body seemed to hum with pleasure. Not the kind of hurried pleasure some of her former lovers would grant her, but the leisurely pace of a lover who had all the time in the world.

And she had no intention of rushing him.

This was a dream she'd give her full and undivided attention to without hurrying the events along. Because every touch was perfection, every contact with her dream lover's hands and mouth a treat as sumptuous as any buffet at the grandest balls in Florence.

Bianca had first become aware of her vivid dream when she'd felt something wet and warm licking over her nipple. Seconds later, firm lips had closed around her little bud and tugged, sending delicious tingles down her skin. That, together with the hand that was playing with the soft flesh between her legs, was making her want to howl. Why could none of her real lovers ever have ignited such passion in her? Why could she only conjure up such feelings in her dreams?

She sighed when his finger slipped over her pearl and ignited her even further. His touch was soft, yet there was enough pressure for her to almost twist away at the intensity of the sensations it produced in her belly. Low and deep it churned in her, as if a fire were building, each flame stoking the fire higher, each touch turning her softer and more receptive. She had rarely ever been able to let herself go and lose herself in the sensations that her body was currently reveling in. She'd always been afraid of losing herself, of giving something she didn't want to give to those men who only wanted her body, who had no interest in her as a person.

But in her dream, she could allow herself to open up to her lover, allow him to truly pleasure her, to show her what heights her body was capable of. When she felt hands on her thighs, she opened wider and sensed him settling between her legs. A moment later, warmth flooded her core: his mouth was on her sex, and he was licking her, lapping up the juices that oozed so freely from her now as if he loved her taste.

Bianca even heard his moans, the deep guttural sound only a man in the throes of ecstasy could make. As if *she* were sucking *him*, not the other way. Yet her dream lover seemed to derive more pleasure from licking her pearl than as if she were sucking his cock into her mouth. Only in a dream, could things be that perfect.

Bianca arched into his touch, silently urging him on to give her more, to drive her higher. He seemed to understand her only too well, because his tongue forged ahead and drove into her quivering slit, filling that gaping void that no other man had ever truly been able to fill. Her back lifted off the mattress as she pressed her head deeper into the pillow, unable to keep her body from trembling.

Perspiration gathered on her skin, the tiny pearls of sweat collecting in the hollow between her breasts before turning into a rivulet and racing down her stomach to pool in her navel. How a dream could make her feel so hot on such a cold night was beyond her. She wouldn't have needed the fire she'd kindled in the fireplace had she known that a talented dream lover would visit her and shower her with his attentions.

His speared tongue alternated between thrusting into her moist channel and then licking over her aching pearl, stroking the bundle of flesh until she was fairly begging for release. But he wouldn't give her any. Whenever she was close to climaxing, he'd pull back and simply stroke languidly over her nether lips and lap up her juices before he'd return to teasing her most sensitive center again. Almost as if he were preparing her for a release of magnificent proportions.

When his tongue circled her pearl again, she reached for him, intent on keeping him there and not letting him escape until he'd brought her over the edge. Her fingers found thick hair that coated his head and buried themselves in it as she cupped him and forced his mouth to suck her harder.

"More!" Bianca cried out.

He succumbed to her order and sucked the little bundle of sensitive flesh between his lips and tugged. A spear of energy bolted through her core, robbing her of her breath. Panting, she praised him, "Yes, yes, that's good."

And as if he understood what she wanted, he tugged harder. At the same time, he drove a thick finger into her channel. She jolted at the intensity—no, two fingers. He'd driven two fingers into her, stretching her tight channel. Her heart beat frantically as he sucked at her pearl then lapped his tongue over it in a rapid rhythm. His fingers took on the same rhythm, pumping into her, and she couldn't hold on any longer.

She felt the waves before they hit her, felt her orgasm approach with a deep rumble and let herself fall. Like a massive ocean current, the sensations drowned her and swept her away until all she felt was the gentle soothing warmth of her lover's tongue as it continued to tease aftershocks from her exhausted body.

It seemed to take ages until he finally lifted his head from her sex and allowed the air to cool her skin.

"You taste delicious."

The deep voice was close and didn't sound as if it were part of her dream. Bianca's body tensed as her eyes flew open. It took several seconds for her vision to adjust to the dark of the room. She was still in her mother's old bedroom, but she was not alone.

A man—a naked man—rose from between her legs. His dark hair was disheveled as if somebody had run their hands through it. His lips glistened with moisture, and his eyes gleamed with arousal.

Her dream lover was real. She had allowed a complete stranger—a man who'd broken into her house—to make love to her!

Bianca looked down at herself and noticed that the little purple robe she'd worn to bed because she'd neglected to pack a nightgown in her haste, was open in the front and her entire body was exposed to the stranger, who still looked at her. His dark eyes were hypnotizing.

"Good, you're awake now. Let's fuck."

His blunt words pulled her out of her momentary trance. She jerked away from him, her back meeting the bed's headboard while she snatched a pillow and pressed it against her front, covering her breasts and her exposed sex, unable to press her thighs together since his hands were still gripping them.

"Who are you?" Bianca cried, her eyes darting to each side of the bed, trying to see if there was anything she could use as a weapon against him.

The stranger sat up, revealing more of his naked body—more than she really wanted to see. Her eyes strayed to his midsection, then dipped lower to where his erection made an unmistakable statement. He'd come to rape her!

"Lorenzo, of course. Who else?" There was a hint of confusion in his tone.

Should she know somebody of the name of Lorenzo? For a second, she searched her memory, but nothing came to her.

"I'm sorry I made you wait," he continued.

"Wait?" Now confusion spread in her mind. What had happened? Had she blacked out? Had she made an appointment with somebody she'd met on her travels? No. She was sure that all she'd done was speak to the solicitor, then come to the house to find the treasure. She hadn't met anybody. And surely, if she'd met this utterly handsome man before, she would remember.

Bianca shivered slightly. Yes, this stranger was handsome. Devastatingly so. Not only were his dark eyes mesmerizing, his lips which were still wet with her juices, were utterly kissable. His dark mane of thick hair had felt soft like silk, and when she looked at his chiseled body, she could only shudder.

"Yes, I'm afraid I got delayed. Had I known that Dante and Nico had hired you for me, I would have been here earlier." His fingers stroked higher on her thigh, and Bianca pulled back, trying to shake off his hand. "But I'm here now, and I'm going to make it up to you."

"Hired me?" A dreadful suspicion crept up her belly. "You think I'm a whore?" Was that what everybody thought of her? Was it written in her face what she'd done all these years? Could everybody tell?

"If you would like to call it something else, by all means," he mumbled apologetically. "Maybe you're one of Dante's and Nico's *friends*?"

"Who are Dante and Nico?"

Lorenzo let out a breath, almost as if he was tired of having to explain something to her for the hundredth time. "My friends. The ones who gave you to me as a housewarming present."

Shock coursed through her. "Housewarming present?" Her voice sounded shrill in her own head. "I'm no housewarming present!"

Tears threatened to come to the surface. Somebody was playing a cruel joke on her. "Get out of my house, Signore! Now, before I call the carabinieri!"

"Your house? Signora, this is my house. So, if anybody is leaving, it will be you."

For a second, Bianca only stared at him. But the realization was soon upon her: this was the man who'd bought her father's house! He was the new owner, and he'd arrived earlier than she'd anticipated.

Now she was truly in trouble. If he was already moving in, how would she be able to continue her search for the treasure? She felt her blood drain from her face as nausea threatened to overwhelm her. She had to think fast. The only thing she could do was to try and bluff her way through this. But she wouldn't leave this house before she had found what she'd come for. No matter the cost.

"Signore, this is my house. I inherited it from my dear father. You're trespassing. Leave!" Bianca lifted her chin in the same way she did to dismiss suitors she had no interest in. When she caught Lorenzo's gaze on her, she was surprised to see a hint of delight in them as well as a little smile playing around his kissable lips.

CHAPTER

FIVE

Lorenzo's heart skipped a beat. The beautiful woman in his bed wasn't a whore. And for some strange reason, this delighted him. However, this newfound knowledge did nothing to bring down his raging hard-on. Having feasted on her sweet cunt and brought her to an earth-shattering orgasm had gotten him even hornier than he'd been when he first saw her in his bed.

"Signorina Greco?"

She nodded. "Bianca Greco."

"Lorenzo Conti, at your service." He bowed his head slightly, but did nothing to cover his naked body. He'd seen the way she'd glanced at his cock, and frankly, he'd liked it. And he wasn't going to deprive her of the sight, decorum be damned.

"May I assume you haven't spoken to your father's solicitor, Signore Mancini, yet?"

"I only arrived today after receiving the terrible news of my dear father's death." She sniffed.

"My condolences, Signorina. However, I have to inform you that this is not your house anymore."

"But—" she interrupted.

Lorenzo held up his hand, suddenly realizing that his other hand was still clutching her thigh. But as long as she wasn't noticing it, he wasn't going to remove it. "Signorina Greco, I purchased the home from your father's estate. In fact, the estate consisted only of debts. Debts that far exceeded the value of this house."

Her eyes went wide with surprise.

"Let me assure you, Signorina, that I've satisfied those debts, but I have taken the house in exchange for those sums of money. It is mine."

"I don't believe you!" She huffed and crossed her arms tighter around the pillow covering her naked body. "You broke in here, and now you're trying to lie your way out of it."

Lorenzo jumped up, outraged. Nobody called him a liar. Jumping off the bed, he marched toward where he'd left his cloak. "I'll prove it to you, Signorina."

He rifled through his clothes and found the piece of paper he'd received earlier. As he walked back to the bed, he noticed her drop her lids, avoiding looking at him. But he'd already caught her. She'd not only stared at his backside when he'd walked away, but also admired his front for longer than any decent woman would admit. And her eyes were shining with desire.

He handed her the paper. "Here's the deed."

Her eyes flew over it before she handed it back to him. Then she met his eyes. Tears brimmed at their rim. "I will not leave. This is my house! The solicitor had no right to sell it."

Lorenzo planted his fists at his hips, fully aware that his erection was pointing at her almost accusingly. And why shouldn't it? She was the reason why he still had this raging hard-on that hadn't been satisfied yet, and which, it seemed, wouldn't be tonight.

"The document is legal, and you know it! This is my house, and I say who can stay and who can't."

"But Signore, I'm still in mourning. I've only just lost my dear father. I'm beside myself with grief." Her eyes looked pleadingly at him.

Mourning? If Bianca was grieving, she sure hadn't shown any of it only minutes earlier when she'd writhed underneath him in obvious ecstasy. If all grieving daughters reacted like this to the death of their beloved fathers, Lorenzo would be stalking every funeral in the city to find his next willing bedmates. If that was how grieving daughters mourned, he wanted a piece of it. A very large piece.

But what he didn't need was a woman in the house. Mourning or not, she had to leave. Not only could he not deal with a woman who seemed to be on the verge of tears, he wouldn't be able to hide his true nature for long. Already now he had to fight his own body to prevent his fangs from lengthening. Her enticing scent and the taste he still carried on his tongue played havoc with his control.

The longer she stayed in his presence the more she would be at risk of him biting her, sinking his fangs into her graceful, long neck and taking her essence into him. And who knew if he could stop? If her blood tasted anything like her sweet cunt, then his control would snap like a little twig under the weight of an elephant. She would have no way of escaping him.

Of course, he could always use his suggestive powers to make her forget the bite, but would *he* be able to forget it, or would he want to come back for more? And he wasn't a long-term kind of man. All he was interested in was a quick fuck and a quick bite, no repeats, no relationships. No emotional commitments. Emotional commitments could get you killed.

They'd almost gotten him killed once already. He wasn't going to make the same mistake twice. It was better to shove this woman out of his life right now and not look back. By tomorrow night she'd be a distant memory. By tomorrow night he'd be in bed with some other doxy before moving onto the next, without even being tempted to have the same woman two nights in a row.

Lorenzo stared at her. She hadn't moved from her position, still clutching the pillow to her chest as if it were a life raft on a sinking ship. The upward tilt of her chin indicated her determination not to let him win. Her eyes gleamed with defiance. She wanted to stay, and she would do anything to keep her home. But he couldn't allow it.

There was only one way to make her leave: he had to make her run from him in panic or disgust. While he could certainly achieve that by flashing his fangs, he couldn't afford that kind of exposure. After the recent attacks by the Guardians, Dante had advised everybody to be more cautious than usual. Lorenzo wouldn't go against that edict.

But there was one other way of making her run away from him. He would show her what a debauched rake he was. And being the well-bred woman he assumed Bianca to be, she would run to save not her life, but her reputation.

"Signorina, the only way you're staying in this house is as my mistress." He looked past her, not keen on seeing the contempt in her face that she must feel for him now. "So, I suggest you get dressed and leave."

He turned away from the bed and reached for his clothes, giving her one last view of his backside before he stepped into his trousers and pulled them up.

Lorenzo congratulated himself. He'd scared her speechless. To do that to a woman was a feat in itself. To accomplish this with a woman who'd given his cock such appreciative glances when she thought he hadn't been looking was a magnificent achievement. He almost felt like patting himself on the back. Nico and Dante would howl with roaring laughter once they heard the story. At least it would make for good entertainment.

It did nothing for his aching cock though.

"What do you expect your mistress to do?"

Lorenzo almost choked on his own saliva. Was she asking him because she was considering his offer? Hell, it hadn't even been an offer. He had no intention of acquiring a mistress. "Signorina—"

"Just tell me what you expect from your mistress."

What would he want from a mistress if he really were in the market for one? "Everything. She has to be uninhibited, open to experimentation, and she has to want it. I don't want a woman who's merely lying on her back. I don't want to fuck a stiff board."

"I understand."

The finality in her words told him that he'd finally managed to dissuade her. He reached for his shirt and put it on. "Fine, then once you're dressed, I'll escort you to a hotel or a boarding house."

"You expect your mistress to live in a hotel or boarding house? I had expected to stay here."

Lorenzo swiveled on his heels, dropping his hands from the buttons he'd been trying to close. He simply stared at her. After all he'd told her, she wanted to be his mistress? This couldn't be happening.

"I would expect you to suck me," he warned her.

Bianca loosened her grip on the pillow and nodded. "I can do that."

Swallowing hard, he pushed his luck further. "I like to take a woman from behind like an animal."

Was he hallucinating, or was the pillow she was holding sliding lower to reveal the top of her breasts?

"So you can get really deep?" Her pink tongue emerged to trace her lower lip. "I like deep."

His legs carried him closer to the bed. "I like to tie my women up so they are at my mercy."

Her hand pushed the pillow further down, revealing one nipple to his hungry gaze. Shocked, he stared at her face. Could he say nothing to shock her? "There are times when I enjoy having somebody else watch me while I fuck my woman."

"Who would you like to watch us?" she asked, her voice low and seductive.

Had she said "us?" Lorenzo felt sweat build on his brow. "A male friend."

"Would he want to join in?"

Knowing Nico, he would, but would Lorenzo want him to? They'd shared women before, but would he want to share Bianca? Hell, what was he even saying? She wasn't his mistress, and she wouldn't become his mistress. Under no circumstances whatsoever!

"Listen, Signorina Greco, I didn't mean—" His next words got stuck in his throat as she moved the pillow and threw it to the foot of the bed, exposing her naked body to him, her legs still spread open, her cunt still glistening from his saliva and her juices.

His brain stopped functioning. Mistress meant sex. Daily sex, hourly sex. Sex whenever he wanted it, without even having to leave the house, without having to go through the whole process of flirting with a woman or without negotiating a purchase.

Lorenzo's gums itched as his sensitive nose filled with her arousal.

"As my mistress you'll live here with me. My house, my rules."

"Rules?" she asked, arching an eyebrow.

"Two rules. Rule one: we sleep during daytime, and the curtains stay closed."

"And rule two?"

"I'll take you whenever and wherever I want, and you won't refuse me."

She looked him up and down, then zeroed in on the massive bulge that tented his trousers. Licking her lips, she purred like a kitten. "Would you like me to try out for the position now?"

CHAPTER

SIX

Bianca knew she'd gone completely mad. His proposal was indecent at best, and no woman in her right mind would have ever accepted it. Unfortunately, she was also desperate. She needed to stay in the house to continue her search, and her ploy of the grieving daughter hadn't softened his heart enough to let her stay.

Now she would stay as his mistress. And maybe that would award her enough freedom to move around the house as she pleased. As long as she pleased him, he probably wouldn't care what she did in the remaining time as long as she kept her real agenda hidden. And if Bianca had learned one thing as a courtesan, it was how to please a man. Lorenzo wouldn't have any complaints, and by the time he tired of her and wanted to move on, she would be long gone anyway. Treasure in hand—whatever it may be.

Bianca watched him as he quickly discarded his clothes and joined her in bed. His eyes swept over her as if he couldn't decide where to start. He looked like a kid who'd received too many presents for Christmas. It appeared that she needed to help him make a decision.

Bianca traced her palm over his cheek and guided his head to her. "Kiss me," she whispered in her most seductive tone and brushed her lips to his.

"And then my body is yours to do with as you please." And only her body. It was all she would give him. This wasn't any different from what she'd done before. For a few more days, she would be somebody's courtesan, but soon, she'd be her own master and make her own decisions. Soon.

His lips were firm as he pressed against her. Then they softened, and suddenly his lips parted, and his tongue swept over her mouth, nudging between the seam of her lips, asking for entry. The moment his tongue slid into her mouth and explored her, she lost all coherent thought. She'd never been kissed like this, not with such fervor, such masterful strokes that left no area unexplored, no corner unclaimed. His mouth all but devoured her as if he was trying to commit her taste to memory to be recalled at will. Relentlessly, Lorenzo tangled with her tongue, licked against her teeth, delved deep into her as if testing the limits of what she would allow. All she could do was cling to him, her arms clutching to his shoulders, her nails digging into his flesh for fear she'd lose her grip on him.

Inside her belly, the fire that had been burning low and steady while they'd talked had reawakened into a blistering inferno, the flames shooting so high, they reached her skin and licked outwards. Did her lover not notice the heat that seeped from her? If he did, it didn't seem to bother him, because his hands roamed freely over her naked skin while his mouth continued its sensual assault, turning her body into a collection of cells controlled only by him.

Wherever his hands went, her body heated under his touch and arched into it to ask for more. Even if she'd wanted to, she wouldn't have been able to stop him. Energy seemed to flow from him and collide with her body's heat, the two forces dancing with each other and engulfing them in a cocoon of lust and desire.

Bianca had never felt so wanton, so absolutely reckless. But instead of every touch and every kiss helping still her thirst for him, it made her want even more. When he ripped his mouth from hers, she felt the loss physically. "No, don't stop," she whimpered. She'd never whimpered before.

"My sweet," he whispered and kissed her throat, tilting it further back so he could reach the sensitive part at the base of it. His lips kissed, his tongue licked, and his teeth scraped against her skin. She shivered involuntarily at the erotic sensation.

"Again," she demanded without thought.

Once more, Lorenzo scraped his teeth against her throat, then pulled back and moved lower. His head dipped to her breasts, taking first one nipple and then the other between his lips. When he sucked the nipple deeper into his mouth and licked his tongue over it, she twisted under his hold, feeling her control slip.

He was turning her into mush. She had to gain the upper hand and show him pleasure. Only then would she remain in control, by robbing his. Her hand slipped down his torso past his muscled, hairless chest, across his ripped abdomen until she reached her destination: the dark thatch of hair between his legs where his cock stood erect.

Bianca wrapped her hand around his shaft, surprised to find that it didn't quite span around his girth.

"Oh, God!" he gasped, temporarily releasing her nipple.

He was too big. Too thick. And long too, she noticed as she stroked all the way down to the base. As hard as marble, yet his skin was as soft as that of a baby. She loved those contrasts in a man, always had. Baby soft skin covering a marble hard cock. The perfect combination. She couldn't wait to feel him inside her and stretch her cunny. None of her former lovers had been that big. But she didn't fear it, didn't fear him.

From what he'd done to her earlier when she'd thought herself in the midst of a dream, she knew he was a patient lover, a considerate one who would make certain she was ready to take him. She'd already orgasmed once under his expert mouth and was again oozing wetness. She was ready for him, her pearl throbbing in anticipation.

But she wanted to drive him wild first. Using all her strength, she pushed against his heavy body. He released her breast, startled, a question already forming on his lips, but it never emerged. A second later, he landed with his back in the sheets as she scooted down his body.

"What?" he gasped and gave her a surprised look.

Bianca didn't waste any time and lowered her head over his groin, guiding his erection to her lips. He stilled instantly, and she could see him watch her as she took her first lick against the velvety soft head.

"Darling," he groaned, his voice hoarse.

"Mmm." Bianca lapped against his cock once more, sliding her tongue all the way down and then back up before she opened her mouth and took him inside. Painstakingly slowly, she slid down on him, taking him as deep as she could. He was more than she could handle with her mouth alone, so she added her hand, wrapping it around the base and pumping him in concert with her lips.

"Fuck!" he moaned out. "You shouldn't..."

Was he trying to protest? Yet, his hips bucked toward her, fucking into her mouth in a steady rhythm. His hands combed through her hair, holding her steady rather than forcing her down on him. Some of her lovers used to direct her head so that they could fuck her face, and she'd always hated it. But Lorenzo used his hands to caress her scalp, to stroke her, not to pound her head against his groin so she would take him deeper.

She appreciated that in him and thanked him by increasing her sucking motion and working him deeper into her mouth.

"Bianca, no. Stop."

Suddenly his hands tugged at her hair, pulling her head away from him, making his cock slip from her mouth. She stared at him, her eyes widening in surprise, and looked into the face of a distraught man.

"I can't do this," he claimed and shook his head.

She gave his cock a pointed look. By her estimations, he was about ten seconds from climaxing. "Of course, you can." Was he anxious about coming in her mouth?

He shook his head and disentangled his limbs from her, scooting to the edge of the bed, where he dropped his legs to the ground, turning his back to her. "I can't do this. I don't want your body."

He'd changed his mind? He was going to throw her out after all? A breath dislodged from her lungs and traveled upwards. She tensed her body, not wanting it to escape sounding like a sob. Had she done something wrong? Did he not like the way she'd sucked him?

"You can stay for a few days until we've figured something out. But you can't be my mistress. Rest. I'll see you tomorrow."

He leapt from the bed and gathered his clothes so fast she had no chance to hold him back. A moment later, the door closed behind him. She was alone. And Lorenzo didn't want her body.

That knowledge was like a slap in the face.

CHAPTER

SEVEN

Something was seriously wrong with him. Lorenzo bolted for the next room and sought shelter from his warring emotions and from the enthralling naked Bianca in the next bedchamber. When had he ever developed scruples about fucking a woman? This wasn't the first time he was taking advantage of somebody, and it wasn't going to be the last.

Exactly, his cock chimed in. *So, let's go back in there and do it.*

Lorenzo stared down at his hard-on and felt like slapping it into submission. He wasn't going back into that bedchamber and take advantage of a young woman who'd had no choice but to offer her body to him so she would have a roof over her head. Not even *he* would sink that low.

He yanked his trousers up and pulled his shirt on, fastening the buttons quickly before he could change his mind. God, Bianca had gone so far as to suck him with those amazing lips, running her tongue along his shaft so tenderly, he'd thought he would burst. While he knew she wasn't an innocent and clearly not a virgin, no decent woman should be subjected to having to service a stranger in such manner, no matter what hard times she'd fallen onto. It wasn't her fault that her father had gambled away all the money.

Lorenzo stopped in his thoughts. He'd left money with the solicitor to give to the daughter so she would have something to tide her over. Had the bastard pocketed the money himself and not given it to her? Was that why she was destitute? No. Now he remembered. Bianca hadn't even seen the solicitor yet. She'd arrived and come straight to the house. No wonder she didn't know about the money, didn't realize she wasn't completely penniless. This could be corrected.

He would send word to Signore Mancini, making him aware that Bianca was temporarily staying at his house and that he should have the money delivered to her there. That would take care of it. Once she had the money, surely, she'd be more than happy to depart and leave him to his debauchery.

Once she was gone, he would be no danger to her anymore. But right now, she was in danger of him taking the last bit of her innocence and if he lost control, the last drop of her blood. And she didn't deserve that, particularly because Lorenzo actually liked her.

Her strength, when she'd been confronted with the news that the house wasn't hers anymore, had impressed him, and her determination to do anything to survive was admirable. He couldn't bring himself to break the spirit of such a woman. It wasn't her fault that she was in the situation she was in. She shouldn't have to be the one to pay for her father's sins.

Lorenzo finished dressing and stalked down the dark stairs, ignoring the enticing scent drifting to him from her bedchamber. He needed to get out of the house for a few hours while night was still upon them. And maybe somehow he could come up with a plan to help Bianca pick up her life and make a new one now that her father was dead.

If he was lucky, he'd find Nico at one of his favorite hells and enlist him in making a few inquires for him.

Half an hour later, Lorenzo marched into a nightspot which was part brothel, part drinking hall, and picked up Nico's scent. He breathed a sigh of relief and headed for the upper floor where small rooms lined the long, dark hallway. The smell of sex, sweat, and unwashed bodies assaulted his senses, making his body aroused and repulsed at the same time. He'd spent many a night at this establishment to slake the unquenchable lust that always coursed through his body. He'd never known any different. It was a difficult vice to control, particularly for a vampire like him. His heightened vampire senses made all temptations that were thrown at him even more irresistible. Once a long time ago, he'd given in and instead of simply giving his body what he needed, he'd opened his heart. Only to have it ripped out in the process.

Elle. He hadn't thought of her in years; he'd suppressed the memory of her quite successfully for a very long time. He didn't understand why he was thinking of her now, other than the fact that maybe Bianca had reminded him a little of her. The same round eyes that could mimic innocence quite effectively.

Elle had been such a sweet and giving woman, and he'd fallen so hard for her that he'd believed that she would accept him for what he was. When he'd confessed to her that he was a vampire, she'd simply closed her eyes for a moment, taken a deep breath, and then proclaimed that she loved him anyway.

What a big lie it had all been. In truth, she'd been disgusted with him the first time she'd surprised him when feeding, but she'd hidden it well. She'd still warmed his bed and lulled him into the belief that she loved him. And if he weren't such a light sleeper, he would have gone to his grave believing in her love.

But he'd woken, finding her standing next to his bed, ready to plunge a stake into his heart. At that moment, his entire world had collapsed. His heart had turned to stone. Yet, he hadn't been able to kill her for her treachery. He had still loved her then. His only option had been to erase from her memory everything that had happened, but there had been too much to erase. Her mind couldn't cope, and she'd gone insane. She'd ended up in an asylum where she'd killed herself a few years later. All because of him.

While he still had to use his skill of wiping humans' memories when he fed from them, he made sure to rarely feed from the same person twice. But he'd never gotten involved with another human woman for fear the fate that had befallen Elle would be repeated. So he'd confined himself mostly to whores from whom he didn't feed so he wouldn't have to use his vampire powers over and over again. A prolonged involvement with a human was too dangerous in his eyes, the repeated erasing of his victims' memories too risky. By separating sex from feeding, he had managed to keep himself under control and lose neither his head nor his heart.

Lorenzo pushed the memories of his past away and inhaled deeply to find Nico's whereabouts. As on so many nights, Nico was hard at work fucking his way through Venice, and Lorenzo had no qualms about interrupting him. It wasn't as if this were a novelty.

He pushed the door open without knocking and entered the dimly lit room. Nico's head snapped toward him, his alert body instantly relaxing when he recognized his visitor.

He winked. "Wanna join in?"

Did he? Lorenzo glanced at the woman, who was sprawled across the bed on her front, her ass high in the air as Nico's hands held her hips tightly while he repeatedly thrust into her from his kneeling position behind her. Lorenzo smiled. It was one thing he and his friend had in common: they liked to take their women from behind for maximum impact.

"She can suck you," Nico offered. "Won't you, love?"

The woman lifted her head at his question and grinned at Lorenzo, revealing a crooked front tooth. While his cock was hard from the scent of arousal in the room, he merely shook his head. He wasn't here for sex. Hell, if he'd wanted sex, he could have had it at home with a much more appealing partner.

Then why didn't we? his over-eager appendage queried.

"Some other time," he assured Nico. "I was wondering whether we could talk."

"Sure, what's going on?" Nico continued plunging into the woman while she dropped her head back down onto the pillow and moaned into it.

Lorenzo rolled his eyes. Fine with him if Nico thought he could concentrate on a conversation as well as on continuing to fuck like a champion. "Can you make some inquires for me?"

"About?" Nico gritted his teeth and grunted, his thrusts turning more ferocious as he went on.

"The house I bought, the heiress showed up tonight thinking it was still hers."

"Oh?"

"I need to find out more about her. The name's Bianca Greco. Can you check with your sources and find out where she came from and why she wasn't with her father? And why she hasn't been to see the solicitor yet."

"Who's the solicitor?" Nico asked and slapped the woman's backside.

"Signore Mancini, his office is—"

"I know where he is. Not a problem."

"I gave Mancini money for her. Have him send it to my house."

"Your house?" Nico frowned.

"Yes, the woman is staying at my new house."

Nico abruptly stopped in his motions and slipped out of the woman.

"What?" she complained.

"Later," he pacified her, then stared back at Lorenzo. "She's at your house?"

Lorenzo knew exactly why Nico was so surprised. Nobody ever stayed with him. All his sexual escapades were conducted at other people's homes, at inns, or brothels. Never in his home. He tried to downplay the incident. "She had nowhere to go."

Now Nico rose from the bed, oblivious to his nudity. Not that Lorenzo cared either way. "You have a woman staying at your house?"

"Don't make it sound as if this is such an extraordinary event." It was, but he wasn't going to quarrel with Nico about it.

"Tell me more. Why do you want me to investigate her? Could it be that you're actually interested in a woman for something other than fucking?"

Lorenzo glared at his friend. "Don't be an ass. I have no interest in her. All I want to know is whether there's something I have to watch out for, considering she's staying for a few days. It's simply a security precaution."

Hell, who was he kidding? Bianca intrigued him, and he wanted to know more about her background. Asking her outright was out of the question—he didn't want to reveal to her that he was even remotely interested in her. What if she was some sort of gold digger, who figured she could get her father's house back if she made nice with him and ensnared him in her net, hoping he'd marry her? He didn't need those kinds of complications. It was better to be prepared.

CHAPTER

EIGHT

Bianca woke around midday. It had been hard to get back to sleep after Lorenzo had left her aroused and unsatisfied. She'd never felt so empty. Why hadn't he finished what he'd started? He'd been hard, and had to have been aching for release, just as she had. Yet he'd denied them both what would have been a night of absolute pleasure.

She threw the covers back and dropped her legs over the side of the bed. Maybe she should be happy that he'd decided to behave like a gentleman after all and not insisted on her paying for her stay by acting as his mistress. In fact, she should be very happy about it. For once, she wouldn't have to pay with her body. It was a welcome change. But it was confusing to say the least.

Bianca knew she had a good body. Plenty of men had told her so, and she'd even seen it in Lorenzo's eyes when he'd gawked at her in her nudity. Had something repulsed him? Had he not wanted her to suck him? Darn, why was she even second-guessing herself? He didn't want her to be his mistress. She should rejoice in that fact. And he hadn't thrown her out yet, which meant she could do what she'd come to do: find the treasure.

With renewed determination, she jumped out of bed, careful not to make too much noise. She'd heard Lorenzo come back before sunrise and enter her father's old room. It appeared that was where he'd made his bed for the night. He hadn't attempted to sneak back into her bed, even though she'd half wished it. Bianca shook her head. It was stupid to think like that. She didn't want him. He was merely a nuisance she had to deal with while she was searching for her father's treasure. Nothing more.

Since she had taken a bath the night before, she washed very quickly with the cold water from the pitcher on the commode, cleaned her teeth and pulled out a clean dress from her bag. If what Lorenzo had said was true—that he slept during the day—then she would have the house to herself to search at her heart's content. She didn't want to waste another minute. The faster she found what she was looking for, the faster she'd be able to leave.

Bianca tiptoed past Lorenzo's chamber and hurried down the stairs. She would start her search in the rooms farthest from where Lorenzo was sleeping. Since she'd already examined the kitchen the night before, and since it was the least likely place her father would have hidden anything, she skipped that room and headed for the parlor. Her father had spent much time in this room, and the ornate decorations throughout it provided plenty of opportunities to disguise a hidden compartment or a false floor.

Systematically, she went to work. What made the work somewhat tedious was the fact that she couldn't simply rip things apart and leave them that way. Because Lorenzo was in the house, she needed to make sure he didn't realize what she was doing. When she pried a loose wooden panel off the ornate cabinet that had been built into the wall and found only dust and cobwebs behind it, she had to jam it back into its old position. Bianca used her elbow to put enough force behind it until the loose panel was sticking again.

Her hands were already dusty as was her dress from sliding against the walls and the furniture, not to mention from crawling on the floor to peek under furniture in case her father had stuck something to the bottom of a piece.

After lifting the ornate rugs in the parlor and finding nothing underneath them, she abandoned the room and went back to the kitchen. Her stomach rumbled. The larder was virtually empty, but the things she'd always liked were there: a jar of olives, hard cheese, and a partial leg of dry cured ham. She inhaled and cut herself thick slices of cheese and ham and spooned a large helping of olives onto a plate.

As she devoured the first slice of ham, she realized how hungry she'd been. Within minutes, the plate was empty, and she felt much better. It was easier to resume her search with a full belly.

Her father's study was her next destination. When she entered the room, it was dim and badly lit. While the window was unobstructed by any drapes, the early afternoon sun didn't reach into the room, as its only window backed up to another home which prevented the sun's rays from reaching it. She couldn't understand why her father had ever chosen such an unsuitable room for his study.

Bianca lit a candle and appreciated its soft glow as it brought light into the room. While the study was small, the walls were stuffed with books from top to bottom. Many were covered with dust. She sighed. It would take her hours to remove book after book to see whether anything was hidden behind them. She set the candlestick with the lit candle to one side onto a shelf, so the light flooded over her shoulder, and went to work.

She'd completely forgotten how many books her father had collected during his lifetime. He'd often read to her as a child, before they'd fallen out, before he'd gotten it into his head to marry her off to the highest bidder. Bianca pushed these thoughts aside and tried to concentrate on the task at hand. The hours seemed to fly by as she handled book after book.

"What are you looking for?"

Bianca shot up from her crouching position and turned in the same instance, her heart beating frantically at the shock of being discovered. Lorenzo, dressed in breeches and a shirt which was open at the neck glowered over her, his eyes narrowed in suspicion.

"I..." She swallowed hard, trying to buy herself some time. "I hope I didn't wake you."

His jaw clenched. "I asked what you're looking for."

It appeared that he wasn't easily dissuaded. Only her talent for acting could help her now. She thrust her chin up and pursed her lips. "If you must know..." Then she cast her eyes to the side and sighed heavily. "I was trying to find an old book my dear father read to me when I was a child." She dropped her head toward her chest, letting out a heavy breath, sniffing in the process. "I wanted something to remember him by."

Bianca forced herself to think of the first few days in Florence, the time when she'd had to live on the streets, the fear and the humiliation. It made the tears come easily—tears she needed now to fool Lorenzo into thinking she was mourning her father.

When she lifted her face back to him, the first tear rolled down her cheek. And with delight, she saw Lorenzo's expression change from suspicion to compassion. Ah, yes, she could still play any man like a fiddle. They had manipulated her for long enough; now it was her turn to manipulate them.

Feeling his fingers stroke over her cheek was more than she had expected. His show of compassion took her off kilter, making her feel something she hadn't felt in a long time: that somebody cared about her.

"I'm so sorry for your loss," he whispered, his hand still stroking her cheek, his body suddenly so much closer, close enough to touch.

She inhaled his scent, the comforting smell of a strong man, a protector, somebody who would take away the pain. When his other hand came up and pulled her closer, she buried her face in his shirt, feeling his hot skin underneath. His arms came around her, pulling her in for an embrace too close to merely comfort. He pressed her against his chest and stroked his hands over her back, caressing her.

"Shh, my darling. Everything will be all right."

She felt his lips on the top of her head, kissing her hair at the same time as his hand loosened the bun at her nape to allow her hair to cascade over her back. His fingers brushing against her neck made her shiver.

It felt so good to be in his arms, to feel protected and safe, even if it was only for a few minutes. Bianca sighed as her tears stopped flowing and raised her face to him. His eyes had an orange glow to them, the candle light reflecting in his irises more intensely than she'd ever seen in anyone's eyes.

Without thinking, she rose on her toes and stretched toward him. His eyes widened in surprise, and a moment later his lips met hers.

Lorenzo's spicy scent seeped into her mouth as she parted her lips for him. At first, he only teased gently, licking against her lips, briefly sweeping his tongue against her teeth, then withdrawing. Was he going to stop again? She couldn't let that happen. She wanted to be kissed by him, to feel him devour her.

Her hands gripped the lapels of his shirt, drawing him closer. Her action elicited a deep groan from him. A second later, his hand slipped to her buttocks, and he pressed her against his loins.

Bianca gasped when she felt the hard outline of his erection pressing into her stomach and rejoiced at the same time: Lorenzo wanted her. His arousal was evidence of his desire for her. Boldly, she snaked out her tongue and slipped it between his lips, searching for its counterpart. Determined not to let him get away, she stroked against him, the texture and taste of him sending tantalizing tingles rippling along her skin and brushing over her sensitive nipples.

A shiver went through her when he responded to her by angling his head and urging her mouth to open wider. His exploration was gentle at first. Licking and stroking, he found his way, dancing with her tongue and teasing white hot sensations from her body. She was on fire.

As an experienced courtesan, she knew how to please men, and she knew how to fake her reactions to them, but with Lorenzo she didn't need to fake any of her reactions. On the contrary, she would have had difficulty hiding them from him. Her body wasn't her own anymore. Under the ministrations of his talented lips, every part of her body became alive with desires she'd never voiced. Desires which were only intensified with the press of his cock against her. For the first time in her life, she wanted to let herself go and respond to a man without pretense, without lies, and without holding back.

CHAPTER
NINE

Bianca was even more pliable in his arms than she'd been the night before. It did nothing to assuage Lorenzo's need to have her underneath him. It only fueled his desire for her. His brain had long ago switched off. In fact, the moment her tears had fallen and he'd taken her into his arms and felt her warmth, he'd been unable to think through his next actions. Now it was too late.

Her kiss was pure abandon, her hands in his hair an unexpected delight. And those voluptuous breasts that were crushed against his chest? They were too tempting not to touch. Without interrupting his kiss, Lorenzo drew back slightly to slide one hand over her torso and cup one breast.

She moaned into his mouth, and he soaked up her excitement, allowing her to get comfortable with his touch before he slid his thumb over the center of her breast. The nipple he encountered through the fabric was hard and stood at attention. Just how he liked it.

Eager for more, he tugged on her dress. A ripping sound alerted him to the fact that he'd been too rough and torn her bodice. But the reward was too sweet to regret the action. Lorenzo freed one breast from its confines and settled it in his palm, cradling the soft flesh as his thumb slid over the hard nipple once more.

A strangled gasp from her lips made him interrupt his kiss to take in a breath. Bianca arched her head back, thrusting her breasts closer to him. Her eyes were closed, and her lips looked swollen from his kiss. Red, moist, and sinful. His gaze dropped to her neck which she so obligingly offered to him. As if she knew what he wanted.

Lorenzo's fangs itched for a bite, for a taste of her sweet blood. But not yet.

He lowered his head to her exposed breast and planted open-mouthed kisses along her skin, nibbling his way to the center, where her rosy nipple waited for him as he rolled it between his thumb and forefinger, making sure it remained as hard as he liked it.

Lorenzo pressed her against the bookcase at her back, rattling a few volumes, as his lips closed around the tasty little bud and sucked. He opened his mouth wider to take more of her flesh between his lips. How a woman like Bianca wasn't flat on her back being devoured by countless men twenty-four hours a day was beyond his comprehension. If she were his, she'd never leave his bed. She'd never get dressed.

As his left hand went for her other breast, he was unable to control his vampire strength. The fabric ripped, making her bodice gape open in the middle. His lips went for her second breast before she could even voice a protest—if she'd wanted to. As he sucked the tit into his mouth and licked its responsive peak, his hands ripped her dress further.

He needed to feel her, to touch her silken skin, to kiss her naked body.

Bianca's hands stroked his chest and tugged on his shirt, sliding it off his shoulders. Lorenzo rid himself of it without thought. All he did was moan out his pleasure at the feeling of those soft hands on his naked skin, touching him, exploring him.

When her palm suddenly cupped his erection through his trousers, he ripped his mouth from her willing tit. Using all his strength, he forced his vampire side back below the surface, his control weaker than it had ever been. Never had sex made him struggle with controlling his vampire powers like this. If he didn't get himself under control quickly, she would realize what he was.

There was only one way for him to regain his control: by taking control of her and slaking the lust that currently careened through his body like a carriage whose horses were charging toward a ravine. Lorenzo's heart raced in concert with those beasts as if wanting to outrun them.

Perspiration had already built on his face and neck, and now rivulets of sweat cascaded down his ripped chest despite the coolness of the room and the lack of a fire in the study. Bianca's body had more fire than he'd ever need to warm himself. Her heat was contagious. Her wanton behavior and her willingness to let him rip her dress to shreds without any protest spilling over her lips, was something that would have appalled decent society.

But decent wasn't what Lorenzo wanted. The more indecent, the more likely he could take what he needed from her. His body ached physically from trying to hold back the monster inside him. The pain his cock experienced wasn't any less severe. Straining heavy against his breeches, the buttons of his flap dug into his flesh. The pain of it was the only thing holding back his orgasm. And he wasn't even inside her yet.

Lorenzo gulped down air when he suddenly felt both her hands on his breeches, releasing the top button. His cock rejoiced at the prospect of feeling her hot hands on him. "Yes," he mumbled. "Take me out."

Moments later, Bianca freed his shaft and wrapped her hands around his hard flesh. For a few seconds, all he could do was breathe, trying not to think of what she was doing for fear it would snap his control entirely. His hand shot to hers, stilling her movements before she could complete her stroking motion.

As he lifted his head from her breasts and looked at her flushed face, he realized she was as mesmerized as he was. Her lids were at half-mast, her lower lip pulled in between her lips, held there by her beautiful white teeth. A shimmer of sweat glistened on her skin, more than any lady would ever want to be seen with. Yet Bianca made no attempt at hiding her excitement.

Unable to resist the woman who so firmly held his cock in her hands, he captured her lips again and held nothing back. Like an ancient Roman, he conquered, cutting down walls that never existed, flattening the territory he claimed. She welcomed him with more enthusiasm and skill than any well-bred young woman should have.

Releasing her hands, Lorenzo lifted her into his arms, ignoring the way she stroked his eager cock. Clutching her to him, he swept the desk clean with one hand, paper and writing implements scattering to the floor, before he laid her on her back, spreading her legs apart as he stepped back.

One last rip and the dress was now in two pieces. His hungry eyes devoured the sumptuous feast before him. Creamy flesh, lush curves, deep valleys. Yet, one valley was still covered by her drawers. He snagged the thin white fabric between his fingers and tore. The sound of ripping fabric echoed in the study. Only Bianca's breathing was louder.

As he pulled the fabric away from her skin and exposed her beautiful cunt, memories of the night before flooded his mind. Her taste, the smell, the way she'd twisted and flexed underneath him. Only this time, he'd explore her body in a different way—much deeper.

Lorenzo leaned over her, pushing back the hair from her neck and sunk his lips onto her pulse. It fluttered in an excited tattoo, tap-tap-tap, faster, and ever faster. As he kissed her neck, his cock settled at her core. His hips moved back and forth, letting his erection slide over her center. With every slide against her flesh, his control moved one iota closer to snapping.

He had no patience for a long, drawn-out lovemaking session. Next time, he'd fuck her slowly, but this time, he had to take her fast. Next time? He wasn't planning a next time. He shouldn't, yet his body didn't seem to agree with his mind in this case. One time wasn't enough.

Good, twice then, he conceded as he fought with himself. He'd fuck her twice, right here, right now. Drawing his hips back, he brought his cock in line with her cunt and pushed forward. With one powerful thrust he seated himself in her tight channel as her muscles gripped him and her juices drenched him.

"Fuck!" he ground out, clenching his jaw. There'd been no barrier, a fact he'd guessed from the way she'd opened her legs for him: not like a shy virgin, but like a woman who knew what was coming. He welcomed the knowledge that she wasn't a virgin. At least that meant he could fuck her hard, because that was what he needed.

His shaft slammed into her, and Bianca let out a moan which was drowned out by an ever more powerful groan coming from him. In a frantic rhythm his cock set for him, he withdrew, then thrust into her again, her legs around his hips aiding the movements when she twined her feet behind his back, locking him in.

Her breasts bounced with each thrust, up and down, side to side. Lorenzo sank his lips onto them, alternately sucking her nipples and licking her flesh. But if he'd thought that by fucking her, he'd gain back control over his vampire side, he was mistaken.

His fangs lengthened, making it impossible to keep the sharp tips hidden in his mouth. They pushed past his lips and nudged against her plump tits. Lorenzo worked his hips frantically, driving his aching cock in and out of her in the hope his release would help him gain control, but the more he fucked her—the more her warm sheath cradled him—the less he was able to exercise control.

Her fingernails raked over his back, holding him firmly to her, and her heels dug into his backside, pushing him deeper inside her with every thrust. Her hips gyrated against his, and the sounds of pleasure that left her lips could not be drowned out by anything but the sound of blood rushing from his fangs down into his throat.

He needed her blood. Now. Only then would he find true release with her. The realization hit him like a ship slamming into a pier.

His fangs scraped against the pink flesh of her tits, grazing her. A drop of blood appeared on her skin. It was miniscule, yet its potency was undeniable.

"Lorenzo, now, please," she mumbled, slamming her hips into him, grabbing his ass with her hands to force him to plunge deeper.

With a roar, he jerked back. No! If he continued, he'd suck her dry, his control all but vanished. Despite Bianca's hands and legs gripping him tightly, he pulled out of her and averted his eyes, tilting his head away from her.

Her protest was instant. "Please, don't stop. Not now."

"I can't," he pressed out and headed for the door faster than if the rising sun were on his heels. The scent of her blood chased him all the way to his bedchamber. And the scent of her cunt was still on his cock, a painful reminder that he hadn't found release, nor had he granted her the climax she'd been so close to.

Bianca was no good for him. She was too much of a temptation. He didn't understand why he lost control with her when he'd never had any problems keeping himself in check when he'd fucked the whores he usually frequented. Instead of sex easing the strain on controlling his vampire powers, it had made it harder to control. He'd always been able to let his vampire side emerge at will—not with Bianca. When he was near her, his entire body screamed for him to claim her.

He couldn't let a woman have such power over him. He'd allowed it once. It had nearly cost him his life. No matter how much he wanted to slake his lust with her, he couldn't risk it.

Bianca had to leave.

CHAPTER

TEN

Almost dizzy, Bianca slipped off her father's old writing desk. With shaking hands, she pulled on the shredded fabric of her dress to cover her torso. The place between her legs throbbed uncontrollably. Frustration made way for surprise, then embarrassment, then anger. How dare Lorenzo fuck her with such raw passion and then leave her before finishing?

Her chest heaved, her body still trying to come down from the peak it had nearly reached. She'd been so close to a most monumental climax only to come crashing down like a wave crashed onto the sandy shore without ever having reached its highest crest.

Bianca wanted to howl in frustration. But what she wanted even more was for Lorenzo to continue. Holding her dress together in the front, she ran out of the study and headed for the stairs. If Lorenzo had lost his erection and hadn't been able to achieve release with her, then she'd do anything to get him back into the right mood so he could finish what they'd started.

She had enough experience to know how to rouse a wilting cock. Lorenzo's words that he couldn't do this could only mean one thing: his manhood had a little problem performing. Even though this seemed some-

256

what strange given that his cock had been harder than anything she'd ever felt, just because he was hard didn't mean he could find release. Maybe he needed more stimulation.

Without knocking, Bianca opened the door to her father's bedchamber and entered.

Lorenzo stood next to the bed, closing the top button on his breeches. His head spun to her instantly, his eyes glaring at her in fury. "Leave! Now!"

His voice was a thunder that would have frightened a lesser woman, but not Bianca. Most dogs that barked didn't bite. Men were just the same. The louder they yelled, the softer they were on the inside.

"No! I refuse to let you treat me like this. And I won't leave!"

The rumble coming from his throat sounded more like the growl of an animal than that of a man. "I apologize for what happened in the study," he ground out through clenched teeth, the cords on his neck straining, ready to snap in an instant. "It won't happen again."

"Well, at least *that* we agree on."

He nodded stiffly then turned his back. "Then please remove yourself from my presence."

"I will do nothing of the sort."

His shoulders tensed visibly as his hands balled into fists, the knuckles turning white. "What do you want from me? A new dress? I'll buy you ten new dresses for the one I ruined."

Bianca took a few steps toward him.

"Don't come any closer!"

Shocked by his harsh tone, she stopped. "I'm not interested in a new dress. But I can help you."

"Help me?" The incredulous tone in his voice was something she had expected. Most men couldn't deal with issues related to their manhood. And if a woman pointed them out, they turned defensive.

"Yes. There could be very simple reasons why you couldn't find release. I can—"

Lorenzo spun to face her so fast, she instinctively took a step back.

"You think I couldn't perform?" His question was turned into an accusation by the way he bit it out. His eyes narrowed, and his jaw clenched. "I assure you, Signorina, if I wanted to find release in your body, I could have done so several times."

Bianca snorted. *Arrogant rake!*

All she was doing was try to help him over his problem, and what did he do? Deny he had a problem. "I don't believe you."

"Signorina! Are you calling me a liar?"

She shrugged, letting her hands fall away to the sides, allowing her dress to gape open over her naked breasts. Lowering her lids slightly, she glanced at his breeches. The bulge underneath it was still visible. He was just as hard as before.

"I'm merely stating what I see. You didn't finish, not only leaving yourself unsatisfied, but also me." Bianca looked past him, trying to appear unaffected by the ever growing erection behind his trousers and the wet spot that had started seeping through to the surface. "I expect a man to satisfy me. Otherwise, I don't see how I can pretend he's a good lover."

From the corner of her eye, she noticed his lips forming into a thin line. She could fairly see him fuming. "Signorina! Watch your words!"

Turning as if attempting to leave, she delivered the last blow. "And you, Signore, are a useless lover."

Before she could take her second step toward the door, Lorenzo grabbed her from behind and lifted her. A moment later, she landed on the bed, face down, her breath rushing out of her lungs.

"A useless lover? I think not!"

His hands stripped the dress from her, and more ripping sounds indicated that he was stripping himself at the same time. Then he latched onto her hips and pulled them back, bringing her onto her knees, before his rock-hard cock plunged deep into her still wet channel.

The force with which he penetrated her would have knocked her off the bed on the other side, had he not held her hips in a vice grip.

"I'll teach you to call me a liar!"

Fury still colored his words as he delivered his next thrust with the same intensity as the first. Bianca gasped, pulling in a breath of air, unable to do anything but receive his cock. None of her previous lovers had ever dared to take her this hard, this fast, this furiously.

"God, yes!" she whimpered, surprised at the intense pleasure she felt as his body slammed against hers repeatedly, plunging deeper with every thrust.

Lorenzo grunted as if in response to her exclamation.

Bianca tried to lift her head from the sheets she was pressed into to get onto her hands, but he pressed a hand onto her upper back, holding her down.

"You had your chance to escape," he hissed and sliced in and out of her.

"No escape," was all she could press out, before needing another breath. "More." Since when did she resort to begging?

His second hand went back to her hips as his erection suddenly pulled out of her.

"No!" she howled. Was he going to stop once more, leaving her unsatisfied? She reached behind her, trying to grab him and pull him back, but he snatched her hand.

"Don't!" he warned. "One touch, and I'll spill."

She felt him pull away, but a moment later, his warm breath was on her sex. He spread her wider, exposing her to him in a way she should have felt embarrassed about. But there was no time for embarrassment, because the next thing she felt was his tongue licking down her cleft.

Her body trembled from the sensual assault, but there was no reprieve. His tongue forged forward, licking over her sensitive pearl. Flames danced on her skin, turning her body into a raging inferno. Perspiration pearled off her naked flesh. And all the while, Lorenzo licked the sensitive bundle of nerves that threatened to turn her into a whimpering woman out of control.

His teeth grazed her folds, sending a shiver through her entire body. "Yes!"

When he sucked her pearl between his lips, pulling it into his mouth, everything shattered. The trembling in her body intensified, indicating the approach of a release he'd previously denied her. She didn't fight it, but greeted its arrival, letting herself fall into the depth of its intensity.

Waves of pleasure poured through her, obliterating everything else in her mind. Only when she felt a widening and stretching of her channel did she realize that Lorenzo's cock was back inside her, riding her hard and fast. Her muscles gripped him, not wanting him to leave her again.

His deep groan and the tensing of his body signaled the loss of his control. A moment later, the warmth of his seed flooded her. And for once in her life, she didn't force him out of her, didn't care about the precautions she should have taken to prevent conception. For once in her life, she welcomed her lover's seed with a greed she couldn't explain with anything but madness. Because it was madness to allow this stranger to take her to such heights and make her submit to him as she'd never submitted to any man.

CHAPTER

ELEVEN

As the last ripples of his orgasm ebbed, Lorenzo felt his fangs retreat by a fraction. They'd descended the moment Bianca had stepped into the chamber. He'd been forced to hide them from her by taking her from behind when more than anything he'd wanted to see her face when he made her come.

"Do you still cling to your previous opinion, Signorina?"

The woman had the audacity to chuckle at his question. Lorenzo dug his hands into her hair and lifted her head from the pillows without dislodging his cock from her soft cave. He wasn't ready to leave that pleasurable channel for a while. Besides, he was still as rock-hard as earlier and needed to get off once more to regain control over his body.

"Do not toy with me, Signorina. As you can see, savage things happen when you provoke me."

"Lorenzo, don't you think it's time you called me by my given name?" She paused and let out a delightful, soft sigh. "Considering you're still inside me and clearly eager for a repeat."

Lorenzo withdrew from her sheath until only his bulbous head was still inside her. Then, painstakingly slowly, he sliced back into her, his movement slow and measured this time. "Not such a useless lover after all, hmm?" Then he tried out her name. "Bianca." And the way it rolled off his tongue and over his lips felt good.

She pulled forward, making his cock slide half-way out before she pushed back into his loins, taking him deep. "Very useful, particularly if he can do this again so soon."

"He can." Lorenzo smiled to himself. Who would have thought the gently raised daughter of a Venice merchant found such pleasure in the carnal arts when she should have no such knowledge in the first place? Had she perhaps been married and was now widowed?

He shook his head. It didn't matter why she responded to him. He wasn't interested in more than just slaking his lust with her. And if she enjoyed this, even better.

His fangs still itched for a bite, but fucking her in such a rough fashion had taken the edge off his need. However, the urge to take her blood hadn't disappeared. Maybe a second fucking would put that need to rest. Only this time, he wanted slow and gentle, but he couldn't change his position, couldn't allow her to see his face. He knew his eyes were still glowing the way they always did when his need for blood was strong. And the sight of his fangs would frighten her and make her retreat.

Not that he didn't like to fuck a woman from behind. He'd always loved it: the control, the view of her round cheeks, and the fact that he could reach deeper into her than in any other position.

"So, you like my cock?" Lorenzo asked, sliding back and forth in her in slow motion. Strangely enough, he wanted words of approval to come over her lips.

"Are you fishing for compliments?" she replied on a moan.

"Just answer the question." He delivered a quick thrust to make his point: he was in charge, and that wouldn't change.

Bianca panted. "Hard. Big. What else can a woman ask for?"

"You find me big?" Damn, he was turning into a hound for compliments. With his hand, he pushed the curtain of her hair aside so he could see her face. It was flushed, her cheeks rosy. The column of her graceful neck glistened with moisture, the scent of her clean sweat enticing him to approach.

He sank over her back, careful to keep his weight off her, and dipped his lips to her nape. As he brushed them against her heated skin, she shivered visibly.

"Very big," she whispered.

Lorenzo nibbled his way along her neck and traveled to her ear. Beautifully shaped and small, her ear was too much of a temptation not to taste. He pulled her earlobe between his lips and sucked.

Another sound of pleasure escaped her lips, making him smile while his cock jumped with joy, relentlessly pumping in and out of her. Her channel was slick and warm with their combined juices. Yet despite the plentiful lubrication, her sheath was gripping him tightly, her muscles relaxing on each inward stroke and squeezing him on each retreat.

"I like what your sweet cunt is doing to me." The words were out before he could stop them. To a whore, he could talk like that, but not to a gently bred woman. Bianca would surely toss him off her back now.

"You mean this?" Her interior muscles squeezed him even tighter.

Surprise rippled through him, quickly followed by delight. Bianca didn't mind him talking dirty. Could he push his luck even further, getting them both even more aroused—if that was possible—by sharing his fantasies with her?

"Darling, where did you learn such tricks?"

Suddenly, she stiffened and stilled her movements. Her hands reached backwards, trying to push him away, but he wouldn't allow his cock to leave her and held her down. "Let me go."

"What's wrong? I thought we were getting along just fine." To emphasize his point, he thrust harder into her, increasing his tempo.

"I don't want any more of this."

Something was seriously wrong. From one second to another, his passionate vixen had turned cold on him. And he was going to get to the bottom of why, even if that meant pulling out of her and interrupting the race to his next orgasm.

Lorenzo lifted himself off her, but before Bianca could scramble off the bed, he turned her onto her back and cradled her in his arms, not allowing her to leave.

"Let go!"

"Shh." He stroked his hand over her back, sliding it down to her cute ass and pressing her against him. Her generous breasts flattened against the hard planes of his chest. Lorenzo enjoyed the feel of Bianca in his arms more than he'd ever enjoyed cradling a woman before. He attributed the feeling to the anticipation his cock exhibited at the thought of fucking her again once he'd figured out why she suddenly wanted to leave his bed. "What did I do?"

Pressing her head against his neck, he made sure she couldn't look at his face, not that she seemed to want to look at him at the moment.

"Nothing, now let go of me." She made another attempt at getting out of his hold, but he only pressed her tighter to him, sliding one leg between her thighs, his cock digging into her soft stomach. Her breath hitched, and he knew he'd won: she wouldn't leave his bed.

"You were all hot for more. So tell me what I did to change your mind, and I'll make it up to you." He sure could think of a few things to pacify her.

Lorenzo slid his hand into her lush hair and buried it there, enjoying the silken softness of her tresses. It smelled sweet, and he sank his face into them, letting himself be engulfed by her enticing scent. He breathed in deeply, taking her essence into his lungs. His cock stiffened further, sending little sensual charges through his body. How simply holding this woman in his arms could send him to such heights was beyond his comprehension. She was a treasure he wanted to plunder over and over again.

"There's no need to treat me like a whore!" Finally, Bianca's response came, and even though he didn't like what he heard, he preferred it to her silence.

"I didn't treat you like a whore. If you remember, I asked you to leave so I wouldn't ravish you, but you left me no—"

"I'm not talking about that."

"Then what *are* you talking about?" Despite the fact that he suspected what this was about, he wanted to hear it from her. He wasn't good at interpreting women, and he wasn't about to start trying now.

"You were implying that I'm a whore."

Lorenzo tilted her head up to him, knowing his fangs had receded completely by now. When he locked eyes with her, he clearly saw the hurt sitting deep inside her. "I did no such thing."

"You asked where I'd learned to..." Her voice trailed off as if she was too embarrassed to talk about what she'd done.

"To squeeze my cock like that?" He smiled down at her, then brushed his lips against hers. "I liked that. A lot. And I didn't mean anything else by it."

"You didn't?" Disbelief still colored her voice.

"No. I only meant to compliment you and show my appreciation. It's rare that I find a woman who can truly please me." He paused for a moment, stealing another sweet kiss. "And you please me."

Lorenzo surprised himself by how soft and tender he suddenly felt toward her. Minutes ago, he'd been randy as a sailor and about as refined as a bunch of hoodlums on a rampage. Yet now he wanted Bianca to understand him. He told himself that it was merely so he could continue fucking her, but even his own mind called him a liar. Deep down in the dark folds of his psyche, something long forgotten was stirring. He didn't want to know what it was and pushed it away before his inner eye could set its sight on it and acknowledge its existence. No, he couldn't let himself feel what he'd felt long ago. There was too much danger in that thought.

A soft smile played around her lips, and the sparkle in her eyes told him he'd found the right words. Could he now immediately go back to ravishing her, or did she need some more pacifying? Not wanting to take a chance, he decided to woo her just a little longer. *Woo?* Where had that irrational thought come from?

"You're a treasure," he whispered and planted soft kisses on her cheek, before trailing further down. The velvety skin below her chin tempted him to nibble. Obligingly, she arched back, offering the white column of her throat to him. Lorenzo's heartbeat spiked. If she knew what he was, she would never expose her vulnerability this way. He was certain of it. Nevertheless, he appreciated the gesture, even though Bianca couldn't know what it meant.

"Too beautiful for me. Too sinful."

Her hummed breath whispered along his temple as he captured her skin between his lips, sucking it ever so tentatively. Visions of biting her and tasting her rich blood danced before his eyes, tempting him to do the deed, to take what should be his. To simply use his powers on her to make her forget, consequences be damned. His vampire side urged him on to forget his scruples, his fangs already lengthening as desire for her blood overshadowed his concern for her safety and even his lust.

Lorenzo opened his lips and allowed the sharp tips of his fangs to emerge. As they grazed her skin, the contact sent a lightning bolt through his body more intense than his previous orgasm. He knew that his fangs were just as sensitive as his cock, yet he'd been unprepared for the sensual assault the contact with Bianca's flesh produced. Never before had he felt such intense pleasure at the contact of his fangs with a human's skin. His mouth opened wider, and his tongue snaked out to lap against her skin, coating it with his saliva so there would be no pain for her. Slowly, anticipation riding him high, he set his fangs and—

"You make me feel safe." Her hushed admission rocked him to a halt.

Safe? What in his behavior had inspired that reaction? Ravishing her on the desk of her late father? Yelling at her to make her leave? Fucking her like an animal?

Bianca wasn't safe with him. But, damn it to hell, if her words didn't make his fangs retract in an instant, as if she'd commanded it so. He couldn't betray the trust she showed in him. If he bit her now, he would sink lower than he ever had. And for once, he didn't want to feel low and dirty. He didn't want the bitter aftertaste of betrayal. He didn't want to taint their encounter with that. Instead, he wanted something pure: pure passion, pure lust.

Lorenzo pulled his lips from her neck and gazed into her eyes. "Sweet Bianca, I have to confess that even though you might feel safe with me, you're not."

Her eyes widened. "I don't believe you'd hurt me."

"I might have already." Could she really be this naïve, not knowing what he'd already done? "I took no precautions."

"Precautions?" she echoed.

"To prevent conception. Surely, you understand what this means." And it confirmed something else for him: a whore would have made sure she prevented an unwanted pregnancy. A young woman like her—while not a virgin—had insufficient experience to do so. Why the thought pleased him, he didn't know.

"Oh." Her lips formed the most perfect little circle he would have loved to kiss, had he not been concerned with offering her reassurance.

"I'm an honorable man." *Since when?* his inner voice asked him. "Therefore, let me assure you, should our encounter result in a child, I will do my duty and support you and the child financially. You needn't worry about that."

It was the first time he'd ever worried about any such thing. The whores he visited regularly always made sure no such accident happened. And in the years since Elle, he hadn't fucked a respectable woman whom he'd had to worry about becoming enceinte. And he'd never kept a mistress. Was Bianca his mistress now?

By taking her to his bed, had he now accepted her as his mistress? Was she expecting him to keep her now? Damn, why had things gotten so complicated so fast? All he'd wanted to do was slake his lust, and suddenly he felt himself embroiled in an affair he wasn't sure he wanted.

Oh, he wanted Bianca, under him, above him, in front of him, naked and panting. There was no doubt about that. But did he want her in his bed every night? Did he want her in his house, his private life?

When he looked at her lovely face again, he noticed that she'd gone quiet. "Bianca, is something the matter?"

BIANCA WANTED to slap herself for her own stupidity. How could she have let herself go like that in the heat of passion, not thinking of the possible consequences? During all those years as a concubine, she'd never once forgotten to prevent conception. What had suddenly gotten into her?

"Bianca?"

As if through a fog, she stared back at Lorenzo, his words still echoing in her ears. He'd take care of her *financially*. Nothing had changed. She was still a concubine. The only difference was that now she was back in Venice where people knew her. So much for starting a new life.

"Everything is fine. I'm sure nothing happened." And if it had, she wouldn't tell him. She wouldn't be trapped. Now more than ever, it was important that she found the treasure, so she could leave and deal with whatever cards she'd been dealt.

Lorenzo smiled at her. "So—" He placed a soft kiss on her lips. "—where were we?"

CHAPTER
TWELVE

Lorenzo peeled himself out of Bianca's arms, careful not to wake her. His sensitive hearing had picked up a sound from the door downstairs. It was an hour before sunrise, but despite the fact that Bianca had only entered his life three nights earlier, Lorenzo's sleeping pattern had been turned upside down. Over the last two days, he'd barely left his bed no matter the time. He was more than comfortable having Bianca sleep in his arms and waking her whenever the need to fuck her became too big—which was often.

Not that he would always wake her. The last time, she'd been so tired and exhausted that he'd not even woken her, but driven his aching cock into her while she was still asleep. Only when he'd started fucking her, had she opened her eyes and moaned out her pleasure and smiled as if she always wanted to awake in the same fashion. And Lorenzo had promised her that he would oblige her only too willingly.

But right now, he needed to let her sleep and allow her tired body to rest while he investigated the sounds coming from outside his front door.

Without making a sound, Lorenzo slipped into his dressing gown, tied the belt around his waist, stepped into his slippers and left the bedchamber. He didn't bother with finding a candle, and descended the stairs in the dark. Another knock on the door indicated that his visitor was getting impatient.

Lorenzo stopped in front of the heavy door, already aware of who was on the other side of it. He turned the key and opened the door.

"About time. Are you deaf?" Nico asked and pushed inside.

Lorenzo closed the door and turned back to his friend, who looked him up and down as if he was looking at a ghost.

"Evening, Nico."

"Were you sleeping? In the middle of the night?"

For a vampire, that was certainly unusual. It was tantamount to a healthy human male suddenly taking an afternoon nap. "Of course, not!" Lorenzo denied.

"Fucking then, I suppose."

He ignored the comment and motioned to the parlor, not wanting to wake Bianca with their conversation. "What brings you here so close to sunrise? I'm assuming it's important."

Nico entered the parlor, then let himself fall into the sofa. "I would have come earlier, but I had to track down Signore Mancini in one of the hells upon his return to the city. It appears he has a little weekend place on the mainland. Anyway, after my chat with him, one thing led to another, and I got distracted." His friend paused. "If you know what I mean."

Since Nico could never enter a hell without partaking in some of the offerings himself, Lorenzo didn't even bother to feign surprise and ignored the comment. "You found Mancini then. What did he tell you? Is he sending the money for Bianca here?"

Nico held up both arms. "One question at a time. Sit down. This may take a while."

Reluctantly, Lorenzo sank into his armchair. "I'm sitting."

"Interesting man, Signore Mancini. Lucky for us that he's just as inter-ested in gossip as a common washerwoman."

"My friend, I know you like drama, but would you please spare me this time. As you so rightly guessed, I have something to get back to, and if I may add, the lady is quite anxious for another helping." The lie rolled off his lips as smoothly as the water flowed under the many bridges of Venice.

It wasn't the lady who was anxious for more, but Lorenzo himself—even if it was merely to hold her in his arms and cradle her as she slept.

Nico's mouth twisted. "If we're talking about the same person—and I'm assuming it is still Bianca Greco who apparently now resides in your bed—then we're not talking about a lady."

Lorenzo shot up from his chair and lunged toward Nico, grabbing him by the collar of his shirt. "I advise you to watch your words. She's a lady despite the fact that she succumbed to my advances. It wasn't her fault. I practically attacked her." Why he felt the need to defend her honor, he didn't want to examine.

Nico raised an eyebrow. "Ah, be that as it may, however, I stand by my opinion." He paused for a second. "As does Signore Mancini."

At the mention of the solicitor's name, Lorenzo loosened his grip and released his friend. "Talk!"

Nico adjusted his cravat and smoothed back his waistcoat. "Are you going to sit down again?"

Lorenzo grunted and sat back in his armchair.

"It appears that Bianca ran away from her father when he planned to marry her off to some rich old aristocrat. Headstrong young woman. Wouldn't give into her father's demands."

Headstrong certainly sounded like Bianca. He'd been at the receiving end of it himself. "I assume she had a beau already and eloped with him?"

Nico shook his head. "Not at all. She left on her own. And your sweet Bianca has never been married."

If she hadn't been married, then some cad had first taken his pleasure with her, and then left her. Why else wouldn't she have been a virgin? "Her lover left her?"

"Which one?"

Confusion spread in Lorenzo. "What do you mean by *which one*?"

"What I'm trying to tell you, my dear Lorenzo, is that the woman currently waiting in your bed is quite at home at what she does there."

A sense of dread filled him at Nico's words, but the full implication of them hadn't sunk in yet. "What are you implying?" Only when the words were out did Lorenzo notice how his voice had risen in anger.

"I'm not implying anything. I'm telling you that Bianco Greco has spent the last few years as a highly-priced courtesan in Florence. She's no lady and certainly no innocent."

Shock made Lorenzo jump up from his chair. Instantly, all their interactions rushed back to him: how she'd responded to him in her sleep, the way she'd demanded he'd satisfy her, and then the way she'd squeezed his cock that had given him so much pleasure. Of course, now it all made sense. She was an experienced woman. And not better than a common whore.

"As for the money," Nico continued undeterred, "she collected it from Mancini the day the deed was recorded."

Lorenzo felt as if he'd been staked. She'd lied to him about everything from the very first moment. "She's playing me."

Nico nodded, his expression grave now. "I'm afraid so. Now, we'll just need to find out what her plan is."

"Her plan?" The wound in Lorenzo's chest widened as the realization of her betrayal sank in deeper and buried itself in his vulnerable flesh. "Isn't that obvious? She wants the house back even if that means she has to service my carnal needs."

"It's simple then. Just show her the door." Nico brushed a dust particle off his immaculate breeches, flicking his wrist in a nonchalant gesture.

"I can't do that."

"Of course, you can. Tell her to get dressed and shove her out the door."

"Nico, you don't understand: I made her my mistress."

Nico's eyebrows rose in surprise. "Well, that's unexpected coming from you. But I'll let you in on a little secret." He edged forward on his seat. "Men dismiss their mistresses at will. Now do it. You certainly don't need a gold digger in your home. Besides, she might get in the way of what we're trying to accomplish. I'm sure neither Raphael nor Dante would be pleased to have a human woman in our midst, who might turn out to be a spy."

Lorenzo dismissed the idea instantly. Bianca was no spy. She was a greedy woman who was after his wealth. After realizing that her father had left her nothing, she'd seen her chance and taken it. Unfortunately, he hadn't seen it coming, and now there was something else that made it impossible for him to send her away.

"I can't dismiss her. I've compromised her."

Nico stood up, agitated now. "She was *already* compromised. You didn't fuck a virgin!"

"I knew that already. But you don't understand: I took no precautions, and neither did she."

Nico frowned. "Precautions?"

Lorenzo rounded his chair and gripped its backrest, suddenly in need of support. "To prevent conception. She could already be carrying my child."

His friend let out an exasperated breath. "I don't believe this. You? You of all people?" Nico's look was scolding. "You've been had!"

Lorenzo cursed. "I know that. Don't you think I know that?" He hit his fist against the backrest of his armchair. "She's planned this down to the last detail: seduced me with her innocent demeanor, lulled me in. And what did I do? I complied. Now she's going to use a child to get what she wants."

Worst of all, if she turned out to be enceinte, he would have to make an important decision: have her bear a human child or make her give him a half-vampire child. His actions during her pregnancy would determine the outcome. If Bianca fed from him while the child was in her womb, the child would draw from his blood, grow up human, yet receive its vampire traits and turn into a vampire when it matured. But if she never took any of his blood into her, her child would be perfectly human and remain so. The choice was his.

"What are you thinking?" Nico cut through his thoughts.

"Nothing."

"Oh, no, you'd better not be thinking what I think you are."

Lorenzo cut him an annoyed glare. "Stay out of this. It's none of your business."

"You're not dismissing me that easily. If you're thinking about whether to make her child half-vampire, I urge you to reconsider. You don't know this woman. In fact, you know that she's devious and scheming."

Despite everything he'd heard about Bianca, he couldn't believe that there was nothing good in her. In his arms, she'd felt better than good. She'd felt like a treasure to him.

"You have no idea how far she will go!"

Something in Nico's words made him pay attention. "What did you say?"

"You don't know what she'll do!"

As an idea formed in his mind, Lorenzo's lips curled up in a smile. "I suppose, I'll have to push her to her limits then."

"I don't like the sound of that," Nico replied, his voice filled with doubt.

Lorenzo looked toward the door, imagining himself walking into his bedchamber. "Oh, but it's going to be extremely pleasurable to find out how far my soiled dove will take it before she gives up and runs as far as her feet will carry her." Even though secretly he hoped that despite what he was planning to confront her with, she'd stay. It was a crazy thought, yet he couldn't stop it from taking residence in his mind.

CHAPTER

THIRTEEN

Lorenzo eased the door to his bedchamber shut, not wanting to make any noise to wake his sleeping vixen. He approached his dressing room which held only a minimal amount of his clothes at this point. His valet had delivered one trunk the night before, wanting to arrange his master's closet at the same time, but Lorenzo had sent him on his way and asked him to take a few days off, wanting to be alone with Bianca. Just as well. He needed no audience or interruptions to what he had in mind now.

He opened the trunk, rummaging through its contents until he felt silk caress his fingers. He pulled on the material, freeing a scarf from the stack. A silk necktie followed. Perusing the two items in his hand, he contemplated adding two more, but dismissed the idea. Two would be sufficient for what he needed.

Lorenzo was about to lower the trunk's lid when his eyes fell onto a small rectangular box. He closed his palm around it, well aware of its contents: French letters. His valet made sure that he always had an ample and ready supply of the pesky skins. For a moment, he contemplated availing himself of one, but quickly dismissed the idea. He'd been fucking Bianca for three days and nights straight without taking any precautions.

And while it was possible that she hadn't conceived during those times, and all could still be saved if he used his French letters now, he was in the mood to tempt fate even more.

Maybe it was to punish her for her deception, or maybe it was simply because his gut told him that the deed had already been done and there'd be no use in taking any further precautions—precautions, which frankly would impede his pleasure. The thought of filling her with his seed once more ignited him to the point of unbearable lust, his cock already tenting his robe, eager to comply.

He released the box that contained the French letters and palmed the one next to it instead. It was larger and heavier.

As he strode back into his chamber and approached the bed, his senses filled with everything that was Bianca: her scent, the soft rustle she made on every exhale, and the way her face looked so peaceful while she was sleeping. There was something about this woman that spoke to him, that told him that she wasn't all calculating and cold. But the things Nico had found out about her spoke against that. Therefore, he had to push her to the brink, so she'd break and confess her true motives.

And if Lorenzo was good at one thing, it was how to lay secrets bare. With Bianca, he'd use his favorite method.

Placing the box on the nightstand, he bent over Bianca. He reached for one of her arms, easing it from underneath the tangled sheets and bound her wrist tightly with the scarf, then pulled her arm up over her head and looped the other end of the scarf through the sturdy wood carving of the headboard, attaching it firmly. Lorenzo tugged on it, making sure it was secured.

Then he proceeded in the same fashion with Bianca's other arm and stepped back to look at the enticing tableau she now represented. By pulling her arms over her head, the sheet covering her breasts had slid down, revealing her naked beauty. Her tits had pulled up, the firm peaks proudly pointing up, moving slightly with every breath she took.

Lorenzo snagged the sheet between his thumb and forefinger and pulled it down to her feet, exposing her nude form to his hungry gaze. Hell, would he ever get enough of that sight? A light sheen of sweat covered her creamy skin, and dew still glistened on her mound. One leg was angled to the side, giving him a full view of the pink flesh between her thighs he'd licked and sucked and fucked relentlessly. And still, he wanted more.

Lorenzo divested himself of his robe and carelessly dropped it to the floor before he slid onto the bed beside Bianca. It was time to wake her and show her what he expected from his mistress.

With his hand, he lightly brushed over her nipples, the globes they topped moving in the process. So responsive, yet she didn't wake, her body clearly too exhausted. It didn't stop him from enjoying a quick lick against her flesh, then a soft tug together with a grazing of his teeth against her breast. But playtime was over.

Lorenzo swung his leg over her, mounting her, his buttocks resting on her upper thighs, so he still had a view of her neatly trimmed triangle of curls. Bianca's breathing changed as he sank part of his weight onto her, her legs behind him trying to find a more comfortable position. He reached for her face and bent down to her, pressing his lips to hers. With his tongue he nudged her lips open and slid inside.

Her gasp told him that she was aware of him, so he eased off and pulled back an inch. Her face lifted from the pillow to follow his lips, and a moment later, she jerked her arms as if trying to reach for him, but was rudely pulled back by her restraints.

Bianca's eyes flew open, her head instantly twisting, her eyes searching for the unknown resistance. Her eyes spotted the bindings that held her trapped, and she snapped her gaze back to him, staring at him in shock. "What? Lorenzo?" The hint of panic in her voice pleased him. He wanted her off kilter.

"Yes, my sweet Bianca?" he asked innocently.

"What are you doing?" There was annoyance in her tone now. She tugged at the ties but couldn't loosen them. "Take these off me!"

Lorenzo smiled down at her and trailed his hand over her breast until he reached her nipple. "I can't do that."

"Untie me!"

He ignored her demand and took her responsive peak between thumb and forefinger, pinching it. A startled gasp was her response. "It's time for you to learn what I expect my mistress to do. And you're my mistress now, aren't you?"

"Lorenzo, please." Even though she was pleading now, her lips pouting like a debutante's, it wouldn't change anything.

"If you remember, we agreed on this when I let you stay here. I warned you about the things you would have to do for me if you wanted to warm my bed. Or have you already forgotten about it?"

Her eyes blinked as her jaw dropped. Yes, she remembered what he'd told her that first night when she'd begged him to let her stay. He would make good on it now.

"I see, you remember."

"But I thought you simply tried to shock me, so I'd leave," she protested in vain.

Lorenzo kept the chuckle that was building inside him where it belonged: hidden from view. The devious vixen was trying to talk her way out of it. Maybe her previous protectors had been so gullible, but it wouldn't work with him.

He *tsk*ed before he lifted himself off her thighs. Her relieved smile died an instant death when he merely scooted up her body so his inner thighs were touching her breasts and his heavy cock nudged toward the valley between them.

"I think I should warn you that in my house my word is law. Whatever order I issue will be followed. And right now, I'm going to have you suck me."

BIANCA TUGGED on the restraints once more, but they were holding, not quite biting into her wrists, but nevertheless firm enough to prevent her from escaping them. What had gotten into Lorenzo? During the last days and nights, he'd been the most passionate, yet considerate lover, and she'd almost forgotten why she was with him in the first place: to find the treasure. Only during those hours when he'd slept deeply had she snuck out of bed to continue her search.

But now as she looked at him looming over her, his body as beautiful as ever, and his cock just as hard and tempting as the many times before, there was a different glint in his eyes. As if a predator lurked behind them.

She'd never allowed any of her lovers to tie her up, yet despite the dominant position Lorenzo had taken above her, she felt no fear. Though her heartbeat had kicked up, a much more powerful emotion than fear was its catalyst: lust. As she trailed her gaze down from his strong chest muscles to his flat stomach, and then lower still to his hard length, her mouth went dry at the beautiful sight. Like a stalk it jutted out, purple veins snaking around it like vines crawling up a castle wall. Its head glistened with moisture coming from the slit on its tip.

Bianca inhaled his scent, so male and more virile than that of any man she'd ever known. During the many hours they'd spent together in his bed, he'd shown her over and over that his sexual prowess was limitless.

"Time to fulfill your duties as my mistress," he continued and scooted up her body, bringing his cock closer to her mouth. "Or have you decided you don't want to be my mistress anymore? If that's the case, say the word, and I'll release you."

Bianca breathed a sigh of relief: he was only teasing her. But with his next words she realized that escape was not an option.

"Of course, then you'll have to leave my house."

Reality slammed into her. She couldn't leave. There were still areas in the house she hadn't searched, and under no circumstances would she leave without her treasure.

Bianca swallowed her pride and gave him a coquettish smile. "If you want me to suck you, my master, then you'll have to come a little closer—" She jerked at her restraints. "—given that I can't put my hands on your... very... very impressive..." She licked her lips, bringing much needed moisture to them. "...cock."

She couldn't interpret the look Lorenzo gave her. Was it approval? Surprise? Or a bit of both? But whatever it was, he nudged forward another inch and, holding his shaft at the root, he guided it to her lips.

"Yes, my sweet Bianca, taste me." His voice had dropped an octave, huskier than she'd ever heard him speak. And his eyes had turned darker, their whites almost completely disappearing. Instead, the light from the candle on the nightstand seemed to cast an orange glow onto them, making them sparkle in the dark.

Bianca parted her lips and extended her tongue to swipe it over the purple head, gathering his pre-cum with it, all the while watching his expression. When she pressed her tongue flat against his slit, Lorenzo's eyes closed and his head fell back, his chest releasing a most animalistic groan. She'd never seen a more tantalizing sight.

Her mouth rocked forward, and she engulfed his length in her moist heat, widening her jaw as much as she could. But he was too big. Only half his shaft fit. Slowly, she moved her head back and forth, making him withdraw, then slide back into her while she swirled her tongue around the underside of his flesh.

With every slide, her own body responded, sending charges of heat to her center of pleasure. She pressed her thighs together in the hope of alleviating the need that boiled up there, but it was no use. She needed to be touched, needed his hand on her to take away the ache.

When she looked back at Lorenzo, his dark eyes were watching her intently.

"God, I love fucking your mouth."

Raw emotions played on his face: desire, lust, and the knowledge that his control would snap soon. His hips flexed as he drove deeper into her, forcing her head back into the pillow. He braced his arms against the headboard above her and thrust in a steady rhythm, his strokes slow and measured, careful not to make her gag, yet deep enough to push her boundaries of comfort.

"See, Bianca, how good it is when you can't get away, when you have to endure everything I want you to do. Does it excite you?"

She wanted to protest, but the lie wouldn't cross her lips. Despite the vulnerable position she found herself in, she couldn't deny the appeal of it. Lorenzo was in charge, and for the first time in her life she felt the need to surrender.

On his next withdrawal, she made a demand of her own. "Touch me."

There was a smile on his lips before he drove back into her. "Not yet, my sweet. Your need isn't great enough yet."

She wanted to protest, tell him that she would burn up if he didn't stroke her pearl and release the tension there, but his relentless cock didn't give her the freedom to speak. So she closed her eyes and concentrated on his body and the beautiful flesh that was hard and soft at the same time, hoping to distract herself from the ache between her legs.

When she thought she couldn't take anymore, Lorenzo suddenly pulled back, breathing hard. Her eyes flew open, their gazes colliding. "Don't stop," she whispered.

He scooted down her body. "I'm not ready to come. But when I am, it'll be in your sweet cunt."

Obviously wishing to shock her, he lashed the crude word at her. But all it did was excite her further. He would fuck her and give her relief. It was all she could think of.

Lorenzo leaned toward the nightstand. Bianca followed his movement, watching as he retrieved a box and opened it. "But first," he announced, "I'll be exploring your body."

When he took a shiny item from the box and turned back to her, she tried to focus on what it was.

"Have you ever seen something like this?"

Shocked, Bianca stared at his hands, which held an object made of a smooth metal. Its shape was unmistakable: it looked like a man's cock, only it was smaller than Lorenzo's, and slimmer as well. She shook her head, both in response to his question as well as to push away the suspicions of what he wanted to do with it.

"No? Well, then I think I have to introduce you to this toy." The wicked grin on his face told her he wouldn't stop until he'd done whatever he wanted.

Lorenzo dismounted and knelt next to her, using his hand to spread her legs in the next instant. She let it happen, unable to fight her own desire. She needed to be touched, and if he wanted to touch her with that toy as he called it, then it was better than not being touched at all. Humiliation be damned.

He led the metal cock to her sex and stroked it against her moist flesh. It was cool and smooth, and the cold metal somewhat eased the fire in her. But then he moved upwards to her pearl. Now coated in her dew, it slid easily against her, the contact sending a flame of heat through her body.

"Oh, God!"

Lorenzo lowered his head to her stomach, trailing open mouthed kisses along her skin. She bucked toward him and toward the metal cock he was holding, wanting more. As if he understood her, he moved the smooth metal rhythmically up and down. Bianca exhaled, allowing the pleasure to spread in her body. Finally, Lorenzo would soothe the ache that had built.

"Yes." It was less word more moan that left her lips.

"Not yet, my sweet," he answered and withdrew the cock.

Frustrated, she pulled on her restraints, rattling the headboard.

"Shh, you're impatient. Have you forgotten that as my mistress you're here to pleasure me? And I decide what gives me pleasure."

An instant later, she felt the metal cock at the entrance to her channel, probing gently, before he drove it into her. Her muscles clenched around it, welcoming the foreign intrusion. Smaller than Lorenzo's cock it nevertheless filled the void. But already, he withdrew it, not allowing her to enjoy the pleasurable sensation for long.

"No! Please, don't stop!"

"I'm not."

Then he pulled her legs up and slid the object further back toward her buttocks. Panic gripped her when she realized what he was about to do. She tensed and tried to push her thighs together, but Lorenzo pried them apart.

"Bianca, I warned you once. These are the things I expect from my mistress." Then he looked at her, his eyes blazing with lust. "If you don't want to be my mistress, tell me now."

Warring emotions collided inside her. But she couldn't give in now. She was too close to her goal. If he dismissed her now, she'd be virtually destitute. Slowly, she eased her legs apart further, pulling her knees up to set her feet flat on the mattress.

Surprise flitted across his face. Then one hand came up to stroke her cheek. "I'll be gentle."

Bianca closed her eyes, steeling herself for what was to come. Instead of pain, she suddenly felt his hand on her pearl, stroking it in a leisurely rhythm, relaxing her further. She arched her hips toward him, and he complied and caressed her with more pressure.

"Yes!"

When he guided the metal cock to the entrance of her dark passage, the moisture it was coated with made the contact smooth and pleasant. Slowly, the cock pressed against the tight ring of muscle. A sense of discomfort spread, but was instantly drowned out by Lorenzo's finger on her pearl.

Gently, he pushed the toy into her, the invasion creating a sense of fullness she'd never experienced. It stretched her. She took steadying breaths to push back the temporary pain.

"That's good, my sweet. Take it slowly."

She should feel embarrassed about what he was doing to her. But when she noticed him watch with rapt fascination how the item disappeared in her dark channel, her pulse flared.

"So beautiful."

Bianca expelled a moan as pain made room for pleasure, the cock in her nether passage sending sensations through her body she'd never felt.

"I'm ready to fuck you now."

Lorenzo let go of the metal cock, keeping it deeply lodged inside her and rose above her, settling between her thighs. With one swift move, he drove his shaft into her cunny. The dual penetration robbed her of her breath. Her heartbeat stuttered.

His head lowered to hers, his eyes boring into hers. "Yes, my sweet, I'm going to make you come so hard you'll faint."

His lips landed on hers before she could reply, kissing her more passionately than he ever had. And as he continued kissing her, he rode her. With every stroke of his hard length, the metal cock in her ass moved, driving her higher every time. It was useless to fight the sensations that crashed onto her like an ocean wave against the shore. So she let herself go and surrendered to him, allowed him to take her and pleasure her without restraints. And despite the restraints that still held her arms captive, she'd never felt more liberated in her life.

"I'm yours," she whispered, her voice echoing amidst his heavy breathing.

"Oh, Bianca!"

His cock jerked inside her, pulsating as her muscles contracted around him, gripping him harder until her body joined his in orgasm, the waves engulfing her until the last one crashed over her and drew her into darkness.

Lorenzo took the sleeping Bianca into his arms and carried her to the bathing chamber where he'd prepared a hot bath for them. He lowered himself into the large tub and arranged Bianca on his lap so she straddled him as he cradled her head against his chest.

Physically, he'd never felt better in his long life. Fucking Bianca while she was tied up had been an amazing experience, fucking her while she had the metal cock inside her sweet ass had almost killed him. Every time he'd thrust into her, he'd felt the other cock against him, adding to the intoxicating sensation of her muscles gripping him. His orgasm had been more intense than ever before.

But while he felt fully satisfied physically, his emotional state was another matter. He didn't know what to make of Bianca. Despite the things he'd thrown at her, she'd played along. Was she really that desperate to attain part of his wealth that she was prepared to engage in any debauched act he could think of? Yet she hadn't simply endured the act. He'd seen the desire in her eyes, the lust, and the pleasure he'd given her despite the apprehension he'd noticed in her at first.

Was Bianca what he needed? Did it really matter that her motives weren't pure? That she wanted him for his money? Didn't any woman hunting for a husband have the same motives? Few people in Venice married for love. It was either for status, money or both. Little else mattered. And frankly, he couldn't even blame women. They had no means of earning their living and depended on a husband to provide for them. So why shouldn't they try and sell themselves to the highest bidder?

Maybe he should even feel honored that Bianca had chosen him. After all, she wasn't stingy with her affections, or offering her body to him more completely than any whores had. Could a man really ask for more? He could do worse than having this hot-blooded vixen in his bed. And so far, she hadn't demanded marriage despite the fact that he'd continued to leave his seed inside her. Maybe all she wanted was a comfortable roof over her head.

Lorenzo reached for the soap and lathered his hands, then started washing the beautiful woman in his arms. He'd never felt so tender toward anybody, except Elle. At the thought of her, he paused. Everything had gone well until he'd told her what he was. He wouldn't make the same mistake with Bianca. If he decided to keep her, he would make sure that she never found out.

So far, he'd managed. He'd had food delivered to the house so she could eat, but he'd never partaken himself, always finding an excuse to briefly leave on an *errand* while she ate. He'd fed plenty on the nearest street person he could find so his hunger wouldn't overwhelm him while he was with Bianca. As much as he wanted to bite her and taste her blood, he knew he could never allow himself that pleasure. Once she knew that he was a vampire, she would become a danger to him, attempting to kill him as Elle had. And wiping her memory every time he bit her was not an option. The memory of Elle in an insane asylum served as a strong enough deterrent.

He would just have to suppress the overwhelming desire to taste her blood. It was the only way he could at least slake his lust with her.

Lorenzo eased Bianca away from his chest, holding her firmly with one arm while he let his soapy hand sweep over her breasts, washing her. As he scooped water over her generous globes, she stirred.

"You've pleased me very much tonight," he whispered and palmed one globe, enjoying the weight in his hand.

"My love." Her whispered endearment was both encouragement and approval.

Lorenzo pulled her back against his chest, tilting her sideways so he could continue to caress her luscious tit. "Sleep, I'll take care of you now."

Bianca's breath ghosted against his wet skin as she relaxed back into sleep. And for as long as the water stayed warm, he kept her cradled in his arms. Safe, for now.

LORENZO HAD TOLD her that he had business to take care of and would be out most of the evening. Bianca gave him one of her sweetest smiles and sent him on his way, assuring him that she was perfectly fine spending an evening on her own.

As soon as the door closed behind him, she breathed a sigh of relief. Finally, she had a few uninterrupted hours during which to continue her search. This would be her first real occasion to search her father's old bedchamber, which she and Lorenzo had been occupying. Even though officially she stayed in her mother's bedchamber, the bed there had remained unused except for that first night.

Lorenzo didn't seem to mind her sleeping in his arms. Her former lovers had preferred to sleep alone once they'd fucked her, and frankly, she'd preferred it too. But strangely enough, she enjoyed being with Lorenzo. Even in his sleep, he seemed to be aware of her and sought an intimate connection. A day earlier, she'd woken only to find that he was sleeping soundly, her back tucked into his front, his hard cock deep inside her channel. None of her lovers had ever done that. Besides, she didn't know any man who'd held an erection for as long as he did.

Only when she'd started to move had Lorenzo awoken and grinned sheepishly, saying that he'd wanted to be connected to her when he slept. It was the sweetest thing anybody had ever said to her.

But Lorenzo had many sides, and she never knew which side she would be confronted with from one minute to the next. Not that it mattered much: she enjoyed each one in its own right. His tender and sweet side made her relax, and his passionate side made her feel wanted. But his dominance unleashed something in her that she never knew she harbored: the need to lose control, the need to surrender and submit. It scared her, yet at the same time, she craved it.

As she swept her gaze around the bedchamber, her eyes caught on the box that still lay on the nightstand, its contents back in its velvet cushion. A shiver raced through her body at the memories of what he'd done with the metal toy. She'd never thought she'd take to such debauched acts, but whenever he opened the box to use the implement in every way possible, her heartbeat accelerated and her center of pleasure throbbed uncontrollably. Then his knowing look rolled over her trembling body, and his cock jerked, oozing with moisture.

Even now with the lid closed, she felt her body prepare itself for the pleasure it was expecting. She should be ashamed of her depraved thoughts, but her heart couldn't fault her for what her body needed. In Lorenzo's arms she felt free, even when he bound her and made her submit to his will. And with this freedom came ultimate bliss and a glimpse of what happiness tasted like.

Bianca shook her head, trying to banish the feelings from her mind. Whatever she and Lorenzo had was temporary. It would last only until she found the treasure or until he tired of her, whichever came first. And she hoped to God that she'd find the treasure in time.

As she set about her task to search her father's old room, she worked methodically, starting in one corner, moving along the walls, peeking behind paintings, crawling under furniture, and opening every drawer. Many of her father's things were still there: his grooming implements, a drawer full of ties, another of stockings and garters. With difficulty, she lifted the heavy mattress of the bed and examined the space underneath, but there was no hidden compartment to be found.

She let the mattress slip back into place, the quick movement creating a dust cloud which settled onto the intricately carved headboard. Bianca took a piece of cloth and wiped it over the carved letters in the center of the wooden piece, removing the dust before she focused her attention on the next area.

The dressing room held only some of Lorenzo's garments. The servant who'd briefly visited a few days ago, had brought his trunk and moved her father's clothes to another unused chamber to make space for his master's garments.

Bianca stared at the trunk. Drawn to it like she was drawn to its owner, she sank to her knees and opened the lid. An assortment of scarves, ties, and smalls greeted her. She should have blushed at the sight of a man's undergarments, but she felt no such sentiment. The intimacies they'd shared had eradicated all embarrassment she could ever feel.

She let her hand run over the soft fabric, caressing it as if she were touching him instead. Her eyes closed, making her remember his touch more intensely when her fingers encountered a hard object. Bianca opened her eyes and looked at the item: a box, smaller than the one that held Lorenzo's favorite toy. She lifted it out of the trunk and opened the lid, curious to see whether it held any other toys. To her surprise, the box contained French letters.

Stunned, she closed the box. Why hadn't Lorenzo used them? After his valet had delivered the trunk, there'd been no reason to continue their carnal pleasures without protection against conception. Did it not bother him that she could soon be with child? And for that matter, why didn't it bother her that she could soon find herself in an untenable situation, having to support not only herself but an illegitimate child?

Bianca shook her head and rose. Was she playing with fire, secretly hoping that there could be more between her and Lorenzo than just a fleeting affair? Was that why she was taking unnecessary risks? She pushed the thoughts aside, not wanting to examine the emotions that drove them.

The search of her father's bedchamber proved fruitless. She'd found nothing. Frustrated, she trudged down the stairs and made her way to the kitchen, where a plate of food was waiting for her. Another one of Lorenzo's elusive servants had delivered it earlier. She wondered briefly why his servants weren't staying at the house with him. Was it because she was with him? Or did he simply like to be on his own?

As she devoured the food, her thoughts drifted back to her father. Had he sold the treasure before his death, and was that the reason why she couldn't find it? Bianca didn't believe it. He'd always claimed that the treasure was worth more than the house itself, yet her father had left a mountain of debt behind. Had he sold the treasure, there shouldn't have been any debt. No, the treasure still had to be in the house.

The slamming of the front door jolted her out of her reverie. She jumped up, eager to be back in Lorenzo's arms. At the kitchen door she halted, alarmed by a second slamming of the same door.

"We're not done!" a stranger's voice echoed through the hallway.

"I didn't invite you to my home, Raphael!" Lorenzo bellowed.

"I'm not leaving until we've discussed this."

Her heart beating in her throat, Bianca strained to hear more, but the two men had moved into the parlor and shut the door behind them.

She knew it wasn't polite to eavesdrop, but something in Lorenzo's voice had alarmed her, and she needed to know what was going on between them. And she knew just the place from where to see everything that went on in the parlor without being seen herself.

As a child, she'd loved to play hide and seek and had found a small storage room located on the upper floor right above the parlor. The room provided access to where the parlor's crystal chandelier was suspended from the ceiling. While the candles could be lit without lowering the chandelier, in order to properly clean the crystals, the area had been made accessible so the heavy item could be lowered with little effort. Holes in the ceiling allowed for a view into the room below to coordinate the lowering of the chandelier with servants in the parlor.

Her stocking-clad feet made no sound as Bianca stooped so as not to hit her head on the beams that carried the weight of the chandelier. She crouched down and slid back the leather patch that covered the hole, allowing her to peek into the parlor.

CHAPTER

FIFTEEN

Lorenzo felt his anger boil over and turned to the fireplace where the embers still glowed. "Nico had no right to tell you!"

"Well, I'm glad he did!"

Lorenzo bent down and placed a handful of kindling on the fire, watching as flames licked up and engulfed it, eager to ignore Raphael's reprimand. His private life was his own. Nobody had a right to interfere in it.

"You have to send her away. She could be a danger to you."

Lorenzo threw another piece of wood onto the fire and rose, turning on his heels to face Raphael. "Bianca is no danger to me, she's—"

"She's human!" Raphael interrupted.

"And how is that any different from what you're doing? Explain it to me, Raphael! Go ahead. Your wife is human. She lets you drink her blood, and don't tell me it doesn't drive you both to ecstasy every time you do it. And you have the gall to deny *me* a chance at the same happiness?" Yet he knew he could never bite Bianca, because he had to hide from her what he was.

"Don't bring Isabella into this. This is very different. You don't know anything about this woman."

"I know enough!"

"That's your cock talking!"

Lorenzo's gums itched as his fangs extended, threatening to push to the surface. "I won't have you insult me in my own home!"

"I'm not insulting you. I'm warning you. Or have you forgotten what happened with Elle?"

At the mention of Elle's name, Lorenzo's fangs pushed past his lips. He snarled and glared at his friend. "How dare you?"

"She betrayed you! Are you going to let the same thing happen again? What will you do once Bianca finds out what you are? Do you trust her enough not to kill you in your sleep?"

As he heard these words, Lorenzo felt the sharp pain of a stake in his heart, almost as though the imaginary weapon his friend had suggested was real. But he wouldn't admit his own doubts to Raphael. "She won't find out. I've hidden it from her so far."

"How much longer do you think you'll succeed?" His friend's voice was calmer now. "And if you really want true happiness with her, then you can't hide this from her."

"I'll hide it for as long as I need to. She'll never know that I'm a vampire." Lorenzo closed his eyes. The promise wasn't meant for Raphael but for himself. He could never allow her to find out. Even if this meant foregoing the ultimate pleasure of feeding from her. If she found out what he was, he'd lose her. And that thought scared him more than being caught outside when the sun rose.

Despite everything he'd done, he'd been unable to protect his heart. Even though he knew what she was—a courtesan, a liar, a woman after his money—he couldn't bring himself to send her away, because whenever he was near her, he felt at peace with his life. And when he was separated from her, a gaping void appeared like the deep chasm of a ravine.

When he opened his eyes, his gaze collided with Raphael's. There was understanding in his friend's eyes now. "God help you. For all our sakes."

Lorenzo nodded, unable to say anything else.

"Guard your back," Raphael cautioned and strode to the door.

Upon hearing the front door close, Lorenzo let himself fall into his armchair in front of the fireplace. He wasn't ready to go upstairs yet to join Bianca, his body still too agitated, his control too close to snapping.

Bianca clamped her hand over her mouth in order not to scream. This couldn't be happening! It had to be a nightmare. But she'd seen it with her own eyes, heard it with her own ears: Lorenzo was a vampire, a vile creature who preyed on humans. She'd heard people talk of them, never truly believing in the gruesome stories herself, but now there was no denying it.

Fangs had protruded from Lorenzo's mouth, and his eyes had glared red as he'd argued with his friend. Seemingly the loss of his temper brought out his hidden vampire side. What if she did something to provoke him? Would he lose control too? Would he bite her? Harm her? Kill her?

Bianca suppressed the sob that built in her chest and threatened to overwhelm her. As quietly as she could, she snuck out of the room and went to her mother's bedchamber, careful not to make any noise. Closing the door behind her, she took in a few steadying breaths. She had to get away. It was the only solution. Not even the hidden treasure could keep her here now. She had to run for her life.

Hastily, she stuffed her small bag with her belongings. There was even less now than before: the dress Lorenzo had ripped in half now lay on a chair. She wouldn't take it. She needed no reminder of what he'd done that day. No reminder of the passion he'd shown.

He could have killed her many times over. Yet, he'd never hurt her, not even when he'd tied her up. All his actions had been those of a passionate and dominant lover, not those of a bloodthirsty beast. But what if he was simply playing with her as a cat played with a mouse before devouring it?

Bianca shuddered at the thought and gripped her bag.

As she negotiated the stairs, trying to avoid those that creaked, her heart beat so loudly she was afraid he'd hear it. A sound from the parlor made her heart stop. Lorenzo was moving, and by the sound of a particularly loudly creaking floorboard, she knew he was almost at the door.

Panicked, she looked around her as she reached the landing, and quickly shoved her bag underneath the credenza and out of view.

A moment later, the parlor door opened and Lorenzo stepped out. He looked utterly crushed, so unhappy in fact that something tugged at her heart.

"Bianca, you're still awake," he noted when their eyes met.

She swallowed hard, trying to push back the lump that was rising in her throat. "I couldn't sleep without you." Would he know that she was lying? Would he see it in her face?

A small smile stole onto his lips as he extended his hand to her. "Then come, and join me in the parlor for a while."

Trembling, she took a step toward him and placed her hand in his palm. It was warm and reassuring.

"You're shaking, my sweet. Are you cold?" Lorenzo instantly pulled her into his arms.

"Yes, yes, I'm cold," she stammered.

"Then let me warm you."

He led her into the parlor and sat down on the sofa. Instead of placing her next to him, he pulled her into his lap and pressed her against his all-too-familiar broad chest. His scent brought back the memories of the intimacies they'd shared. And despite what she'd seen only a short while ago, her body didn't recoil from his touch.

"I've realized something tonight." Lorenzo's hand stroked over her hair, then he planted a soft kiss on top of her head.

"Yes?" With bated breath, Bianca waited for his response. Had he decided that it was time for him to bite her, that he couldn't deny his nature any longer and needed to drain her of her blood? Would she have the strength to pull free from him and run? More importantly: would she want to?

"I realized tonight that I need you."

"Need me?"

"Yes. When I have you in my arms, it feels good."

"You mean when we have... relations," she corrected him. What man didn't like to fuck? Surely, a vampire wasn't any different in that way.

His hand nudged under her chin, tipping her face up to look at him. Bianca couldn't evade his penetrating gaze.

"It's not about that." Then he grinned. "Even though, I've never felt a more intense pleasure than when I'm inside you." As if his body wanted to make a point, Lorenzo shifted her so she suddenly felt the hard outline of his erection against her hip.

"Oh."

His hand dropped to her bodice, where he tugged at the laces. "It's been too long..." He expertly freed her breasts from their confines, pushing her bodice below them.

"But we only... it was only a few hours ago." How could he want her again so soon? And why was her own body responding to him, her nipples pebbling under his touch, when she knew what kind of monster he was? Out of nowhere, the words Lorenzo had hurled at his friend echoed in her head: *She lets you drink her blood, and don't tell me it doesn't drive you both to ecstasy every time you do it.* Did this mean that his bite wasn't fatal, that it was in fact *pleasurable*?

"A few hours is too long," he whispered against her skin before he sucked one taut nipple into his mouth. His teeth grazed her sensitive skin, causing alarm bells to ring in her head. She shivered, and a moment later he let her nipple pop from his mouth.

"Take me out of my breeches," he ordered, his voice husky, his eyes dark with passion.

Without thinking, she obeyed. The moment she held his erect shaft in her hand, he groaned. The sound mesmerized her. "Now, lift your skirts."

Releasing his cock, Bianca reached for the seams of her skirts and pulled them up at the same time as Lorenzo lifted her up and settled her over him so she straddled him.

"Tell me you're wet."

When she answered him, it wasn't a lie. Because she was wet, her cunny readying itself for his invasion. Then she felt him, the thick head of his cock nudging at her entrance. She lowered herself and took him inside in one smooth glide. Before she could move any further, Lorenzo locked his arms around her and stopped her, breathing hard.

"See, now I feel better again."

Seeing a chance for a question, Bianca asked, "Were you not feeling well earlier?"

He shook his head. "I quarreled with a dear friend."

"What about?"

He stared past her into the distance. "It doesn't matter. What matters is that he was wrong."

"And you were right?" she challenged.

Lorenzo met her eyes. Long seconds passed before he spoke again. "Would you ever hurt me?"

Her heartbeat rose at his question. Would she? Trying to buy herself time, she stalled. "I don't understand."

"Would you have the heart to hurt me?" His gaze was intense, penetrating now.

"Only if you hurt me," she hedged, easing off him slightly, prepared to flee if she had to.

His arms pulled her back, his cock driving deeper into her. "I'll never hurt you, I swear by everything that's dear to me."

Was he trying to tell her that he wouldn't bite her, that she wouldn't have to fear him? Had he heard her sneak around upstairs, eavesdropping on him and his friend?

"Your heart is beating faster." Lorenzo's hand stroked over her breast.

Swallowing hard, Bianca tried to find the right words. "Because you're inside me. It excites me."

"Then ride me if it excites you."

CHAPTER

SIXTEEN

With Bianca sprawled over his half-clothed body, Lorenzo lay on the sofa in his parlor, one arm around her back, the other stroking over her delectable naked backside, her skirts hiked up to her waist. He'd never felt better. The fight with Raphael was forgotten, and all he could think of was the pliable woman in his arms.

"Tell me about your life," she suddenly demanded.

"There's not much to tell." And the things that mattered, he couldn't really talk to her about for fear of giving away his secrets.

"You jest. You must be the first man I've met who doesn't like the sound of his own voice."

Lorenzo chuckled. "I'm not like most men. I'm very private."

"Is that why you don't have the servants live with you?"

"I don't have many servants, only one permanent one really, my valet, and he normally resides with me. I've given him a few days off. The others spend only several hours a day with me when I need them."

"That's very peculiar."

"Not if you don't like others to nose around in your private business."

"What is it you have to hide then?" Bianca teased.

He gave her a playful slap on her bottom. "*If* I had anything to hide, I'd hardly blurt it out just because you're asking."

"What if I ask more nicely?"

Lorenzo responded in the same playful tone she'd used, "How nicely?"

She wiggled above him, grinding her body against his cock.

He let out a hearty laugh. "That's very nice indeed. But don't you think you've had enough for tonight?"

"*You* never seem to get enough."

He lifted his hand from Bianca's backside and brought it to her chin, tilting her face up so he could look at her. Her lids were half-lowered, the eyes behind them sleepy, and her lips were plump and red from his kisses. By God, how he loved that sight.

"Of you, my sweet Bianca, I don't think I'll ever get enough."

"You say that now, but—"

He put his finger across her lips. "No *but*. With you, everything is perfect. I've never been in want of a mistress, but now that I have you, I can't seem to remember how I ever did without."

His answer seemed to please her if he interpreted her sweet smile correctly. "You know that you don't have to charm me if you want to have your way with me again. I'm not likely to refuse you."

"The way I recall it is that you were having your way with me. Or aren't you the same woman who just rode me as if the Devil were chasing her?" He'd never seen a woman with such enthusiasm to please him.

"You didn't like it?" Her smile told him that she knew his answer full well. He'd loved every second of it.

Lorenzo reached down to her bottom and gave it a quick slap. "I think somebody is in need of a little disciplining. It'll teach you not to mock your master."

When he glanced at her face, he caught a flash of fear in her eyes. He instantly stilled his hand then stroked gently over her soft flesh. "Don't fear me, Bianca. I promised you I'll never hurt you. You believe me, don't you?"

He held his breath as he waited for her answer, hoping he hadn't scared her with his demands. Despite the fact that he'd started out by trying to push her to her limits to make her confess about her deception, his need to have her tell him the truth about her past and her motives for being with him had made way for the delight he felt when he realized that she didn't shy away from even the most debauched acts he shared with her. It didn't matter anymore that her motives for being with him weren't honest. Bianca had made up for it with the uninhibited passion she allowed him to tease out of her.

It seemed like an eternity until her lips finally parted and her breath ghosted against his skin. "I trust you."

BIANCA LET the words roll over her tongue and realized the moment they hit the air that she spoke the truth. She trusted Lorenzo, the man she knew to be a vampire, the man who could kill her so easily if he wanted to.

Yet instead of fear, another emotion coursed through her like blood rushing through her veins: excitement. Lorenzo wanted her, not simply to fuck her, but to keep him company. And he'd confessed that he couldn't get enough of her. The way with which he looked at her now, desire and affection equally occupying his gleaming eyes, she truly couldn't imagine that he'd ever hurt her. Even when she recalled the way he'd looked when he'd quarreled with his friend, when his fangs had shown and his eyes had burned like molten lava, no fear emerged in her heart.

On the contrary, knowing what power he kept leashed inside him made her desire for him even more intense.

Bianca brushed her lips against his. "You won't hurt me."

"And you won't hurt me," he whispered back before he took her lips and kissed her more tenderly than he ever had before.

And if a vampire could be tender, then she had nothing to fear from him, she knew it in her heart. Her only fear now was that he would tire of her, because what she wanted most was to stay with him, not to continue her search for the treasure, but to be with Lorenzo.

When he carried her to bed that night and cradled her in his arms, Bianca didn't sleep for a long time. Instead, she watched him sleep, watched how his chest fell and rose with each breath. He was a living, breathing man, full of passion and tenderness. And he had power over her, just as she had power over him.

His friend's words echoed in her ears. *"Do you trust her enough not to kill you in your sleep?"*

Bianca looked at Lorenzo's sleeping nude form and stroked her hand over the place where his heart was. It beat against her palm, strong and steady.

"My love," he mumbled in his sleep.

No, she couldn't hurt him, even if he turned out to be a terrible monster. So she hoped with all her heart that whatever it meant to be a vampire, it was nothing more than an affliction that required him to drink blood, but that apart from that gruesome act, he was as humane as she thought herself to be.

"Sleep, my love, you're safe," she whispered and snuggled into the curve of his body.

CHAPTER

SEVENTEEN

Ever since the night he'd quarreled with Raphael, Lorenzo thought that Bianca looked at him differently. Whenever she thought he wasn't watching, he caught her perusing him in a most peculiar fashion as if she couldn't believe her own eyes. It would have been unnerving, had she not at the same time become even more wanton in bed, inciting him to drive them both to the point where control shattered and ecstasy ruled supreme.

"Tie me up!" Bianca urged him now as she lay writhing underneath him, already bathed in sweat from their lovemaking, but eager for more.

He pulled his rock-hard erection out of her, more than willing to comply with her request. As he reached for the ties which had taken up permanent residence on his nightstand and proceeded to tie her wrists above her head, Bianca impatiently rocked her pelvis against him.

"Yes, show me how powerful you are. Make me submit to you." Her words were interspersed by heavy breathing, her voice sounding almost delirious. And her eyes watched him with untamed lust, her tongue licking her lips the way she always did when she wanted to suck him. God, he was one lucky son of a bitch having Bianca in his bed.

Once he'd secured the restraints around the headboard, he lowered himself over her again, playfully sliding his cock over her pearl. She hissed out a breath and arched against him, but he withdrew too quickly for her.

"Oh, no, my sweet, I'm your master now. I'll control your pleasure."

She lowered her gaze to his cock. "Let me suck you. I know how much you like that."

Despite the fact that she was right about how much he enjoyed his cock in her mouth, he shook his head. "It's your pleasure I want."

Then he reached for the black scarf. "Now be a good mistress and close your eyes."

There was a glint of surprise in her look before she lowered her lids and let herself be blindfolded. He'd never deprived her of her eyesight before, but he'd never seen her acting with such abandon as tonight. If she ever agreed to this, it would be tonight.

"What are you going to do?" she asked. He heard no fear in her voice, only excitement.

"Do you remember when I told you that on occasion I would want somebody else to watch us?"

Her breath hitched as her muscles tensed. "Who is it?"

Lorenzo smiled. "You haven't met him. And it doesn't matter who he is. All that matters is that you know that a stranger is looking at you while I'm pleasuring you."

He rose and swung his legs to the side of the bed. "He's waiting downstairs. I will go and fetch him now." Then he stood and walked to the door and opened it, glancing back over his shoulder. He noticed how Bianca's chest rose, her breathing more uneven than before. "Don't be concerned, my love. He may only watch, not touch."

Then he walked into the corridor and closed the door behind him.

Bianca felt her heartbeat escalate. The thought of another man watching them both scared and excited her. But it was too late to do anything about it. She was tied up, willingly at that, and unable to move. Maybe it was best this way: she could live out her wildest fantasies, things she would have never dared before.

When she heard steps on the stairs, she braced herself. Moments later, the door opened and closed.

"I'm back, Bianca. My friend here will stand to the right side of the bed so he'll have a good view of what I'm doing. I've asked him not to speak so that you won't be able to recognize his voice when you meet him in polite society in the future."

The notion that one day she might face this man suddenly made her panic. "Lorenzo, maybe this isn't a good idea."

"Nonsense. Just forget he's even here."

When Lorenzo's hand stroked over her thigh, Bianca jolted.

"Easy, my love, easy. I thought you wanted to do something new. And look—" He paused, trailing his fingers to the apex of her thighs, dipping one digit into her wet cave. "—how wet you are at the thought of this." Then he inhaled audibly. "I need to taste you."

Lorenzo pushed her thighs further apart, then settled between them. His hot breath blew against her moist flesh a moment before his tongue swept against it, lapping up the juices that oozed from her throbbing cunny. His moans reverberated in her body, driving any sane thought out of her passion-clouded mind.

"Oh, God," she let out. "More."

Lorenzo lifted his head from her flesh, cold air wafting against it in the process. But it didn't douse the fire that was already burning inside her. "Can you smell that, my friend? Yes? She tastes even better. Shame really, that you can't have any of it. Isn't that right, Bianca? Or do you want him to lick you too?"

Shocked, Bianca pulled on her restraints. "NO!"

She heard the grin in Lorenzo's voice when he answered. "Good answer, because had you said that you wanted him too, I would have had to kill him, friendship or not." Then he drove one thick finger into her, making her muscles clench around him. "Because you're mine alone. Not to be shared. Not to be touched by anybody else."

"Yes," was all she could whimper as he continued to finger-fuck her, adding a second digit to the first. But the contact left her wanting, not giving her enough friction, not filling her the way she needed to be filled. "I need more."

"I know that, my love. You'll have to learn to ask for what you want. So, ask for it."

She swallowed, apprehensive about another person besides Lorenzo hearing her voice dirty words. "I want you inside me."

"I *am* inside you," Lorenzo emphasized and drove his fingers in knuckles deep.

"Your cock!"

"Ah, you want my cock."

"Yes, fill me with your cock!"

"How do you want it? Slow and gentle?"

Bianca writhed against him, her pearl in desperate need. "Hard, fast." When he withdrew his fingers, she sighed in anticipation. His body settled over her. "Touch me first," she begged, unable to still the burning need at her core.

A moment later, his hard cock slid over her pearl. Relief flooded her. "Yes!"

But a second later, his erection nudged at her cunny and sliced into her with a move so powerful, it shifted her entire body closer to the headboard.

"Is that how you like it?" he grunted.

"Yes!"

Lorenzo withdrew, then slammed back into her. She braced her bound hands against the headboard feeling the carved letters underneath her fingertips as she prepared for the next impact. Instead, she felt his hand rip the blindfold from her eyes.

"I want you to look at me when you come." His voice was raw.

Her eyes darted to the right of the bed, searching for the stranger who was watching them. She saw—nobody. When she spun her head back, her gaze collided with Lorenzo's.

"You didn't think I would allow any man to see you this way, did you? You're mine. Nobody else has the right to see you like this."

His words broke the wall around her heart down as if it was merely a paper screen. She locked eyes with him. They had a glint in them now, a red-orange glow. Previously, she would have dismissed it as a reflection of the candlelight, but now that she knew what he was, a vampire, she understood that he stood at the tether of his control. And at that very moment she realized what she wanted.

Her lips parted, and the words she thought she'd never utter spilled over her lips. "Then bite me and make me yours."

Lorenzo's heart stopped as his body jolted backwards of its own volition, virtually catapulting him off the bed so fast he realized his vampire side had taken control. Bianca's words echoed over and over in his head: *bite me*. She knew! Bianca knew!

His heart started beating again, faster now. He gulped down air, expanding his chest, his body ready to fight.

"Lorenzo, please, come back."

Bianca's plea made him snap, turning his gaze back to her. Still tied up and utterly vulnerable in her nudity, her eyes hadn't lost the desire he'd seen shining in them earlier.

"I... you... you're mistaken." His brain couldn't produce a coherent thought. It felt as if his brain was being disassembled.

"I know what you are."

He shook his head. Denial was the only solution. "You know nothing."

"You're a vampire. I saw how you changed."

"No!" He took a step back.

"That night you quarreled with your friend... I saw your fangs, I saw your eyes. I know what you are. I heard you say it."

Lorenzo ran his hand through his hair and took a tentative step toward the bed. "You eavesdropped?"

Bianca nodded. "I'm glad I did."

"You didn't run. Why?"

"I wanted to. But then you came out of the parlor."

Slowly, he approached the bed, watching for signs of fear from Bianca, but there were none. "You could have escaped later."

"No. I can't escape you. Not then. Not now. You've captured me and my heart. You looked so distraught that night, so sad. I didn't have the heart to leave you. And when you told me you needed me, I…" Her voice trailed off, but her eyes continued her sentence.

Could it be real? Did she truly love him? How could he know for certain? He had to offer her a choice. "You're free to go, Bianca."

Lorenzo stopped next to the bed and reached for her wrists, untying them swiftly. Then he stepped back. "Leave now. I won't hurt you. All I ask is that you keep my secret."

Bianca sat up, shaking her head in the process. "No. I can't do that."

He closed his eyes for a moment. She wouldn't keep his secret? God, no! Why did she have to force his next action? He didn't want to wipe her memory of all that had happened, but now he knew that he had to. Anguish swept over him at the thought that the same fate as Elle's would befall Bianca. "I beg you."

Bianca slid off the bed, her bare feet making barely any sound on the wooden floor. With two steps, she crossed the distance between them and laid her hand on his chest. "I won't leave you. I want you, now more than ever."

He put his hand over hers. "It's madness, you should run while you still can."

"My heart's already made its choice. I want you. But if you have tired of me already—"

He placed his finger on her lips. She wanted him? Was this even possible?

His heart spoke for him as he parted his lips. "I'll never tire of you."

She gifted him with a ravishing smile. "Then bite me. I know you want it. I can feel it every time your teeth graze my skin."

His cock stiffened at the thought of sinking his fangs into her. He pulled her into his embrace. "My love, you can't even begin to understand what this means to me." To be allowed to feed off the very woman who had captured his heart was more than anything he'd ever hoped for. "I've been craving your blood ever since you stepped into my home. And I've fought it every day."

"No longer," she whispered and tilted her head to expose her graceful neck.

"Don't be afraid."

Lorenzo lifted her into his arms and carried her to the bed, laying her onto it before moving over her and positioning himself between her thighs.

"I want to make love to you at the same time." He stroked his hand over her face, smoothing back a strand of hair. Then he moved his hips and slid into her, exhaling sharply as his cock sank deep into her hot channel.

Bianca panted, her eyes closing.

"Look at me."

When her eyes flew open, Lorenzo willed his fangs to extend. He felt them push past his lips and noticed how Bianca gazed at him in fascination. There was no fear.

"I love you," he whispered and bent his head, connecting with the soft skin on her neck. He licked over it and felt her shiver.

"Do it, my love."

Lorenzo opened his mouth wider and pressed his fangs into her skin, piercing it, before he drove deeper. As he drew the first drops of her blood, his head swam. Her essence was pure and sinful at the same time, more intoxicating than he could have ever imagined. Without haste, he sucked on her vein, taking the life-giving essence into his body where it rejuvenated his cells and recharged his power.

At the same time, his hips moved, and he slowly withdrew his cock from her sheath only to thrust it back into her. Her muscles gripped him tightly, shuddering as he plunged deep. But he needed more, an even closer connection to the treasure he held in his arms. And for the first time in his life, he opened his heart and laid its contents bare, sending his emotions out to her.

He knew when she pressed her hand against the back of his head to hold him tighter to her neck that she felt the connection between them.

"Oh, God, Lorenzo!" she moaned on a shallow breath.

Lorenzo released her neck and licked over the puncture wounds, closing them instantly and turned his face to her. Her lips glistened and beckoned him to approach. As he brushed his bloodstained lips against hers and licked against them, she parted them. He swept his tongue inside and kissed her, claiming her as his, while he continued to send his feelings to her, his mind and heart pouring out of him so she would understand the depth of his need for her.

Her hands came around him, gripping him tighter, urging him on to take her harder. He complied and drove deeper into her until her interior muscles spasmed around him, sending him over the crest and into paradise.

EIGHTEEN

Bianca felt Lorenzo's lips on hers and slowly opened her eyes.

"It's called the little death," he explained with a smile as he caressed her cheek with the back of his index finger.

"I fainted." She'd never passed out in bed with a man.

"It happens sometimes when the pleasure is too much to bear." He planted a soft kiss on her lips.

If she'd had any decency left, she would have blushed at his words, but as it was, all she could think of was what it had felt like when he'd bitten her. Her entire body had been afire. But not only that: she'd sensed him, his emotions, the love he had for her, almost as if she'd been inside his mind.

"I felt something strange when we made love," she started.

Lorenzo took her hand and led it to his lips to kiss it. "I know. I opened my heart to you so you could feel what's inside me."

So she hadn't dreamed it. "How?"

"My vampire powers allow me to reach out to you and send you my thoughts and my feelings without speaking."

"Does that mean you can read my mind too?"

He shook his head. "I only know what you show me or tell me, but I can't see into your heart. But what you've shown me tonight, what you've given me by offering me your blood, has told me everything I need to know."

His eyes shone with the evidence of his affection for her. It made her chest feel heavy with the secrets she still kept from him. But she couldn't share them now.

"And your blood." He inhaled deeply, closing his eyes for a moment. "My sweet Bianca, I've never tasted anything as pure as you."

Pure? She wasn't pure. Panic gripped her for a moment. What if he ever found out about her past? About her life as a courtesan? Would he still consider her pure then? Her pulse raced at the thought that if he ever discovered her secret, he might change his mind about her. And then? Would he toss her aside, bitter about her deception?

If she confessed everything now, would he forgive her? She had to try. "Lorenzo, there's something I need to say..." She paused, not knowing how to go on.

"Bianca, before you say anything else, I need to explain one thing to you. It's about what you overheard that night. About Elle."

At the mention of that name, Bianca remembered his friend's words about a betrayal. An uneasy feeling rose from her stomach. "Yes?"

Lorenzo rolled to his side and let his head flop onto the pillow beside her. Then he pulled her into the curve of his body, cradling her against him. His breath was at her ear when he finally spoke. "I loved a woman once. She was human, and her name was Elle." He sighed. "I trusted her, and I believed that she loved me. And maybe she did. But her love wasn't strong enough."

"What happened?"

"She betrayed me. When I confessed to her what I was, she pretended that she didn't mind, that she could live with it. I should have seen it. She'd hidden her feelings in plain sight. One night, I awoke to find her bending over me with a stake. She almost killed me."

A heavy gasp escaped her as tears formed in her eyes.

"Oh, Lorenzo, I'm so sorry." She realized then that he wouldn't be able to forgive another betrayal. "What happened?"

"I had to wipe her memory of any knowledge of me. But it was too much for her mind to take. She became insane and died soon after."

Bianca's heart stuttered to a halt. Having felt how he'd projected his own feelings into her mind, the knowledge that he could wipe away memories didn't surprise her as much as it might have otherwise. Yet, there was something else that didn't make sense to her. "But, I don't understand. How could she not have accepted you? Why would she forego the kind of pleasure your bite brings? Why would—"

"I never took her blood. She didn't allow it. At the time I thought if I was patient, maybe she would change her mind. But sometimes we just don't want to see what's in plain view. She didn't love me."

A sob escaped her.

"You, my love, are the only woman who's ever freely offered her blood to me. And for that, I cherish you even more."

His words choked her, because she knew she didn't deserve his adoration. She'd deceived him just as Elle had, and while Bianca had no intention of ever hurting him, she knew if he found out about her past, he would feel the same kind of betrayal that he had gone through with Elle. She couldn't stop the next sob from escaping her throat.

Lorenzo stroked over her cheek. "You weep for my heartbreak, my love? There's no need for it anymore. My heart is mended now. I've given it to you, and I can't imagine a more worthy woman to keep it safe for me."

As her tears flowed freely, Lorenzo's hands caressed her and lulled her into sleep and the comfort she didn't deserve.

LORENZO LEANED back in the armchair in Nico's rooms and stared into the fire.

"Then why don't you tell her that you know about her past?" Nico asked and took a seat next to him, stretching his long legs toward the fire.

"Things have been so perfect the last couple of days, I don't want to upset the status quo."

"And what *is* the status quo?" his friend asked pointedly.

"I told you already. She knows about me now. And she accepts me as I am. Hell, every day and every night, she offers me her blood. Freely, without restraints. I can't tell her that I've been looking into her background. What must she think?"

Nico smirked. "That you're a cautious man? Who has reasons to be cautious, if I may add. Surely, she can't fault you for that. She showed up in your home, unannounced and—"

"Which reminds me," Lorenzo interrupted, "what *was* my house-warming present to be if it wasn't Bianca?"

"Ah, that!" Nico grinned. "We were planning on organizing an orgy for you, with exotic belly dancers fresh from the Orient, but seeing that you're so infatuated with this woman, I suppose we shall purchase a piece of furniture instead."

"Much appreciated." The thought of an orgy had no appeal for him at all. Not when he knew that Bianca was warming his bed.

"Now, to get back to my point: *she*'s the one who deceived you, yet *you*'re the one feeling guilty for investigating her background. Why do I think that's odd?" Nico made a near comical face, underscoring his sarcasm.

"Because you're an unfeeling ass, Nico! If you understood women at all, you'd see clearly that I'm in a quandary here. How am I going to show her that her past has no bearing on my feelings for her when I don't want to let her know that I already know?"

With his hands, Nico made circles in the air. "As you so eloquently stated, that is a quandary. And you're quite sure, you're not willing to admit to your little indiscretion about inquiring into her past?"

Lorenzo shot him an annoyed glare, and Nico instantly threw up his hands.

"Very well then. And since I *do* know women a little, thank you very much, I have a suggestion."

Lorenzo edged forward on his chair. "Let me have it."

"I haven't met a woman yet who won't forgive a little sin like yours as long as the reward is big enough."

"Reward?"

Nico nodded, his right index finger pointing at the fourth finger of his left hand. "Yes, reward. And don't tell me the thought hasn't crossed your mind yet."

Indeed, the thought had crossed his mind.

CHAPTER

NINETEEN

Bianca tossed and turned. Vaguely, she registered that at some time during the wee hours before sunrise, Lorenzo had returned from visiting a friend and joined her in bed. He slept soundly now, but her own sleep was agitated. Her dreams tormented her.

Scenes from her time in Florence flitted across her mind, reminding her of what she didn't want to go back to. Pictures of her former lovers mingled with those of the suitors her father had entertained, laughing at her now that she was a fallen woman. All of Venice knew. She found herself on the streets, her dress torn, walking across Piazza San Marco barefoot and with not a *lira* to her name. The people she passed turned away from her. But their whispered words carried to her nevertheless.

A whore.

Her lover found out and tossed her out on the street where she belongs.

She lied to him.

It's an open secret.

All for a treasure that was hidden in plain view.

Bathed in sweat, Bianca woke with a start. Her chest heaved with the effort to breathe. She glanced at Lorenzo, hoping she hadn't talked in her sleep. But he was sound asleep, the reflection of the flames from the low fire dancing on his skin.

As quietly as she could, she slid out of bed and walked to the sideboard, which held a pitcher of water. She poured herself a glass and gulped it down, trying to cool her heated body.

She couldn't go on like this. She had to tell him about her past and why she was here. Maybe he would forgive her for her deception. If he truly loved her the way he showed her every time he drank her blood, maybe he could find it in his heart to forgive her.

Bianca took a tentative step toward the bed. The fire behind her threw bizarre shadows over Lorenzo's body and the headboard behind him. As she walked closer, the shadows shifted and moved, pulling her gaze to the intricate carving on the wooden headboard. She stared at it, her eyes suddenly focusing in on the delicate workmanship.

Her heart stopped when she saw it. There, in large carved letters it was written: *Tesoro*. Treasure. Her feet carried her to the edge of the bed, but there was no mistake. The carving said treasure.

Bianca crawled onto the bed, careful not to disturb Lorenzo, and kneeled in front of the carving, letting her hands run over the letters. She'd felt them before when Lorenzo had tied her up, but she'd never paid them much attention. But now that she knew what they spelled out, she pressed against each letter, holding her breath. The last letter gave way and depressed. An instant later, a section of the carving not larger than a book sprang open like a little door.

Behind it was a dark space. This was where her father's treasure had to be hidden.

Excitement coursed through her as she reached her hand inside, unable to see its contents for lack of proper lighting. Her fingertips brushed against a piece of paper. She pulled it from the small cave and held it up so the light from the fireplace fell onto it.

Disappointment swept over her when she looked at it closely: underneath a symbol of a cross with three horizontal waves, all that was written was a list of names. No treasure map, no instructions on where the real treasure was buried. She tossed the useless item onto the pillow next to her and reached into the hidden compartment once more.

Her hand encountered a small item made of metal. She pulled it out and perused it. It was a ring. But it wasn't shiny nor did it hold a large precious stone. Instead, the ring was rather ugly, its black stone carrying the same symbol she had noticed on the paper she'd found. This wasn't any treasure! It was a near worthless piece of jewelry, which didn't even please her eye.

There had to be something else in the treasure trove. Could this really be all her father had left her? Had he sold the remainder and gambled the money away?

Disheartened, Bianca reached into the dark compartment and swept her hand systematically from left to right and top to bottom when her palm encountered a stick. She wrapped her hand around its smooth surface and brought it out into the light.

Her heartbeat doubled as she looked at the item that her hand gripped tightly: a stake! She was holding a wooden stake. A gasp escaped her. Had her father hunted vampires? Had he killed men like Lorenzo?

But she had no chance to think on it further, a movement to her left entering her vision. As she turned her head, Lorenzo vaulted himself onto her and wrestled her onto her back, his strong arms gripping her wrists and pressing them against the mattress to both sides of her head. At the same time, he straddled her, pinning her to the bed so she was unable to move.

When she caught the look on his face, she shrieked. His eyes were glaring red, and his fangs were extended. He growled low and dark.

"You too? How could you?" Disbelief carried in his voice. "You devious bitch! I trusted you!"

She knew what it must look like, and knowing what his former lover had done, she could only too easily understand his anger. "Lorenzo! Please, don't hurt me! Please, I didn't—"

He flashed his fangs at her and snarled. "You tried to kill me!" Then he threw his head back. "And to think that I loved you! What an idiot I am!"

"No, no!" she pleaded. "I didn't try to hurt you."

He let out a bitter laugh. "Oh, no? The stake in your hand says otherwise." He wrung the offending item from her palm and tossed it off the bed.

"I found it! It's not mine. It was with the treasure!" Bianca closed her eyes, willing away the tears that threatened to burst to the surface. He wouldn't believe her tears. Her only chance at making him believe her was to tell him the truth, all of it, every ugly detail.

"What treasure?"

She swallowed hard before she opened her eyes again. His gaze was as angry as before, yet she'd never thought him more beautiful. And she would lose him now. Once he knew of her past, he would toss her out onto the street. At least she would be alive, even though she couldn't imagine living without Lorenzo. He'd come to mean everything to her in the last few days.

"My father, he told me of a treasure he'd hidden in this house. He said it was worth more than the house itself."

Lorenzo huffed, but said nothing.

"I came back to find it so that I could finally start a new life. I'm not a lady. I'm not the gently bred daughter of a Venice merchant anymore. You deserve to know what I did. I've deceived you. I've hidden my shame, and I'm sorry. But when my father tried to marry me off to some old man I hated, I had to run. I had to escape."

She closed her eyes and allowed a tear to escape. "To survive I became a courtesan. I'm no better than a common whore."

"Bianca—"

"No! Don't say anything now. Hear me out. I tried to escape my lot. When my father died, I came back to find the treasure he'd spoken to me about so many years ago. But then Signore Mancini told me that the house had already been sold. I let myself in, hoping the new owner wouldn't move in until the next week. By that time I would have been gone with my treasure. But then you came that night—"

"You weren't at the house hoping to seduce me so you could stay and snag yourself a rich husband?"

She shook her head. "No! Of course not. All I wanted was to search for my father's treasure and leave to start a new life where nobody knew me."

Lorenzo eased his grip on her wrists. "Go on."

"You know the rest."

"No. Tell me why you stayed and allowed me to seduce you into my bed."

She averted her eyes, feeling embarrassment sweep over her at the memory of their intimacies. "At first, I stayed merely to continue my search. But then—"

"Then?" His eyes were back to their normal color now, and his fangs had retreated too.

"I stayed because I didn't want to leave you. I felt something I'd never felt before."

LORENZO'S HEARTBEAT slowed as his anger started to slowly dissipate. "If you have feelings for me, then why did you try to kill me?"

"I didn't. I found the stake. There." She pointed past him toward the head of the bed. "It was with the treasure." She gave an unladylike snort. "And what treasure it was: a stupid ring and a piece of paper. Worthless! Now I have nothing."

Lorenzo turned to look behind him and saw the opening in the headboard. A secret hiding place and cleverly done at that. He'd never noticed it, not that he'd given the piece of furniture more than a cursory glance before. Every time he'd been in this room, his entire attention had been lavished on Bianca, and he'd never really taken in any details about his surroundings.

As he was about to turn back to Bianca, his gaze fell onto the pillow. The black onyx ring contrasted against the white linen.

"Hell!" he cursed and picked up the evil item, snapping his head back to her. "This was the ring you found?"

She nodded.

"Do you realize what this is?"

"It's just a worthless ring. It's not even a diamond." The disappointment in her voice told him that she really had no idea what she'd stumbled upon.

"This, my sweet, is the ring of a Guardian."

She gave him the most confused look he'd ever seen her wear. "It's ugly."

He suddenly felt compelled to smile. "That it is. It appears your father was a Guardian, a member of the secret society that hunts our kind."

Bianca gasped. "He hunted vampires?"

"It appears that way."

"I don't understand. Then where's the treasure he spoke of? Was he just telling me tales to entertain me as a child?"

Lorenzo held the ring in front of her face. "This *is* a treasure. Was this all you found?"

"There was a piece of paper too, with names."

"Names?" Lorenzo spun around to pick up the sheet of paper he'd ignored earlier and looked at it now. As his eyes ran over the long list of names, his head spun. The list could only mean that those named were Guardians.

He looked down at Bianca, realizing that he still held her captive between his thighs. "This is the real treasure. The list. The names."

"Worth more than this house?"

He nodded.

"That's what my father always claimed. He said if he sold the treasure to the right people, he would be a rich man."

"He was right. Any vampire in this city would pay a vast sum of money to get his hands on this list. Knowing these names, we can finally defend ourselves and know our enemies."

"So you believe me now that I didn't want to kill you?" she asked, her voice resigned now. Why did she not join in his joy?

"Yes, my sweet, I believe you." He lifted himself off her and pulled her up to sit.

"Then I should pack my things and leave."

Lorenzo's heart stopped. "Leave?"

"Yes. You do understand that I can't stay here any longer. You know my secret now. You know what I am. A whore. Not worthy to be your mistress anymore." She moved to slide off the bed, but he snatched her arm and pulled her back.

"You're right. You can't be my mistress anymore. It wouldn't be right." Then he leaned toward the nightstand where he reached for the little box he'd placed there upon his return home. He opened it and took out the item it contained and turned back to Bianca.

"I wouldn't want the woman I love to merely be my mistress." Then he took her hand and slid the brilliant ruby ring onto her finger. "Be my wife."

A gasp came from Bianca's mouth, but no words came out even when she opened her lips and worked her throat. Her eyes went wide, and tears stood at their rim. Her gaze darted from the ring on her finger back to his face, and still she didn't say anything.

"Bianca, please say something. Don't keep me in suspense. I need to know your answer. You know I love you. You've seen my heart, you've felt the depth of my commitment to you, now please tell me you want me as your husband."

Suddenly her hands came around his neck, and she pulled him to her.

"Is that a yes?" he asked.

She nodded, a sob escaping her. "Yes."

His heart felt like bursting as he pulled her into his arms and kissed her passionately. But there was a tiny twinge of guilt inside him that he couldn't suppress. Separating his lips from hers, he inhaled deeply before he spoke.

"Bianca, my love, I have to make a confession."

Her eyelids rose, and her gaze collided with his. "Yes?"

"I've known about your past all along."

She pulled away further. "You what?"

"When I found you in my house that first night, I had my friend Nico make inquiries. I'm sorry I didn't tell you earlier, but I was afraid you'd be angry at me for investigating you."

"You knew I was a whore?"

"Shh. You're no whore. You're pure."

"I'm not pure. I'm soiled. I'm—"

He laid his hand on her heart. "In here, you're pure. It doesn't matter to me what lies in your past. You're what I want. Be mine. Let me make you happy."

"You mean this, don't you?"

He simply nodded. A moment later she threw herself into his arms and held him tighter than he'd ever been held.

"I love you, Lorenzo."

He lifted her chin up to brush his lips against hers. "For eternity." Then he lowered her back onto the sheets and moved over her, sliding in between her spread thighs. "My love, if we ever make it out of this bed, I'll shower you with every treasure you can imagine."

"And what can I give you?"

He smiled. "I already have my own treasure. You."

CHAPTER

TWENTY

Three weeks later

"The men on this list don't exist," Raphael proclaimed, holding up the infamous piece of paper Bianca had found.

As murmurs of disbelief rippled through the dozen friends who were assembled in Raphael's parlor, Lorenzo felt disappointment settle in. He'd been so sure the list showed the members of the hated Guardians of the Holy Waters, the group who'd been hunting him and his friends for years.

He let his gaze travel to Bianca, who sat on the sofa next to Isabella and gave her a reassuring look. While Nico, Raphael, Dante, and the latter two's wives had already met Bianca three weeks earlier, today Lorenzo had introduced her as his wife to the remainder of their closely knit group. Rumors about his nuptials had already traveled like ocean waves through the canals of Venice, and his friends had been eager to set eyes on the woman who'd stolen his heart.

"Then why would Signore Greco hide it with a ring of the Guardians? Is it to try and throw us off their trail?" Andrea asked.

"A ruse, I assume," Dante explained. "I assure you, Raphael and I have investigated each and every single name on this list. Without any success. The names are false."

"And incomplete." Isabella's words made Lorenzo snap his gaze to her.

"How can you know that?" Lorenzo took a step closer to her.

"Because neither my late husband's nor Massimo's name is on it."

"Nor Salvatore's," Viola, who stood next to Dante, added.

Lorenzo remembered all too well what had happened to the three men: Giovanni, Isabella's first husband and a Guardian had drowned. Massimo, another Guardian, who'd threatened to kill Raphael had been shot dead by Isabella, and Salvatore, the Guardian who'd nearly killed Dante and had forced him to turn Viola into a vampire to save her from certain death, had been shot and killed by Raphael.

"Maybe they're not on the list because they're dead," Lorenzo voiced his observation.

Bianca shook her head. "I don't think so. The ink on the paper looks old and worn. My father didn't write this list in the last few months before his death."

Raphael looked at the list in his hands again. "I agree. This is older than merely a few months. Hence it's impossible for those three men not to be on the list. Signore Greco couldn't have known about their deaths when he wrote down the names."

"Maybe they are on the list after all." Everybody turned at Nico's words.

"How so?" Lorenzo asked, curious whether Nico had figured something out that the rest of them had overlooked.

"A code."

Raphael's gaze swept over the paper in his hands. "By God!"

"Yes," Nico continued, "what if they all have code names they call each other by, so that if they are being overheard, their true identities won't be revealed?"

Lorenzo's spirit lifted. The find hadn't been for naught. "Then we simply have to figure out the code. Knowing that Massimo, Giovanni and Salvatore have to be on the list, if we can decipher what their code names were, we can get behind the logic of it and figure out the remaining names."

Nico grinned. "You're taking the words right out of my mouth, my friend."

"Excellent!" Dante slapped Nico on the shoulder and looked into the round. "Let's get to work then."

As his friends huddled together to pore over the list, Isabella rose from her seat and approached him. In a low voice, she addressed him. "Lorenzo, I think you should take your wife home. She seems unwell."

Instantly, his gaze shot to his wife, and indeed she looked somewhat pale. "Thank you, Isabella." He took her hand and kissed the back of it before he strode to Bianca.

"My sweet, let's go home."

Bianca gave him a grateful smile. "If you need to stay, I can go by myself."

Lorenzo pulled her up to stand. "I'd rather spend the rest of the night with you than with my friends." Then he snaked his arm around her waist. "Now come, you need to rest."

"I'm perfectly fine."

He smiled at her attempt to brush off his concern and made his excuses before he led Bianca out of the house. Glad that his house was only steps from Raphael and Dante's, he lifted her into his arms and carried her, ignoring her protests.

"I can walk."

He pressed a quick kiss on her lips to stop her from talking, then carried her into their home and up the stairs. "I like having you in my arms."

In their chamber, he gently set her on her feet. She instantly swayed, then ran for the commode which held a pitcher of water and a bowl.

"Oh, no!" she wailed, before she bent over the bowl and cast up her accounts.

With two steps, Lorenzo was behind her, slid his arm around her waist and supported her. Despite the fact that she was unwell, he couldn't suppress his smile. His sweet little wife was giving him the most amazing present.

With his free hand he poured her a glass of water.

"I'm sorry. I don't know what's wrong. Maybe the meat I ate was spoiled."

"Drink."

She took a gulp of water, washing out her mouth, then spit it out. "I'm better. I'm sorry you had to see this."

Lorenzo's hand slid possessively over her stomach, and his lips went to her ear. "My sweet, I'll be here whenever you need me. And now that we can be relatively certain that you're *enceinte*, we have a decision to make."

"*Enceinte?*" Bianca gasped and turned to face him.

"Yes, my love. There can be no other reason for your sickness. And if you need any more proof: you've not once rejected my advances in the last weeks and claimed to have your courses."

"Oh, my God." She looked down at herself and pressed her hand onto her stomach, then looked back up at him with wonder in her eyes. "A child."

"Yes, our child. But we have to—"

She grabbed his hand. "Lorenzo, will it be a vampire like you or human like me?"

"That is for you to decide."

Bianca gave him a confused look. "But how?"

"If you decide you want a human child, there's nothing for you to do. But should you decide you want a child that's half vampire, half human, for it can never be fully vampire, you have to drink my blood while the child is in your womb. You have until you're four months along to decide."

Would she want a child that was part vampire? Lorenzo knew what he wanted.

"What do you want?" Bianca asked.

"It doesn't matter what I want. This is your decision. Your choice." He didn't want to influence her with his own preference, so he didn't voice it.

"If it's half vampire, will it be hurt in the sun?"

"No. A half vampire, half human child will be able to walk in the sun and the shadows, having the traits and strengths of both species. It'll be stronger than either."

"But will it age?"

He understood her concern and was glad to be able to lay it to rest. "Yes, the child will grow and age as any human child. But as soon as it reaches maturity, it'll stop aging, just as any vampire's age is frozen at their turning."

Bianca nodded, clearly contemplating his words. Then she looked at him, her eyes going to his neck where his vein throbbed uncontrollably. She licked her lips. "What does blood taste like?"

Lorenzo's heart leapt. "Are you sure this is what you want?"

She nodded.

He drew her into his embrace. "You don't know what this means to me. Nobody's ever accepted me as you have. And now, to know that you're prepared to have our child be half vampire, you're making me the happiest man in the entire world."

"I love you, Lorenzo," she whispered and pressed herself closer. "Make love to me and let me drink your blood."

And there was nothing else he'd rather do in that instant.

Venice Vampyr

Sensual Danger

NEW YORK TIMES BESTSELLING AUTHOR

TINA FOLSOM

CHAPTER

ONE

enice, Italy – early 1800s

Nico hit the heavy knocker against the massive oak door and waited, his eyes darting down the dark alley. While it was not polite to call upon a virtual stranger after dark, particularly when such a visit was possibly not welcome, he didn't exactly have a choice about the time of day he could venture out. Unfortunately, a mid-afternoon appointment was foolish and potentially deadly—for a vampire.

On occasion, he'd braved a few seconds in daylight, but only in emergencies, and then only covered in a heavy black cloak and running as fast as if the devil were chasing him, always hugging the shadows of the buildings and avoiding direct sunlight. But even then, he'd sustained burns. He wasn't desperate enough for a repeat any time soon.

Nico heard the sound of a creaking staircase as footsteps approached the entrance door. A moment later, the lock slid back and the door opened a fraction. The first thing he noticed was a long, straight nose before the rest of the footman's face appeared. He was dressed in livery, his white gloves gleaming in the dark.

The man looked down his nose, crinkling it slightly. Nico, instantly reminded of the story of Pinocchio, wondered whose breathing apparatus was longer: this servant's or the wooden boy's. He would bet a few Lira on the snooty servant for sure.

"Yes?" The man's drawn-out inquiry conveyed his displeasure more than any rude remark could have.

Nico casually pulled off one dark glove. "I'm here to see Signore Lombardi."

A raised eyebrow was followed by a quick glance up and down Nico's person. Luckily, he didn't give a fig about what a lowly servant thought of his late arrival. But if the man displeased him, Nico didn't have any scruples about using his powers of suggestion on him to gain access to the house. Either way, he'd see Signore Lombardi tonight.

"And who may I say is calling?"

"Nicholas Angelotti," he answered and pulled off his second glove.

"One moment, signore." The servant nodded and made a motion to close the door, but Nico inserted his boot between door and frame, then nudged it forward.

"Ah, excuse me." He pushed the door open farther and entered the foyer, much to the obvious consternation of the unpleasant footman. "Terribly damp outside tonight."

With a glare, the man turned on his heel. "If you'll be so kind as to wait here." As he disappeared into the parlor to his right, Nico allowed his superior hearing to listen in on the announcement the servant made to his employer. Luckily, Signore Lombardi was a curious man and could not be dissuaded from receiving his late-night visitor.

When the door opened a few moments later, the footman motioned to it. "Signore Lombardi will see you now." With a barely perceivable nod, he stepped aside and let Nico pass into the room, closing the door behind him with a loud thud.

Nico took a short bow and studied the elderly gentleman who stood in front of the fireplace dressed in dark breeches and a burgundy house vest with matching coat, its belt tied to one side. His hair had grayed at the temples and was thinning on the top—a fact very easily observed since Nico was half a foot taller than his host. The spectacles Lombardi wore gave him the air of a confused *professore*, yet the intelligent mousy-brown eyes behind them belied that notion: the man was as alert as they came. And most likely a shrewd negotiator.

"Signore Lombardi, I'm grateful to be received despite the unusual hour."

"I don't believe we know each other, Signore Angelotti, or is my mind betraying me?"

"Indeed, it is not." Nico took a few steps closer.

"Pray, sit then." Lombardi slunk back into his armchair and pointed toward the sofa opposite. Nico obliged him even though he would have preferred to stand. He always liked to conduct business while standing.

"I'm assuming this is not a social visit," Lombardi said with a glance at the large Biedermeier clock that adorned one wall.

Nico inclined his head a fraction and allowed a gentle smile to play around his lips. "Let me be straightforward with you, signore, and not waste your time."

"I'd appreciate it, given the hour."

"I have come for some business."

"Which involves...?" Lombardi fished.

"The rumors that you're interested in retiring to the mainland and leaving Venice."

The man visibly relaxed and leaned back in his armchair, allowing his arms to rest on his lap as he crossed his ankles. "Ah, *those* rumors." He chuckled to himself. "About time somebody listened to them. Took me long enough to spread them."

With a start, Nico sat forward on the sofa. Had he come on a fool's errand? "Are you telling me that they aren't true?"

"They could be."

"They could be what, signore?"

"Either true or not true."

Frustration spread in Nico's gut. "Which one then?"

The old man smiled. "That depends entirely on you and your offer."

Nico relaxed. His immediate instinct about the man had been right: he was an excellent negotiator. However, how he knew why Nico was here was anybody's guess. "I see."

"Indeed. It appears properties in this area have increased in value. Several homes have changed hands in the last few weeks, and from what I hear, at considerable prices. Shall we say at more than what the bricks and mortar seem to be worth?"

Nico smiled. "I think you and I will get on splendidly during our negotiations."

"I shall hope so." He pointed toward the sideboard where a decanter beckoned. "Grappa?"

In order not to appear impolite, Nico nodded. He'd only recently fed on the rich blood of a tavern wench, so some alcohol on a full stomach wouldn't harm him. As a vampire he could imbibe liquids without any adverse effects. Alcohol was a little more difficult and on an empty stomach could easily impair his senses. They would still be sharper than a human's but with alcohol he would have nowhere near his normal fighting capabilities and perceptive skills.

"Three fingers," Lombardi indicated and motioned toward the decanter. "If you don't mind, young man, but my bones." He pointed toward the outside. "The damp, you know. It's much warmer and drier on the mainland."

Nico poured two glasses and handed one to his host before he took his assigned seat on the sofa. He raised his glass. "To your health, signore."

His host brought the glass to his lips and sipped. Nico did likewise, allowing the burning liquid to coat his throat. It was nothing like the smooth texture of the blood he'd so recently consumed. This liquid was harsh and unpleasant, yet by the look on Lombardi's face and the contented sigh he released, it seemed the grappa was of the highest quality. Feeling he had no choice to do otherwise, Nico allowed a fake sigh of enjoyment to pass his lips.

"Ah, I see you're a man who appreciates his spirits," Lombardi commented, looking pleased. "I would hate to do business with anybody who doesn't enjoy a good glass of grappa."

Nico smiled, still recovering from the burn of the alcohol. He would have to go for a second feeding tonight just to get the awful taste out of his mouth. "An exceptional vintage." Did they call grappa a vintage? He hoped so.

"Yes, yes." Lombardi set his glass on the little mahogany side table next to his armchair and glanced back at the clock once more. "May I ask the reason why you're interested in acquiring this residence?"

Nico cleared his throat, trying to buy himself some time. He hadn't expected Lombardi to ask such a personal question. Nico's hackles instantly rose. No reasons were ever given for business transactions such as these.

"Maybe your wife is in need of a larger home?" the old man suggested.

"I'm a bachelor."

Instantly, his host's face lit up, and he sat forward on his chair. "A man of your obvious breeding is still unmarried?"

Nico nodded curtly, neither wanting to alienate the curious man, nor willing to give away any of his personal circumstances. "Entirely so. But to get back to this house. I understand that you have direct access to the canal via a covered entrance?"

It was one thing Nico had noticed instantly when he'd scoured the houses on this block for one he wanted to make a bid on. On the side facing the canal, an archway had been built into the house, making it possible for a gondola to move into the interior of the house and out of the rays of the sun. If using a closed gondola, it would afford a vampire the ability to enter and exit without exposing himself to the rays of the sun. Nico couldn't pass up this opportunity.

While there were many homes in Venice that possessed this feature, on the block that he and his fellow vampires had decided to buy up all homes in order to establish a stronghold only two houses possessed such a covered entry: this and the one Dante and Raphael lived in with their wives. It would be a boon to snatch this house up before anybody else did.

"Yes, yes, it has a covered space for our gondola." He made a dismissive hand movement as if he didn't care about the feature. "But let me ask you something. Are you in need of a house because you've recently become engaged?"

Nico narrowed his eyes. Why was the blasted man so interested in his personal life? If there were another house like this available, he would leave Lombardi right now. His questions were getting downright rude. "No."

Another smile crossed the man's face. "Ah, excellent, excellent. Well, in this case, shall we discuss the purchase price? I assume that you're in possession of liquid funds?"

Nico sighed with relief. "My funds are liquid and can be dispensed at the shortest notice."

Lombardi nodded. "That's what I thought. As for the price, are you aware of the amount Signore Greco's home fetched only recently?"

"I'm indeed intimately aware of it." Lorenzo, one of his friends had purchased the house.

"Good. I would like twenty-five percent more."

Nico's jaw dropped. "Signore, you can't possibly be serious. This house isn't any larger than Signore Greco's."

Lombardi took another sip from his grappa. "Signore Greco's home is drafty and in need of repair. This house isn't."

"Ten percent more," Nico conceded.

"This home comes with its entire contents."

Surprised, Nico almost spilled his grappa. "You're selling the furniture with the house?"

"Not just the furniture, everything."

A terrible thought settled in Nico's gut. "Not the footman!" He wouldn't tolerate that insolent man.

"Of course not. Adolfo, the footman you met, will come with me to the countryside. Everything else stays, including the other servants: a second footman, a maid, and the cook."

Even though Nico would hire his own servants later, he nodded and looked around, assessing the furnishings. They were in good condition and of good quality. "Is the rest of the house furnished comparably?"

"It is. You may assure yourself of it personally in a short while." Lombardi took a deep breath. "Do we agree? Twenty-five percent more."

Nico didn't have to think about it. While the price was a little high, knowing he didn't have to deal with furnishing the house, plus the knowledge that it had a covered entry for a gondola more than made up for the outrageous sum Lombardi demanded.

He rose and offered his outstretched hand to Lombardi. He took it with a surprisingly firm grip.

"Now to the arrangements for the ceremony," Lombardi added.

Nico's stomach lurched as instant panic filled his body. "Ceremony?"

"Yes, the marriage shall be performed with utmost haste. And as soon—"

"Marriage?" Nico croaked.

Lombardi's beaded eyes looked at him as if Nico was dimwitted. "Yes, the marriage to my daughter of course."

"I'm sorry, signore, but there seems to be a misunderstanding." Was the man senile? "We discussed the purchase of your house."

"Which we agreed on for a fair price. And this price includes a marriage to my daughter. I thought you knew."

"Knew what?" Nico felt like tearing his hair out. How many glasses of grappa had the man had tonight?

"Everybody in Venice knows that I'd never part with the house unless my daughter gets a husband in the bargain. I've been waiting for a long time to make a match for her. I must say, I never figured that she would get such a dashing, young man as her betrothed. I would have settled for somebody much older and less handsome than yourself."

Lombardi's words told him everything he needed to know: his daughter was ugly and without any skills or graces to recommend her. And Nico would be the last man to accept a woman like her as his wife.

CHAPTER

TWO

"He wants you to do what?" Dante repeated for the second time.

Nico glared at him. "Are you deaf?"

Dante exchanged a grin with his brother Raphael who was lounging in his armchair in front of the fireplace, one leg casually swung over the armrest while the other was stretched out in front of him. Only in his own home could a man be this relaxed.

While Nico was always welcome in Dante's and Raphael's home, at present the feeling of comfort he normally sensed at the brothers' house escaped him. Inside, he was agitated and wondered whether he was making the biggest mistake of his life. Had he made the right decision?

"You could do worse than get a wife in the bargain," Raphael said.

"It would merely be a marriage of convenience in any case. A minor annoyance," Dante added.

"Don't let your wife hear that, or she might stake you instantly." Nico pushed a strand of hair out of his face.

"As all of us here know, I married for love. But then we can't all be that lucky. Besides, I didn't think you believed in love, Nico."

"Of course not. It's all a big lie."

"Then I don't really see why you object this much," Raphael inter-

336

jected. "If you don't believe in love, you've got nothing to lose by marrying this young woman and—"

"Young woman? Her father looks ancient. For all I know she's well past her prime. Maybe even in her thirties!"

"God forbid." Raphael chuckled.

Nico nodded. "That's right! And most likely she's as ugly as a piss pot. Or why else would she still be unmarried in her mid-thirties?"

"Now she's in her mid-thirties?" Dante asked and tossed his brother a sideways glance. "Give it another half hour and she's an aging spinster in need of a walking cane."

"And who is to say that she isn't? Her father is well off. He can provide her with a decent dowry. So why, I'm asking you, has nobody stepped forward to claim this *prize*?" Nico looked from Dante to Raphael, but the two did well to suppress their answers. Their smirks were another matter. "I tell you why: because a forty-year-old spinster with a nose like a hawk and a walk as graceful as a washerwoman on her last leg is the last thing any man worth his salt would want to warm his bed."

"Who says she has to warm your bed?" Dante loosened his cravat and opened the top button of his crisp white shirt. "Why can't you just send her to your estate on the mainland and have her live there while you stay in Venice?"

"Send the hag to the country?" Nico contemplated the idea. It wasn't bad at all. And he wouldn't even have to give her a reason why. She would have to obey her husband's orders. It would be simple. "She could travel to the mainland the day after the wedding."

Raphael tossed him a disapproving look. "Don't you think that's a little harsh? Sending her away the day after your wedding night?"

"Wedding night?" Nico echoed. "You don't expect me to fuck a woman who looks like a wicked witch?"

Dante laughed. "I'm afraid, Nico, you'll have to at least consummate the marriage. Nobody expects you to enjoy it."

A cold shudder ran down his spine at the thought of bedding Lombardi's daughter. If she had inherited any features from her father, she would be the ugliest woman he'd ever fucked, and that included some of the cheaper whores he'd frequented on occasion. Sure, he wasn't all that choosey when it came to bedmates, but at least the few less-than-handsome women he'd been in bed with had made up for their lack of beauty with their knowledge of the carnal arts. Those women had sucked cock better than the pretty ones.

He swallowed hard. "Easy for you to say. Your wife is beautiful. Who wouldn't want to—"

"Don't say it," Dante warned, his voice low and dangerous. "One word of disrespect toward Viola out of your mouth and I'll toss you into the canal myself."

Nico's eyes widened instantly. Landing in the waters of the canal was a death sentence for any vampire. Their cells were so dense and solid that as a result their bodies were much heavier than water and therefore sank like a rock. He would drown. "My apology."

"Apology accepted." Dante nodded swiftly. Then his expression darkened. "Don't think I don't understand your plight. But we need this house. We need every single house on this block to build a sanctuary for us and our fellow vampires. The Guardians are on our heels, and without a stronghold affording us safety and security, our numbers will diminish. We need to be strong to fight them."

Nico understood only too well. The Guardians of the Holy Waters, a secret society of Venetian noblemen and merchants, had made it their mission to eradicate each and every vampire in their midst. They had killed many of his friends in the last few years. It was because of this ever increasing threat that the vampires had decided to band together and purchase all houses on the block where Dante and Raphael lived, and to connect them with secret walkways, creating in effect one large fortress in which they could move around safely.

"Have we still not been able to glean any information from the list of names Lorenzo's wife found?"

"I haven't heard anything about Marcello having found the cipher yet." Raphael gave a hopeful smile. "But he's a smart man. I'm sure he'll find something."

Nico nodded. It had been very fortunate that Bianca, Lorenzo's wife, had found a list with the names of the Guardians in her father's house. It appeared that her late father had been one of them and prepared the list possibly in an attempt to use it to make a fortune. And for certain, any of his fellow vampires would have paid a pretty penny for it. However, it had turned out that the names were written in some sort of code that Nico and his friends hadn't been able to decipher yet.

"Good. I hope so. I'd hate for us to be sitting ducks, not knowing who our enemies are."

Dante let out a deep breath. "Patience, patience. But in the meantime, we have to continue what we've started. Enrico just bought the house at the end of the alley. Andrea is in the middle of negotiations for the house between ours and Lorenzo's, and Carlo thinks he has a lead on another one. We're making progress."

Nico picked up the gaze his friend sent him and read the question in it. Could he be relied upon to do the right thing and take over Lombardi's house despite the burden it came with? Nico felt perspiration build on his neck and felt the urge to pat himself dry but resisted it. He didn't want to admit to his friends that the entire situation caused him stress. Instead, he looked away and changed the subject.

"Maybe I should call on Marcello and see if he needs help. Four eyes see more than two."

"Suit yourself," Dante said, sounding slightly annoyed. "But your time would be better spent returning to your negotiations with Signore Lombardi. The man is clearly interested in ridding himself of the house and his daughter in one transaction, and there are plenty of men around who might find the offer tempting."

"Tempting?" Nico snorted. "Marrying an old spinster whose face is so disagreeable no man in his right mind would want to be in her presence at daylight? I don't see how that can be tempting."

"Tempting or not, what's your objection? You prefer the night anyway. Just blow out the candles." Dante made it sound easier than it was.

"Just imagine she is somebody else when you fuck her," Raphael advised. "You probably do that anyway when you visit your whores. So what's the difference?"

Nico shrugged. Was there a difference? In the dark, weren't all women the same? Well, maybe not entirely. They all tasted and smelled different. And maybe, just maybe Lombardi's daughter had an agreeable smell to her. Then fucking her in the dark wouldn't be as disagreeable after all.

Nico rose from his seat. "I'd better get going. There's much to be done." He walked to the door, then glanced back over his shoulder. "I trust you'll be at my wedding?" When he saw both brothers' jaws drop in surprise, he couldn't suppress his grin.

"You already decided?" Dante asked.

"Of course. The house is worth it. The wedding is scheduled for Friday night. You'll attend with Viola and Isabella?"

"That's two days from now."

"No need to waste time. The quicker I get the ceremony behind me, the faster I can send her to the countryside."

And that was exactly what he would do. He'd marry the ugly spinster on Friday night, consummate the marriage post haste and send her on her way to his estate by Monday. Despite his plan, Nico felt as if he'd made a decision which would change his life forever. But he wouldn't allow it. Once his wife was safely tucked away in the country, he'd resume his bachelor life, fucking whatever woman he wanted and feeding from the sweetest blood available. Nothing would change. Nothing!

CHAPTER

THREE

Nico had insisted on an evening wedding, and Lombardi hadn't objected. The parlor of the home that would officially become his after the ceremony had been decorated with flowers. Furniture had been removed to make space for the wedding party. Nico had invited only a few of his friends, mostly so as not to raise any suspicion with Signore Lombardi. A man without friends was not to be trusted.

In addition to the brothers Dante and Raphael and their wives Viola and Isabella, Lorenzo had come with his wife Bianca. Both Marcello and Carlo couldn't be dissuaded to stay away once they'd heard of his impending nuptials. The two bachelors were clearly here to gloat.

Nico nervously shifted from one foot to the other when he finally heard the bride's footsteps on the stairs as she descended from the upper floor. He cast a look through the open door and saw her walking on her father's arm. Her gown was of cream silk, making her appear as if she floated on a cloud.

His mouth went dry. This was Oriana, his bride? He looked back up the stairs to reassure himself that no other woman was following the procession. But no, the female on Signore Lombardi's arm was the only woman apart from his friends' wives.

Once more he shifted, this time not because of nerves, but to adjust his stiffening prick—for his bride was the most gorgeous woman he'd ever set eyes on. Her hair was a dark chestnut color and was piled high on her head, leaving her graceful neck bare.

Temptation coiled through him. He could see himself taking out the pins from her coiffure, allowing her hair to cascade over her pale shoulders while he dug his hungry fangs into her neck and thrust his insatiable shaft into her quivering sex.

As he tried to find some semblance of composure, a question penetrated his lust-drugged mind. Why was Lombardi so keen on marrying her off by practically throwing her in with the sale of the property? For certain, a stunning beauty like Oriana had suitors aplenty. What was wrong with her?

STILL SEETHING about her father's orders to marry a man she'd never met, Oriana did not turn her head to look at her future husband and instead stared at the priest who officiated the ceremony. She'd had no choice but to bend to her father's will. He owned her, just like her husband would own her the moment the marriage vows were spoken.

At least while she'd been subject to her father's wishes, she'd been able to circumvent his orders often enough: in secret and with the help of the second footman, she'd been able to conduct her scientific experiments. This was her life's work. It had started two years earlier: one night after a masquerade, she'd returned home accompanied by her footman. In an alley, she'd observed a man bent over a woman as if he were kissing her neck. At first she'd been embarrassed and had looked away, but when she'd glanced back, she'd noticed that the woman's neck was bloody. Shocked to the core, she'd fled from the scene, her footman chasing after her, surprised at her behavior.

After a night during which she was plagued with nightmares about what she'd seen, she'd woken with a purpose: to prove that she hadn't imagined the scene from the previous night. She had seen a vampire feeding from a human. For weeks she'd ventured out after dark, always accompanied by her footman, and had searched for the supernatural creatures, until one night, she'd seen one. She was certain now: vampires existed, and they were using humans without their consent. The far-away look in the eyes of the woman the vampire was feeding from was proof of it: he'd somehow drugged her so he could use her. Oriana had felt compassion for the young woman who was no older than herself. And then she'd recognized her: the girl was the maid her father had fired after a few pieces of linen had disappeared. Was she living on the streets now? Had she been easy prey? Her heart had clenched, and she'd searched for a way to help, but she'd been too afraid to approach, scared that the vampire would attack her too.

Ashamed, she'd returned home, and after a sleepless night, she'd woken with the determination to do what lay within her powers. She'd started devouring every scientific book she could lay her hands on and started her research. Now she was at a point where she had a machine which, if it worked, would alert her to the presence of a vampire.

When her father had found out, he'd been furious at first, claiming that it was no decent occupation for a lady. Luckily, he only knew that she was tinkering with scientific instruments—had he known she was trying to ferret out vampires, he would have locked her in an asylum for the insane.

Her father had started contemplating what to do to make her stop in her endeavors. Clearly, he'd found a solution: to marry her off to some rich gentleman, thus killing two birds with one stone. Not only would her father finally be rid of her, making her scientific interests her husband's problem, he would also be enriching himself in the process, taking the money Signore Angelotti paid for her to live a carefree life on the mainland.

Everything was working out perfectly, at least for her father and her new husband. She alone was carrying the entire burden. And as if the loss of her freedom wasn't enough, she was certain her husband would insist on his marital rights and make her share his bed. The very thought of having to offer her body to a man she didn't know and allow him to do whatever god-awful things he wanted was disgusting.

A shiver ran down her spine, and she felt herself sway. She was tempted to look at the man who now stood next to her, but she fought it. It would only increase her feeling of disgust further. Pushing down the bile that rose, she automatically answered the priest's questions and repeated his words. She wanted no conscious memory of this ceremony and not be reminded of the moment her life would change irrevocably.

A husband—she'd never wanted one. She'd seen too many of the women she'd grown up with stuck in arranged marriages with older men in order to save their family's waning fortune. She'd prayed to escape the same fate, but alas, her prayers had not been answered.

Now all she could do was bear her lot. But this didn't mean that she would make it easy for her new husband. She could brush him off as if he were merely a dust particle on her pristine white gloves and make certain that after a few unsatisfying nights in her bed, he would seek his pleasures elsewhere. Maybe she should suggest he take a mistress so he wouldn't bother her with his carnal desires. It was the best solution for both of them. After all, he'd agreed to marry her without even seeing her. It confirmed that he was only interested in the house, not in her. Surely, an arrangement by which he wouldn't be encumbered by her presence, nor feel obligated to perform any marital duties, would suit him just as much as it suited her.

"...by the power vested in me by God, I pronounce you husband and wife," the priest suddenly said. "You may kiss the bride."

For the first time, Oriana lifted her head and turned it toward the man standing next to her. Shock made her rock back on her heels, almost robbing her of her balance. The man she'd exchanged vows with only seconds earlier wasn't at all what she'd expected.

He was young, perhaps only five to seven years older than herself. And handsome—extraordinarily handsome. Instantly, her mouth went dry and her stomach quivered. Why had this man married her? Why would he possibly marry a woman he'd never seen? Something had to be wrong with him.

But she couldn't continue her thought process, because her husband stepped closer, bringing his head close to hers. His eyes locked with hers, and the brilliant green in them struck her, sending another flutter through her core. She'd never been one to faint, had always despised the debutantes who did so at the slightest provocation, but now she herself felt as if her knees would give way at any moment.

Yet, she knew she wouldn't fall because Nicholas Angelotti, the man who was now her husband, laid his hands on her waist and drew her against his body. His lips parted. Then he pressed them onto her mouth, kissing her softly.

She inhaled his masculine scent, drawing it into her body, opening her mouth in the process. As if seeing this as an invitation, she felt his warm tongue slide over her lips, licking gently before dipping inside her. It took her by surprise, so much so, that she instinctively gripped his shoulders. But instead of pushing him away from her, she pulled him closer.

Like a wanton woman, she tilted her head to the side, allowing him deeper access. A moan came over his lips as he danced with her tongue and explored her. She should be ashamed of herself for allowing him such liberties, but her body didn't react to her commands. His kiss was passionate and seductive. It was indecent! Did all husbands kiss their wives like this? Her female friends had never mentioned anything like it. No, this was all wrong. She had to stop this. But her lips continued responding to him, relishing the firm pressure with which he captured her mouth, the seductive slide of his tongue and the sinful way with which his hands burned through her gown.

When the clearing of several throats entered her consciousness, he finally released her.

"Oriana, my sweet wife," he said for all to hear. Then he bent to her ear and whispered, "I promise you, our wedding night will be more passionate —and last much longer."

She gasped for air, shocked at his insinuation. At the same time, heat rose to her cheeks, making them burn as if somebody had doused her with scalding hot water.

"Signore!" was all she could exclaim.

When he pulled his head back to look at her, he smiled knowingly.

Outraged at his arrogance, she pressed her lips together. If he thought he could simply waltz into her life and turn her into a quivering female who would bend to his will, she would show him!

CHAPTER

FOUR

Nico couldn't wait to see the back of his wedding guests as he ushered them out the door. Unfortunately, they had taken their time and lingered after the ceremony, accepting the beverages his new father-in-law had offered. But finally, after what seemed like an eternity, not only his friends but also Oriana's father had departed with his dreaded footman. Only the second footman, a maid, and the cook remained in the house.

In effect, he was alone with his wife.

Oriana took his proffered arm, and he led her to the stairs. Her face remained expressionless, and he could only imagine that she was afraid of what would happen in the marriage bed. As it happened, her mother had died many years earlier, and at the ceremony no elderly female relative had been present who could have talked to his bride about the goings on between husband and wife. It appeared Nico would have to explain things to her himself. Since he wasn't in the mood for a lengthy conversation, he would have to show her instead. That prospect pleased him more than anything else.

At the top of the stairs, she motioned to the left, and he followed her indication until she stopped at a door.

346

"May I?" he asked politely and opened the door for her, letting her enter.

Nico caught a glimpse of the room. It was lit by several candles, and warmth emanated from it, indicating that a fire was burning in the fireplace. But before he could peruse the chamber further, Oriana turned and blocked his entry.

"I bid you good night, signore," she said with a quick bow of her head.

Taken by surprise for a split second, he almost had the door slammed in his face, had he not reached out his hand and stopped her from shutting it. Jerking it open wider, he took a step into the room.

"Signore," she protested, her cheeks flaming. "This is my chamber. Yours is next door."

Nico sighed. It appeared he had more explaining to do than he expected. Exactly how innocent could this beautiful woman be? Was it possible that she knew nothing about the relations between married couples?

"I beg your pardon, my dear wife, but it appears you may have overlooked something. I can only guess that the lack of a mother has made you oblivious to the concept of a wedding night. Surely, were your dear mother —God rest her soul—alive, she would have explained to you about—"

"Signore," she interrupted him with an icy voice. "Let me be clear, since it appears that a subtle hint from me will not suffice."

Nico raised a surprised eyebrow, both at her tone as well as her words.

"You married me because you wanted to purchase this house, and my father would only sell it if he could arrange a marriage at the same time. Neither you nor I are interested in this arrangement. Therefore, I propose that you and I carry on as before this unfortunate event and live together in quiet ignorance of each other. I shall play the obedient wife in public as long as you make no demands on me in private. I shall turn a blind eye to any mistresses you may wish to entertain and can assure you that you will find no fault in my virtuous behavior. I trust this is agreeable?"

She raised her chin and looked at him as if she had just made an arrangement with the butcher about which cuts of the venison she would like delivered. No emotions played across her face.

"But my sweet wife, you're mistaken. I admit, at first I was, shall we say, *surprised* since I had no plans of entering matrimony; however, in light of the circumstances, I'm more than happy to carry out my husbandly duties." He dropped his gaze to her mouth, then lower to where the swells of her breasts heaved as she took more air into her lungs. The creamy flesh her modestly cut dress revealed looked inviting.

"Signore, I—"

"Nico," he interrupted. "I would like you to call me by my given name. Trust me, it would be more than awkward if you continued to call me *signore* when we're engaged in... marital relations."

Her eyes narrowed, and he could firmly see how her spine stiffened. "You don't seem to understand. I relieve you of your marital duties, *signore!*"

Nico took a step closer. "I'm afraid it is you who doesn't understand. Maybe I'm not making myself clear enough: I *wish* to exercise my marital duties."

Suddenly she fisted her hands at her hips. "If you believe I'll let you mount me as if I were a broodmare, I advise you to turn around and find your filthy pleasures elsewhere."

Part relief, part anger flared through him. "Ah, so I see, you *are* aware of what happens in the marriage bed." At least he wouldn't have to explain the details.

"I know more than enough. And I can assure you that I have no interest in it. Find yourself a mistress and perform whatever unpleasant activities you have in mind with her. I'm certain she'll welcome you with open arms since your physique is not disagreeable. A man of your looks should have no problems finding a willing bed partner."

Nico smiled involuntarily. "So you find me good looking?"

A shocked gasp came over her red lips, and a furious blush suddenly stained her cheeks. "I merely meant to say that a gentleman of your age, looks, and means will not be rejected by those women who offer their favors to married men. So please take your leave. You have my blessing."

"Your blessing?"

Her words made him want to chuckle, but he kept himself in check, not showing how much he enjoyed her sharp tongue. He hadn't expected her to resist in such a way. Particularly if she was attracted to him. Well, she'd said he was good looking, but didn't that amount to the same thing?

"My dear wife, it's not your blessing I seek."

Quite deliberately he swept his eyes over her body, lingering on her bosom for more than a few seconds. He wanted her to be aware of his intentions, because he wouldn't be swayed. When he lifted his eyes to meet hers, a twinge of fear flickered across her face.

Oriana's voice trembled almost unnoticeably when she continued, "Signore, surely a gentleman like you wouldn't force himself on a woman who doesn't welcome his attentions."

As she backed farther into the room, he followed suit. His eyes fell onto the large four-poster bed that fairly invited him to throw her onto it and make her his.

He leaned closer, making his chest connect with her bosom. At the contact, his body heated, but the sensation lasted for too brief a time, because his reluctant wife sidestepped him, intent on escaping his attentions.

Slowly, he moved his head from side to side, giving her a chiding look. "Did I mention that a wife has duties too?"

With defiance glaring from her beautiful blue eyes, she took a deep breath. "No gentleman would force a woman, even if she was his wife. Is that what you want, signore? To bed a wife who is disgusted by a man's—" She hesitated, her gaze drifting away in embarrassment.

"...prick?" With satisfaction, he heard her release an outraged huff. He'd used the vulgar word on purpose, wanting to coax a reaction from her. "There's nothing disgusting about it—not if he uses his manhood well. And let me assure you, I know how to please a woman with it."

"Hah!" she cried out, then lashed an angry glare at him. "From what I've heard, there is no pleasure to be had by a woman. It is merely meant to satisfy a man."

He chuckled. "From what you've heard? Pray, my sweet wife, what is your source for this untruth?"

"Are you calling me a liar?" She threw her head back, a curl escaping her beautiful coiffure in the process.

Nico gave a cursory bow, smiling to himself for the brief moment his face was turned away from her. He hadn't expected to spar with his bride during their wedding night, at least not verbally. "Far from it. I only question the validity of your sources. Once a piece of information changes hands too many times, it is often distorted."

"My information comes from a woman who has experienced this first hand!"

"A married woman?" he asked politely.

"Yes! And from the complaints I've been made to listen to during her visits, I daresay the poor woman is suffering dreadfully, having to endure her husband mounting her for his vile pleasure, leaving her in pain and shame on a nightly basis." She lashed an accusatory glare at him. "I don't care to share the same fate!"

Relieved that Oriana's objection to the marriage bed lay only in misinformation and was something he would be able to remove quickly and swiftly, he smiled.

"I apologize, my dear Oriana. Of course, I would never subject you to shame and pain. No husband ever should. I fully understand your concerns now, and let me assure you that I have no intention of doing what your friend's husband is subjecting her to."

He heard her sigh in relief, and noticed how her shoulders relaxed. "Thank you, signore. I'm pleased to know that you understand. I'm sure with this obstacle out of the way, our marriage will be an agreeable one."

Nico shook his head lightly, realizing that she had clearly misunderstood his words. "Agreeable? It will be more than that. And the obstacle that you speak of has not been removed. It has merely been pushed to the side for tonight." With two long strides, he crossed the distance that separated them. "Because I promise you, when I take you to bed, you won't feel shame or pain, you'll feel pleasure and desire. And you won't refuse my advances, because you'll be begging me to drive into your sweet body and make you mine in every sense of the word."

Oriana's face turned ashen. "Oh God!"

Taking her hand, Nico brought it to his lips and placed a soft kiss on her knuckles. "For tonight I'll let you rest, but tomorrow, I'll show you how a husband treats his wife properly. And I promise you, when your married friend visits again, you won't have any complaints to share with her. Whether you'll want to confide in her how your husband makes you scream with pleasure, is for you to decide. Maybe, if she's a good friend, you would want to give her details she may pass on to her husband, so she too may experience pleasure instead of shame."

Then he bowed and left her chamber, pulling the door shut behind him. Leaving her tonight was the hardest thing he'd ever had to do, but he knew it was necessary, because his wife had to be seduced—thoroughly. And in her current frightened state, she wouldn't respond to him. He had to catch her off guard.

CHAPTER

FIVE

Oriana tossed and turned half the night. Her husband's words had shaken her. He wasn't at all what she expected a husband to be like. First of all, he seemed utterly unconventional, repeatedly calling her by her given name and asking her to do the same. She'd refused and stoically continued to call him *signore*, even though she'd wanted to try out his name on her tongue.

"Nico," she whispered now that she was alone and nobody could hear her.

But the words he'd said to her, his promise to take her to bed and that she would even beg him for it, were outrageous. She couldn't allow this. From Ilaria, her friend, she knew how humiliating the experience was, and how painful at the same time. She wanted no part of it. And for certain he was hallucinating if he thought she would ever beg for it!

Tonight, she would lock her door as well as the connecting door between their chambers so he wouldn't be able to gain access to her. Surely if she continued this long enough, he would give up and pursue his pleasures with some trollop he found in a tavern. But she, Oriana, would never allow him to touch her that way, despite the fact that he was neither as old nor as ugly as Ilaria's husband.

Having formed a plan, she fell asleep, but woke early. Like every day, she rose and performed her ablutions. Then she dressed herself without calling for the maid—she would put her corset on later—and snuck out of her room to find her way downstairs, carrying a candlestick with a lit candle to help her along in the darkness. Through a hidden door in the first floor hallway, she entered a secret corridor. It smelled musty and stale in the dark space, but Oriana had gotten used to it. It took her only seconds to reach the only room in this hidden part of the house.

She entered it and lit more candles in the room. They reflected in the mirrors she'd collected over the years and aligned along the walls. She'd acquired a large amount of scientific knowledge during her years of study and understood the principles of most disciplines. Since light reflected in mirrors, she'd decided to brighten the room with their help, thus using only a minimal number of candles.

It had helped her hide her activities from her father, who would have noticed if she had used up more candle wax than he believed she should. Nevertheless, he'd discovered her activities one day. That was when he'd decided to rid himself of her by way of marriage and make her another man's responsibility—and problem.

For quite a while now, she'd been working on an apparatus that would make it possible to detect supernatural beings. Even before her chance encounter with a vampire, she'd been interested in science and had tinkered with it. Later she'd taken everything she'd learned about physics, chemistry, and biology, and combined it with the knowledge she'd gleaned from myths and legends. Thus she had come up with the formula of what would identify such a creature.

She was constantly fine-tuning her equipment, then testing it again and again out in the dark streets of Venice. She was no fool of course, knowing that if she ventured out on her own, she could fall victim to some cutthroat, so she'd let the second footman, Giuseppe, in on her secrets and found him to be not only a great protector when out on Venice's dangerous streets, but also a talented assistant in her clandestine lab.

Oriana looked up from her work bench when she heard a sound

coming from the corridor. As always on such occasions, she tensed until a soft knock sounded at the old wooden door.

"Come," she answered, already knowing who asked for entry.

When Giuseppe entered, lowering his head as he stepped through the low door, he bowed briefly.

"I didn't expect you to be down here so early, Signorina, or I would have come earlier to assist you."

She smiled, but didn't correct him when he still called her *Signorina*, when now she was a *Signora*, a married woman.

"Where else would I be?"

He shuffled closer, embarrassed about something. "Your wedding, signorina, I mean signora. I would have expected..." His voice died, then he cleared it loudly. "I wanted to let you know that cook has prepared breakfast."

"Is it that late already?" she asked, surprised, since she hadn't noticed the time pass.

"Indeed, signora. And cook delayed it by two hours already, given the fact that this is the morning after you wedding n-n-night." Whenever he was nervous, his stutter was more pronounced.

"Well, then I'd better not disappoint cook. Has my husband risen?" The word *husband* sounded so foreign in her ears that she wondered whether she was still asleep and merely dreaming.

"He hasn't rung for any assistance yet."

Good. At least she could have breakfast in peace and quiet before returning to her lab.

"And, uh..."

She looked at Giuseppe when he didn't complete his sentence. "Yes, is there something else?"

He nodded quickly. "Do you remember when I mentioned a fortnight ago that I'd heard of some group who's equally interested in the supernatural as yourself?"

Curious, she froze. "Yes."

"It appears that this group is very interested in exchanging information with you. In fact, they would even be willing to pay money for seeing your research."

Her heart stopped. "They know about my research?"

Giuseppe dropped his head, and his fingers played nervously with a button on his livery. "Well, the thing is, in order to find out what they know, I had to tell them a little bit about what you know." He raised his eyes quickly, uncertainty about her reaction to this news written in them. "I didn't say much, but I alluded to the fact that you may know how to identify preternatural beings."

Frantically, the wheels in Oriana's head began to spin. Had her footman put her in danger by revealing something about her research to strangers? Or could these people help her further her work?

"Do you know what specifically they're looking for?" she asked.

"Vampires, just like you. They are interested in finding out how to detect one."

"Have you told them about my machine?" she asked, raising her voice and stepping closer.

Instinctively, he shrunk back from her. "No, not really. Not specifical-ly." He hesitated, shifting his weight from one foot onto the other, while she stared at him intensely. "I may have said you have a way of knowing."

"What *exactly* did you tell them?"

He swallowed visibly, his Adam's apple jumping. "I may have said that you're working on an apparatus..."

Oriana sighed in frustration. "I don't even know if this machine works yet. I'm still tinkering with it. It's too early to tell anybody about it. If it fails, I'll be the laughingstock of all of Venice! Giuseppe!" she cursed.

"I apologize, signorina, uh, signora!"

"Never mind that now. You'd better go back to them and tell them that I'm still testing the equipment and I'm not ready to reveal it yet."

Giuseppe scratched himself on the back of his head. "I don't really know anybody of the group directly. They seem to be very secretive."

"Then how did you relay information to them?" she asked, confused.

"There's this footman I know; he knows one of them."

"Well, then talk to him and tell him what I've told you: I'm not ready."

Then she brushed past him and left her laboratory, calling for her maid to help her put on her corset, which was one piece of clothing she couldn't lace herself into. Once dressed properly, she headed for the dining room to partake of her breakfast.

CHAPTER

SIX

Nico was awakened by the various sounds in his new home, and had risen despite the fact that it was still daytime, and by the looks of it, even before midday. He could say with certainty that in his entire time as a vampire, he'd never been up this early.

He sleepwalked his way through his morning ritual, nevertheless taking great pains to wash with the cold water that a servant had left in a pitcher the night before. He would call for a bath at a later time. For now, he was eager to find his wife and reassure himself that the face he'd dreamed of after returning home in the early hours of the morning was as beautiful as he remembered.

After Oriana had refused him access to her chamber and her enticing body, he'd left the house, knowing full well that staying while she slept in the room next door would make it impossible for him to sleep one wink. Besides, he was a creature of the night and could be found in a bed during night time for only one reason: to bed a woman.

With stealthy steps that were second nature to him, he stalked downstairs and inhaled deeply, taking in the different scents of the house that was now his home. One scent among the many different ones tickled his nostrils, eliciting the same reaction as when he'd first smelled it the night before: Oriana's pure scent.

He followed it as it carried him toward the dining room. When he approached the door, he heard the faint tinkling of cutlery. Oriana's scent was strongest here. Filling his lungs, he opened the door and let himself in, closing it silently behind him.

Knowing he only had a second to take in the lovely sight, before his wife would be alerted to the intrusion, he looked his fill: her lips were red and plump, her fingers holding a fork ever so delicately, her back straight, and her eyes fixated on something in the distance.

Despite the two windows, the room was rather dark because the house backed onto another, slightly taller building, which robbed this side of the house of sunlight. He appreciated this fact, because it made it easy for him to move around. In fact, many Venetian homes were rather dark, since they were only separated from other houses by narrow alleys that didn't allow much light to penetrate.

When he pushed himself away from the door and took a step into the room, Oriana's head suddenly whipped in his direction. Her eyes widened, but within a split second, she had herself under control again, hiding her outraged expression. She could have fooled any man and made him think she was indifferent to his presence, just not Nico, because at the same time he could hear her accelerated heartbeat as it beat a frantic tattoo against her ribcage. Her bosom heaved in concert with it.

"Good morning, Oriana," he greeted her and approached as slowly as a tiger its prey.

"Good morning, signore," she answered and turned to look at her plate, stabbing her fork into a morsel of biscuit, before she brought it to her lips and chewed longer than was necessary.

Clearly a ploy so she wouldn't have to converse with him. Little did she know that he hadn't come to talk.

"I trust you slept well," Nico continued and took a seat opposite her, reaching for a biscuit and putting it on his plate even though he had no intention of eating it.

He'd long ago mastered the art of moving food around his plate without anybody noticing that he never actually ate any of it. He distracted those who watched him with conversation and by cutting the food into smaller pieces, then rearranging it on his plate so that it looked as if he'd eaten some of it.

Not that he would even make a pretense of it today. He had, after all, more important things to do: he had to seduce his wife.

"Yes, very well. And you, did you sleep well?"

Her voice was a soft trickle, and he wondered how she would sound when she lay in his arms, panting in ecstasy. Would her voice be even more breathless? Even huskier? Or would she still pretend that he didn't affect her?

"I slept terribly, my sweet wife, and I hope to remedy this situation very soon."

When he lifted his lids and looked straight at her, he noticed a pink blush spread over her cheeks, but she didn't raise her eyes to meet his gaze and instead stared at her empty plate.

Then she removed the napkin from her lap and folded it, placing it neatly next to her plate. "If you'll excuse me. I have things to attend to."

She rose swiftly, but he was faster. Before she could make two steps away from the table, he had her cornered between it and the paneled wall.

"Signore! If you'd please let me pass," she requested, her voice tight.

"My name is Nico." He took another step closer, bringing his body flush with hers.

"Signore..."

He shook his head.

Finally, she seemed to understand. "Nico, please, would you let me pass?"

"If that's what you truly want, Oriana." He closed the distance between their heads, allowing his lips to hover mere centimeters above her mouth. His action had caused her to press herself against the wall behind her, leaving her nowhere else to go.

"Y-yes," she stammered.

Nico leaned in closer. "How can you know what you truly want, my sweet, when you don't know what options you have? Why don't I show you some of them? Maybe then you can choose what you like best."

And he hoped her taste was similar to his.

His lips met hers, pressing softly against them. He wasn't going to behave like a barbarian and force himself on her. No, he'd rather tease her with his touch and coax a reaction from her. Sliding his lips gently across her mouth, he slanted his head a little to the side. Without haste, he inhaled her scent and tasted her skin.

She was rigid beneath him, not moving at all: neither to push him away nor to pull him closer. But he knew how to elicit reactions from women, even from a woman who believed sex to be a painful and dirty undertaking—she wouldn't remain frozen like this for long.

Slowly, Nico brought his hand to her neck, sliding it to her nape. His fingers pushed up into her hair, while his thumb caressed the soft skin below her ear. Her pulse beat against his thumb as loudly as a drum. He sensed her tremble under his touch, yet she didn't turn her head to sever the contact.

"Oriana," he whispered against her mouth, before he parted his lips and licked his tongue against the seam of her lips.

A gasp escaped her.

Combing his hand through her hair and in the process disturbing some of the pins that held her coiffure up, he slanted his lips over her mouth, licking over it again. Under light pressure, she parted her lips. She finally understood what he wanted. Or had she simply wanted to take a breath? It didn't matter, because all he could think of was the warm and moist cavern he now explored. With gentle and measured strokes, he delved into her mouth, ever so softly licking over her teeth, before touching her tongue.

A bolt of lightning charged through him, turning his insides into an inferno in an instant. A groan came over his lips before he could stop it. Just like he couldn't stop another bodily reaction: after having been semi-erect ever since entering the room, his cock swelled to its full size, the blood pumping into it bringing it to near bursting. His eager appendage pushed against the flap of his trousers, pressing into the buttons. He could only hope that the thread with which the buttons were sewn was strong enough, or he would burst from his trousers and make a fool of himself.

Trying to push away those thoughts, he captured her mouth more fiercely now, kissing her with more passion and determination. To his surprise there was no resistance. This was easier than he'd imagined.

Sighing, he allowed his hands to roam her body. As one of them reached the round swell of her breast and cupped it, Oriana ripped her mouth from his.

A split second later, a sharp pain in his foot made him jump back. Shocked, he stared at her. Oriana had driven the heel of her slipper into his foot.

"How dare you?!" she cried out.

Anger charged through him.

SEVEN

Oriana saw the fury blazing from Nico's eyes and instinctively shrank back. His eyes darkened and his jaw clenched.

To her utter shock and dismay, she'd enjoyed his kiss. Or maybe she'd been so surprised by it that she'd been unable to react the way a lady would—with indifference. But when she'd felt his hand on her breast, her brain had suddenly started working again, and she'd done the only thing she could: defend herself.

Narrowing his eyes, Nico approached. "Oh, I dare even more, my sweet wife!"

Suddenly afraid, she froze. She'd unleashed a wild beast in him. Now he would truly hurt her! Before, he would have simply taken her dignity, now he would do much worse. Her heart beating into her throat, she squeezed her eyes shut, not wanting to see what was coming.

A moment later, she felt herself lifted up, then she heard dishes and cutlery crash onto the floor. When he deposited her on the table, she steeled herself for her fate: he would take her right here on the table. She wouldn't even get a bed to cushion her back, instead he'd use her like a common whore. Oh, the indignity!

"No!" she cried out, but Nico didn't stop.

He pushed her skirts up to her waist. Then she felt his hand on her drawers. He ripped them, laying her bare to his view. Shame flooded her. Nobody had ever seen her like this.

"Oh God, you're beautiful." His voice sounded anything but angry—it sounded reverent.

Her eyes flew open. She'd expected to see him opening his trousers to take out his manhood so he could do what men did, but instead she saw him look at the place between her legs, legs he now spread wider.

"And I'm sure you taste as beautiful."

Before she understood what he meant by his words, he sank his head between her legs and brought his lips to her sex. For a long moment, she was frozen in disbelief. What he was doing was impossible. Maybe she had fainted so she wouldn't have to face what was happening to her.

She sensed him inhale sharply, pressing his face into the triangle of hair that guarded her woman's place. It was really happening. She hadn't fainted.

When she felt warm air blow against her, she realized that he was kissing her there. Kissing a place that was unthinkable. Forbidden. Her friend Ilaria had never mentioned her husband doing anything of the sort. Surely, this was not done!

Oriana was about to protest, trying to lift herself up from her lying position, when his fingers parted her female folds and something warm and moist swiped against them.

"Ohhhhh!" she sighed.

Nico was licking her with his tongue! It was outrageous, but she couldn't gather the strength to push him away, despite the fact that his hands weren't holding her down. He was using no force on her, his fingers too busy caressing her instead. She could easily push him off her and free herself. So why didn't she? Why was she allowing him to do this to her? To kiss her in such a scandalous way?

As if it had been turned off, her mind gave no answer to her questions. Instead, her body dictated her reaction. Like a wanton woman, she moaned, her body writhing against his mouth and tongue, her pelvis tilting toward him to achieve a closer connection.

Her body was aflame, burning from the inside out. At the same time, her nipples were chafing against her corset, begging to be freed, yet there was no way of doing so. But she needed relief. Without thinking, she rubbed her palms over her breasts, cupping and squeezing them as much as was possible through the fabric. It wasn't enough to give her any sense of relief, so she allowed her fingers to trail higher, ignoring the little voice in her head that called her "wanton" and instead touched the part of her skin that was exposed. Then she hooked her thumbs underneath the corset and pushed it farther down. Another pull, and her nipples popped over the rim of the corset. Cool air blew against them, making the hard tips even harder.

She moaned in response. At the same time, Nico licked with more intensity and pressed harder against her exposed flesh. She felt liquid pool there. With it, embarrassment swept through her. What was she doing? How could she allow him to see her like this, to touch her like this?

And on the dining table of all places! That thought sent a shockwave through her body. What if one of the servants entered and saw them?

"We can't..." she stammered.

Instead of an answer, Nico moved his position and licked higher up, reaching a spot where her heartbeat pulsed violently. He licked over it, sending a charge through her body as if she'd been hit by lightning.

"Ohhh!" she cried out, pleasure racing through her.

No, she didn't want him to stop now. She wanted more of this, more of what he was doing right now. Whatever he was doing. She had no words for it. But it didn't stop her from begging, "More. Oh God, more!"

She knew there had to be more of this kind of sensation, this joy that traveled through her body and made her toss her inhibitions out the window and into the canals below. There was something she couldn't put a name to that was just beyond her reach. Something wonderful, something pleasurable. Her body knew it as if it was a primal instinct. And her body now drove her toward it, ignoring all manners and decorum.

Nico was doing this to her. Her husband was giving her something she'd never experienced. Was this what married couples really did? Then why had Ilaria made it sound like it was all pain and shame? The shame she could understand, because even now she felt ashamed at her lusty behavior, like that of a common trollop and not the lady she was. But there was no pain. Nico's fingers stroked her gently as if he knew what she needed, where she wanted to be touched. Indeed, he seemed to know better than she did, because his caresses reached places before she even knew she needed his touch there.

Just like he now stroked along her folds while his tongue licked over the small bundle of nerves that was so sensitive she felt she might explode any moment. But whenever she thought it would happen, Nico pulled back and decreased the pressure. Over and over he did this, varying the intensity with which he licked and stroked her, as if he wanted to hold off the inevitable.

Oriana felt one finger probe at the entrance to her body, sliding between the moist folds. Instinctively, she spread her legs wider and pulled her knees up so they pointed toward the ceiling. She didn't care that no lady would ever expose herself like this—all she cared about was that she gave him better access to her sex.

Nico's next groan reverberated through her, and at the same time his finger slid into her. The invasion was foreign at first, her muscles clamping around him instantly. Before she could decide whether she liked what he did, the pressure on her center of pleasure intensified and she let out an involuntary moan.

She barely noticed how Nico's finger moved in and out of her, because the pleasure from him licking and sucking her drove every sane thought out of her mind.

Her hands went back to her breasts, strumming her nipples while her hips bucked against Nico's mouth, encouraging him to go faster. Her chest heaved, and small beads of sweat built on her face and neck. She ignored them and instead squeezed her breasts harder.

"Yes, yes, yes," she chanted without thinking.

Who was this lusty woman who'd taken over her body? Who was controlling her now? Because for certain it wasn't the studious young woman who'd never shown any interest in men.

A grumble came from Nico. "Yes, my wanton wife!"

Then everything changed. Nico sucked her sensitive flesh into his mouth and pressed his lips together. At the same time, his finger drove deep and hard into her. With a cry, she exploded. Waves of pleasure raced through her body, threatening to incinerate her. But no flames consumed her body, instead she felt as if floating on a cloud. Weightless. Without any thoughts, without any worries in the world.

Her vision blurred, and she realized that tears were running down her cheeks.

When she finally floated back down, her limbs felt boneless. She was overcome with emotions, but of one thing she was certain: she wanted more of this, and more of Nico.

Nico's head lifted and he looked at her. Concern spread over his face when he noticed her tears. His hand reached to wipe one off her cheek.

Then, with a pained expression, he turned on his heel and stormed out of the room.

"Nico!" But he was already gone.

CHAPTER

EIGHT

After receiving a missive from Marcello in the late afternoon, Nico grabbed his hooded cloak and left the house in his closed gondola. Marcello's note had sounded urgent, and it gave Nico the perfect excuse to leave the house and not face his wife.

He'd made her cry! Even though she'd climaxed under his lips. He'd felt it; there had been no mistaking the shudders that had made her body tremble. Her interior muscles had spasmed around his finger, squeezing him so tightly that he'd nearly come in his smalls.

Had he not been so close to his own climax, he would have stayed and tried to find out why she was crying, but male pride had made him flee so he wouldn't embarrass himself in front of her like a green kid who'd never had a woman.

Still, the moment he'd reached his bedchamber and opened the flap of his trousers, he'd spilled into his own hand with only one single thrust into his fist. So much for his legendary control! One day of marriage, and he had turned into a complete and utter fool. What had made him think even for one minute that taking his wife on the dining table was a good idea? It was the way he took a whore, not a lady like her! But when she'd defied him by driving her heel into his foot, he'd seen red. That he hadn't taken out his aching cock and fucked her with it, was a miracle in itself. But what would happen next time? Would he rape her? No, he couldn't allow that to happen.

There was no way to mend what he'd done already, he was sure. And he didn't want to face this now, so he was glad that he had other things to think about right now.

Nico reached Marcello's house after negotiating several corners and tied the gondola to the covered dock. Then he dashed inside, not wanting to remain outside any longer, even though the rays of the late afternoon sun were already dipping behind the neighboring houses.

Marcello's house was more a palace than a house. Bordering on a small canal on one side, it stood four stories tall. It was flanked by smaller houses on each side, and its front opened to a small piazza. Marcello employed a number of servants to maintain the house. All of them were humans. However, they came from families who'd worked for him for generations, their loyalty beyond question. In exchange, they lived privileged lives—no servant in Venice received better food, better clothing, or better accommodations than Marcello's.

Nico allowed the footman to take his cloak and followed him as he ushered him upstairs. Surprised, Nico raised an eyebrow. Normally Marcello received his visitors downstairs, rather than in his private rooms.

"Ah, there you are, always the last," Marcello's deep voice boomed from the open door to his private study as Nico stepped over the threshold. "Even though today you have a good excuse: I'm sure it wasn't easy to pull your prick out from between the clenching thighs of your blushing bride."

Raucous laughter followed. Everybody was assembled: Silvano, Francesco, the brothers Dante and Raphael, Lorenzo, Andrea, Carlo, Paolo, Enrico, and of course Marcello himself. And not an eye remained dry as all of them laughed about Marcello's raunchy comment.

Not wanting to give his friends any reason to believe that his wedding night hadn't gone according to plan and that his marriage was already in shambles, Nico shut the door behind him and added, "What if it wasn't her cunny I was having trouble disentangling myself from? What if her lips were so tightly sealed around my prick that I couldn't pull out for fear she would bite me if I left her?"

He should be so lucky, he thought, as his friends erupted in yet another round of laughter. A woman like her would never suck his cock. She'd never debase herself like that. After all, she was a well-bred woman, and he was as debauched as they came. He couldn't even get her to accept marital relations; teaching her to enjoy other diversions such as sucking his insatiable cock would be an impossible feat. It was best to accept the inevitable and admit that his wife was disgusted with him.

"But enough of the fun and games," he heard Marcello cut through his thoughts. "We have a serious matter to discuss."

Everybody looked expectantly at Marcello. Nico leaned against the door and crossed his arms over his chest, curious why Marcello had demanded this meeting, which after all, was taking place in broad daylight.

"My spies have heard of a vicious rumor. Apparently, somebody in this city has come up with a contraption, some sort of device that makes it possible to identify vampires."

Nico dropped his arms to the side, his body hardening and straightening instantly. Air rushed from his lungs, and he took another breath. He noticed the same sort of reaction in his fellow vampires. Shock rippled through them.

"How can that be?" Dante asked.

"Are you sure?" Raphael added.

Marcello nodded gravely. "You all know that my spies are reliable. I bloody well pay them enough. I believe it to be true. This rumor has been circulating over the past week and only just came to my spies' ears. And if *we* know about this, then it's safe to assume the Guardians know about it too."

"And they'll want the machine," Nico added calmly, even though he felt agitated. If the Guardians of the Holy Waters, a secret society of Venetian men who wanted to eradicate vampires, got hold of a means to detect vampires more easily, it would put them all in danger.

"What if it doesn't work?" Andrea threw in.

Silvano tossed him a concerned look. "What if it does?"

Marcello lifted his hand. "No matter whether the answer is yes or no, we have to find the machine first. If it falls into the Guardians' hands and it does indeed work, then we'll have a very hard time remaining in hiding. None of us will be safe. Once they have one device, they can duplicate it. Soon, all Guardians will have one and hunt us down."

His friend had a point. Every time one of them ventured out of their houses, the risk of detection would be multiplied. So far, vampires only had to be careful when out hunting for blood, so they wouldn't be detected when they drank from a human. But if the Guardians had another method of recognizing them even though their vampire side was hidden, then a simple walk in the evening would become hazardous.

"What are we going to do about it?" Nico asked, looking at his host. "Do your spies have any information as to the whereabouts of this detection device?"

"Nothing concrete so far. As we speak, they're using their contacts to find out more. But they're being careful, because we can't risk their questions being traced back to us."

"Marcello," Dante suddenly threw in. "Tell them what you told me about the list of names earlier."

Marcello cleared his throat. "As most of you know, the list is a parchment with the presumed names of the Guardians of the Holy Waters that Bianca found hidden in her late father's house. Only, the names don't exist: they're made up. Code names. We know this because we know three dead members from this list: Giovanni, the first husband of Raphael's wife, Massimo, her cousin, as well as a known rake, Salvatore. They aren't on the list, even though they were members of the Guardians."

Marcello looked dejected. "Unfortunately there's no logic behind the way they chose their names. Even with using common ciphers and searching for the most common letters appearing in the list, I wasn't able to figure out what names those three known Guardians chose. I'm not sure what else to try."

Lorenzo nodded. "I worked on a copy of the list, but haven't come up with anything either. There might not be any code hidden in the list. It could be a hoax."

Nico balled his hand into a fist and slammed it against the door. "Damn!"

"Never mind that now!" Raphael cut in. "Let's deal with the problem at hand. I suggest that at nightfall each and every one of us search out his trusted contacts in the city and see what else he can find out. Somebody must know something else. Nothing remains a secret forever in this city. Servants talk. Let's use that to our advantage. Let's find the ones who'll tell us what we want to know."

The others nodded, mumbling their agreement to Raphael's plan. Nico did likewise. At least it gave him something to do rather than go home.

He wasn't ready to face his wife and find out the reason for her tears, for he guessed it: he disgusted her, and she hated his touch. Having his suspicion confirmed would only force him to act upon it: he would have to do what he had planned all along. Send her to the mainland. Why this revelation didn't make him feel relieved, he didn't know.

After all, sending her away would mean he could resume his old life: fuck a different whore every night. However, that prospect made him recoil. He didn't want to fuck a whore, he wanted to bed his wife. On clean sheets. In their marriage bed. Every night. And every day.

Something was seriously wrong with this picture. Because Nico liked variety, he liked the conquest, and he liked his women experienced and adventurous.

Not virginal. Not shy in bed. Not disgusted with him.

So why did his cock rise every time he thought of Oriana? Why did his heart beat faster when he caught a whiff of her scent?

"Nico!"

Dante's voice pulled him out of his daydreams. Nico rolled his shoulders. "Yes?"

"I said, if you want to spend the evening at your home—I mean considering you're practically on your honeymoon—nobody is going to fault you for it."

Nico shook his head. "There's no need. I'll do my part."

At the very least, it would distract him, though roaming the city at night wouldn't dull the hunger he felt for his wife. The hunger for her luscious body and her rich blood. A hunger she would never allow him to still. He had to end this charade now: he would send her to the mainland as planned. At least that way, he wouldn't make her cry again. She would get what she wanted, and he would simply return to his bachelor life. If he could get Oriana out of his mind.

CHAPTER

NINE

Oriana couldn't believe that her husband had simply left without a word. He hadn't even told the servants where he was going or when he was coming back. Cook had looked at her almost accusatorily when she'd served Oriana's supper and Nico still hadn't returned by then.

She'd waited impatiently, but when the clock in the sitting room had chimed the twelve strokes of midnight, she'd yawned and ascended to her room. After her maid had loosened Oriana's corset, she sent her to bed. She continued undressing, draping her dress over the screen. When she was wearing only her chemise and drawers, she let her hands glide over her torso. Instantly, the same desire flared up in her again as when she'd lain on the dining table being pleasured by Nico.

Would this remain the only time he touched her like this? Had she done something wrong? Was that why he hadn't come back yet? He'd called her his wanton wife. What if she had disgusted him with her behavior? After all, he'd married a lady, and he'd gotten nothing better than a trollop dressed in lady's clothing.

How she could have behaved like this, Oriana couldn't explain. Maybe some temporary insanity had gripped her and controlled her. Would it happen again? Would she again lose all her good senses and behave like a whore the next time her husband tested her like this? Because that was all it could have been: a test to assure himself that she was the virtuous wife she'd promised him she'd be.

Surprised at herself why she was even concerned about what her husband thought of her, she shook her head. She didn't care what he thought.

Liar! she chided herself.

At the very moment when he'd looked at her with such untamed passion in his eyes while taking her on the dining table, something had changed. Even now she felt her heart race at the thought that he wanted her. A rush of power surged through her. Confusion followed. She'd never been so torn in her life. One minute she wanted to throw herself into her husband's arms, the next she wanted to profess her virtuousness and assure him that she would never again behave in such a lusty way.

While she tried to understand what was happening to her, Oriana turned to the chest that contained her finest garments. Among the items was a negligee she had saved from her mother's things. Why she'd taken it before her father had given all of her mother's things away after her death, she wasn't sure, because the garment was positively scandalous. She couldn't imagine that a proper lady like her mother would have ever worn such a thing.

Yet, she couldn't resist the temptation to take it out, look at it, and wonder what she would look like wearing it. Would it even fit her? Feeling the silk between her fingers, a yearning came over her. Maybe she could simply try it on, only to see it for a moment. Afterwards, she'd slip into her virginal nightgown, the one that reached up to her neck and covered her completely.

Oriana rid herself of her chemise and drawers and slipped the silken negligee over her head. To her surprise, it fit her perfectly, clinging to her aching breasts and hugging her bottom. A large slit ran all the way up her thigh, making it possible for her to take normal steps.

She walked around the screen and looked into the mirror, seeing a woman there she'd never seen before. A woman who personified lust and passion. She felt different, more alive, more aware of her body. Wicked thoughts invaded her mind—of things that she couldn't find words for. Things no decent woman should want. Her craving for those wicked things grew stronger with every second she watched herself in the mirror.

What would Nico do if he found out about them?

Nico closed the heavy door of his new home behind him and walked upstairs, treading quietly so as not to wake the whole house. The sun would rise in two hours, and he needed sleep if he wanted to face his wife tomorrow.

He entered his bedchamber and threw his cloak onto a chair, then stepped out of his shoes. His jacket followed. When he opened the top button of his shirt, he cast a look at his empty bed. If only the beautiful Oriana were waiting in it for him. But that would never happen. He sighed and turned his head to the door that connected their rooms.

Surprise made him stumble backwards: the door was open!

Without conscious thought, he moved toward it until he could peer into Oriana's bedchamber. His eyes instantly fell on the bed, but it was pristine and unused. Shock made him storm into the room. Had she left him?

Frantically he gazed about the room, when he saw her lying on the settee in front of the fireplace. He almost didn't believe what his eyes perceived: his wife wore a scandalously low-cut negligee that not only made her bosom practically spill out, but the cut in the long skirt reached so high up her hip that he could get a glimpse of her bottom. Why was she sleeping on the settee? And why was she wearing such a revealing garment?

His legs carried him to her, and he crouched down in front of her. Oriana's hair was fanned out, her long chestnut tresses spilling over the couch. He buried his face in her hair and inhaled her heady scent. Instantly, his cock stiffened and his hand palmed one breast.

Underneath his touch, she stirred. Quickly, he removed his hand. He wouldn't do anything against her will. He'd done enough damage already.

"Nico?" she asked in a sleepy voice a moment before she opened her eyes.

When their gazes met, she rose to a sitting position, her face flushing. As a result of her hasty movement, one strap of her negligee slid off her shoulder, making the fabric that covered her left breast slide down. It was caught by her nipple before it could slide down all the way.

Nico's eyes were drawn to it, and an involuntary groan escaped his throat.

Oriana gasped in response and pulled back, quickly adjusting the strap.

Her reaction confirmed that he was making the right choice: she didn't want his attention, and sending her away was the only solution. Nico rose to his feet and looked down at her. Unfortunately, this position gave him a perfect view of her plunging neckline. More blood shot into his cock—a cock that was now eyelevel with her. Could the situation possibly get any worse?

Quickly he whirled around, facing the fireplace instead.

"I beg your pardon, my dear wife. I wouldn't have intruded on your privacy had I not seen the door open and been worried about your safety. But now that I see that everything seems to be in order, I shall take my leave."

He took a hesitant step toward the door, unable to tear himself away completely. This would be the last time he saw her like this.

"About what happened earlier today," she started.

He stopped in his tracks. "We can talk about it tomorrow." Because for this one night he wanted to go to bed and dream that she was his. Even though he knew she never would be.

"No."

Surprised at her insistent tone, he turned to face her. If she wanted this to be done and over with tonight, then so be it.

"Signora," he said formally. "I made you cry today. And a husband should never make his wife cry. It appears that I'm not suitable to be a husband. Therefore, I shall agree to your earlier proposal. As you suggested, I will take a mistress and spare you my advances. In exchange, I beg only one thing. That you'll move to my estate on the mainland. It's a large property with a house grander than this. You'll have a large number of servants to take care of you."

She stared at him, stunned. "But..."

He raised his hand to interrupt her. "It's the only way I can guarantee that I will keep my end of the bargain."

She rose from the settee and took a few steps toward him. "And why is that?"

He motioned to her garment. "Signora, no hot-blooded man can resist a beautiful woman like you. Even less so when she's dressed like this." He averted his gaze, his body already turning halfway to be ready to flee from her presence.

"Oriana, my name is Oriana," she said softly, her hand all of a sudden finding his forearm.

Slowly, he turned his head and stared at her. She met his gaze without pulling back. When she licked her lips, he almost came.

"Would it help if I weren't dressed like this?" she asked.

"A little," he confessed. However, in the state he was in, it wouldn't make a difference. Even if she wore an old rag, he'd find her sinfully tantalizing.

"Then maybe this garment wasn't such a good idea." She dropped first one strap, then the other from her shoulders and allowed the fabric to slide down her breasts and pool at her waist.

"Fuck!" he cursed, his eyes hungrily roaming her naked bosom.

He swallowed hard, his throat suddenly dry as sandpaper. Then he tried to shake the image from his mind: clearly, he was hallucinating.

"But I made you cry," he repeated.

"I couldn't hold back the tears because of what you did to me."

Nico dropped his gaze to the floor. "Because I forced you."

She took his hand and guided it to her breast, making him cup it. He felt the soft flesh—it was too real to be a hallucination. His head shot up.

"No. Because I was overwhelmed by what you made me feel. I've never before felt like a woman. I didn't know that this is what married couples did. My friend… she never mentioned…" She hesitated for a moment, searching his face. "But if you're disgusted by my behavior, I'll agree to your wishes and leave for the mainland tomorrow."

Had he heard correctly? "Disgusted?" How could she have even thought such a thing? Every man worth his salt would welcome a woman who responded with such passion.

Of its own volition, his hand kneaded her breast. Oriana's head fell back in response, and her lips parted on a moan.

"I would never be disgusted with a woman who gives herself so freely. As long as she gives herself only to me."

Nico pulled her into his arms, lifting her off her feet, and captured her mouth with a hungry kiss. If he was still hallucinating, it was a damn good hallucination, and he didn't want it to end.

Her full, soft breasts pressed against his shirt. He felt their warmth seeping into his body. Her arms wrapped around him, clinging to him as if she was afraid he'd drop her. Little did she know there was no way in hell he'd allow her to escape from his embrace tonight. Not until they were both thoroughly sated. And even then, he wouldn't let go of her.

Her breath still tasted of the toothpowder she must have used earlier, and her lips were warm and receptive to his demanding kiss. He'd been prepared to send her away, but when she'd exposed her luscious breasts to him, he'd known instinctively that he would never be able to send her away, no matter what happened—even if she found the actual sex act painful and distasteful. Even if she cried because of it. Because to have a wife with a body as sinful as that of the most experienced courtesan, yet live separate lives would be unthinkable. He'd be a fool to let her go.

It left him with only one option: he would have to make sure she felt neither pain nor disgust tonight. He would have to be a patient lover and be more considerate than he'd ever been. He had to forget his own pleasure and only think of hers. Only then did he have a chance.

CHAPTER

TEN

Determined to do this right, Nico carried her to the bed and placed her on the coverlet. Without undressing, he joined Oriana on the bed, not covering her with his body, but simply lying next to her with his body turned toward her.

As she looked up at him, her eyelashes fluttered. He watched her bosom rising and falling.

"So beautiful," he whispered, kissing her already-bruised lips again, then let his hand find her breasts again, kneading and squeezing the responsive flesh.

Her torso arched off the mattress, and her eyes fell shut when more sighs escaped her lips. Without haste, he moved his hand lower to where her negligee had bunched at her waist. He traveled over it until he reached the apex of her thighs. When he rubbed softly against that precious spot, Oriana bucked against him, moaning as he released her lips.

"Oh, yes, my sweet wife, tonight you'll feel me here. Inside your wet cave." He pressed against her mound, cupping her, feeling the heat that emanated from her. As if a furnace were burning inside her. If they weren't careful tonight, the house would burst into flames and they would find themselves amidst a fire that would consume them both.

When he released her sex, a disappointed mewl came from her. He suppressed a chuckle. His virginal wife was quickly developing a knowledge of what her body wanted. He was glad for it, and more than willing to comply. But this time skin-on-skin.

Nico tunneled underneath the fabric, reaching first the thatch of coarse hair, then dipping lower to where her arousal made her flesh slick. Without further coaxing, she spread her thighs wider, allowing his hand to dip between them.

He coated his fingers in her juices, stroking softly over the plump flesh that was begging him for a touch. With slow circular strokes, he explored her womanly folds, parting them to dip lower. He watched her face for her reaction. This morning, he'd had his face buried in her cunny and had been unable to watch her face, but this time he would make sure he found out immediately if there was something she didn't enjoy. He was determined to do everything right.

Keeping his touch gentle, careful not to be too rough, his eyes wandered over her flushed face. Her skin glistened, and beads of sweat formed on her neck and forehead. He'd never seen a lady sweat—plenty of whores, yes, but not a well-bred woman. It was frowned upon in polite society, yet Nico decided that it was becoming of her. In fact, Oriana looked positively ravishing—no, more than that, positively wanton—the way a thin sheen of moisture built on her skin.

He wondered what it would be like once she rode him. Her petite body would be aflame, and their bodies would glide against each other smoothly, helped by the moisture that was building on their skin. But not only Oriana's skin was getting increasingly moist, her sex was now saturated with her arousal, the enticing scent of it spreading in the bedchamber like an expensive perfume the trade ships had brought from the East.

He inhaled it, taking it into his body as if it were nourishment. And maybe it was, because it doubled the power and wildness that lived within him. At the same time, it made his cock ache more intensely.

He hadn't undressed yet, and he wouldn't until Oriana was good and ready for him. Because once his cock was let out of its confinement, he would plunge it into her within seconds, unable to hold back any longer. He'd never been so randy in his life. Was it because tonight he was going to fuck a lady, not one of the whores who normally saw to his needs? Needs that were becoming more urgent by the second.

But while he couldn't satisfy them yet, he could do something else he'd always enjoyed. Talking to a woman while he pleasured her. But not in polite words, rather words no well-bred woman knew. Could he risk it with Oriana?

Before he could even make a decision, his mouth was already open. "What a beautiful cunny you have."

A hushed breath rushed from her lungs, and her eyes flew open.

He hesitated, but she didn't pull back. Instead, she gyrated against his hand that had stilled, clearly urging him to continue. Locking eyes with her, he not only stroked his finger upwards to her pearl, but he also spoke again. "Yes, the sexiest cunt I've ever touched."

Her eyes widened, and the blush on her cheeks darkened.

"The tastiest I've ever licked."

She moaned, her lips parting and her tongue darting out to lick them. He groaned. "And when you came apart this morning, I felt your pussy clamp down on my finger as if you wanted to pull me deep inside you. Was that what you wanted?" He probed at the entrance to her body. "Was it, Oriana?"

Her sex arched toward him, but he didn't push inside her. Instead, he circled her slit.

"You have to tell me what you want, my sweet. Do you want my finger in your cunt?"

She dropped her lids halfway, avoiding his insistent gaze, but he wouldn't let her get away with it. He lifted his hand from her pussy and slid farther up, attempting to free his hand from under the silk fabric.

"No!" she cried out.

He stopped in his movement, leaving his hand where it was, barely grazing her pubic hair. "Yes, my sweet?"

Lifting her lids slowly, her gaze crashed into his. Her eyes were dark with lust and passion, her voice breathless, when she finally answered, "I want your finger inside my... c-c-cunt."

He gave her what she wanted, sliding his hand back between her legs and extending his middle finger. Then he parted her folds and pushed inside her tight sheath.

A contented sigh came over Oriana's lips. He bent over her face, his lips hovering over hers. "See, my sweet, the things I'll give you if only you ask."

Then he withdrew his finger and pushed back inside, making her gasp for air. She was tighter than anything he'd ever felt. He knew that she would scream out in pain if he tried to plunge his cock into her and rip her hymen, which he was probably already partially perforating with his finger.

There had to be a way of distracting her from it. Damn it, he'd never slept with a virgin. He had no idea how painful it would be for her. Would she feel it like a pinprick? Or was it as if somebody drove a knife into her? How much pain would she feel? And how long would it last?

Maybe he could do things gradually.

Releasing her lips, he dropped his head to her neck, kissing her tempting skin. Underneath his lips, her vein pulsed, the rhythm tempting him to taste her. But he couldn't risk that. One other task was more urgent at present: to deflower her without causing her pain.

"Sweetling, I'm going to make you feel the way you felt this morning," he whispered to her. "Remember when your body came apart as if you were lifted in the air?" At least he hoped that was what she'd felt.

"Yes, it was . . . " Her voice died.

" . . . magical," he ended her sentence for her. "And I'm going to make it magical again. But I want you to do something for me too."

Her body froze for a moment, and he immediately rubbed his thumb over her pearl, while keeping his finger inside her. She relaxed into his touch.

"I need to stretch your beautiful cunny. You'll have to take two of my fingers. It'll feel uncomfortable at first."

"But, it's already . . . " Again, she didn't finish her sentence.

Nico made small circles around her center of pleasure and moved his finger gently inside her. "I know, my love. That's why I want you to bury your face in my neck and bite me if it's painful. That way I know to ease off."

"Bite you? But I can't possibly—"

He lifted his head and looked at her. "Please. I want you to."

She eyed his neck, and slowly he dipped his head so that her lips connected with the spot where his neck and shoulder met. He shivered involuntarily. If she were a vampire female, she would know that it was normal for lovers to bite each other during the act. It would heighten their arousal. Even though Oriana was human, she would heighten his arousal despite the fact that her blunt human teeth would never break through his tough vampire skin.

When she nibbled gently, he sighed and resumed finger-fucking her while his thumb rubbed over her pearl with faster strokes. Her breathing became more uneven, her body writhing under his ministrations. Her cunny rained more juices onto his finger, the lubrication making it easier and easier to drive his finger in and out of her. On the next stroke, he added his index finger and slowly pushed both fingers forward. Simultaneously, he caressed her clitoris faster. He felt her hold her breath, her back arching off the bed, then he slid both fingers into her.

Oriana's teeth dug into his neck. Pleasure speared through him, and at the same moment he felt her muscles spasm around him, gripping him tighter, pulling him inside her with a force astounding for a woman.

He felt her climax violently against his hand, her teeth releasing his neck too quickly for his liking. Knowing this meant that she wasn't in pain anymore, he continued to slide his fingers in and out of her. More gently now in rhythm with her orgasmic spasms. Her pussy relaxed, opening wider for him and allowing him to finger-fuck her. Without thinking, he added a third finger to the first two. And she took those three without any complaints. All she did was gyrate her hips against his hand, moving in synch with him.

Relieved, he pulled his head from her and gazed at her. "Are you ready for my cock now?"

Her eyes opened wide, a twinge of fear clearly visible in them.

As Nico pulled his hand from her, he noticed a few drops of blood on it. He'd ripped her hymen—good, it would make things easier from here. He took her hand to bring it to the massive bulge that pressed against the flap of his trousers, realizing too late that moisture had already leaked from it. When he pressed her hand against it, a choked sound came from her throat.

"I've already had three fingers inside you, love. This isn't going to be much more." Who was he kidding? His cock was at least as thick as four times his largest finger. And even though she was now without a hymen, he would still cause her discomfort.

Oriana squeezed his hard-on, making him jerk back. "Fuck!"

Immediately, a frightened look crossed her face and she scooted away from him. He reached for her, pulling her closer.

"Don't be afraid! I'm sorry, but if you touch me like that, you'll make me come in an instant."

"Come?" she murmured.

He smiled and slid his hand over her sex, the silk fabric a thin barrier. "Yes, come." He pressed against her still pulsing folds. "Like you came just now. You'll do the same to me if you touch me like that."

Confusion turned her forehead into a frown. "And you don't like it? I thought men—"

"Oh yes, men do like that. More than anything," he interrupted. "But you know what I like even more?"

She shook her head.

"When your sweet cunt squeezes me, just like it squeezed my fingers. So tell me, my wanton wife, will you grant me that?"

Her eyes dropped back to his erection, then her hand slid over it, stroking his entire length as if she was measuring him. "Yes."

CHAPTER

ELEVEN

Oriana watched with fascination how Nico undressed in front of her as if he'd done so a thousand times: without shame or embarrassment, while he continued to look at her with such intensity that her body heated once more.

She still felt the shudders that had gone through her body when he'd touched her with his expert hands. Now those same hands opened the buttons of his shirt, revealing a ripped chest and flat stomach. A light dusting of dark hair covered his torso, growing stronger farther down until it built a dark line of hair that disappeared into his breeches. Almost as if it were meant as a guiding sign. She was drawn to it instinctively.

Her eyes dipping lower, she stared at the heavy bulge that was hidden behind the fabric. Earlier, she'd felt its heat under her palm. She'd felt it pulsate against her hand and had never before felt so alive when touching it.

When his hands went to the buttons of his flap, her mouth went dry. One-by-one, he eased the buttons open, then slowly pushed his trousers down, stepping out of them. His smalls followed while she lay there motionless. Only her chest moved: up and down in quick succession, her breathing having sped up. The heat she felt was unbearable. And she knew why: because she was staring at a naked man whose body was so perfect and beautiful, she couldn't believe that he was her husband.

Even before this night, she'd known what a man's physique was like: she'd seen depictions of the statue of David, a nude male chiseled into marble by the artist Michelangelo. But Nico was different. More beautiful, more perfect, and... bigger.

The hard, veined shaft that curved toward his belly was almost purple in color, attesting to the blood inside it that made it stand erect like a flag pole. Beneath it, a sac hung heavy, the oval pieces of fruit inside clearly visible.

A groan made her lift her eyes to meet Nico's gaze. His eyes had a golden sheen to them now, the natural green in them suddenly gone. Maybe the light from the candles and the fireplace played this optical trick on her.

Nico took a step toward her then reached for the fabric of her negligee where it pooled at her midsection. He pulled on it, lifting her bottom in the process, and stripped her naked. Instinctively, she covered her sex with her hands. But he gripped them and pulled them away.

"Never hide anything from me," he warned, his voice a low growl.

The mattress dipped under his weight when he joined her on the bed. His hands pushed her thighs apart.

Oh, God, now he would mount her, and it would be painful—no way would his massive manhood fit inside her, just the way her friend Ilaria had told her. Oriana squeezed her eyes shut and steeled herself for the inevitable.

A heavy sigh came from Nico. "Open your eyes, Oriana."

She obeyed.

"You're still scared. That won't do."

She turned her head away. "I'm sorry. I'll bear it. I promise. Mount me and—"

"Mount you? Is that how you still see it? That I'll mount you like a stallion to take my pleasure without any regard for yours?"

"You've already given me pleasure. It's only right that you receive the same. I won't resist you."

Nico shook his head. "That's not how this works. I won't mount you. Not like this."

"But—"

She was unable to finish her sentence, because Nico suddenly turned onto his back and lifted her onto his body. Her legs fell open, straddling him. His shaft pulsed against her stomach.

"*You* will mount *me*."

"W-what?" Shocked at his suggestion, her heart began to pound frantically.

"You heard me, my sweet. You'll be the one to decide when I'll enter you, and how deep and how hard I'll thrust. You'll be holding the reins."

"But surely that's not how it's done. I mean, my friend, her husband—"

Nico placed his finger over her lips. "Your friend's husband is not worth his salt if he can't show his wife the pleasures of the marriage bed. And just so you know: there are hundreds of ways a man can make love to a woman, and few include mounting her. I have every intention of teaching you every single one of them."

Surprised and at the same time relieved about his revelation, she dipped her head to his. "Will you teach me how to please you?" Because a man who showed such consideration for his wife had to be rewarded.

"My love, you already please me more than you can know. Now all we have to do is learn to please each other at the same time." Nico placed a gentle kiss on her lips. "Now ride me, my wanton wife. Slide your pearl against my cock, and when you're ready, then take me inside you and bear down on me."

His hand cupped her nape, his thumb stroking her cheek.

"Yes," she whispered.

With her hand she sought his shaft and pressed it against her sex. Then she started moving up and down, the moisture that pooled from her coating his erection and making him slide smoothly against her. The spot where he'd touched her earlier, her pearl as he'd called it, throbbed at the contact.

Oriana threw her head back, sitting up straight. Supported by her

knees and Nico's hands on her hips, she continued her tentative movements. She noticed Nico's breathing become more ragged, his groans more
guttural. The cords in his neck bulged, and his jaw clenched as if he was
fighting against something.

It excited her to watch him like this, to see him submit to her touch.
When she squeezed his shaft and pressed harder against him, he cursed.

"Fuck! Oriana! Have mercy with me!"

She understood what he meant, and though it still scared her, one part
in her wanted to feel him inside her. One part of her wanted to feel being
taken by him. To submit to him.

She lifted herself on her knees, high enough so she could guide his
shaft to her female folds. When she felt the crown of his manhood press
against the entrance of her body, she shivered, not with fear this time, but
with excitement. She wanted this, wanted him.

Taking a deep breath, she sank down on him, impaling herself on his
rod until he was completely submerged in her. The fullness she felt was
overwhelming at first, robbing her of her breath. For a second, she didn't
move, trying to adjust to the foreign invasion, then she felt him move
underneath her, his hips pulling back, then pushing upwards again.

A breath escaped her and joined the moan Nico released. His eyes were
shining back at her, a red rim around his irises. Stunned at what she saw,
she froze for a moment, but then Nico's hands on her hips distracted her,
urging her to move. At first, she moved slowly, but with every second that
passed, her body heated more, and her rhythm took on a life of its own, not
listening to her brain anymore, but simply responding to nature's demand.

Beneath her, Nico thrust upwards each time she bore down on him,
intensifying the impact. Her pearl vibrated with each movement, driving
her to continue.

"Oh, God, Oriana!" Nico cried out, before he reversed their positions,
rolling her onto her back.

Suddenly she found herself underneath him, her legs spread wide, and
his cock pounding into her.

"But I thought," she managed to croak.

He grinned down at her. "My turn to ride you."

She found herself wrapping her legs around him, pulling him closer, adding to the power of his thrusts by digging her heels into his backside.

"Just like that," he mumbled near her ear. "Let me fuck you hard and deep."

To her surprise, she felt no pain or discomfort. All she felt was the lust that danced between them, the passion that ignited with every thrust, and the fire that burned around them. The heat that filled the room. She loved the feeling of being at his mercy, unable to get out from underneath him, unable to escape his relentless thrusts, his insatiable cock.

He stretched her wide, yet the fullness she felt was exhilarating, the sensations that raced through her body addictive. She wanted more of this. She wanted all of him.

His hands gripped her hard, probably leaving bruises on her delicate skin, but she didn't care. As long as he touched her and looked at her with such passion, she didn't mind. Because right now he made her feel like the most important person in his life. He only saw her. Nobody else existed.

When he sank his lips onto her neck and licked and kissed her there, she shivered, feeling a tingling sensation running through her body. As it reached her pearl, she lost all conscious thought. She was flying, her body weightless.

In the distance she heard Nico's shout, a last thrust by him, and then a rush of warmth flooding her womb.

"Fuck, yes!!" he cried out, before he collapsed on top of her.

Her legs released him, falling limply to the sides. Before she could complain about his heavy body on her chest, Nico rolled onto his back, taking her with her, his cock slipping halfway out of her. As she lay on top of him, her body too weak to move, his hands went back to her hips, pushing her down on him completely and driving his cock deep inside her again.

She buried her face in the crook of his neck, inhaling his masculine scent.

"My love?"

"Mmm?" she answered.

"I hope you're not too tired."

She lifted her head to look at him. "Why?"

"Because I'm not done."

"But you... I mean, I felt..."

He grinned sinfully. "Oh, I came. But if you remember I promised to show you all different ways of how a man can make love to his wife."

"Tonight?"

He brought his lips to hers. "We'll start tonight. But we won't finish tonight."

CHAPTER

TWELVE

"I have business to attend to tonight," Nico said as he rose and got out of bed.

It was early evening, and Oriana and he had spent most of the previous two days and nights in bed. She'd never imagined that such bliss was possible. No married woman had ever mentioned enjoying marital relations, let alone engaging in them with such frequency. By daylight even!

"Oh?" She made a disappointed face.

Nico smiled and bent to her for a soft kiss. "I'll be back after midnight. Don't wait up for me. Sleep."

"Will you come to my bed when you return?" Two days ago she would have never thought that she'd ever make such a demand, but after all the things that she and Nico had shared in the last few days, she had developed enough confidence to ask for what she wanted.

"You'll awake with my cock thrusting inside you, my hands on your breasts, and my lips on yours."

Her heartbeat accelerated, her body unashamed of the desire that coursed through her at his words. "Would you really take me while I'm asleep?"

Nico leaned closer. "Yes, and you know why?"

"Why?" she echoed.

"Because you want me to. Because just thinking of it now gets you all wet. Am I right?"

His hand reached under the sheet and slid between her legs, legs she spread for him willingly. His finger probed at her moist core, then plunged inside her. She panted, instantly aroused and wanting more.

"Ah, my wanton wife. Who would have thought that you would turn into such an insatiable wicked woman?"

"You find me insatiable?"

"Oh yes, quite." He withdrew his finger from her body and licked it, looking at her with hungry eyes.

The sight made her womb clench with need.

"Later, my wife, I'll teach you something new." His eyes dropped down to his cock. "I'll teach you to love the taste of my cock."

The thought should disgust her, but it didn't. Nico had put his mouth to her sex several times, licking her, sucking her. Yet so far, he hadn't asked her to do the same to him, even though she'd been curious. More than curious in fact. She was craving it, but hadn't voiced it, because she wasn't sure whether it would be too shocking a proposition. But now...

"Tell me, my wicked husband, why don't you give me a little taste now before you leave?"

Nico groaned, his eyes darkening. "Because if I let you suck me now, I'll never leave this room."

Then he turned abruptly and went into his own bedchamber, closing the connecting door behind him.

Oriana sighed. She hated waiting. Knowing she would get bored if she remained in bed, she rang for her maid. Since her husband would be out of the house for the entire evening, she could attend to her own business. She'd neglected her research in the last few days, and it was important that she returned to it.

Tonight, she would venture out with her trusted footman Giuseppe and take her apparatus with her to test it. It was something she couldn't do in her laboratory. She had to roam the dark streets of Venice in search of vampires and hope her machine was working.

She'd tested it as much as she could in her laboratory, using herself and Giuseppe as test subjects. When a human touched the rod that protruded from it, the center of the machine would emit an orange glow. Her research led her to believe that the physical composition of a vampire was vastly different from a human; therefore, the machine wouldn't emit that same glow when coming in contact with a vampire. She expected it to glow blue instead, or maybe green, but not the warm color of a living, breathing human.

Tonight, she would try to find proof for her assumptions.

NICO SANK his fangs deep into the woman's neck, closing his eyes so he could imagine it was Oriana he was drinking from. But neither did the whore who was plying her trade in the back streets of Venice have the young and pliable body his wife possessed, nor did she smell as enticing. Rather, the smell of the filthy streets clung to the woman he'd coaxed into a dark corner, using his mental powers of suggestion, a skill every vampire possessed. Maybe subconsciously he'd chosen a victim who looked and smelled nothing like his wife so he wouldn't turn delirious thinking he was drinking Oriana's blood.

While the blood was as nourishing as any blood he'd had in his long life as a vampire, it didn't give him the satisfaction he'd hoped for. He knew why: after making love to Oriana for two days and two nights, he craved her blood more than anything. Had he stayed another minute, he would have attacked her and taken her blood no matter how much she protested. Luckily, he'd had just enough strength left to flee the house and her tantalizing scent.

However, even now her scent seemed to follow him. Even in the dark streets of Venice, where some of the canals smelled viler than others, Oriana's scent filled his nostrils, as impossible as it was.

Knowing his body had gotten all the nourishment he needed, he let go of the woman's neck and licked the tiny incisions with his tongue, closing them instantly. Then he pressed a few coins into her palm—more than she would have earned had she serviced a dozen men tonight—and wiped her memory of the event.

Nico exited the alley and walked to a small piazza. On one side, a small fountain provided water. He cupped his hands and filled them with the cold liquid, then splashed his face and neck to wash away the whore's scent.

When he dried his hands and face on his cloak and lifted his head again, his nose twitched. Oriana's scent was back in the air. Clearly, his own body still smelled of her after he'd practically bathed his hands and mouth in her arousal for hours on end. He'd never been so crazy about a woman, and he'd certainly never thought he'd take to marriage so quickly and with such enthusiasm.

Turning away from the fountain, he crossed the piazza and walked over the small bridge that led in the direction of his home. Like a beacon, Oriana's scent guided him, but when he reached another fork and would have turned right to continue to his house, Oriana's scent seemed stronger to the left.

He hesitated when a scream suddenly echoed through the narrow alley.

Oriana!

It was her voice, he was certain. His entire body went on alert, and he ran in the direction from which the scream had come, her scent becoming more intense with every step he took. When he rushed around the next corner, he saw her: his proper wife was engaged in a battle with a thug, who had his hands on an item Oriana was gripping with both hands. He focused his eyes: it was some sort of apparatus he'd never seen, and it was emitting an orange light.

A few steps away from her, Giuseppe, the footman he'd inherited from her father, exchanged blows with a second man.

Not losing a second, Nico barreled toward them, his hands clenching into fists. He charged the man who was attacking Oriana, and, in slamming him backwards against the wall, broke his hold on the item he and Oriana were fighting over.

Behind him he heard Oriana scream once more, then he heard a crash. He swiveled, his hands releasing the thug, when he saw Oriana fall. Her hands were flailing as she tried to hold onto her balance, but she was still holding onto the apparatus as she fell backwards.

He rushed to her and reached for her, but all his fingers caught was a rod sticking out from the item in her hands. At the same time, he noticed that the glow it emitted now changed to blue. He pulled on it, thus lessening the impact of her fall, but her head hit the wall behind her nevertheless.

"Oriana!" he screamed.

Her hands released the machine and it rolled to the floor beside her.

"Run!" he heard one of the thugs shout to his accomplice, and from the corner of his eye he saw the second thug push Giuseppe to the ground then run out of the alley, following the other one.

Fury coursed through him, and he was ready to kill those two, but there was no time. His wife was injured, and he had to take care of her.

Nico crouched down next to her, frantically touching her head and torso to feel for any injuries. He smelled no blood, a fact that filled him with relief.

"Oriana, my love, can you hear me?"

But she didn't respond. He placed his hand on her chest, feeling for her heartbeat. It was as strong as always. He released the breath he'd been holding. Oriana was alive.

"Signore Angelotti?" the footman said from behind him.

He turned and glared at the man, pointing his finger at him. "You!"

How could his servant allow his wife to leave the house in the middle of the night?

"I'm s-s-sorry, signore. They c-c-came out of nowhere."

"Not another word now! I'll deal with you when we're at home!"

He picked up Oriana in his arms and rose, then his eyes fell onto the contraption she'd fought over so bravely. Why?

"Giuseppe, pick it up. Follow me!"

"Yes, signore," the servant answered meekly.

Listening to Oriana's breathing and heartbeat, Nico carried her out of the dark alley.

CHAPTER

THIRTEEN

After assuring himself that Oriana's heartbeat was strong and she had no external injuries, Nico placed her on her bed and called for the maid to tend to her needs. His senses told him that the shock of the attack, together with the violent encounter with a wall, had knocked her unconscious. He picked up no other signs of a serious injury.

When he closed the door to her chamber behind him, he walked down the stairs. In the foyer, the footman stood, hanging his head, still holding the contraption Oriana had fought over in his hands. Only it wasn't glowing anymore.

"Follow me. And bring this... thing!"

Nico marched into the parlor and heard Giuseppe follow him and close the door behind them. He turned slowly, fury still charging through his veins.

"Look at me!" he ordered, his voice building like a distant thunder.

Giuseppe raised his head, his eyes displaying fear. "Y-yes, signore."

"Tell me what you think you were doing out there!" He pointed toward the window, indicating the dark streets past the safety of his walls. "Have you no sense? How could you take my wife out there in the middle of the night, subjecting her to the vermin that roams the streets at such an hour? How could you put her in such danger?"

The footman trembled. "I'm sorry, signore. B-but your wife, she demanded—"

"Demanded?" Well, Nico could picture only too well what it looked like when Oriana demanded something. He'd been subjected to her sharp tongue on their wedding night. "I don't care what my wife demands! You should have come to me!"

"B-but, signore, you were o-o-out."

"Ah, well, yes." Nico took a quick gulp of air. "Then you should have made her stay until I was back! There is no excuse for allowing her to put herself in danger."

"But the other t-t-times," he stuttered. "Nothing happened before."

Nico glared at the man. "The other times?" He took a step closer. "What are you saying? That my wife has done this before? That she goes out on her own on a regular basis?"

"Never alone," Giuseppe assured him. "I'm with her a-a-all t-t-the time."

Nico clenched his fist. "Yes, and we all know how well that worked out tonight! Had I not come upon her, that cutthroat would have seriously hurt her, maybe even killed her!"

As he said it, he felt a stab in his heart as if somebody had driven a stake into it. In that moment he realized that losing Oriana would mean losing his heart. Because he loved her. For an instant, he froze, stunned at the realization. How could this have happened? How could he have fallen in love with his own wife when three days ago he'd fought tooth and nail against this marriage?

"Why was she out there?" he thundered, then pointed to the contraption in the servant's hands. "And what is this? Why was she fighting with that cutthroat over this thing?"

The servant's eyes widened, and he nervously looked around the room as if looking for a way to escape his master's scrutiny.

"Speak! Or I'll make you regret the day you were born!"

Shaking, Giuseppe's mouth opened. Only a croaking sound emerged.

"Now!"

"Y-y-your w-w-w-w-wife she has a l-l-l..." His voice died.

Nico's heart stopped. "A lover?" How could this be? She'd been a virgin until he'd deflowered her only two days ago. With disbelief, he stared at the stuttering footman. "I swear, man, I'll crush you with my bare hands if you don't tell me the truth immediately."

"L-l-laboratory. Your wife has a laboratory," Giuseppe answered.

Relieved and confused at the same time, Nico questioned him again, "What do you mean, a laboratory? For what purpose?"

"The signora tinkers."

"Tinkers?"

Giuseppe raised the apparatus in his hands. "With s-s-science. She built this to prove that v-v-v-vampires exist."

The room suddenly began to turn before Nico's eyes, as if the earth beneath him were shaking. "No, no," he mumbled breathlessly. It was impossible. His wife? She was the one who was rumored to have a way of ferreting out vampires? "No," he repeated.

"Y-yes, signore. I speak the truth. You have to believe me."

Nico looked at him, then dropped his gaze to the machine. "Show me."

"Show you what, signore?"

He made a throwaway gesture. "Everything: her laboratory, her science, how this contraption works. Everything!"

Meekly, the servant nodded. "There's a secret passageway." He motioned Nico to follow him as he stepped out into the hallway.

A secret passageway? What else was in store for him? He was unable to even contemplate what this news would mean for him. If his wife was the person who was trying to find a way to discover vampires, then she was their enemy. He couldn't live with his enemy. One day she would find out what he was. One day she would discover his secret and kill him. Because there could only be one reason why she had built this machine: to aid the Guardians of the Holy Waters, the vampires' sworn enemies. Maybe she was even one of them! Who was to say that the secret society of the Guardians only consisted of men? What if women had joined their ranks?

With a heavy heart, Nico followed his servant through a hidden door in the paneling in the hallway. It led him along an old, musty, narrow corridor to a single door. Giuseppe reached above the sill of the door and pulled a key from it. Unlocking the door, he pushed it open and entered. Hyperaware of his surroundings, Nico entered behind him.

The room was dark. Nico heard a match being struck, then watched Giuseppe light a candle. The light now illuminating the room revealed a multitude of bottles, jars, and tools, as well as an abundance of scientific books and papers.

Nico pointed to the machine Giuseppe now placed on a workbench. "I saw it glow when we were in the alley. It's not glowing now. How does it work?"

Giuseppe pointed to a cylinder in the middle of the contraption. "Your w-w-wife fills it with a l-l-liquid and when a vampire touches it, it will g-g-glow a certain color. If the p-p-p-person is human, it glows a d-d-different color."

Nico nodded. He'd seen the machine in action: it had glowed orange when the cutthroat had tried to take it from his wife, but when Nico had touched the rod that protruded from its front, it had started glowing blue. But he wasn't going to share this revelation with Giuseppe, since he was almost certain that the servant had been too engaged in fighting off the second thug to have had an opportunity to observe what had happened.

"Why doesn't it glow now?"

"The cylinder is empty. M-m-maybe the liquid spilled, w-w-when your wife fell."

Nico stretched his palm out to Giuseppe. "The key to this room."

Giuseppe quickly obeyed and placed the key in Nico's hand.

"Nobody enters this room. And not a word to my wife that you told me about this. Do you understand?"

"What if she is looking for the k-k-key?"

"Then you know nothing!"

Giuseppe nodded. Nico shooed him out the door, then after following him, locked the door behind them and put the key into the pocket of his waistcoat. In the hallway he turned to his servant once more.

"I will be back shortly. In the meantime, you're responsible for seeing that nobody enters or leaves this house. That goes for everybody, especially my wife. If my orders aren't followed to the letter, I will find you, I promise you that."

A frightened look on his face, Giuseppe nodded quickly. "E-e-everything will be done as you w-w-wish, signore."

But at this point, Nico wished only one thing: for this nightmare to be over. However, it was a wish his servant didn't have the power to grant him.

CHAPTER
FOURTEEN

A sudden silence fell over the parlor in Dante's and Raphael's house, where the two brothers, their wives Viola and Isabella, as well as Marcello, Lorenzo, and Bianca were assembled. They had been poring over the list of Guardians' names once more.

Nico nodded gravely. He'd arrived ten minutes earlier and relayed what his footman had told him and what he'd observed with this own eyes when coming upon Oriana in the dark alley where she'd been attacked. "It's true. My wife is the enemy we've been hunting for the last few days."

The enemy—the word sliced through his chest.

Raphael sighed. "There can only be one reason why your wife was attacked." He exchanged a look with Marcello.

"The cutthroats you chased off must have been working for the Guardians," Marcello continued. "Nobody else has a reason to want this machine."

Nico shifted restlessly from one foot to the other. "But why attack her if she's working for them?"

"Maybe she isn't. Maybe she's working on her own and will sell the machine to the highest bidder. If the Guardians are aware of that, they'll want to intervene before somebody else gets hold of it," Raphael ventured a guess.

Marcello made a hand movement, indicating his impatience. "Be that as it may. It's clear what we have to do: destroy the machine and erase her memory."

Nico's heart began to race, but before he could even protest, Lorenzo rose from his seat and protested, "No!"

All eyes landed on him.

"You know my position on this. Erasing a human's memory should only be done if it is to erase a single moment in time, not entire weeks or months of a person's life. It's too dangerous. You all know what can happen."

Nico locked eyes with Lorenzo, knowing only too well what lay in his friend's past. He'd been forced to erase his lover's memory after she'd tried to stake him. Elle had ended up in an insane asylum, her mind destroyed, because of the amount of memories Lorenzo had erased. Ever since then, Lorenzo had cautioned all of them not to make the same mistake.

"I can't do this to my wife," Nico said quietly, reassuring himself that he wasn't the kind of monster to hurt the woman he loved.

"Then what are you planning to do?" Marcello took a step toward him, poking his index finger into Nico's chest. "Why do you even care? Weren't you the one who was planning to send her to the countryside after the wedding? Or have you suddenly changed your mind?"

Surprised that even Marcello knew about his original plan, he glared at Raphael and Dante.

Dante shrugged. "You never said it was a secret."

"Never mind that now," Marcello continued. "You know as well as each and every one of us that your wife presents a danger to us. We have to deal with it. Swiftly, before things escalate and the Guardians succeed next time and snatch the machine from her."

Nico's anger surged. "There won't be a next time. I'll destroy the machine!"

"That won't be enough!"

It had to be, because the other thing his friends expected him to do, he couldn't do. "It will have to be enough!"

"And what if they snatch her?" Marcello challenged him. "What if they force her to build a new machine?"

"She won't."

While Nico's voice was strong and filled with determination, his mind was anything but. How would he stop his wife from betraying them? He couldn't keep her locked up day and night. He would have a mutiny on his hands in short order. A headstrong woman like his wife wouldn't submit for long. Eventually, she would resent him for curbing her freedom. And she would try to escape.

"There's no way of making sure of that," Marcello disagreed.

Lorenzo, leaning casually against the fireplace, cleared his throat. Nico snapped his gaze to him.

"There is one way," Lorenzo claimed.

Nico raised an interested eyebrow.

"Show her what you are."

For several seconds nobody spoke. Then Nico shook his head. "It'll never work. She hates vampires. Why else would she build a machine to be able to identify us? If I reveal what I am..." Nico couldn't finish his sentence.

Oriana would recoil from him in disgust. Instead of wrapping her legs around him and pulling him closer, she would kick him off her, searching for the nearest weapon to kill him. And then he'd be forced to kill her. And by God, he could never kill the woman he loved.

"Nico." Lorenzo's urging voice penetrated his thoughts.

He looked up to meet his friend's gaze.

"Nobody's heard from you in the last two days and nights. It leads me to believe that you've been... shall we say, busy with your wife?"

Nico narrowed his eyes. "What is your point?"

"If she's invited you to her bed and you stayed there for two days and nights, I can only assume that she enjoyed your company as much as you enjoyed hers."

Nico clenched his teeth. "Get to the point."

Lorenzo smiled nonchalantly. "But that *is* my point."

"Would you care to elaborate on that?"

His friend laughed. "I didn't think you needed tutoring lessons in seduction."

Nico fisted his hands at his hips and widened his stance. "It's one thing to seduce a woman into your bed, it's an entirely different one to make her accept me as a vampire. She'll recoil from me in disgust."

A soft female chuckle interrupted him. He turned his head to stare at Isabella and Viola.

"For a moment maybe, until she's overcome the initial shock!" Isabella claimed. Then she let her eyes wander over her husband's body. "But once she realizes what it means to have a vampire for a husband, she'll be yours forever."

Nico looked at her. He couldn't help but notice how her chest suddenly heaved when Rafael looked at her, his eyes blazing with lust. Would Oriana react the same way once she knew what he was?

Marcello grunted and pointed at his fellow vampires. "If I leave it up to you besotted idiots, our entire race will vanish in no time. I say we destroy the machine and erase her memory now. It's the only sure way!"

"No!" Nico protested. Marcello's reaction was forcing him to make a decision. "I'll follow Lorenzo's suggestion."

Marcello glared at him. "Fine. You have twenty-four hours. If you can't bring your wife in line by then, we're doing it my way. Any objections?" He looked at the brothers, then at Lorenzo, daring them to protest.

Lorenzo threw up his hands in capitulation and rolled his eyes. "Whatever the big brute says."

Raphael and Dante exchanged a quick look, then Dante replied, "One day and one night." He tossed Nico an encouraging look. "I doubt you'll need that much time."

Wishing he could display the same confidence his friend possessed, Nico turned on his heel and left the house. He would have to conjure up all sensitivity and tact he possessed to aid him in the most difficult mission of his life. To convince his wife that he wasn't a monster.

CHAPTER

FIFTEEN

"The signora is awake," the maid informed Nico the moment he entered his home.

With a curt nod, he acknowledged her words. "My wife won't need you any longer tonight. You may go to bed."

She curtsied and withdrew.

Taking a deep breath, Nico headed for his wife's bedchamber. When he reached it, he hesitated for a moment. He would have to be as calm as possible to achieve his goal.

He opened the door and entered, finding that the maid had added more wood to the fire to warm the room. An oil lamp was lit next to the bed and threw an orange glow over Oriana, who sat up in bed, wearing a virginal nightdress that reached almost all the way to her neck.

She turned her head when she heard him enter and looked at him, then quickly averted her eyes.

"How are you feeling?" he asked politely.

"Perfectly well."

Nico approached the bed and sat on its edge. "Good. Then maybe you'd like to explain to me what you think you were doing out there." His words came out a little harsher than he'd intended, but he couldn't take them back now.

Oriana sucked in a quick breath, her chest rising under the white fabric. "I was merely taking an evening stroll when those men attacked the footman and me."

"A stroll?" He narrowed his eyes, anger boiling up at the fact that his wife was blatantly lying to him. "I would advise you to tell me the truth!"

She straightened her back. "Are you insinuating that I'm lying?" Outrage colored her voice.

Oh, what a magnificent actress his wife was!

Nico leaned in, making her shrink back into the pillows. "I'm doing more than that. I'm also telling you that from now on you won't go out at night unless it's in my company. You won't put yourself in danger like this anymore. Do we understand each other?"

She huffed angrily. "If you think that simply because I submit to you in the marriage bed, I shall allow you to curb my freedom, let me make one thing clear, *signore*! I am not your property!"

Her cheeks were aflame, and her lips trembled.

"Ah, my dear wife, that's where you're wrong! You're my responsibility now. You might have fooled your father, but don't think you can play the same games with me. I've found you out! I've seen your so-called laboratory!"

She shrieked, her eyes widening in shock.

"Oh yes! I know what you're up to, and I'm telling you it'll stop this instant!"

"You can't do this!" she cried out. "My work! My research!"

"Research?! Do you have any idea what you're getting into?"

"But I have to continue. I'm at a breakthrough. I'm certain I can make my machine work. Don't you see? With it I can detect vampires."

He glared at her, grunting low and dark.

"You might not believe it, but they exist. And I can make others aware of the danger they present. Venice will be safer for it!"

"There'll be a bloodbath if you continue!" Because once he and his friends were exposed, they would be forced to defend themselves. It meant killing those humans who attacked them. Venice wouldn't be safer.

"No, you don't understand! Please, Nico, you have to let me continue," she begged.

"No!"

She raised her chin and set her jaw. "If you don't, you won't be welcome in my bed any longer."

At her threat, his mood darkened even further. She was going to deny him her body? The beast inside him growled, roaring its disapproval. "Careful with your threats!"

"I mean it!" she bit out. "Either you let me continue with my work, or you'll be banned from my chamber!"

Furious at her mutinous behavior, he gripped her shoulders and pressed her against the headboard. "If I let you continue, you'll be putting me in danger. Is that what you want? To hurt your husband?"

"How would that hurt you? By not having a submissive wife? Yes, surely that will hurt your ego!" she mocked.

Nico felt his fangs lengthen. "You might as well paint a target on my chest! Because everybody will know what I am." He stared right at her and allowed his fangs to descend fully, opening his mouth in the process so she could get a good look at them.

Slowly, her eyes widened, and her breath rushed from her lungs. Her pulse instantly tripled, and she tried to escape from his grip. But he was infinitely stronger than she and didn't release her from his hold.

"Yes, look at me! I am what you seek. I am a vampire, the very creature you wish to expose with your machine. I shall destroy your machine, but what happens to you is up to you."

She squeezed her eyes shut for an instant, then opened them again. "Oh God, oh no! Please don't kill me!"

~

FEAR SURGED THROUGH HER. How could this have happened? How was it possible that her husband was a vampire? Nico, the man who'd so passionately made love to her for the last two days and nights. Her short moments of bliss were at an end. Not only that: her life would end tonight. He would bite her and drain her.

Frantically, she shook her head, trying to wake up from this nightmare. Against all odds, she hoped that she was dreaming, even though she knew she wasn't.

"Please have mercy!"

Nico tilted his head to the side. "Mercy? Why? You were going to sell the machine to my enemies so that they could eradicate my friends and me."

"Who? What enemies? I wasn't going to sell the machine."

He gave a bitter laugh, ignoring her question. "Why do you hate vampires so much? What have they done to you?"

"They hurt people."

"How would you know that? Has any of them hurt you?"

She glanced to his hands that clamped around her upper arms, holding her in a vice grip. "I saw one of them feeding from a human. Biting. Hurting."

Slowly he shook his head. "From that you think we hurt humans? You have no idea what a bite does. How much pleasure it can give." His gaze drifted to her neck, and his nostrils flared. "How much sexual pleasure I could give you with a single bite while I make love to you. More pleasure than you've experienced in the last two days combined."

Her breath hitched. Farther south, her womb clenched at the thought of feeling him inside her again. No! She couldn't allow that! He was a vampire, a vile creature, a monster. Why was he talking about making love? Was he trying to trick her into feeling safe?

"Never!" she vowed. "I'd rather die!"

"Die?"

He suddenly chuckled, making his features instantly much softer, despite the sharp fangs that were protruding from his mouth. Suddenly they didn't look as scary anymore.

"Before you make a monumental decision like that, I would like you to understand all options. As we both know, the last time you made a decision without knowing the other side, you very quickly changed your mind when I showed you what options you were dismissing so casually."

She gasped. How dare he remind her of the words she'd hurled at him during their wedding night? She'd told him that she wasn't interested in sharing his bed because it led only to shame and pain. Of course, he'd convinced her otherwise. But this didn't mean he could convince her again. Accepting marital congress was different from accepting a vampire as one's husband.

"Do not even attempt such a thing!" she cried out, her fear turning into outrage. How dare he treat her like this?

"Are you challenging me?"

She noticed amusement in his eyes. Angry that he was clearly not taking her seriously, she raised her chin in defiance. "It is not a challenge. It's a command! I command you to unhand me and leave."

He grinned and appeared as sinful as if he were introducing her to a new way of making love. How could this be? How could she still see him as the lover he'd been, when now he was different, when now he was a vampire?

"Ah, but my sweet wife, I'm afraid you still haven't learned that I don't take commands from you. They only inflame me even more. And right now I'm in the right mood to bend you over my knees and spank your bottom for your insolent behavior toward me."

Enraged by his suggestion, she tried to twist from his grip. "How dare you?!" She was no child that needed a spanking.

"Wrong answer, my sweet!"

CHAPTER

SIXTEEN

With one move, Nico flipped his wife onto her stomach and jumped behind her on the bed. Then he grabbed her virginal nightgown and ripped it all the way to the bottom, exposing the creamy skin on her back and ass.

Oriana tried to escape him, but he pinned her down with his knees over her thighs.

"You've been bad, disobeying your husband."

He stroked his hand over her firm cheeks, eliciting an outraged grunt from her.

"Lay one finger on me, and you'll pay for it!" she threatened.

"One finger?" he asked, his mind already forming an idea.

Painstakingly slowly, he ran his hand over her bottom, then slipped it between her thighs. Oriana tried to squeeze them together to deny him access, but her legs were spread wide enough for him to dip his finger to her female folds. To his delight, she was wet there.

"This finger?" he asked and probed at her slit, slowly thrusting inside her.

She moaned into the pillow. Satisfied at her reaction, Nico withdrew his hand. "Now that we know that your body is still welcoming me, let's commence your punishment."

"Why don't you just kill me now? Do you have to humiliate me too?"

He gently stroked over her beautiful flesh. "Kill you? My love, I have no intention of killing you now or later. Nor humiliate you. All I want is for you to accept me for what I am. Your vampire husband. And we're not going to leave this room until you do."

He punctuated his words by delivering the first slap on her ass.

She cried out, sounding more outraged than in pain. "I'll never accept a vampire as my husband!"

He smiled to himself, noticing that even though she was verbally still sparring with him, she wasn't trying to twist away from him.

"That's too bad, considering we're already married."

"I'll get an annulment!" Oriana claimed.

He answered her with a second slap. "Out of the question!"

Then he gripped her hips and pulled her onto her knees, so her bottom was in the air. He slipped one hand between her legs, cupping her sex, then slapped her ass cheek with the other.

She moaned, panting heavily, and he felt her cunny quiver under his touch. Moisture trickled onto his fingers, and he slid them along her warm flesh, pushing upwards to find her pearl.

His next slap coincided with the pad of his finger pressing onto her pleasure button, and an uncontrolled cry came from her throat.

"See, my love, how pleasurable punishment can be?"

"Stop," she begged, but her sex gyrated against his hand, asking for more friction.

"No," he answered. "Let your body do your thinking for you." He rubbed his finger over her swollen pearl, the juices that were oozing from her making the movement smooth and gentle.

"There," he coaxed and slapped her once more. "That's what you need. A good spanking from your vampire husband, so you'll behave." He deliberately reminded her of what he was, wanting her to hear it while she was experiencing pleasure so she would associate the word vampire with passion and pleasure.

Nico slipped one finger into her warm channel, while continuing to stroke her. "Do you want to come for your vampire husband?" He pinched her clitoris and delivered another slap on her bottom at the same time.

Oriana panted, her hips moving frantically to rub herself against his hand. He could feel how close she was. Over the last two days he'd learned to recognize her body's signs. And he wanted to join her.

With his free hand, he opened the buttons of his flap and pushed his trousers and smalls past his groin, enough to free his cock. He was as hard as he'd ever been.

"That's good, my sweet. You're all wet and ready for me." He pulled his finger from her and brought his cock to her pussy. "You know what that is, my love?"

She breathed heavily, her body pushing back toward him.

"It's a vampire's cock. Because a vampire is going to fuck you now. Just the way you like it." Oriana had developed a taste for being taken from behind. She'd confessed to him that she liked to be dominated by him in that way, and he'd greeted the confession with enthusiasm.

Nico plunged inside her, driving his cock to the hilt.

"Oh, God!" she cried out, her interior muscles clenching instantly.

Already he could feel the waves that hit his cock as she spasmed around him. "Not yet! Oriana! Fuck!"

But it was too late. She climaxed, igniting him as if his cock were made of dynamite and her arousal were the fuse. On his next thrust, he shot his seed into her, coming without warning. For a few more movements, his body thrust as if driven by an invisible force, then he collapsed onto her. Before he could crush her with his weight, he rolled to the side, pulling her with him, wrapping his arms around her to prevent himself from sliding from her body. This was where he belonged.

His breathing was ragged, and his cock still pulsed. His fangs were still extended and he now scraped them against her neck, hungry for her blood.

∼

ORIANA SHIVERED when she felt his teeth connect with her skin. Yet her body felt too lethargic to be able to move, her sex still dealing with the after-shocks of her release. She'd never felt so good. So thoroughly pleasured. To her surprise, the spanking had added to her pleasure, the shocks the slaps had sent through her body traveling directly to her pearl and igniting it. It was the reason why she'd been unable to stop him, even though she'd tried at first.

"My love," he murmured. "Was it so bad to be loved by a vampire?"

She hesitated, unsure how to answer, when she felt Nico's hand slip from her belly farther down. He combed through her pubic hair until his moist finger slid over the spot where her center of pleasure was hidden.

A sigh escaped her. "Oh!"

Then she felt his hips move, delivering the tiniest of thrusts. "Tell me, is loving a vampire as disgusting as you thought?"

"No," she finally confessed. "But will it always be this way?"

"No."

Her heart stopped. She'd feared as much. He would be the gentle lover now, but one day he wouldn't be able to hold back his violent vampire side anymore and he'd hurt her.

"It'll be better," he whispered into her ear while his finger rubbed in circular motions over her pearl, stoking the flames that she'd thought had already died in her body. But the embers were still glowing, and now, with as little as a gentle caress and slow thrusts of his still hard cock, they were igniting again.

"Ah, my wanton wife, how I love it when you show such passion."

His lips sank onto her neck, kissing her. Then she felt his sharp teeth scraping against her delicate skin. A shiver raced through her, making her tremble.

"Don't be afraid! I'll never hurt you. How could I? I love you."

Surprised by this revelation, she turned her head to stare at him. A golden hew shimmered from his eyes, and there was nothing frightening about it, because all she could see was the affection he held for her.

Their eyes locked.

"Yes, Oriana, I love you. And by God, I had no intention of falling in love. It happened nevertheless. I'm at your mercy now. Because if you can't love me and accept me for what I am, I have no life worth living. I need you. As my wife, my lover, my companion. I have no intention of robbing you of your freedom or the things you enjoy, but I'll do everything to protect you. Because you're precious to me. Without you, I'm simply an empty shell."

Oriana turned fully to him, making him slip from her body. Nico didn't move and let it happen. Her hand came up to touch his cheek.

"Can a vampire truly love?"

He closed his eyes in lieu of a nod. "As intensely as a human. And our hearts can just as easily be broken."

She dropped her hand to his chest and laid it over the spot where his heart was. It beat into her palm, strongly and evenly.

"It beats for you now."

She lifted her lids, looking into his eyes. "The bite. Will it hurt?" She was crazy even asking such a thing, but when he looked at her like this, love shining back at her, nothing else mattered. She wanted to be his in every way, even if it meant accepting him as a vampire.

"No. There'll be no pain."

"Will it turn me into a vampire too?"

"No. You'll remain human. But you don't have to make a decision now. As long as I know that you'll think about it, I won't make any demands on you. I won't push you. I won't force you. When you're ready, you'll tell me. Then, and only then will I drink your blood. Because once you do accept me, once you let me bite you, there'll be no going back."

Oriana felt her eyes grow moist. Nico was giving her a choice. He wasn't going to force this on her now, despite what he'd said earlier. He loved her enough to give her the freedom of choice. Overwhelmed by his words, she could barely choke out her next words. "I love you."

Then she pressed her lips onto his and kissed him.

CHAPTER
SEVENTEEN

Oriana knew that her happiness wouldn't last if she didn't remove one last obstacle. Nico had told her that her machine would have to be destroyed, but in her heart she knew it wouldn't be enough. The Guardians already knew about the machine. And they knew who she was; otherwise they wouldn't have sent the two thugs after her to steal the apparatus from her. Even if she destroyed it now, Nico's enemies wouldn't give up. They would eventually catch her and force her to replicate it—unless they could be convinced that she was a fraud.

She contemplated telling her husband about her plan, but dismissed the idea quickly, remembering what he'd told her before falling asleep.

You'll never get anywhere close to a Guardian again.

He would stop her, and Oriana knew she was the only one who could execute her deception. It was better if Nico didn't find out about it. She'd heard his protectiveness shine through his words. He would only stop her. No, this was something she had to do on her own.

During daytime, while her husband slept deeply, she snuck downstairs, but found her laboratory locked. It didn't take much to realize who had locked it and taken the key. It didn't matter: after losing the key once before and not finding it for several days, she'd tried out all other keys in the house and discovered that the key to the cook's pantry fit the lock to her secret laboratory. Nico wouldn't be able to keep her from her machine.

Before she went to the kitchen to retrieve the key, she looked for the footman, finding him in the parlor tending to the fireplace. He rose when he heard her enter.

"Signora." He bowed briefly.

She closed the door behind her and addressed him quietly, not wanting to be overheard. "I need you to arrange a meeting with the group who is interested in my apparatus. It's of the utmost importance."

"B-but signora." His eyes darted to the door, and he shifted nervously. "You're not to leave the house, and c-c-considering what happened, Signore Angelotti would n-n-not w-want me to—"

She cut him off with a hand movement and a glare. "Never mind that now. Do as I tell you! Arrange the meeting. For today."

He sighed. "And w-what do you want me to tell them why you want to m-m-meet them?" Giuseppe asked, sounding resigned.

"Tell them I want to demonstrate the machine to them."

Her servant's eyes widened. "They will try to steal it from you. We have to a-a-arm ourselves."

Oriana shook her head. "You're not coming with me." She had to do this on her own. Besides, Giuseppe hadn't been much help the last time. It was better if he stayed at home and made certain that Nico wouldn't follow her. She wanted him nowhere near a Guardian. It would only expose him.

"B-but—"

"Do it! And not a word about this to my husband. Or I'll make certain you'll never find another position in Venice." She hated threatening him, and she'd never follow through with her threat of course, but she needed his compliance.

Shock registered on the footman's face, but he nodded in agreement.

"Good." Oriana turned on her heel.

After retrieving the key, she let herself into her laboratory and went to work. She prepared two vials, each with a different chemical component and tested the machine. Her heart pounded so loudly, she was worried Nico would be able to hear it from the bedchamber.

Then the waiting began.

~

Nico had slept like a log. It was still daylight outside when he stirred and reached for Oriana, only to find her side of the bed empty. He shot up to a sitting position. Her scent still clung to the sheets. He looked around the room, but the bedchamber was empty. Maybe she had gone downstairs to eat. After all, he'd exhausted her the night before, and she had to be hungry. He too needed to replenish, and the thought of gorging himself on the blood coming from the thick vein on Oriana's neck made his fangs lengthen. How long he would be able to hold back his hunger for her until she made a decision, he wasn't sure. He could only hope that she would realize soon that she had nothing to fear from his bite. After all, she was making love to him with the full knowledge of what he was. It wouldn't take long until she would accept every part of him.

Smiling contentedly, he rose and dressed quickly.

He walked downstairs, listening for any sounds in the house. From the kitchen he heard the cook going about her work. Other than that, it was quiet.

Nico opened the door to the dining room and peered inside, but it was empty. There were no signs or smells that would indicate that Oriana had been there and eaten a meal in the last few hours.

Wondering where else she could be, he crossed the hallway and walked into the parlor. Nobody was inside, and the smell of a freshly lit fire over-shadowed any other smells, making it impossible for him to know whether Oriana had been here.

Unease crept up his spine. There weren't many other places in the house where she could be. When he stepped back out into the hallway, his gaze fell onto the wooden paneling behind which the secret passageway led to Oriana's laboratory. He approached the door slowly, his suspicion rising with every step.

A faint whiff of her smell drifted to his nostrils. He cursed under his breath. He squeezed his eyes shut for a short moment, trying to push down the rising anger. Oriana had gone to her laboratory, going against his wishes. Had she not understood that she couldn't continue her research? That doing so would endanger him?

He should have destroyed the machine instantly when he'd had a chance, but instead he'd spend the last hours in bed with his wife, making love to her to convince her that she could trust him not to hurt her. And as soon as he'd been asleep, she'd snuck down here behind his back to continue her work. How could she?

Fuming, he jerked the door open and entered the musty corridor, rushing along in the darkness until he reached the door to the laboratory. The door was unlocked, evidence that she'd gone against his wishes. He pushed it open, ready to give his wife a tongue-lashing she wouldn't forget for a long time.

The room was empty. His eyes focused on the workbench where Giuseppe had set down her machine. He froze. It was gone.

His hands balled into fists, and he slammed them into the nearest wall.

"Oriana!" he screamed and turned on his heels, running back into the hallway.

"ORIANA!"

But there was no reply.

Then a sound coming from the butler's pantry made him whip his head in that direction. Giuseppe's dropped shoulders and his lowered head told him everything he needed to know. He charged the man and slammed him against the wall.

"Where is she?"

The footman trembled. His lips moved, but nothing came out.

"Speak!"

"She w-w-went t-t-to m-m-m..." His voice died.

"Where?"

"Th-the group who is i-i-interested in her r-r-research. She's meeting them to show them the machine."

His heart turned to ice. After declaring his love for Oriana, she'd betrayed him. And he hadn't seen it coming. He hadn't seen her deception. How blind he'd been, how utterly blind!

"Where?" he repeated, his voice dead calm.

He knew what he had to do now. There was no other solution. And simply wiping her memory wouldn't be enough. There was only one answer to such a betrayal.

As he listened to the footman giving him the location where Oriana would meet a representative of the Guardians, Nico glanced toward the small window over the entrance door. Almost an hour of daylight was still left, but he couldn't wait for nightfall. This situation had to be dealt with without delay.

Throwing his black, hooded cloak over his shoulders, he headed for the sheltered dock that held his closed gondola.

CHAPTER

EIGHTEEN

Oriana's hands trembled slightly when she inserted one vial into the metal holder in the center of her machine. Nothing happened at first.

"What is it supposed to do?" the man barked, his face concealed by the hood of his cloak.

They stood in an archway that led through a row of houses to a bridge crossing one of the many canals. It was quiet in this mostly residential part of Venice. There were no shops, no street vendors, no passersby. She'd realized too late that the location the Guardian had chosen to meet her was remote. Unease settled in her belly. What if she was mistaken, and the machine didn't work the way she wanted it to?

Trying to keep her voice from revealing her nervousness, she said firmly, "When a human touches the rod which protrudes from the front, the center of the machine will glow orange, indicating a human's warmth."

"And how does that help with detecting a vampire?" he asked impatiently, suspicion rolling off him like rain water off the smooth tiles of a roof.

"I was coming to that." Her hands fumbled underneath the machine, partly concealed by the dark cloth she'd attached to its bottom before leaving the house. "But first, I need to ask a question."

"Mmm?"

She swallowed nervously. "Who knows about the machine?"

He chuckled unexpectedly. "All my uh... brothers do."

"Yet, you're the only one who wanted a demonstration of it?" she countered, hoping to get more information from him.

"A wise man doesn't share his sources."

"I beg your pardon, signore?" Could this possibly mean what she thought it meant?

"Every society has its hierarchy. To climb, one needs advantages."

The wheels in her mind clicked. "You're the only one then who knows who I am?"

"As I said, no man has ever risen to the top by sharing all his secrets with his competitors. But enough of that. Explain the machine! You said it would be glowing if a human touched it. I don't see it glowing now, and you're touching it."

"I simply have to establish the connection from the vial to the rod by way of a tube." She felt for the tube underneath the fabric and shoved it into an opening. Then she touched the rod with one hand, and the center of the machine instantly started glowing orange. "See?"

The man shrunk back a step, then curiosity made him move closer again.

She removed her hand and slipped it underneath the machine again, and the glow dissipated. Underneath the cloth her next action remained hidden from his eyes.

"Would you like to try it out too?" she asked, keeping her voice indifferent, so as not to make him any more suspicious than he already was.

FROM HIS HIDING place across the bridge, underneath a sheltering archway, Nico watched his wife demonstrate the machine to the hooded man. His heart broke into a thousand pieces at having her deception confirmed. She was there to sell her apparatus to the Guardians, thus giving them a valuable tool to help them eradicate him and his fellow vampires.

Still, he waited, unable to do what he had to do: kill her and the man with whom she was striking the despicable trade. Why hadn't she simply staked him in his sleep? It would have been a kinder death than letting him suffer like this. Suffer, because the woman he loved was betraying him to his enemies. Was that what he was waiting for, to hear her tell the stranger where he could find a vampire on whom to test the machine?

His throat constricted, allowing no more air into his lungs. For an instant, he closed his eyes, wishing for this nightmare to end, but when he opened his eyes again, he was still standing at the same spot.

Yet one thing had changed: the machine suddenly glowed blue, the same way it had glowed when he'd touched it that night. Only, the person who touched the apparatus now, was the Guardian!

Panic surged through him. He couldn't see the face of the man. Was it possible that one of his fellow vampires had tricked Oriana into believing she was meeting with a Guardian? And once he knew the machine worked, would he then kill her?

Oh God no!

"I'm not a vampire!" he heard the man yell furiously. "It doesn't work! The machine is a useless piece of garbage! How dare you waste my time?" He raised his hand to strike.

Too many emotions collided in Nico, rendering him unable to make a decision. His body made it for him: no matter what she'd done, how she'd betrayed him, he couldn't allow Oriana to get hurt.

Nico charged out from his shelter and barreled over the bridge, feeling the late afternoon sun's rays on his back. Even though he was covered head-to-toe by the heavy hooded cloak, he could feel the heat instantly as it tried to penetrate the cloth and reach his skin.

In the seconds it took him to cross the bridge, one thing became instantly clear: the man wasn't a vampire—now that Nico was close enough, he could not only smell the man's human blood, but also see that he wasn't surrounded by the telltale aura that identified a vampire to other vampires.

In the distance, a question emerged: why then had the machine glowed blue instead of orange? He had no time to find an answer, because at that moment, the man's fist struck down on Oriana, knocking her toward the narrow stone stairs that led down to the canal next to the bridge. She stumbled backwards, crying out.

"Nooooo!!!!" he roared, drawing the Guardian's attention on himself.

But he couldn't deal with the man right now. Oriana was falling backwards, her feet getting caught in her petticoats and her hands flailing. She'd dropped her machine to the ground the moment she'd been struck. Nico jumped toward her, reaching his hand out from under the protection of his cloak.

Muted sunlight hit his skin. He ignored the burning sensation, his eyes focused on his wife as her back crashed against the metal handrail. Her hand gripped it, but the metal made a cracking sound. Without a conscious thought, he lunged for her, reaching for her with both hands. He'd neglected to wear gloves, and now the skin on the back of his hands was blistering. He ignored the pain and got hold of one of her arms just as the handrail gave way, and she fell.

Oriana's scream was a mere croak. Nico felt her full weight, now only supported by his hand clasping tightly around her forearm. From the corner of his eye he saw the Guardian approach. Nico whipped his head toward him and saw the blade he now wielded.

"I'll teach you to cheat me!" he ground out and lunged toward them.

With one hand holding onto Oriana, trying to steady her swaying body, which hung suspended over the canal, he reached for his own knife under the cloak, realizing too late that he hadn't armed himself before leaving the house.

The Guardian barreled toward him. Nico kicked his leg out, grazing his attacker's thigh as the man sidestepped him. Knowing he was at a disadvantage, both because he was still holding onto Oriana, and because the late afternoon sun was quickly robbing him of his energy as it damaged his skin, burning through the upper layers, he made a split-second decision.

He turned away from the Guardian and reached for Oriana with his second hand, gripping her other arm. He heaved her up, depositing her onto the steps, just as a knife sliced into his back.

Pain seared through him. He knew the knife wound wouldn't kill him, but in his current state, it debilitated him further. Swinging around, he faced the Guardian. This time, his attacker sliced through Nico's cloak. It got tangled up with the knife, and as the Guardian attempted to pull his knife from it, he inadvertently ripped the protective cloak even further, pulling it halfway off Nico's body.

Instantly, Nico felt the sun's rays on his body, his white shirt and thin waistcoat providing no adequate barrier.

Stunned, the Guardian stared at him, seemingly only now realizing that he was fighting a vampire. With an evil grin, he pulled on the remainder of the cloak, pulling it clear off Nico. Now he was fully exposed. His face and neck instantly started to blister. From his damaged hands smoke already started to rise.

Despite the pain, Nico lunged at his attacker, knowing that if he couldn't defeat him, the Guardian would kill Oriana. He landed a punch in the man's face, wiping the grin off it. But Nico immediately realized that his strength was already waning. Under normal circumstances, his fist would have knocked his attacker unconscious. Now it only numbed him for a short moment. Already, his attacker was fighting back.

Nico eyed the archway. He had to push the Guardian back toward it so he could fight him under its shelter and avoid any more damage by the sun. Ramming his entire body against the man, he managed to get a few feet closer to the shaded area, but then a kick to his stomach pushed him back toward the bridge again.

The scent of charred flesh rose to his nostrils. Nico caught sight of his right hand, the one that had been exposed to the sun the longest and saw that the back of it had turned black like charcoal. Shit! He didn't have much time left or the damage would be irreversible.

The Guardian's hand holding the knife flew toward him. Nico twisted, avoiding it by a hair's breadth, then landed a punch in his attacker's neck, throwing him off balance. The Guardian tumbled for a brief moment, but caught himself and aimed his knife again.

Nico saw it coming toward him and tried to avoid it, but his movements were slowing, and his breath deserted his lungs. He was done for. The sun was killing him. He'd failed. The knife came closer. The Guardian didn't need a stake to kill him now; he knew that: by debilitating him sufficiently so Nico wouldn't have the strength to crawl inside, the sun would finish the job for him.

Nico's eyes darted to where he'd left Oriana, hoping for one last glance at her, but she was gone. Disappointment and relief collided in him. At least she had escaped. Nico's vision blurred.

Suddenly the Guardian froze. There was a movement behind him. His hand holding the knife dropped, then blood seeped from his neck.

Nico focused his eyes just as the Guardian fell. Behind him, Oriana stood, still holding her machine with both hands, blood dripping from the metal rod that protruded from its front.

Stunned, he stared at her.

Concerned eyes looked back at him. "We have to get you out of the sun."

She rushed to him, put an arm around his waist and dragged him toward the archway. His feet barely cooperated, his knees already buckling, but Oriana didn't give up. A moment later, he found himself sitting in the darkest corner of the archway, away from the sun.

His body still smoldered, the damage to his skin and flesh severe. He needed blood, and he needed it soon. But he needed to know something else first, otherwise his heart would never rest.

"Why did you save me after you betrayed me?"

A tender hand stroked over his chest. "I didn't betray you."

He closed his eyes, unable to look at her. "You demonstrated the machine to a Guardian."

"I did. To prove that it doesn't work."

"But it works. The night you were attacked, it worked. You didn't see it, because you fell, but when I touched it, it turned blue."

"As it did when the Guardian touched it a moment ago," she confirmed. "I secretly connected the machine to a different chemical to make sure he would think it doesn't work."

He stared at her, not understanding. "Why?"

"Because they'll never give up if they think there's a machine out there that's working."

Nico motioned his head toward the bridge where the dead body of the Guardian still lay. "But he's dead. He won't be able to tell his fellow Guardians that the machine doesn't work."

"But he was also the only one who knew who I am. The others don't know. They'll never find us."

"How do you know?"

"He was using the knowledge of who I am as leverage with the other Guardians. He said, a wise man never reveals his sources. He was too greedy to share the information. We're safe." She sighed. "Now, let's get you home."

He shook his head. "I won't make it."

Oriana's breath hitched. "No! Don't do this to me! Don't die on me!"

He shook his head. "What I meant to say is that I won't make it home without blood. My body is too damaged to sustain another moment in the sun. I left our gondola on the canal parallel to this. I won't make it that far unless I have a chance to heal first. To heal I need…"

His eyes dropped to her neck, and he saw her shiver.

Then a smile suddenly curved her lips. "I suppose it's the least I can do after you saved me from the Guardian." She inched closer.

"Yes, it's the least you can do," he confirmed, smiling too.

Oriana tilted her head to the side, exposing her pale neck. He raised his hand to brush over her skin, then caught sight of the charred surface of it, and pulled it back.

"I'm sorry, I'm not much to look at right now."

"I don't look at the exterior, my love," she murmured. "Because I can see your heart." She pressed her hand over the spot where his heart was pounding out of control. "You risked your life for me."

Then she brought her neck to his lips. He inhaled her scent.

"Drink from me."

His fangs lengthened and nudged against her neck. He opened his mouth wider, then drove the sharp tips into her skin. A momentary tensing of her muscles was the answer, but then she relaxed against him, and he began to pull on her vein.

Her blood was rich and sweet. Greedily he drank from her, feeling how her blood spread in his veins, nourishing him, healing him. His cells restored themselves, the charred skin falling off him and new skin covering the exposed flesh. His hair grew, replacing the strands that had been burned off.

With every drop of her blood, his strength returned. And with it came the desire for her. The desire to have her. He pulled her up, having regained his full strength, and without removing his fangs from her neck, pressed her against the wall.

Then his hands pushed her skirts up and pressed the fabric into her hands to hold it up. She complied without complaint. Opening his breeches a moment later, he freed his cock. He was hard.

His fingers found the slit in her drawers, and he pushed inside her, seating himself to the hilt. Oriana moaned in response. The sound echoed in the archway and accompanied the thrusts with which he claimed her and made her his in every way.

CHAPTER

NINETEEN

They had disposed of the Guardian's body in the canal, weighing it down with a few stones and wrapping his cloak tightly around him, a task Oriana performed without flinching.

Nico couldn't feel happier, knowing that his wife had allowed him to drink her blood.

"Did you like it?" he murmured now as they lay in bed, her naked body wrapped around his, their limbs entangled.

She chuckled softly, and the sound warmed his heart. "Do you really have to ask?" Her hand trailed down to where his cock was already swelling again. She wrapped her hand around him. "If you need more…"

He laughed softly. "If you're worried that my cock won't be hard enough for you, my wanton wife, then don't be. For the important things, I always have enough energy."

"I just want to make certain that you're completely healed."

"I am." He pressed a kiss on her lips. "Thanks to you. And now it's time to thank you for it."

Her cheeks blushed. "But you already thanked me. First under the archway, then here."

Nico pulled her closer, caressing her soft backside. "Oh that? That was only a reflex to reassure myself that I'm still alive."

"Oh!"

"Thanking you is going to take a little longer."

Her eyelashes lifted, almost crashing against her eyebrows. "How long?"

He brushed his lips against hers. "Eternity."

Oriana suddenly pulled back and sat up. "For you maybe, but I don't have eternity. I'm human."

Nico sat up and faced her. "You have a choice, my love. But not now. Not yet. I want us to have children first."

"Children?"

"Yes." He stroked his hand over her stomach. "I want my seed to grow in you. Once we've filled this house with our children, you'll have to make a decision whether to join me and become what I am, so we can live together for eternity."

Oriana opened her mouth. "Ah—"

Nico placed his finger over her lips. "Not now. I want you to learn more about us first, so you'll know what your decision means. You're a scientist, are you not?"

She nodded.

"Then you'll want to examine all issues before you come to your conclusion."

"Examine?" she murmured and turned her gaze to his midsection.

A bolt of lightning charged through him. Yes, he had a wicked wife with a sinful disposition. And he wouldn't have it any other way.

"May I start with the examination now?"

He leaned back into the cushions and pushed the bed linen down all the way, baring himself to her. "You may do anything you want, my love."

She scooted down and eyed his cock, then licked her lips suggestively. "Anything?"

He groaned. "Yes, and particularly that."

She glanced at him. "How do you know what I intend to do?"

Nico smiled. "Because I can read it in your face." Then he pointed to his cock. "Are you going to make me wait forever?"

Oriana bent over his groin. A moment later, her tongue darted out, and she licked over the head of his erection. His entire body went rigid.

"Oh, I'm going to enjoy this," she claimed.

"Not as much as I," Nico prophesized.

A second later he lost his ability to speak when Oriana's lips wrapped around him and slid down his hard length, taking him inside her warm and wet mouth.

And for a long time after that moment, nothing else mattered.

ABOUT THE AUTHOR

Tina Folsom was born in Germany and has been living in English speaking countries since 1991. Tina has always been a bit of a globe trotter. She lived in Munich, Lausanne, London, New York City, Los Angeles, San Francisco, and Sacramento. She has now made a beach town in Southern California her permanent home with her American husband and her dog.

She's written 50 romance novels in English most of which are translated into German, French, and Spanish.

https://tinawritesromance.com
tina@tinawritesromance.com

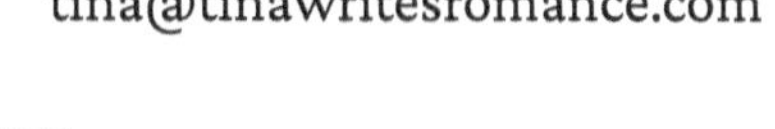 facebook.com/TinaFolsomFans
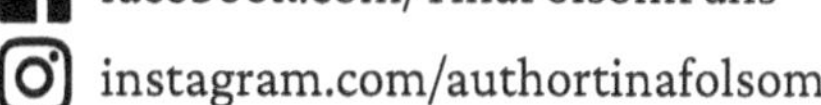 instagram.com/authortinafolsom

www.ingramcontent.com/pod-product-compliance
Lightning Source LLC
Chambersburg PA
CBHW051311190726

48290CB00001B/96